THREE ESCAPED CONVICTS.
ONE OBS
A MURDER SP
A PATH
ACROSS THE A

"A SLAM-BANG ACTION NOVEL."
—*The Baltimore Sun*

"AN EXCEPTIONAL THRILLER."
—John Sandford, author of *Night Prey*

STEPHEN HUNTER

dirty white boys

Island
BOOKS

ISLAND BOOKS
Published by
Dell Publishing
a division of
Bantam Doubleday Dell Publishing Group, Inc.
1540 Broadway
New York, New York 10036

ISBN: 0-440-22179-X

Reprinted by arrangement with Random House, Inc.

Printed in the United States of America

Published simultaneously in Canada

December 1995

10 9 8 7 6 5 4 3 2 1

OPM

**Dedicated to the five friends who helped me
the best when I needed it the most:**

Mike Hill
Bob Lopez
Lenne Miller
Weyman Swagger
Steven Wigler

There is a paradox at the core of penology, and from it derives the thousand ills and afflictions of the prison system. It is that not only the worst of the young are sent to prison, but the best—that is, the proudest, the bravest, the most daring, the most enterprising and the most undefeated of the poor. There starts the horror.
—Norman Mailer's introduction to
In the Belly of the Beast
by Jack Henry Abbott

No one knows what it's like to be the bad man.
—Peter Townsend, "Behind Blue Eyes"

dirty white boys

CHAPTER
1

Three men at McAlester State Penitentiary had larger penises than Lamar Pye, but all were black and therefore, by Lamar's own figuring, hardly human at all. His was the largest penis ever seen on a white man in that prison or any of the others in which Lamar had spent so much of his adult life. It was a monster, a snake, a ropey, veiny thing that hardly looked at all like what it was but rather like some form of rubber tubing.

Therefore he was Number One on the fag hit parade, but the fags knew to stay away and could only dream of him in private. Lamar wasn't a fag, although, when the spirit moved him, he was a buttfucker. He wasn't a boss con's fuckboy, either, or a punk, or a bitch or a mary or a snitch, and he carried a simple message in the graceful economy of his movements: to fuck with me is to fuck with death itself.

It helped, of course, that he was also protected by Daddy Cool, the bullet-pocked biker king who ran the Mac's dirty white boys; with Daddy's special mojo protecting him and his own reputation as a man-killer, almost nobody, con or guard alike, messed with him. And it helped that his hulking cousin Odell stood ready to back him up on the dime if it went down hard. But mainly it was just Lamar and his attitude. He was the prince of the Dirty White Boys.

It was four o'clock in the afternoon, on a day like any other in the institution's melancholy history as Oklahoma's toughest prison. In the guard quarters, through two levels of security off the D corridor, Lamar turned on the shower and let the water hit him. Its blast struck his bulging muscles, washed the sweat away. This was his favorite moment of the day, and as a ranking lifer, he had earned the right to a private second or two in the hack's shower before lockup. It meant as much to him as a million dollars in the bank, and he knew he'd never have a million dollars in the bank. What he had was a nice, fresh bar of Dial soap, which he'd just unwrapped: none of that green liquid disinfectant soap the regular cons used in their showers.

Lamar Pye was thirty-eight years old, with a tangle of thick hair, which he generally wore braided down his back or in a ponytail. Though he had an open, friendly face and warm eyes showing over a nose that had seen much wear, he also had F U C K and Y O U ! inscribed across the knuckles of his left and right fists and BORN TO KICK ASS on his left forearm, all in the spidery and uncertain blue ink of a free-hand convict tattoo artist. On his right forearm, in the same wobbly line, was a pictograph of a dagger jammed halfway to its hilt into the flesh. A stream of red droplets wiggled out of it. On his left wrist it said SHADOW OF DEATH under a crude but unmistakably effective rendering of a skull. On the top of his right hand, it said WHITE GREASED LIGHTNING, with a rat-tailed squiggle in fading blue indicating a lightning bolt. Lamar couldn't even remember getting that one. He must have been drunk or high or something. He just woke up one goddamned day during a two-year slide for assault with intent up at Crabtree State in Helena and there it was. Craziest damn thing.

The water felt so good when it blasted against the swollen bulges of his muscles, with the contrast between the hissing steam and the sense of cooling. Two hundred curls with the seventy-five-pound bar, two hundred squat thrusts with the two-hundred-pound bar on his shoulders, a long goddamned time under the chest machine, hoisting two hundred pounds of dead weight until he was swollen like a tire on a hot day. When the water hit his muscles and deflated him, man, that felt so cool!

Lamar contemplated his chest in the hissing steam. Looking downward he saw an endless field of possibility. His chest was wide and white and not particularly hairy. It was wide open. You could put anything on it you wanted.

It was Richard who'd got his head turned in this direction. Newboy Richard was so scared of them he hadn't said a thing for a week, and Lamar at first wanted just to torture him for a while before he fucked him and sold him to Rodney Smalls's niggers for cigarettes, but goddamn Richard was so weak it wouldn't have meant a thing. All Richard would do was sit there with a pencil and some kind of tablet, his hand flying over the surface of the paper, as if by concentrating so hard he could make it all go away. Or read funny little books with no pictures, underlining things furiously. Though he clung to Lamar's shadow like a dog whenever Lamar went into the yard.

Finally Lamar had said, "Goddamn you, boy, what is that shit you're working at?"

Addressed directly, Richard had seemed to melt. His puffy face trembled as the color fled his cheeks. He quivered like a leaf in a high breeze. Then he said, "Art."

"Art who?" Lamar demanded.

"Art *art,*" said Richard. "You know. *Art.* Pictures. What the imagination can show."

"Fuck all that shit," said Lamar. Now he really wanted

to hurt Richard. He hated when somebody threw a word at him. *Mag-i-nation*. Fuck that. But weirdly curious, he bent over and looked at what Richard had been diddling.

Goddamn, it was Lamar! It was Lamar himself, fearsome as a lion, scared of no man, looking like some kind of ancient king or Viking. Under a frosty moon. Lamar, with a mighty sword, ready to slay enemies by the thousands. The whole thing had a spooky feel to it, some kind of magic or something. Somewhere inside, Lamar felt a little thing move.

"The fuck," he said, "that ain't the way it is. I'm a hardtimer goddamned inmate buttfucker. I ain't no goddamned he-ro."

"I—I just drew what my mind saw," said Richard. "Please don't hurt me."

"Ah," said Lamar, stumped. He went back to his *Penthouse*.

Yet the image had somehow jiggered something in Lamar. It troubled his dreams, bumping aside for a while the stroke-book blondes who gave their rosy asses to him every night until he came and could relax. Not that night. And the next day he wanted Richard to show it to him, and the next and the next. He thought about it for nearly another week, and then he started dreaming about it.

"You know that there picture?"

"Yes," said Richard.

"Could you do another one? From what I told you. You wouldn't have to see it or nothing. I could just fucking *tell* you. You could make it?"

"Er, yes, I suppose. I mean, of course."

"Hmm," said Lamar, thinking hard. "You know, what I truly like, is lions. But a lion not in no jungle but in a castle. You know. And a bitch, blond, with really big tits. And, somehow, she love the lion. She love him like a *man,* not like no *pet*. Now, I don't want no picture of the lion fucking her, but the lion *could* fuck her if he wanted to.''

"Ah, I think I see what you're getting at. He's, like, an *archetype* of a certain aggressive masculine power.''

"Huh?''

"Ah, I mean—''

"He's a *lion* and he's got a *bitch*. And she has *tits*. And it's all a long time ago. Got that?''

"Yes sir.''

Richard got busy. For days he huddled in the corner madly dashing away. He'd throw pictures away, cursing. He even went to the prison library and got books with lions in them. And then finally—

"Lamar? Is this what you had in mind?''

He held out a sketch. The lion was a god, the woman a slut with huge tits, her nipples taut as bowstrings. It was master, she was slave.

"Goddamn,'' said Lamar. "Look-a-that! Man, like you got that outta my head! Damn, ain't that a goddamn piece of work! Only, now, wouldn't it be better if the lion was taller? And maybe the gal's tits weren't that big? That's too big. It don't look *real*. I want it to be *real*. I like the castle though.''

Richard took the criticism like a man and spent another week on revisions. When he made his final submission, Lamar was quite pleased.

"Goddamn, Richard. You got a gift, if I do say so myself. Now, say, I wanted you to try other things. You know, other things I see in my head, could you do it?''

"I know I could,'' said Richard.

"Goddamn, ain't that something. I want you to draw what I tell you. You do that, I'll look after you. Got it?''

"Yes sir,'' said Richard, and the deal was done.

Why was it so satisfying? He didn't know. But it was,

and it was a newfound source of pleasure. He could just dream something up and Richard would make it appear on paper. It really made him happy. So Lamar swelled a little with pleasure, taking happiness from the pleasures of his well-ordered world. Everybody feared him. He could fuck just about any of the white boys and half the niggers if he so chose. He had a percentage of three dope smuggling operations, including a methamphetamine lab in Caddo county that muled in a pound of crystal a week. He had his cousin Odell about as happy as that poor boy could ever be. He had Richard to draw whatsoever he chose. He was a wealthy man.

But then, ahead of him, something moved in the vapor, and it all changed, it all went away.

Lamar, startled, looked up. No-goddamned-body was supposed to be in here. He paid Harry Funt, the hack, four cartons of cigarettes a week to make sure nobody disturbed him in his private time.

"Who's that, goddammit?" barked Lamar.

A huge, dark shape emerged from the steam, just as buck naked as Lamar, gleaming and globular.

"Goddamn, Junior, ain't nobody supposed to be in here. I bought this goddamn time, fair and square."

Junior Jefferson went close to four hundred pounds, and naked, his giant body seemed like something out of a movie, especially the way he shone in the light. He had a goddamned strange look in his eyes, too. Lamar didn't like this at all. His feral instincts came alert. Junior was a known rapist and child molester, and perhaps the only man in D block who didn't fear Lamar or his monster cousin Odell.

"You know the goddamn rules, Junior," said Lamar, backing up just a bit. "It's mine, I paid for it. Paid Harry Funt. It's the goddamned rules."

"Rules be shit," said Junior and reached down and grabbed his cock to show Lamar. It was stiff as a bat and strangely blue.

"Git me some white pussy," said Junior. "Git me some whiteboy asshole, yas, I am."

"You fucking nigger, you stay away. We got a gang truce and you is over the limits."

"Your dumb motherfucker cousin O-dell, he done dissed Daddy Cool and so Daddy Cool sold your ass to Rodney Smalls who done give it to me. You gonna service the niggers for a month."

Lamar knew in a second it was possible. That Odell! That boy was born without a brain in his head! It wasn't just the soft part of his mouth and lip that was missing but a goddamned part of his thinker, too! But if he dissed Daddy, there was no sense in disciplining him, because he was too dumb to know pain from pleasure; worse yet, he had no ability to *mag-ine* fear. So to punish Odell would be pointless; Daddy must have decided to punish Lamar in his place, and Lamar saw the terrible justice in it: he was responsible for Odell. Odell was family.

"You got something wrong, nigger. I don't take it in the ass. I give it in the ass, but I don't never take it there."

Junior said, "I asked for you special, Lamar, 'cause you so pretty."

Lamar had seen Junior kill a bitch in D yard once, just by squashing him against a wall. A snitch, the bitch deserved it; still, Junior just rammed him against the wall, capturing the bitch's face in his huge belly and sloppy, saggy chest. The bitch beat and chirped, but it was over in two minutes. That's how fast it could happen in the yard.

Junior advanced on him like the earth itself, set on swallowing him up. Lamar had no weapons; his shank was in his shaving kit in the shitter. He had no boots to kick with.

He was outweighed by a good two hundred pounds of meat and, though strong, was not near strong enough. But he wasn't scared. It was funny: he *never* got scared. He laughed a little bit. He liked having his back to the wall and everything on the line. It was exciting.

He paused, gathering strength as the giant wobbled in, arms spread, fingers grasping. Just as Junior closed, he hit Junior a powerful blow right above the heart, his F U C K fist driven forward like a steam piston, and the blow sent the echo of meat pounding meat against the hiss of the showers. He followed up with a Y O U ! to the solar plexus, but it didn't slow Junior a goddamned bit, he just butted Lamar with his belly back against the wall and leaned on him.

"Drain you of air, then when you half dead, do you like a doggy. Then you be movin' to my cell, yes sir. You gots a busy night ahead."

Junior's rich laughter filled the air as his arms squished around Lamar, his immense bulk flattening Lamar's ribcage, crushing his heart. Lamar felt his head bobbing like that of a dying fish flopping on the dock for the amusement of small boys. With a ham hand, Junior grabbed hold of Lamar's hair and quieted the head and then, beaming with pleasure, bent to give his victim a little kiss.

Deoxygenated, Lamar watched helplessly as the nigger lips gathered to form a dainty seal, then felt a scream of helplessness erupt from his lungs, which shocked Junior a hair, giving Lamar a whisker of a chance. His neck snapped upward, unfolding almost like a turtle's, and in a second he'd sunk his teeth into Junior's nose. He bit and bit, almost choking on the blood, and he couldn't hear Junior scream. But scream Junior did, pulling away, his hands flying reflexively to the torn appendage. Lamar spit some gristle out, bent in a flash and struck upward, another piston stroke that landed in Junior's balls, crushing one testicle.

Junior staggered, seemed to lose it, then flared up in rage just as Lamar drilled him a savage F U C K in the throat, this time with a quarter fist so that his knuckles were sharp like a blade. They roared through the flab covering Junior's larynx, but they reached that treasure and crushed it. Junior went down to his knees, gasping. He begged for mercy with his eyes, but Lamar was not into mercy; he quickly flanked the giant and with another open hand drove F U C K into the back of his neck. Junior jerked forward as if the blow had a charge of electricity with it and put up a weak arm to ward off more punches, but Lamar kept hitting him in the high spine and the neck, a F U C K and then a Y O U !, using the heel of his palms so that he would break none of his own bones, over and over and over, until the big man lay still.

Lamar stood up from his handiwork, breathing hard. His hands hurt. He was shaking involuntarily. The blood raced and thundered in his brain.

"Fuck with me, see what it gets you," he explained.

Like a great beached whale, Junior somehow rolled over. Blood gushed from his mouth and nose. Horror showed in his eyes. A great slobby arm came up, as if to ward off any more blows from the smaller, tougher man. The water beat down, the steam heaved. Red liquid lapped at Junior's blackness.

"Don't hurt me no more," he said. "Please."

Lamar stared at him. You could pound on someone like Junior for a year and maybe you'd fuck him up, but you wouldn't really kill him. He took a lot of killing, more killing maybe than Lamar had in him.

"Oh, god," moaned Junior. "You done hurt me bad. Git some help. I can't hardly breathe none."

Lamar felt next to nothing. Only: Problem—how to shut this fat nigger up? Then: Answer. He reached into the soap dish and took the new bar of Dial in his hand. Then, quickly, he knelt to Junior.

"I think you got something stuck in your mouth," he said. "Better open up and let me see."

Obediently, Junior opened his mouth, and quick as a snake, Lamar jammed the soap bar into it and with his strong thumbs forced it in deep. Junior's eyes bulged and he lifted a feeble hand toward his mouth, but Lamar slapped it away and shoved the soap still deeper, forcing it down the throat. Trapped beneath it, Junior's tongue rolled and unrolled. Unusual sounds came from him—*"Ulllccccchhhh! Ullguccchhhhhhuch!"*—and he began to buck on the wet floor of the shower. The water cascaded onto them both. Junior struggled and struggled, eyes wide, noises wet and revolting, farts and shit ripping out of his ass, filling the shower with filth and stench, as under his blackness his skin seemed to turn almost blue.

At last the big arm went limp, and his head fell heavily to the left. His eyes stared into nothingness. He was still in his own shit.

Lamar stood back.

"Get up, you fat nigger," he said. "I want to hurt you some more." But Junior's eyes had filled with water.

Now how the fuck am I going to wash? Lamar wondered.

Then he took a deep breath and realized he had to get out or either Rodney Smalls and the niggers or Daddy Cool would kill him before nightfall.

Richard Peed hated the last hour before lockup the worst of all. In the yard, he could hang close to Lamar or Odell and in that way be protected from the predators. After lockup, he could more or less keep the two Pye boys at bay by seeming to go so limp and formless he wasn't there. That passivity somehow made them uninterested in hurting him. And now that he'd reached some kind of provisional deal with Lamar about the drawings, he felt he'd made a real step forward toward survival for the three months that he was destined to spend in the Mac before the deal clicked in and he was removed to the minimum security joint called El Reno Federal Correctional Facility, twenty miles west of Oklahoma City.

But at four, Lamar went to the guard's shower after working out for two hours. And Odell went back of the kitchens to feed his cats. Richard had at least an hour of vulnerable solitude to survive. He had taken to going to the cell and sitting as still as he could in the shadows, thinking about this painter or that, anything, just to get through it.

He was always scared. He knew he was food. Really, that's all he was. Food. A weak white man with no criminal skills, no natural cunning, no weapons whatsoever, and a stark terror of violence: He was the lowest thing in the McAlester foodchain. He was plankton. If God didn't want him eaten, why did he make him so weak and then contrive, due to no fault of Richard's own, to put him in a penitentiary?

Richard knew himself to be a uniquely talented individual. It was merely others conspiring against him that kept him from achieving that greatness. But somehow he saw things that others didn't see and felt things that others didn't feel. It may have been that he was too damned sensitive for his own good, that he saw through so much, that made people hate him so.

But that was the burden of the artist. In a society of philistines, he had that cross to bear. He could do it.

Richard, thirty-one, had a pillowy bouffant of blond hair and a face strangely smooth for his age. He had a long, soft body and an extremely quiet way of walking, as if his feet were somehow more delicate than others'. He was by profession an art teacher, with a master's from the Maryland Institute of Art in Baltimore, but by passion an artist, who had spent the better part of the last two decades trying to master certain intricacies of the human form. It was a problem he had never quite worked out, but now, with 877 prison days ahead of him, he thought if he concentrated, he might find some way to—

"Richard, goddamn, boy, get your ass up."

Richard, jerked from his reverie, looked up to see Lamar, his hair soaked, flying into the cell.

"Uh, I—"

"Listen, here, got to move fast. You go out behind the kitchens and bring goddamn Odell back here. Do you understand?"

The terror blanched across Richard's face. He swallowed as if ingesting a billiard ball. The yard was a land of terror if a rabbit like him went unescorted. The blacks would rip him up. The Aryan Brotherhood would make him a hood ornament. The homeboys would make fajitas out of him. The fags would fuck him in every orifice. The Indians would burn him at the stake. The hacks might use him for target practice.

"Richard!" barked Lamar, "now you got to be a man today. Had to kill me a big nigger in the hack showers and—"

"You *what!* You *kil*—"

Lamar was on him, rammed him backward, and got his hand around Richard's mouth to shut him up fast.

"Listen here, Richard. I am dead by nightfall if I don't get out of this place and so is poor baby Odell. And with the two of us gone, little brother, what you think they gonna do to you? You'll be the fuckboy to end all fuckboys. Someone gonna tattoo FOR RENT on your asshole, son. Now I cain't be seen out there, 'cause I'm supposed to be riding

Junior Jefferson's dick right now. We got to get out of here.''

''Out?''

It was inconceivable to Richard.

''That's right, boy. We goin' on a little vacation before all fucking hell breaks out.''

It was all attitude, Richard knew. All it took was a certain carriage, a manly posture, a strut that stank of violence and warned all who saw you that you were the stone stud.

He puffed himself up and strutted down the corridor to the yard entrance. He stepped into the blazing light, his chest stout and his shoulders back. He was a man. Nobody could fuck with him.

''Here, kitty, kitty, kitty,'' a black man sung at him.

Someone else made wet kissing sounds.

A giant tongue licked its lips, smacking with the anticipation of violent sex.

Richard melted. His knees began to shake; his breath came in terrible spurts that he had to fight to get in and out of his chest. His vision grew woozy. He walked straight ahead, pretending to be oblivious to the shouts that rose to greet him, while he ached to cry. There was no comfort in this universe, none whatsoever, nothing, nowhere. It was all Darwinism, Darwinism gone spectacularly exponential. The strong didn't just eat the weak, they ate the strong, too. It was a primal sink, a festival of eating.

''Mrs. Lamar Pye, you sweet thang, be on your ass like a big dog,'' someone called, ending in a glissando of poochy sounds.

It had stunned him most of all that they had so much freedom inside. Prison? He'd imagined it as being in little cells the whole day, where you could get some constructive reading done. But no. The cells came open at seven A.M., after headcount, and then it was pretty much anything goes. Only a few of the inmates, the connected ones, had jobs; the rest milled and seethed in the yard, or worked out, endlessly pumping iron or playing some weird version of handball against the wall. Violence broke out casually, randomly. It was pure Bosch, a landscape of degradation. The white walls loomed overhead, cupping the seven-hundred-odd inmates in an arena built for three hundred, and the solemn guards, with their automatic rifles, paid only nominal attention to what was going on.

"Hey, pachuco, hey, gringa, Romeo's got something for you to suck on, my pretty one."

It was the Mexicans. *Cholos,* they called themselves. They were as bad as the blacks. Sexy, graceful men, so full of laughter, eyes flashing with passion, weirdly stylish under their red bandannas and hairnets. Blinding, bleached-white T-shirts. The blacks had their ways, too: they brought the steamy urban music of their culture to their space, and you could hear the soul sounds blasting out twenty-four hours a day. They were like superb ebony warriors, with hard muscles sculpted from sheer anthracite coal, glistening with sweat, so wonderfully graceful and body proud. Scary. So scary. And then the red gang, calling itself N-D-N-Z, with those letters elaborately tattooed around their biceps in some picturesque calligraphy that was clearly the work of a genius. They looked at him with flat eyes, as if his lifeform didn't register on their radar screens. They never teased or challenged, but only watched him with their savage, indifferent eyes, and he knew they were imagining hurting him out of sheer boredom.

But none of the gangs was as bad as the white boys, who really ran the Mac, the tribe of mutants and scum, tattooed and slobby, their hair greased up like Vikings on a raid, their squirrely eyes narrow with evil cunning. They would fuck you or kill you in a second, as if it made not a penny's worth of difference to them. Fat, with bulging white bellies and purple wreaths of convict tattooing proudly inscribed on their chalky skin, they were the outlaw elite. Goatees, full hillbilly beards, ponytails; hair, at any rate, in its many forms. Deviance was their religion, indifference to pain, their own or others, its highest form of expression. Some of them even had some teeth.

In his terror, Richard yearned for Lamar's protection, yearned even to see the idiot Odell. He knew he didn't dare disappoint Lamar, who could be a stern disciplinarian. So somehow he kept himself on track, pushing ahead through the mob, waiting for his heart to go into vaporlock.

The Mac without Lamar? Jesus, it terrified him. He'd be—

"Wi-shud."

He looked up. It was his other savior. It was Odell.

Working quickly, Lamar went down two cells to Freddy the Dentist's, where Freddy was painting the engine of some twin-engined World War II fighter plane model, and sent Freddy off to find Harry Funt, the hack. Harry Funt was the absolute centerpiece of the scam he had already, with stunning speed that no IQ test could ever hope to measure, conceptualized in his mind by drawing upon the immense archival wealth of data he held in his head about the Mac.

Lamar looked at his watch. Twenty till. The men would start filing back in shortly. Goddamned Harry better show.

He went to his cell. He took his best shank out from under the toilet bowl, a wicked two-incher cut down from a butter knife. Cost him two cartons. Would kill a man in one swipe if you got him right. He'd done it, twice, too. That made him feel a little better. He'd go down fighting at least.

Been fighting his whole goddamn life. Cards always against him. But it didn't matter, he was a man, he'd do the job. He could get through anything. Once, when he was nineteen, a couple of Cherokee deputies in Anadarko had worked him over for three long days, broken his nose, his jaw, his cheekbone, four ribs, and the fingers of his left hand. They thought he'd raped this squaw girl. He had, and several others too frightened to complain, but he never gave them the goddamn satisfaction of hearing him admit it. That hadn't been the first time he'd spit teeth and blood.

He went to his collection of stroke books, dug through *Juggs* and *Leg Show* and *Dears and Rears* and came at last to the November 1992 *Penthouse.* He took it out gingerly, opened it to the centerfold, and there he discovered the Picture.

It was Lamar the Lion and his bitch princess. He looked at it, seeing his own features in the king of the jungle and the submissiveness across the woman's beautiful face that was the highest form of love. Richard had finally gotten her tits right. They weren't real big floppers. He hated floppers. He liked them kind of tight, muscley, so they'd move when she ran but wouldn't bang. The lines around the central form were heavily etched, because he'd ran over them with a pencil himself, hoping to find out how Richard had done it. But his lines somehow made it heavier.

Something in the picture he liked so very much. Nothing had ever pleased him quite that much. He folded it up and put it in his pocket just as Harry Funt came in. Harry, the oldest of the hacks, was in his blue uniform, with a walkie-talkie and a baton but no firearm.

"Lamar—" Freddy said.

"We're getting out. Now. The three of us, Richard, Odell, and me—and you."

Harry just looked at him. He gulped. Some water came into his pale old eyes.

"Lamar—"

"Had to kill me that nigger Junior Jefferson in the showers. He was going to fuck me. Now I know you got annex forms in the office and you can get us out of the cellblock and by security, at least into the A corridor and into Admin Two."

There was nothing in the old man at all, no guts, no outrage, just a sense of wiltedness, like a flower in the frost, waiting on a cold night's death. He looked down, begging for mercy.

"I can't, Lamar. Please don't make me. Got a wife needs a operation. My granddaughter got one of them breathing problems, we got to keep her—"

But Lamar had never been into mercy.

"Oh yes you can, Harry. 'Cause when they find Junior, all hell's going to break out and the niggers will kill me. I can't let that happen to me and mine. I'll turn snitch, and you been muling in scat for Daddy Cool *and* copilots and phennies for Rodney and nobody knows you're working both sides but me. You even do a load of crystal meth now and again. Right? Now, let me tell you how fast I will sell you to both of them, old man. Just that fast. There won't be enough of you left to feed Odell's cats."

Harry threw a fast, nervous look at his watch. He had about twelve minutes until lockup. Then he gave it up, exactly as Lamar's shrewd calculus had predicted.

"Okay," he said. "But it would help if you'd conk me one, too. It won't look so bad. I might even get a medal."

It wasn't that Odell was big. It wasn't that he had a cleft palate and the gap under his nose was like the dark fissure of the Mariana Trench. It wasn't that his arms were abnormally long, and it wasn't that his teeth were black or that, owing to his physical deformity, he was a mouth breather and issued raspy wheezes wherever he went.

More than anything it was the strange, almost lozenge shape of his head as it soared outward, almost exploding from the pointy little chin into a broad, pale forehead topped, most absurdly, by a flame of red hair. He had freckles, like any Huck Finn, but his eyes were almost always devoid of emotion.

He held out a dead cat. It had just stopped moving. He had been holding it tightly a few minutes earlier. He shook it to bring it back to life, but it remained still and even floppy.

Kiddy, he thought. *Kiddy no no. Kiddy no mew? Kiddy sleepytime. Kiddy. KIDDY be jumpy! Kiddy jumpy jumpy jumpy. Make kiddy be jumpy-jump. Dell no like em kiddy ust no no. Sleepytime kiddy baby.*

Standing nervously before him, Richard thought, *Jesus, who framed thy fearful asymmetry? William Blake himself couldn't have thought this guy up.*

Everyone gave Odell a wide berth, even the blacks and the warriors of N-D-N-Z, because Odell was known to have no fear. Even in this behavioral grease trap, he could inspire fear because he literally had none. Only Lamar could control him or even reach him, and Lamar rented him out to Daddy Cool for disciplinary tasks. Odell would walk into a crowd of blacks without noticing them and maim the man among them who'd earned Daddy's disapproval. Then he'd walk away, his face implacably impassive.

"Odell, Lamar needs us. He sent me to get you. Come on, quick."

"Na kiddy ust dud," Odell said impassively, face slack and dull, as if he hadn't heard what Richard just said. Richard was beginning to understand Odell, which had him worried: My kitty is dead.

Odell held up the tiny cat, limp in his huge hands. The fur between its ears was strangely wet, as if he had been licking it.

Richard thought he'd puke. Odell was a squalid mountain of man-child, with the brain of a fish, and the docile demeanor of an old beagle until Lamar told him to act otherwise.

"That's too bad, Odell, but Lamar wants us now. It's an emergency."

"Mergy?" asked Odell.

"A hurry-hurry-Odell," said Richard, aping the strange language in which Lamar communicated with Odell.

Awareness flickered behind Odell's dim eyes.

"Huwwy huwwy," he said, then made a half smile that increased momentarily the terrible gap in his skull. He tucked the cat in his shirt—Richard wanted to gag—and sped off. The masses parted to let him by. Nobody would dis Odell or stand against him. And in the blessed safety of his wake, Richard hurried after, feeling almost heroic.

They didn't even reach the cell but instead were intercepted by Lamar just inside the D block door.

"Okay, boys, time to go," said Lamar.

"Lamar, I—" began the very nervous Richard.

"Now you just shut up, Richard, and be a good boy. Odell, if Richard talks, you make him no-talk."

"No-talk, Mar," said Odell, love blooming in his eyes, and he turned toward Richard as if to crush his skull.

"No-talk, Wi-chud," he said.

"No-talk," said Richard.

They headed to the lieutenant's office, which was empty:

the lieutenant would be in the guard's lounge having a cup of coffee. Inside, a nervous old Harry Funt waited.

"Lamar, I got the forms, but I don't know if this is going to work. You boys have to put on irons and chains."

"We'll put them on, goddamn it, Harry."

"You're going to conk me good?"

"Real good."

"You want to mess up the office? This'd be where you jump me."

"You can tell 'em we did it clean. We don't got time for the office."

"Okay, Lamar, if you say so. And you won't say nothing about my participation if it doesn't work?"

"It's gonna work, Harry. This is Lamar talking. You believe it, Harry. Now here, you take this."

He handed over the shank, a short, evilly sharpened blade embedded in a plastic haft.

"You don't need no weapons, Lamar," said Harry. "You ain't going to hurt nobody, are you?"

"No sir, I am not," said Lamar. "But I may have to face somebody down and a goddamn shank gets a man to thinking about what it'd feel like to get cut up bad, it surely does. Now you take it, because nobody's going to throw the metal detector on you, Harry. Hurry now. We got to get moving."

Harry took the blade with a shudder, sliding it into his hip pocket as if he didn't know what it was for.

Quickly the three prisoners put on leg irons, waist chains, and handcuffs. They were not allowed to move out of the cellblock area without the bondage—it was McAlester's oldest and strictest security arrangement.

"Now Lamar, s'pose I get asked how come I'm bringing all three you boys? Regs say only move one at a time through the chokepoint into the desecure zone."

"You just wink, like you got three fish on a goddamn line. You caught three big-uns. We're gonna give something up the warden hisself has got to hear. You gonna be a hero, Harry."

"He-wo," said Odell.

Now Richard was really scared.

Harry sullenly pushed his chained trio down the corridor.

"Take out your club, Harry," said Lamar. "It'll look more serious."

Harry swallowed and did just that, and in a second they came across two hacks heading down to supervise lockdown.

"Harry, what the fuck is this?"

"Uh, you know. Lamar's got a beef with somebody and he wants to sing to the lieutenant. Won't talk to nobody less."

"You wanna sing to me, Lamar?"

"Bubba, you ain't got the heat to get me no deal. I'm gonna give the warden some names, but I need protection for me and mine and only the warden has the clout."

"Watch him, Harry. Lamar's too fucking smart to go on the snitch. He's playing some fucking angle, I swear to you."

"Lamar's a good boy, ain't you, Lamar," said Harry, through dry lips.

"Lamar's inmate scum, Harry, don't you put your trust in him. It'll come to grief, I swear."

But the guards slid on down the corridor, heading to the cellblock and to their duties.

The little party reached the stairway that lead up to the cellblock exit, and Harry took out his walkie-talkie.

"Ah, Control, this is Mike-Five, ah, coming through

with three inmates, the two Pye boys and their cellmate, ah—''

"Peed," said Richard.

"Yeah, Peed," said Harry into the thing.

"What's the dope, Harry?" the radio crackled. "The lieutenant okay this?"

"Say he did and you can check with him," said Lamar.

Harry swallowed again, seemed to lose half a shade of color, and then lied badly into the radio, "Yes, he did, Control. You can check. Got me a canary wants to do some singing.''

"You need an escort?"

"No, got me a pussy newboy and two soft old boys, that's all. No sweat."

"You watch that fucking Odell," said the voice. "He's as crazy as a goddamned loon."

"Cleared?"

"Cleared, but you gotta show paperwork."

Harry led the three men up the catwalk. At the top, they could turn and see the whole cellblock behind them, a cube cut with cells situated inside the larger cube of the housing building, with catwalks called shooting ways strung out parallel to each level, so that the screws could watch or blast away with water, buckshot, or .223s, as it fit their purposes.

Lamar looked at it. His home. Knew every cell, every nook and cranny, every hiding place. Only place he'd ever been happy. Where he belonged, really belonged.

"Mar," said Odell. "Go home see mamma?"

"That's right, Odell. Odell go see mamma. You just do what I say, and it'll all be fine."

Odell, Lamar realized, was scared. He was leaving something that he knew. He probably couldn't even remember the outside, so small and cramped was his sad little mind.

With his elbow, he gave Odell a little nudge of affection. "Lamar going to take care of Odell, make it all right," he said.

The main security gate at the highest level opened.

The three inmates stepped into a cocoon of professional attention. Guards flew to them, patted them down. One of them waved a Garrett Super Scanner metal detector up and down in search of the telltale hum that revealed a hidden hatpin or razor; none came. Meanwhile, another man gave Harry's paperwork the once-over.

"Harry, this don't look like the goddamn lieutenant's scrawl, though goddammit, the man can hardly write his own name."

"When he drinks a bit his hand gets scratchy," Harry said. "Whyn't you call him for the okay?"

The moment hung in the air. Richard had some trouble breathing, but Lamar was as slick as they come.

"You damn boys are making it so hard on me I just might change my goddamned mind. Don't want to think too long 'bout what I'm set to do. Might change my tune."

"Lamar, you have more shit in you than a goddamn out-house," said the guard. "Go on, Harry, get 'em out of here. I can't believe Lamar's turning snitch. Thought you was a tough con, Lamar."

"Getting old," said Lamar. "Can't get it hard no more. Warden's going to get me a softer joint, you know, a country club. Maybe I can get me some pussy."

"Get 'em out of here," said the supervisor. "Hope the goddamned warden knows what he's in for."

Harry escorted them down the hallway beyond the security checkpoint. It seemed like a different world suddenly; the hallway was bright and airy, though the windows had mesh screens; it was just possible to see the green plains of Southeast Oklahoma outside as they fell away toward Oklahoma City a hundred-odd miles off, all farmland and low hills. And horizon! Richard saw the horizon between the two red turrets of the rear gate, accessible only from Admin Two, the building they were now in.

The outside world: Richard had forgotten such a place existed. The weight of the prison was its totality, its immensity: in its grip, all other possibilities diminished, even disappeared. He had a brief and sweet image of his life before, of the freedoms he'd had, the pleasures, the small idiotic rights. A blast of pity for himself and his helpless ways swept over him.

"In here," said Lamar, putting his shoulder quickly against a locked door and bucking it open without a sound.

The four men were suddenly in the darkened office of the prison's medical administrator, Dr. Benteen. Benteen, who was brother-in-law to some powerful state senator, was almost a total no-show these days, with a bad drinking problem, much loathed by everyone in the prison community but untouchable.

Quickly Lamar took the keys from the hapless Harry and sprang himself; he tossed them to Odell, who did the same, and finally it was Richard who got them. By the time he was out, Lamar had taken up a post at the window. They were two stories up. Jesus Christ, Richard thought, what were they supposed to do, parachute?

"Yeah, he's still here, goddammit," said Lamar. "Parked where he always parks. That gets us ten feet less to jump. You ain't afraid of a little jump, are you, Richard? Say twenty feet. On a nice, soft van roof."

Richard looked: Twenty-five feet below he saw the flat roof of a white van. How had Lamar known it would be there?

"Goddamn guy comes to put Hostess Twinkies and HoHo Cakes in the guard's vending machines every goddamned Tuesday this time. Now we jump onto that, I can hot-wire the goddamned thing, and we off. Good thang them damned hacks love their HoHo Cakes so fucking much!''

Lamar knew the prison up one side and down the other. Just knew it cold.

"Fall long," said Odell. "Boo boo fall. Hurt Odell."

"Now Odell, you can jump it, you know you can. See mamma, get out, okay Odell?" He turned to Richard. "This boy loved his mamma. She was the only one ever treated him decent till I come along. We got to get him to her grave just once before he dies. Now Odell, want you to bend this goddamned metal screen out, so we can get ourselves out of here. Got to move fast—that guy's going to be moving along soon enough."

"Lamar, you want I should tie myself up," said Harry. "I don't think I can get it tight enough. You may have to tie the knots for me."

"Sure, Harry. You go on. Use your belt and the cord from that drape or maybe you can find some tape. Odell and I going to get this screen out. Richard, son, you just hang loose a sec, we may need you."

But they didn't. Odell gathered up a length of curtain and cushioned his hands, then proceeded to punch the glass out of the window. Then he upturned the doctor's chair, pulling it apart until he had a metal strut. Inserting it in a small gap in the metalwork, he pried enough of the window mesh from its screws to get leverage; finishing with the strength of his own arms, he bent the screen back savagely, until a man could easily crawl out.

Meanwhile, Harry Funt scavenged through the office until he found some masking tape.

"This here tape'll work just fine," he said. "Should I gag myself, Lamar?"

"Yeah, Harry, that's great. You know, it's them little touches that make it real. This here thing is working out just great, ain't it, Richard?"

"It's great," said Richard. "Really very, very nice."

"Almost ready, Odell?"

"Weddy," said Odell.

"Lamar," said Harry, "I did my ankles and legs. I'm going to put the gag on now. Can you do my wrists? Not too tight or nothing. And when you hit me, just enough to bring some blood. Nothing dramatic. I'm too goddamned old for drama."

"Why, sure, Harry," said Lamar. He waited as the old man put some cotton balls in his mouth and then ran a length of tape around his mouth to the back of his head. Then Lamar bent behind the old man who eagerly offered his wrists behind his back and Lamar swiftly ensnared his wrists. Then Lamar wrapped several more lengths of tape around Harry's mouth.

"That's kind of tight, isn't it?" asked Richard.

"Well, maybe it is," said Lamar. "But we want it real. Harry don't mind. Do you mind, Harry?" he asked.

Harry, gagging a little, shook his head no.

"Good," said Lamar. "Well, then, boys, we are all set. Oh, wait, just this one little last thing."

He bent to Harry.

"We want it real, don't we, Harry. All the details just right?"

Harry nodded.

The shank magically appeared in Lamar's hand, and he cut the old man's carotid artery.

CHAPTER 2

The phone pulled Bud Pewtie from a blank and dreamless sleep, and he awoke in the dark of his bedroom, his wife breathing heavily beside him. All through the house it was quiet, except for the sounds of his two sons shifting and squirming under their blankets down the hall.

He picked it up.

"Yeah, Pewtie here."

"Bud?"

Bud immediately recognized the voice of Captain Tim James, the Zone Five area commander and his boss. Bud felt the edge in Captain James's voice. A bad one on I-44, kids smeared on the pavement, propane burning, gas leaking, a schoolbus burned? Bud had seen them all.

"Bud, we got a call-out. It's a big ten-ninety-eight. Up at goddamn McAlester, three tough-ass inmates. They capped a guard, another convict and probably a guy they stole a truck from."

"Yes sir," he said.

Bud was secretly relieved. He'd seen a lot of random destruction on the highway, what speed and metal can do to the innocent or the stupid. Twenty-five long years in, he knew a certain part of himself was wearing away: that part that could look without flinching at young lives crunched into bent metal.

Russell ''Bud'' Pewtie was forty-eight, a strong, large man with short, graying hair and brusque ways. He wasn't exactly an emotion machine, and his profession had conspired to drive what few public feelings he had even deeper behind the set lines of his squarish face. No one could read much on Bud. He was a sergeant and Zone Five assistant commander of Troop G, of the Oklahoma Highway Patrol, that is, for Comanche, Caddo, Grady, Cotton, Stephens, and Jefferson Counties, as well as for the long northeast-southwest run of I-44 down from Oklahoma City on the way to Wichita Falls, Texas.

''Affirmative, Captain,'' he said. ''I'm rolling.''

''Bud, nobody's riding alone on this one. Oklahoma City's orders. These boys are too goddamned mean and you can bet their first stop's gonna be a gun store or some hunter's basement. We're partnering up and traveling cocked and locked.''

''Who'm I partnering with?''

''I see you broke in that kid Ted Pepper. He lives near you, don't he?''

For just a beat, Bud paused. He tried to clear his head, but yeah, it would be Ted. Somehow, it had to be Ted.

''Yeah, Ted's about ten minutes away on the other side of Lawton.''

''Okay, you double with Ted. This is just an ad hoc thing, but we're setting up roadblocks on all the majors between here and McAlester. Gonna be a meeting up in Chickasha in the highway maintenance shop. Can you get there by oh-seven-hundred for roadblock assignment? I want you and Ted to represent our troop, and I'll rotate others in as I can.''

"Yes sir," said Bud. "I'll call Ted."

"Bud, I know you'll do damned good. But be careful. These boys are trash."

Bud rolled out of bed, pausing just a second on the edge to collect his scattered wits. It felt cold, as if a terrible wind were blowing, but it was just a random chill.

"Bud?"

It was Jen, in the dark.

"Yes?"

"What is it?"

"Oh, it was Tim. A goddamn call-out. Escaped cons. I'll be sitting on a goddamned roadblock or running up and down the highway, that's all."

"You be careful, Bud."

"I always am," he said.

Bud went down to the kitchen and, after just the faintest pause, dialed Ted Pepper's number. He knew it by heart.

It rang three times.

"Hello?"

Ted's wife Holly answered. He knew her voice too well. He swallowed hard. On the phone she sounded like syrup; there was a low vibration, a hum, that still made him a little woozy. She was twenty-six. How complicated things can get!

"Holly?"

"Bud! You shouldn't call me here. He—"

"Holly, is Ted there?"

"Of course he isn't here. You know that. He's in the other bedroom. I'll get him."

"Good, you do that, Holly."

Thirty seconds later Ted came on.

"Bud?"

"It sure is," said Bud heartily, and gave Ted the news. "I'm swinging by in fifteen, and I want to find you with all your creases straight and your AR-15 locked and loaded. Got that, son?''

"Oh, Christ," said Ted. "I only just went to sleep."

"Well, now, I know you have it in you."

"Christ, Bud, you got all the damn answers. You're goddamn happy, I can tell. See you in twenty."

"Fifteen, young trooper," said Bud.

He was so merry with Ted. Old trooper sergeant, all the damn answers, full of laughs and teasing and the subtle insistence of obedience. Before he'd won his stripes, he'd been "the kid" to a dozen tough old sergeants, and now, here he was, a sergeant himself.

Bud hit the shower, was out in a flash, and rushed through the rest. Then, stepping into his closet, he found his next day's uniform spring-fresh on the hanger. He pinned on the gold badge, an Indian shield with two wings above it, and the words TO PROTECT AND SERVE. To a lot of the younger men, the badge meant nothing. But he still felt as if it symbolized his membership and acceptance in an elite society: we enforce, it said to the world. We protect.

He pulled on his socks and a Galco ankle holster, then stepped into his taupe, striped slacks, still thirty-sixes. The brown shirt, with its flashy gray epaulets and pocket flaps, fit him like a glove. Its three yellow chevrons stood out bright as daisies, just below the yellow-piped arrowhead shoulder patch that said Oklahoma Highway Patrol. Nineteen years to make that rank, even if he'd passed the test up at the top the first time, when he'd only done a decade. He buttoned it up, swiftly tied the tie.

"Bud, you put your vest on!" Jen called from the bedroom, where she should have been sleeping.

It irritated him, but most things Jen said irritated him these days.

"That goddamn thing's heavy as a washing machine."

"Still, you put it on."

"Of course I will," he lied. He hated it. Made him feel like he had on a girdle.

Last, Bud slipped into his black patent oxfords and tied them tight.

He stepped out of the closet.

"Bud, you don't have that vest on, I can tell. You're going to get yourself killed, and leave me with a mountain of bills," Jen said.

"Nobody's killing me," he said. "Now go back to sleep."

"I swear, you are an ornery man these days," she said sullenly.

She settled in under the blankets, rolling over.

He stepped into the short hallway. Not much of a house, but nobody'd ever complained. It was dark, a blue dark, but Bud knew every square inch of it. He walked a bit, and leaned in to look at Russ, who snoozed with some trouble; he was restive in sleep as in life. Russ's hair, mottled and tangled, ensnared his handsome face; above him the specter of some rock performer made up like the devil himself rose on a poster, stark white and psychotic. He looked like a PCP zombie Bud had once seen a DEA team blow away on 44 the other side of OK City. But Bud didn't worry about Russ. Russ, who was seventeen, looked like six kinds of shit, with all that damned hair and the black clothes he wore and a little glittery something in his earlobe that Bud didn't even want to know about, but Bud somehow knew he had too much of his mother in him to do anything crazy. He still got mostly As. He had a chance to go to a fancy Eastern university if certain things worked out right.

Across the hall, he looked in on the younger boy, Jeff. Jeff was the smaller at fifteen but the tougher. He had a pug face and an athlete's wiry, muscley frame. The room stank ever so slightly of stale sweat socks, moldy jocks, ten pairs of sneakers. He was the jock wannabe, no genius, not a reader, but on any kind of field a hard and earnest plugger who yearned to do well and almost never did. There was something tragic in Jeff's wanting and continual air of disappointment in himself. Bud felt a wave of love and melancholy wash across him, so intense that he felt he could bend over and kiss the young man on the cheek. Jeff seemed to need him so.

I'm going to leave this young boy? he asked himself, feeling the weight come onto his shoulders. But leaving was being discussed. It was a possibility up ahead on the road. Scared the hell out of him. Am I really getting ready to pull out?

Well, maybe I am. Maybe they'll be all right.

"Daddy?" Jeff had stirred, seeing his father.

"Yes, Jeff, what is it?"

"What's going on?"

"Oh, they need me. Nothing much."

"You don't have your vest on. I can tell."

"It's nothing," he said. "Don't you worry a bit. You're just like your mother. Get on back to sleep now."

Bud put his family behind him and walked downstairs to the end of the hall to a closet. He opened it to face his gun vault. Quickly, he turned the familiar combination.

His heavy patent-leather belt hung on the pegboard inside the door; he peeled it off, ran the belt around his waist, and pulled it tight, third hole. A belt was important to a policeman; it carried so much: cuffs, can of mace, a baton if he was working crowd control, a sap as some of the boys carried, a radio jack, a speedloader pouch, and the gun, of course.

Of course the gun. A four-inch Smith & Wesson M66 .357 Magnum. He took his off the shelf and gave it a quick wipedown; its stainless steel ugliness gleamed in the low light, but the damned thing felt so good in the hand. It fired six murderous little Federal 125-grain hollowpoint bullets, with a one-shot stop rating of 93 percent. Bud went to the range twice a week; he was a very good shot.

He opened the cylinder and quickly dropped in six Federals from the open box; he had two speedloaders, each charged with six cartridges for quick refills. Unlike many state officers, Bud laboriously practiced with the speed-loaders, and could get his six empties out and have six new shells deposited in the cylinder in less than two seconds. He'd never had to do so, just as he'd never shot a living man, but it was better to be able to do it fast and not need it than to need it and not be able to do it. He secured the pistol in his holster, snapping the thumb snap. Then he reached into the gun safe and removed a tiny Smith & Wesson 640, a two-incher, flicked the cylinder open to assure himself it carried five +P .38-Special hollowtips, locked the cylinder, and slipped it into his ankle holster, left inside ankle, again securing it with the strap.

He locked the safe up tight and pulled his Smokey off its top. The dark green flatbrimmed hat was perched just so atop his head, its brim just edging off the top of his vision, as it was supposed to. Maybe that's where it started for him, all those years back. Goddamn, he still thought it was the best-looking hat he'd ever seen; it was the only hat he'd ever wear. He wanted to be buried in it, or at least with it.

He stepped out of the house and went to the cruiser parked in the driveway, a gleaming Chevy Caprice, in the black-and-white tones of the state. Firing up the engine, he picked up the mike and pressed the send button.

"Ah, Dispatch, this is six-oh-five, I'm ten-fifty-one to Officer two-eleven."

"Got you, six-oh-five," said the woman's voice, the

night duty dispatcher. "Advise you switch to Police Inter-city Net for updates as they come through."

"Affirmative, Dispatch. Any news?"

"Big zero, so far."

"Okay, Dispatch, off I go."

He switched to the intercity net, 155.670 MHz, eased the big car out of the driveway, and headed to Ted and Holly Pepper's.

The Pepper trailer, alone on its grim little street, was lit up like a turnpike gas station. Ted, fully uniformed, stood outside with a rifle case in one hand. He was a tall, good-looking youngster, perhaps too handsome; if there was weakness to his character it was that as a young man things had been given to him too easily, without his ever quite acquiring the lessons of humility and hard-ass work. If you're a blue-eyed boy with a button nose, things just show up on your plate. But he was all right. Ted just didn't have the gift—that special instinct for human deviance, that cunning about motive, that twitch for the truth under the lie, and finally, the will to do the job flat out—that marked a great cop. But there weren't too many great cops left, and Bud knew he himself fell short in a bunch of areas, too. He had only this on Ted: He'd been around a bit more.

As Bud pulled in, the door opened, and Holly came out in a housecoat with two sealed 7-Eleven plastic cups that presumably held hot coffee. Her freckles stood out now, without makeup; her straw-colored, almost reddish mass of hair looked like she'd been electrified, but, dammit, that was Holly, she was a cute one.

Ted was in a surly mood, Bud could tell, and Holly kept her distance.

"Hi, Bud," she chirped. "You and Ted off on another excellent adventure?"

"Holly, for Chrissakes," Ted said. "Howdy, Bud."

"Ted, you locked and loaded?"

"Yes sir, and I got three mags with the sixty-nine-grain hollowpoints. Eighteen in each one, as per."

"Good man. Let's get her in the trunk and get on the road. Morning, Holly."

"Oh, don't notice me or anything there, Mr. Sergeant Bud Pewtie."

He laughed. Holly was a flirty thing.

"I made you boys some coffee. I hope it helps."

"Anything helps," said Bud, opening the trunk. Ted put the rifle case in next to Bud's own rifle case, where a Mossberg 12-gauge pump gun with an extended magazine was concealed.

"You boys could start yourself a war," said Holly.

"Ain't gonna be no shooting," said Bud. "These trashy boys just want to stretch their legs before they go back. It's just a little vacation."

"Way I hear, they already killed three people," Holly said.

"Okay, so, they're a little testy," said Bud. But then he turned to Ted.

"Ted, I want you to go back and get your vest on. This is a vest day if ever there was one."

"Bud, you know I hate the goddamn vest. You ain't wearing one."

"No, I ain't. That's because I figure if there's any shooting, you going to be a hero while I sit in the goddamn back seat and pray. So I don't need no vest. You do, young trooper. You don't want to widow this beautiful young woman, do you?"

"Ah, Bud—"

"Now, Ted, don't make me pull hard rank in front of your wife. You just go on and do it. And don't think you can shame me by calling me a hypocrite, because I already know I am one and goddamn it, son, I am *proud* of it!''

Like a chastised child, Ted went sullenly into the trailer from where, presently, the sound of things being tossed and doors being slammed arrived.

''It's his day in the barrel, I guess,'' Bud said.

''He'll be fine, once he gets the coffee in him. Bud, how are you?''

''Oh, Holly, you know.''

He and Holly met at least twice and sometimes, depending on hunger and possibility, five or six times a week at various sites around the motel-rich greater Lawton area and made love with a desperation and a purity that Bud could never remember having felt in his life before. He hadn't made love to Jen in over two years. He could hardly remember making love to Jen. But he could never forget making love to Holly.

And what was going to happen next? Hell if he knew. It had the sense of a high speed chase to it: going faster and faster, and something bad was bound to come of it, but once you start, in some terrible way you have to finish.

''You said you'd work it out and I think you will. You'll be a man. Somebody has to be around here.''

''He is upset about something, isn't he? Could he know—''

''Bud, that boy hasn't paid no attention to me in a year. If I turned green, he wouldn't notice. So no, Bud, he don't know a thing.''

''Okay. I don't want him getting hurt. It's important we tell him when we tell Jen. So nobody gets hurt any more than necessary. We'll work this out. I promise. I swear.''

''You never want anybody getting hurt, do you, Bud? That's what I like so very much about you. But you should be wearing your vest.''

"Well, Ted's right. I'm too old to itch that much all day, though you're the third person who's told me to wear it in the past twenty minutes."

"Bud, you should. You really should."

"Nobody's shooting this old boy, that I promise you."

"Bud, I love you," she suddenly said, as if she had to get it in quick. Then Ted, looking stiff with the seven pounds of Kevlar-reinforced fiberglass that now girdled his torso under his uniform shirt, came back out.

"Okay," said Bud, "time to get humming."

He shot Holly a secret look as Ted climbed into the car, then climbed in himself, backed out of the driveway, and sped out of the trailer park, heading crosstown to pick up Gore on the way to the 44.

Ted was silent.

"Well," Bud finally said, "looks like we got a hard couple of days coming up. Nobody goes home on these jobs till it's over. I remember back in 1978, there was this con who—"

But he glanced over and saw that Ted had settled back involuntarily and begun to breathe the heavy breath of sleep.

Middle of the night! thought Bud, and put the pedal to the metal, goosing the 350-cube engine, shooting through the deserted city as the sun just began to edge into the eastern sky.

It was full dawn when Bud pulled into the Chickasha highway maintenance barracks forty miles up the 44 toward Oklahoma City from Lawton, and Ted had slept the whole way. It was no big deal; Bud would have just talked to hear himself talk. If it made Ted sharper later on, so be it.

He entered the lot, not at all surprised to see cruisers not only from his own outfit but half a dozen others: the county sheriff's offices, the Lawton and Chickasha municipal police, MPs from the Fort Sill reservation whose vastness abutted Lawton, as well as a couple of black sedans that were the trademark of the OSBI, the Oklahoma State Bureau of Investigation, the state's own down-home FBI.

Oh, Christ, Bud thought: Osbies. Always think they know just that much more. Somehow always a little bit better protected than us poor old Patrol Smokies.

"Okay, bub," Bud announced. "Let's go git the particulars."

"Huh! Oh, Christ, sorry, Bud, didn't get much sleep last night. That goddamned wife of mine kept me up like you wouldn't believe. Hard to believe a scrawny girl like that needs it twice a night."

"Oh, to be that goddamned young again," said Bud, completing the circle of the lie. Ted had stopped sleeping with his wife thirteen months ago, for no known reason at all—just stopped; Bud had started sleeping with Ted's wife two months ago, and he knew the reason.

They got out and headed in, finding the place hopping, as was to be expected. He saw a lieutenant from Troop M over in Altus talking to two heavy-lidded types in ill-fitting suits who had to be OSBI. The two men in suits had Remington 700s with scopes hanging over their shoulders. In fact, looking about at the law enforcement types milling in the corridor, Bud saw that nearly everyone packed extra heat.

"Get yourself a cup of coffee," the lieutenant said to him. "We're waiting on goddamn C.D. for a briefing."

"I thought that old coot was dead," said Bud, acknowledging the mention of the legendary lawman.

"C.D. ain't ever going to die," said the lieutenant. "He's too pickled in bourbon to pass on."

He and Ted found coffee and a big tub of Dunkin' Donuts, and Bud passed on the pastry while Ted took a sugary one. Suddenly Bud noticed guys streaming by them into the duty room as if everyone just knew that it was somehow time to get the word. Bud filed in, too, and the place that was sparsely filled when a twelve-man rotation got its shift briefing was now chockablock with cops.

A state officer made a few introductory remarks, but Bud, like all of them, paid no attention: they were eyeballing the legendary old Lt. C. D. Henderson, sitting there in a string tie and Tony Lama boots, and a definitely nonregulation Colt automatic in some kind of ancient, blackened, multistrapped and -buckled shoulder rig under his suit coat.

C.D. was the most famous detective in the state of Oklahoma and a hardcore police gunfighter who went back to great days when the Oklahoma City police pistol team sent its best men into the FBI to handle all violent duties. He himself, it was said, had been trained in the art of close-in shooting by the legendary D. A. "Jelly" Bryce.

But he looked so old. Rumor had it that he was a secret lush and would have been long since retired off the force if he didn't have photographs of well-known politicians with prostitutes or something.

"Well, my compliments to y'all, can't tell you how damned impressed I am with how fast you boys got here and how many of you there are," C.D. said as he took over. His face was a prune left in the sun an extra week and the suit, khaki with cowboy piping, seemed to have been originally bought for a much larger man in the unenthusiastic way it hung off his scrawny geezer's frame.

"Anyway, the goddamned Department of Correction dumped a bad one on us, and here's the latest I have, and I just got off the phone with Oklahoma City. Pass the bulletins out, please."

A couple of lesser lights walked among the men, handing out three-page sheets.

"At about eighteen hundred hours last night, that is, thirteen hours ago, a bad old boy named Lamar Pye led his cousin Odell and a poor newboy stiff named Richard Peed out of McAlester State Penitentiary. The first bad news is, it was only discovered at ten P.M., when they did a headcount, learned that the three boys were gone, and began to search. Found a goddamn treasure chest of bodies—an old guard was found with his throat cut. A big black inmate named Willie Ralph Jefferson, Jr., stowed in a closet, with a bar of soap shoved down his craw. Odell's work, probably. We learned quickly that a vending machine delivery guy whose last stop was the prison never came back. Now that's bad because they were out over four hours before they were discovered missing, which means roadblocks and bloodhounds in McAlester area ain't apt to turn up much."

He then narrated some colorful details of the escape, including a description of the van they purportedly made their getaway in, an eighty-nine Ford Econoline with HOSTESS PRODUCTS emblazoned on it, and the license number and a description of the poor missing driver, a Willard Jones.

"What you see before you now is the rap sheet on the three inmates. Lamar's the baddest bad news. He's a goddamned professional inmate and criminal. Been breaking the law since he was ten years old. His daddy, matter of fact, was killed in a shootout with an Arkansas state trooper back in fifty-five, when Lamar was just a lump in his mama's belly. Raised in reform school. B and E, assault, assault with a deadly weapon, armed robbery, distribution of narcotics, he just put his hands in everything, working out of Tulsa and Oklahoma City. He shot a convenience store clerk dead in 1974. Just shot him, point blank. That's Lamar. Anyway, it was goddamn plea-bargained down to murder two, and he was paroled in 1980. Then he and his cousin, poor dumb old Odell, they commenced to rob banks, fast-food restaurants, hell, they even robbed a yogurt shop in Tulsa mall. They're both shooters. We also believe Lamar pulled the trigger on a couple of snitches who were ratting out the Noble Pagans motorcycle club, on contract from the Pagans. Here's something you won't see on no bulletin: they say this boy's hung like an ox. They say he makes Johnny Dillinger look like a sprout in that department. So if you have a suspect, you can always check his pecker, and if you need two rulers to measure, I'd say you got your man!''

There was tide of laughter in the room.

''Now Odell's like Lamar's body servant. Dumb as a stump and can't hardly talk. Retarded, probably. Anyway, in 1985, Lamar and Odell decided to rip off a Noble Pagan road captain who was dealing and they took him out beyond Anadarko and shot him in the head. Well, he didn't die soon as they thought, and he named them first, which is how come the boys ended up in the Mac.''

Bud looked at the pictures of the two men and saw what he'd seen so many times before—the look of billytown trash, hard-burning eyes smoldering with either some obscure grudge against the world or utter stupidity. Minds that worked different from most minds, that's what they were like, as if in some way they were hardwired different. Killers, manipulators, ruthless, savage—and yet, goddamn them, always brave. So much sheer aggression. So used to violence, so comfortable with it.

Odell's eyes were like coal lumps; not a goddamned thing in them; he just stared out from the photograph, his strange-shaped head seeming to come from a different planet, a black smear where his upper lip should have been.

Lamar was different: his face was wider and more open and held some charm to it. In a certain hard way, he was a handsome man; but the eyes had such a glare to them, such a fuck-not-with-me attitude. There was something tragic in them, too; the hard cons, the real pros, always had a glimmer of talent. They could have been something else, something better.

"My guess is, here's how we'll catch him," said Henderson. "Sooner or later he'll run to his own kind—outlaw biker scum, punks, hardcases. Hell, he's been affiliated with half the gangs in Oklahoma; he's done time with all the hardcore convicts and professional criminals in the state. He'll go to them and somebody'll rat him out, you just watch."

"What about this other boy?" a voice called.

"Peed is hard to figure," said C. D. Henderson. "He ain't your inmate material, or so it would seem. No priors. Some kind of art genius, went to that high school for the gifted they run in Tulsa—his daddy was a oil executive— and he went out East to some kind of art place. A painter, they say. Anyway, back he comes when his mama gets sick and he spends ten years nursing her. Meanwhile, he's teaching art at Oklahoma City Junior College, but mainly he's painting."

Bud looked at this Richard Peed. Under the puffy, pillow head of hair, he beheld a face remarkable in its softness. No harsh lines attended Richard Peed at all; he seemed raw material, unformed, callow, a child-man. His face was dough, waiting for experience to stamp an imprint upon it. The eyes were fuzzy and slightly weak, and even in the picture, peering over the new rack of inmate's numbers and bled of all nuance by the harshness of the flashbulb, he radiated fear; he was a rabbit. The joint would kill him.

"What'd this he-man do?" a deputy sheriff asked. "Rob a goddamned lemonade stand?"

But Bud could see the only mark against him was an assault with intent to kill, three to five. That almost never got a fellow time in a hard joint like the Mac. Any first-year law student could get a body with no priors out in two months.

"Well, because he was white and rich, they had to make a big show of going hard on him. But the deal was, he'd do his three months at the Mac, and then be transferred to the Federal playground at El Reno. What he did, though, was plumb right crazy sick," said Lt. Henderson. "He had this art show and he thought all the reviewers were going to say how great he was, only nobody came. His poor mama was giving him a hard time. So he stabbed her."

If C. D. Henderson meant to shock his audience, he failed. All the men there had encountered more grotesque atrocities in the billytowns and black townships of Oklahoma, but Henderson wasn't quite done yet.

"Stabbed her, that is, in the eyes. Put his own mother's goddamned eyes out. Blinded her."

CHAPTER 3

Another rabbit was learning about the wolves.

It was nearly eight, getting on to darkness. Bud Pewtie would not receive his phone call for a good six hours yet. But in a van heading at just five miles under the speed limit west down State Route 1 toward Ada, the lesson progressed.

This rabbit's name was Willard. It said so on a little oval on his pocket. WILLARD, in script.

Lamar thought: *Whatever happens, I ain't never going to have to wear no shirt with my goddamned name in a little oval so all the square johns can say, Oh, hello, Lamar, check the oil, Lamar, put that thing over there, Lamar, I take sugar in my coffee, Lamar.*

Willard had already pissed in his pants. He couldn't stop weeping. But that's what rabbits did. That's why they were rabbits.

"Now, Willard," said Lamar, "tell me again about your plant."

"Mister, please don't hurt me, Christ, it's just a goddamned plant."

"How many trucks?"

"Jesus, mister, I don't know, I never counted."

"Now listen careful, Willard. I don't want to have to hurt you. Just tell me. How many trucks? Answer my questions or I'll have Odell hurt you like he done before."

Odell had already broken four of Willard's fingers. He sat now, his big arm necklaced around Willard's scrawny, shivering neck, eating Twinkies. He'd eaten about fifty of them.

"Dink-ies," he'd say occasionally.

"Richard," called Lamar, "you just keep going straight on toward Ada. Don't do nothing stupid. You're right at the speed limit, son, I can feel it."

Richard, driving the van, tried to appear nonchalant, but the rabbit's terror was like the smell of decaying flesh in the air, and it made him sick.

"Yes, Lamar," called Richard. They rolled through jerk-water towns where Richard had always wondered how people made a living, across rolling green fields strewn with barrellike rolls of hay, across a landscape that could have been a portrait of Farmland, USA. He tried not to listen to what was going on behind him, but only concentrate on the speed limit, on staying right at sixty.

"Maybe twenty-five trucks," Willard was saying, his voice wobbly and occasionally falsetto with fear. "We got accounts all over South Oklahoma. We do all the grocery store deliveries, we got vending machine accounts in VFWs in every town over five thousand, we do cop stations—cops eat a lot of HoHo Cakes—we do gas stations, every place a man might eat a Twinkie or a HoHo Cake, that's where we are."

"Dink-ies," said Odell.

"Please, please, I got a wife and two kids. Sir, I never hurt nobody and never did no wrong."

"Never you mind, Willard. You just work with me and I'll see if I can't cut you a little slack with Odell, okay?"

"Yes sir," sobbed Willard.

"Twenty-five trucks? Now, when you pull in, they all park together or what? Is it fenced? You checked in? Does anybody pay any attention to you? You go into an operations shack, or what?"

"Y'all park together, sir," said Willard, concentrating very hard. "There ain't no fence or nothing. Nobody checks you in. The drivers go into the office with what stock they got left, and unload. Then they check out."

"If you didn't check out, would anybody notice? Would it be a big thing? Who would know?"

"Oh, Christ. You're going to hurt me."

"I am not going to hurt you, 'less you make me hurt you. I want this shit, Willard. Willard, help me, goddammit. We can work together on this goddamned thing, can't we?"

"I guess round about eight, maybe they'd begin to wonder what-all the hell I been up to. Maybe if I don't git back by ten, that's when they call the cops. But drivers and vendor service guys, you know, they always go off, do the goddamndest things."

"But not you, Willard. You do good work."

"Yes sir."

"Now, Willard. You got any money?"

"Sir, I only got 'bout ten dollars on me, cash. And I got lots of quarters. Maybe five hundred dollars in quarters and loose change."

"Ah," said Lamar, calculating. "What about a bankcard? You got a bankcard, Willard?"

"No sir. I only make fourteen thousand dollars a year. I don't have enough money for no bankcard."

"Do you have any money at your house?"

"Please, sir, don't go to my house. I got two little girls. Oh, Jesus, why is this happening?"

It was as if Willard's need to know *why* finally exasperated Lamar beyond endurance. He felt no man had the right to ask such elemental questions of him.

"Here's why, Willard. You see what it says here?"

He held out his big right fist, the one that said F U C K. Willard nodded.

"Yes, you do."

And he held out his big left fist.

Y O U ! it said.

The fear radiated from Willard's eyes like heat. Lamar liked that in a man.

"Do you get it, Willard? Do it make sense now?"

Desperately, Willard nodded.

"Yes. *Now* it makes sense. Odell, break his goddamned thumb."

Odell cakey, cakey good. Sweet. Cakey like mama, sweet.
Cakey, all cakey in whole wurl. Lookie cakey! Lookie!
   Truck full cakey. Cakey white, cakey good brown,
   cakey milklike cakey.
Mar like loud up sudden "Odell break his goddamned
   thumb."
Hurty man Odell do. Hurty bad hurt hurt. Thumb no go.
   Thumb no go! Thumb no go!
Thumb go like pop!
Pop go thumb.
Now me cakey Mar. Mar like now you go cakey.

Willard screamed while Odell broke his thumb. He screamed so loud it irritated Lamar, who crawled forward, below eye level, to talk to Richard.

"How you holding up, Richard?"

"Do you have to hurt him so?" Richard asked.

"Hurt him? Hell, you ain't seen a thing, Richard, in your short life if you think that's hurting." Lamar gave a little chuckle at the stupidity of Richard's observation.

"Anyway," he continued after a pause, "I think you'll be wanting to hit the turnoff up ahead, into Ada, I do believe. Then we look for Davis Street and when we head down, you give me a call."

"Lamar . . . where are we going?"

"Don't you worry, son, I got it all figured out. Now, what was that about the wrists, boy? Remember, the other night you was telling me about the wrists."

Willard was still screaming; he sobbed and heaved and begged, but Odell kept him captured with a single immense hand while eating Twinkies with the other.

The wrist? The wrist? Now what the fuck?

Then he had it: art. *Art!*

"Oh, yeah. Well, I think actually, ah, you see, what makes a painting or a drawing so fluid, actually, so lifelike, is the flexibility of the wrist and the exquisite relationship of the articulate muscles of the wrist and hand to the vision and the imagination. That's why a free-painted line is always called a living line."

"Goddamn," said Lamar, rapturous with delight. "Yessir, you sure can talk. You can talk and you can draw! You are a goddamned interesting young man, ain't he, Odell?"

"Awoooooah," said Odell Pye, his broad, crippled mouth knitting up into a smile, his lips crusted with flecks of weightless white custard filling, Willard weeping in his grasp.

"Well, now, Richard, boy, you be thinking on your next drawing. I think I want to go back to lions. I liked the eagles and I liked the tigers, but damn, there's something about that old king of the jungle that just tickles me where I itch the worst!''

Richard watched as a black-and-white Highway Patrol car flew by across the way. He checked his watch. Clearly they hadn't been discovered yet.

Lamar had one more item on his agenda. He crawled back into the rear of the van. He reached over and lifted the rabbit's head, so that the man's face looked into his. What he saw was what he expected to see: no surprises at all. Fear. The eyes were stone bright, like the rabbit had been high on crank, but the drug that made him so mad was just the fear. You could now do anything to Willard the Rabbit. You could fuck him, fuck his daughters, kill his wife, set his house a-fire, and he'd just look at you like that, baby lips aquiver. He wasn't no man, goddammit. He was a rabbit. Even a nigger will fight you, you push him hard enough or corner him. But not a rabbit. Rabbit just look you over while you decide which part of him to bite on. He may even help you make that decision. And he will sell you anything, anything at all.

''Now, Willard, listen here, I need some more help.''

''W-what?'' said Willard.

''Guns. I need some guns. Man like me, man with enemies, got to have a gun, you know. Not to hurt, to protect. Now, Willard, you got any guns?''

''I hate guns,'' said Willard.

''Gwus,'' said Odell. ''Bangy like bangy.''

''Son, that doesn't surprise me.''

''I know where there's a gun store,'' said Willard, trying to help.

''Now, Willard, I can see you're trying to get with it. But a gun store don't fill the bill. How can I rob a gun store if I don't got no guns? And if I had a gun, I wouldn't need to rob no gun store. Plus, these days, you run into your scum in gun stores. Them boys all pack and they just looking for excuses to shoot a man. Read about it in gun magazines, they want to blow someone away. Peckerwoods, trashy boys, your basic Okabilly scum. No sir, gun store ain't no place at all. I need a citizen with guns. A man who keeps guns, a hunter, something like that. Willard, I know if you think real hard, you'll be knowing somebody who's got guns."

Willard scrunched up his face in despair until at last a little light came on behind his eyes.

"Mr. Stepford says his father hunts," he said. "Says his old man sends him a haunch of venison every fall."

"Hmm," said Lamar. "Now who would Mr. Stepford be?"

"Mr. Bill Stepford, regional vice-president for Hostess Baking Division of Oklahoma. My boss's boss. He give me the job. He said his father been up in Canada hunting elk, been to Mexico to shoot them doves, wants to go to Maine to hunt bear before he dies."

"Where his father live?"

"Uh, he's a big farmer. Owns a spread out near Ratliff City."

"Do this old man have a first name?"

"Sir, I don't— You're not going to hurt him, are you? He's an old man. Fought in World War II as a bomber pilot. He was a hero. He was a—"

"Do he have a first name?"

"I don't know," said Willard. "Except that now that I think it over, I kind of think Mr. Bill Stepford is a Mr. Bill Stepford, Jr. You're not going to hurt that old man, are you?"

"Now, Willard," said Lamar. "I cut a square deal. You helped me, I didn't hurt you. Would I hurt that old man? Do

I look like that sort? Odell, don't hurt him none. Makie still.''

"Yoppa-yoppa," said Odell.

And Odell didn't hurt Willard. He strangled the young man to death as peacefully as he could, though the young man squirmed and bucked.

The van accelerated to close to ninety. Lamar turned and yelled, "Goddammit, Richard, you slow this thing down, you stupid little cocksucker, you get us chased by the police and I will have your ass for breakfast."

Richard tried to get control of himself. The boy's struggle had at last ceased. He checked the mirror as he dropped back down under sixty-five, and saw no red flashing light. He was all right. He tried to breathe slowly.

"Dink-ie," said Odell.

CHAPTER
4

The world had ceased to make sense back in the seventies, and it just got worse and worse and worse: crazed kids with automatic weapons, crimes against children and women, these nutcase whiteboys who thought they were God's chosen, niggers gone plumb screwball on delusions of victimization and fearfully nursed grudges. Sometimes he believed the communists or the trilateralists or somebody, some agency—the CIA, the FBI, the KKK—was behind it all. But still Lt. C. D. Henderson clung to certain convictions against the mounting chaos. Primarily, he believed in logic. He was a detective, that most specialized and refined and renowned type of lawman, the most famous detective in Oklahoma, a celebrity at police conventions, a consultant on cases far and wide. His core belief was that if enough data could be assembled, a clever fellow could find a pattern in it somehow and make sense of it, and bring it to its logical conclusion.

He was sixty-eight years old, and still a lieutenant. He'd always be a lieutenant, just as inevitably as when they needed someone to run an investigation, they'd always call him. Careers had been built on his intelligence and insight, and still he made less than forty thousand dollars a year. The men he'd broken in with were mostly dead, the men he'd trained had retired or gone to other, better jobs, and he was now primarily working for rude young people. But he still had the gift: he saw the connections the others missed, he was willing to do the dreary work, the collating, the sifting, the endless examination of details.

"These kids," he often lamented to the Missus, "these damned kids, they just don't want to do the work. Get a wiretap, bust a raid, go to SWAT, sweat an interrogation, call forensics. They ain't got the patience to nurse the answers out. They won't look at the stuff and just *figure* it out."

"Carl," she'd say, "they ain't worth a glass of hot gravy in July."

It was the bitterness, mainly, that drove him to the loving arms of I. W. Harper. With his daily pint of Harper's resting comfy and promising in a brown paper bag in his right inside pocket, he could get his mind loose and fluent and quell the seething anger that dogged him like a mean little dog. Maybe he made a few more mistakes, maybe he missed a trick or two, maybe the younger men could smell the whiskey on his breath and knew to leave him alone after four in the afternoon, it didn't matter. It was drink or eat the gun, he knew that.

Now acolytes and cynics had gathered around in a hangerlike facility at the Oklahoma Turnpike Authority in Chickasha, as a whole flood of men in the second day of the Pye cousins manhunt came off duty and tried to grab some rest and perhaps seek advice. He'd run a manhunt or two in his time, it was said.

"So Lieutenant," someone said, "got me a gal I'd like to git back to. What do you think the chances are we gonna git off this detail soon?"

"Most of 'em just wander around with no damned idea of what to do," he began, staring out at the young, unformed faces, "and they run into a roadblock in the first few minutes or hours. They're easy, they're the ones the roadblock system is designed to catch. Then there's those who have some kind of organization sponsoring them, and can count on it for support—transportation, weapons, new IDs, that sort of thing. But sooner or later, somebody rats them out, when there's an advantage in doing so.

"But every now and then," he continued, "every now and then you get a smart one. One who's full of natural cunning from the get-go, you know, has the *gift* for such a thing. Add to that, he's been calculating the angles for years, he's thought over all the mistakes he made, he's been smart enough to pick up tips from the older inmates. And let me tell you, he gives you a run. He gives you a goddamn run."

"C.D., you think this Lamar is going to give us a run?"

"Well, now son, it's early yet. But he has been out forty-eight hours and he seems to have goddamn disappeared. That's very impressive, I have to tell you. So maybe Lamar is your boy, your hardcore bad man on a hot streak, getting bolder and bolder. And I'll tell you this—if he is, he'll be hell to catch."

"C.D., if the governor asks you for advice, what will you say?"

"I'd solve it like any crime. I'd say, 'Look for the third piece of evidence.' Sometimes you can do it on two. You can't do it on one, that I know from long and bitter years of trying. Sometimes, maybe, just maybe, two will set you on your way. I've seen it happen a time or so. But this here is just an investigation. Every damn case, whether it's some SWAT team hoedown in the city or a domestic dispute or a goddamn high-speed motorized chase along the turnpike, it's still fundamentally an investigation and the fundamental rules apply. And it's that third piece of evidence that takes you where you want to go every damn time. That's how I got Freddy the Dentist.''

It was C.D.'s most famous case; it had even been written up in a magazine, and there'd been talk about making a movie, though nothing ever came of it.

But no one shouted: Tell us about Freddy the Dentist, C.D.

At least not for a bit.

''Wasn't that—''

''That's the one,'' said C.D., and he was off. The old glory unrolled before his eyes. Lord, how he wished for a drink to ease the telling, but tell it he would, to show these young men the way.

It was 1975, American Airlines Flight 354, Oklahoma City to Chicago, twenty minutes into its trip: *Ka-boom!* One hundred twenty-one souls vanished in a thunderclap. Body parts over four counties. The FBI highhanding it. It didn't take them long to determine an explosive device, generic as all get-out—four sticks of dynamite wired to a drugstore clock—had blown the guts out of the plane before it even reached altitude. They figured whoever had done such a thing had done it strictly for the money. Thus they made a rapid assumption that it was a crime for profit, and quickly examined the data on newly acquired life insurance policies over $100,000 on the victims. That was their first piece of evidence. This yielded twenty-three suspects; they then cross-referenced against engineering or demolitions experience on the theory that building such a device was a sophisticated enterprise, demanding expertise. This was the second piece of evidence, and damned if in a day they didn't arrest a forty-four-year-old petroleum executive who'd done fieldwork for Phillips in the Choctaw Fields, where dynamite was regularly employed for sonar testing.

But C.D. just didn't buy it. The man *always* took out a short-term insurance policy on his wife when she flew, as far back as 1958 when they were married. There were no accounts of marital difficulty, and the fellow was a deacon in his church. And he was screwing a secretary, probably his true crime, but one so easily uncovered it would have pointed the finger at him so quickly he could never have hoped to escape it. But the most important thing: he wasn't a handyman. C.D. visited the house after the arrest and didn't see a single piece of home-built furniture, not even a bookshelf. In the basement there were no tools at all, just boxes. He knew there was a vast gulf between men who did things with their hands and men who didn't: he didn't believe a man who didn't would actually take it upon himself to build a bomb.

"The FBI was all over the newspapers with their big triumph," C.D. said. "But to me, the thing smelled to high heaven. They couldn't find no trace of explosive residue in the house or office. I don't know much about bombs, but if they're trying to tell me he built it, I got to satisfy myself that he'd have the confidence in his manual skills to do such a thing without leaving a crater over one half of Cleveland County."

So C.D. set to work: first piece of evidence—insurance policies over $35,00, not over $100,000.

"To city boys like the FBI, used to working organized crime, white-collar crime, drugs, that sort of thing, nobody'd do nothing for less than a hundred grand. But to a country person or a small-time middle-class shopkeep or just-barely-making-it professional man who's not got by on much his whole life and is way deep in debt, thirty-five thousand or so can sound pretty damned big."

This yielded him not twenty-three names but forty-seven.

Now he cross-referenced for some kind of explosives experience or exposure and achieved . . . nothing. None of the new names had any identifiable explosives experience.

So he figured the person must have gone to the library to learn. He called the Oklahoma City library and learned that of the forty-seven, thirty-one held cards in its system; computers were just coming in to use, and he was able to examine the records of the thirty-one cardholders. He discovered that one of them had checked out a book two months earlier called *Principles of Explosive Exploration: a Guidebook for Petroleum Geologists.*

This happened to be one Freddy Dupont, thirty-eight years old, of Midwest City, Okalahoma . . . a dentist.

"A dentist, I thought," C.D. told his listeners. "Now why the hell is a dentist checking out books on oil field explosives? And isn't a dentist by the very goddamned nature of his job the kind of manual tinkerer that would have the skill necessary to put something like a bomb together?"

But it wasn't enough. He needed a third piece of evidence.

So he took the book to an oil geologist he knew and said to the man, "I know what this book tells me. What *don't* it tell me?"

The geologist examined the volume for several minutes, scanning the table of contents and the index, and then said one word that sent a shiver down C.D.'s spine.

"'Fuses.' That's what he said. It didn't say nothing about *fuses.* How to set the thing off."

"Where'd a feller go to learn about fuses?" C.D. had asked him.

"Only one place I know. The military," was the reply.

"He ain't been in the military." But then C.D. had a

moment. The military puts every damn thing it knows into
. . . field manuals.

It was pretty easy after that. Calling the U.S. Government
Printing Office, he learned that a dental hygienist named
Rose Fluerry, in Dr. Dupont's office for less than a year,
had ordered a field manual entitled *Special Forces Impro-
vised Field Munitions Detonation Techniques.* An examination of the book yielded a blueprint for "Timing Device
Simple, with Expedient Materials," which looked pretty
goddamn much like the one the FBI said blew the airliner.
A day's worth of surveillance revealed that in fact the dentist had moved in with Rose Fleurry; another day's investigation showed he'd moved in the day after the blast that had
claimed the lives of, among others, his wife and three children.

C.D. had picked up Rose, interrogated her gently for an
hour, and she had rolled over on her lover just that fast.
Turned out she didn't care for him much anymore by that
time. He didn't put the toilet seat down. And the fifty thousand dollars in insurance money on the wife and three kids?
Strictly an afterthought, a little fun money for a fling in
Mexico that he never got to take.

"Put him in the death house, proud to say, though goddammit, the sentence was later reduced to life. The funny
thing is, when we arrested him—he had model airplanes
everywhichgoddamnwhere. He *loved* airplanes. But it was
that *third* piece of evidence that done the trick."

This final observation fell on largely deaf ears, for by
now the old man had begun to bore the younger crowd.
C.D. felt it happen all the time. They pretended to want to
know, but somehow they just didn't have the patience, the
concentration.

As they turned away to sleep for tomorrow, C.D. pretended to go back to the data, the OSBI file on Lamar.

But he reached into his coat pocket and slipped out the I. W. Harper bottle. The lid was loose; with deft fingers he removed it. He hunched, seemed to shift in his old man's dry-boned way, and managed to draw a large, fiery swig from the bottle. It tasted like charcoal, gun smoke, and old plums. It knocked him where he wanted to be, which was into a state of blur.

Bud rolled over, trying to get to sleep. On this job it was six on the damn block, peeking into cars, then twelve on the road for what was called "aggressive patrolling," and then six off, and his six off was three gone and goddamned if old C.D. wasn't holding court with a bunch of Bureau boys a couple of bunks on down the goddamned way. There were dog teams outside, yowling, just in case. An OSBI helicopter made a buzz overhead every once in a while. The communications center, in one corner, crackled and yammered. Men were cleaning guns that hadn't yet been fired. Sleep was a hard bargain tonight.

Yet Bud wasn't an unhappy man. He and Ted alternated on the driving, and after close to twenty-five years of driving himself, Bud hated it when someone drove him. And was it his imagination, or was Ted's ambivalence about his life somehow expressing itself in his driving? Made Bud pretty itchy to sit there while the boy diddled with the accelerator. You go trooper, you got to *love* to drive a car, because that's 98 percent of the duty day: you'll see death in all the ways it can come to drivers and you'll give chase and maybe kill, but it all turned on the powerful automobile. You had to love that bitch on wheels or get another line of work.

But in three hours it would be his day to drive again. A certain secret part of him responded to the pleasures of the

wheel, and he hoped they wouldn't nab those goddamned
boys until after he had his eighteen.

But that was only a surface thing. Truth was, Bud felt
another deeper pleasure, though he could put no name on it.
For now, in the temporary suspension of normalcy that the
statewide manhunt brought, he felt something singing and
vibrant. It was freedom, or the illusion of freedom, from It.

That's how he thought of it: It. It was It, that was all It
was.

It, being the thing, the mess, the situation. It, meaning
Jen and the boys and the placid pleasures of duty versus the
sweetness of renewal as experienced in young Holly, and all
the pleasures it promised, all the places to go, all the ways
to be.

Bud was no romantic. His idea of reading was the new
Guns & Ammo or *Car and Driver,* and his idea of fun was
to go to a high school baseball game and watch Jeff play or
to zero in the .270 for deer season. He went to the movies
once a year, which was one time too much. He didn't watch
TV since they took Johnny off for that other goof, and it
still pissed him that they went and did such a goddamned
fool thing. Mainly, he just did his duty as he saw it, hard
and fair, and expected otherwise to be left alone.

Then It happened and all craziness broke out. Three
months ago he'd been cruising 44 near to shift's end and
had pulled off at a favorite place, a diner called Mary's in
the little town of Cement, where the coffee was hot and
black and the hash browns crispy, the way he liked them.

He was sitting at the counter, taking his twenty, when he
heard his name.

''Bud? Sergeant Bud Pewtie?''

He turned, and there she was. He remembered now.
When he'd been partnered up with Ted during Ted's six-
month provisional, he'd met Holly off and on, and when

Ted got his First Class stripe, he and Jen had the younger couple over to dinner to celebrate with a barbecue. But then as Ted changed, he'd drifted away, and he hardly ever talked to Bud anymore.

"Holly, how are you? Damn, what brings you up here?"

The part of Bud that he no longer thought he had reacted first. It wasn't that Holly was just pretty; some other secret thing under her surface just teased him in a strange way. Her youth, her boyish body, those freckles, that bright smile, but most of all it was something behind her eyes, something secretly merry and conspiratorial. She was a plotter, all right.

"Well, Bud, truth is, I came looking for you."

"Well, sit yourself down and I'll buy you a cup of coffee. You ever hear of such a thing called a telephone? Real easy to operate. You just drop a dime in and push some buttons and, like magic, you're talking to the man you want."

"Well, Bud, thanks for the tip, but it ain't so easy. I wanted it private."

"You got it. But this isn't some sad song I heard on the radio a hundred times and still can't say Jack Jump about? That damn fool Ted's found a new girl, or some such. I know I look like Ann Landers but I don't have her wisdom. My idea would be: I'll loan you the gun and you go shoot him. I don't think Ann would ever tell you that."

She giggled at old Bud.

"Oh, Bud, you love to flirt and make all the girls laugh, don't you? I'll bet you were a pistol back in high school."

Not so; he'd been a fullback, big and awkward and a little smarter than people thought when they considered his bulk, but no showboat with the girls. He'd married the first pretty one that was nice to him.

"Sure I was."

"Well, anyway," she said, "you're not far wrong. But I

don't think it's a girl. It's just a thing. He's just not there anymore. I was wondering if something's going on in the patrol or on the road I should know about.''

It was true. Ted had drifted off. He went his own way, put in his hours and disappeared. He was no longer a part of the elaborate Smokey culture—the gym, the shooting range, the optional SWAT exercises, the speed pursuit course—and when you took yourself out of that, you sort of guaranteed you'd stay at First Class for a long time.

''Oh, he's probably working some things out.''

''That's what he says, when he says anything.''

''It can be a hard life.''

''But Bud Pewtie didn't let it turn him sour.''

''Well, old Bud Pewtie, he went through his dog days, too. Holly, give him some room. Maybe he ain't made to be a policeman. That's okay. No shame in that. There's other things that he can do and make you and himself proud, I swear it. It's a hard life and more than once I've regretted the path I chose.''

''Well, you're so John Wayne I find that hard to believe, but I love the way you tried to make me feel good.''

She laughed and it suddenly occurred to Bud how easy it would be for him to like her. He wished sometimes he'd stopped it there and just frozen that moment in his heart forever: her laughter, his pleasure in it, her blinding beauty, his sense of having done the right thing.

But a couple of weeks later, having thought pretty much of nothing except her, he'd just up and called her one day and made up some pretext about Ted's problems and one damn thing led on to another; it became It.

''Bud?''

It was Ted, in the next bunk.

''Yes, Ted?''

''Bud, I can't sleep. I'm gonna go sit in the car.''

"Ted, you need your sleep."

"But I can't."

"Ted, you have to be sharp. Is something bothering you?"

"I'll tell you about it sometime, Bud. You'll know what I should do."

Bud watched Ted go on out. He tried to feel something for Ted. Shouldn't he feel awful, partnered up with the man whose wife he was sleeping with? But he didn't. Ted had made his own bed with his strange ways. Bud couldn't believe a bad thing about Holly, and some of the things she'd told him made him sick. Ted watched dirty movies on the VCR alone late at night. Ted didn't seem to even think about touching her anymore. Ted just didn't care; he was letting it drift apart.

Ted, partner, you made a dumb mistake. I wish I were man enough to help you out, but I got too much involved.

They were on the swing between I-44 at Chickasha and Anadarko, where the Pye boys hailed from, and where they just might head (though Bud thought not; whatever Lamar was, he wasn't that dumb) when Ted finally broke his silence.

"Bud, I got a thing or two on my mind."

"Well, that's no place for a thing or two. Spit 'em out."

The young trooper's face seemed to knit up in pain as he struggled for the words. But then finally he relaxed a bit and just said it.

"Ah, Bud . . . something's been eating me alive for months now. I even went to a psychiatrist, through that employees' assistance program the Department of Public Safety runs. But you're the first real person I breathed a word to."

"Well, then you'd best get it out. Just flat say it, and we'll pick up the pieces and see what we got."

"It's this: I don't think I got the guts for this line of work. The pure guts."

So that was it. The moment hung in the car. On either side, the countryside, like a green river, flowed by, rolling yet mountainless, the wheat fields and pastures and alfalfa fields all green in the sunlight. Soon Anadarko would come up, an ugly, desolate little town, with its customary bright strip of cheesy fast-food mills, a mile off the dead center of town.

"It's a scary job, Ted. Every one of us feels it when we strap on the gun. You run into a crazy, a hopped-up Tulsa gangbanger, a bad Okabilly with an attitude, you could stop a slug. I feel it, too, specially in these crazy days, where every goddamned body has a gun."

"No, Bud, you're just talking about duty anxiety. That's what the shrink said. But it's something deeper."

"Well, okay, Ted, if you say so. But I think everybody in our profession feels the horsecollar."

"About a year ago, I had a bad ten-seventy. I got good radar on a Nova about twenty miles below Oklahoma City. Pulled him over. It was around three in the goddamned morning. Not a soul about. Couldn't even see any lights on the horizon. I did a run through Dispatch and found there was no paper on the driver. Still, I don't know why, I was scared. A trooper in Maryland got one in the head just that way a few years back."

"I remember, Ted. I went to his funeral."

"Anyway, I approached the car. . . . It was four blacks. You know, in the X caps, the workout suits, and, man, that car just reeked of grass. They'd been having a *high* old time, I like to got buzzed just standing there. So I ask for the license and the guy hands it over. And I feel these eight eyes on me. And I look. And they're just staring at me, the reefer smoke just pouring out of that car, and I'm all alone and I'm thinking . . . *I'm dead.* I'm sure they were hauling a load. And they were just *staring* at me, waiting for me to make a move, daring me to make a move. And then I saw the first gun. An AR-15, like mine, only with the shorty barrel. It came up on the off-driver's side. One of 'em gets out. He's got a fucking *Uzi*! I see the guy in the back seat fiddling with something I couldn't even ID! Some weird thing with ventilation holes in the barrel shroud, a red-dot scope, a goddamned banana magazine. And here I am with a Smith and six cartridges. Goddamn, Bud, my dad fought in Vietnam and his dad fought in Korea and World War II and on down the line us Pepper boys have stood up and been counted. And all of a sudden it came over me so hard I thought I'd faint: I don't have it.''

"Ted—"

"So anyway, I just handed the license back. Apologized for stopping. And watched them go away. They laughed. I could hear them laugh as they pulled away. I went back to the cruiser and I just cried. I sat there and I cried.''

Ted just sat there, face slack, eyes dull. Burnt out, used up. He'd let the thing eat him alive.

"Well, Ted, you're a fine young officer,'' Bud finally said. "I think it would be a shame to let a thing like that worry on you too much. Sometime you got to back down. Those boys had you cold. What was the point of getting killed for nothing? They've probably killed each other by now anyway. Why not just pass it as done, and swear to do your best from here on out. That's all.''

"Bud, haven't you ever made a mistake? Don't you ever feel guilty? No, I don't suppose you do. You just are naturally the kind of man who goes through life without screwing up. God, I wish I could be like you. Sometimes I think

Holly wishes I could be like you. Bud this and Bud that. That girl has a thing for you, Bud. And for a while I hated you on account of it.''

"Ted, I—''

"No, Bud, it's not your damned fault. Well, anyway, that's it. You got it. I don't.''

"Well, Ted, the truth is, I have never done a courageous thing in my life. I don't have no idea how I'd be if there's lead flying about and I hope never to find out. And there's all sorts of things about me you don't know," Bud said.

"All units, all units," came the squawk over the statewide intercity net on the Motorola.

Both men suddenly started to listen.

"OSBI has just confirmed the location of the van thought to have been stolen by the inmate escapees Pye and Peed. It was found in the parking lot of a Hostess bakery and distributorship in Ada, where it had apparently sat for over thirty-six hours, unnoticed.''

"Goddamn," said Bud.

"Body in the back identified as Willard Jones, twenty-four, of Ada. We think we're looking for victim's car, a blue eighty-seven Dodge Dart, plates Lima-X-ray-Papa five-niner-seven," Dispatch said.

"Goddamn," said Bud, "that old Lamar's a smart one. Only place nobody'd notice a Hostess van is in the Hostess parking lot. He's outside the ring now. And nobody knows where the hell he's heading.''

A quiver passed through Bud.

Lamar was smart and he was bad. It was the worst news.

"Goddamn," said Ted, "glad you made me wear this damned vest.''

CHAPTER 5

Richard knew he was smart. He read at three. He was in gifted and special classes all the way through school, with grades way off the charts and an IQ that always opened eyes. And his talent: eerie, vivid, almost supernatural. A special, precious kind of boy, who impressed all exposed to him, all the way through.

But Lamar was *smart*.

Put Richard on the street and he's dead. Put Richard in jail and he's dead. Put him in Russia, in ancient Rome, on Mars, in the Marine Corps, all those places—he's dead. Not Lamar. Lamar ends up running most of them, or in their prisons, running them. Lamar just *knows*. Always, always figuring. Show him a problem and he breaks it down fast and right, though not the way a normal man might: He breaks it down so there's more for him and less for you. That's his one moral law, and having accepted it, he has no qualms or doubts. He works this law passionately and with straightforward conviction. What is Yeats's line? "The worst are full of passionate intensity"? That's it. That's Lamar. A sly genius at disorder, a prince of chaos.

These thoughts rocketed through Richard's oh-so-busy

brain as he drove the little trio in Willard Johnson's four-year-old Dart west of Ada toward Ratliff City, toward Mr. Bill Stepford, Sr.,'s place, where Mr. Stepford, Sr., and family had some guns that they would take, by any means possible. Richard tried not to think of that part. These poor people were condemned: Hurricane Lamar would hit them, abetted by Cyclone Odell, and wipe them out. They were the dead, sitting there in their little farmhouse even now, watching the television, finishing up the peach cobbler, wondering about the upcoming Grange meeting, deer season, and the possibility of Oklahoma ever getting some sort of major professional sports franchise. They had fought in wars and paid taxes and said their prayers for sixty-odd years and loved each other and the land that supported them, and they were dead. The existential majesty of it overwhelmed Richard.

Both Lamar and Odell were asleep in the back. He could hear them breathing, the even-odd-even-odd rhapsody of their snores, broken now and again by a belch or the rippling percussion of a smelly fart (Odell farted all the time and then smiled and said, "Odell makey stinky.") Their presence held not only terror but squalor and banality as well: They were so crude, bald, itchy, raw, unvarnished, brutes of the id. Richard looked out the window at the silent alfalfa fields of Oklahoma, the long and dreadful wait in the van at last over. He fought down a sob and studied a patch of sky, riddled with stars.

Richard thought: I could do it. I could slew the car off the road, throw the door open, and run, run away, flee. The police would find me eventually. I could explain. Just like the other thing: It's not my fault. Really. I was made to do it, I had no choice.

But he knew this was complete illusion. He could no more get away from Lamar than he could face him down and kill him. Lamar was everything. Lamar would run him down and break his neck with those strong hands, watching him with those superficially charming but ultimately empathyless eyes; then, as he was dying of asphyxiation, his spine having punctured his lungs, Lamar would fuck him in the ass, laughing; that would be how Richard left this world.

He wouldn't do it, of course. It made him nervous to even consider such a thing. If Lamar could see what he was thinking, Lamar would kill him for thinking it. Lamar was an absolute god: he demanded obedience as sternly as the figure in the Old Testament.

He looked out the window again.

"Be easy, wouldn't it, Richard?" Lamar asked softly from behind him. It startled Richard; he jumped.

"You scare so quick, Richard," Lamar laughed in a whisper. "But it would be easy, wouldn't it?"

"What, Lamar?"

"You know. Dump us. Take off. Go on, admit it. You thought of it."

"It's not my nature to be bold."

"No, it ain't. I could see that from the start. But I will change that. Richard, I swear to you, you stick with me, I may not make you rich or even free, but by God, you will be a man. Do you read me?"

"Yes sir," said Richard.

"Don't you 'sir' me, boy. I ain't no goddamned officer. I'm your friend, Richard, do you believe me? Your only friend."

"Yes, Lamar."

"You don't like the killing, do you?"

"No, I don't."

"Son, what that means, you raised in a different place than Lamar and Odell. Where Lamar come from, you hadda fight like shit every damn day or someone take it all from you. I do not enjoy it. I am not a low-down, trashy man. But a man has to do what he has to do to look after his people. Do you understand?''

''I do.''

''That's good. That's very good.''

No, it was very bad, because in the glare of their headlights a solitary mailbox stood against the glinting black tarmac before it and the fields of wheat country, now fallow in summer, behind it. It said simply STEPFORD.

''Party time,'' said Lamar.

It fell to Richard. Lamar explained patiently.

''This old farm lady, she take a look at me and she's on the phone to the county sheriff. I got something about me scares people. You, Richard, you got no tattoos and a girly body, you couldn't hurt a flea. So you knock on the door and get us in and when I come in, you make sure that old man don't make it to no gun.''

They parked halfway down the farm road. Richard could see the house, its windows glowing, standing in the middle of a barnyard, the barn towering nearby. It looked like a Christmas card. He yearned for moral destitution, some sign of country decadence, so that there'd be some sense that these people deserved what Lamar had in mind for them; but no. It was too pretty, a banal quaintness, possibly too studied. A farm from a Potemkin village.

Odell split off back; he'd come in the rear when Lamar came in the front. It was about ten o'clock. Why were the old people up so late?

''Y-you won't hurt them if you don't have to?'' Richard asked.

'''Course not,'' said Lamar. ''I ain't low-down. Only, see, we do need these guns. Suppose Johnny Cop pulls down on us. Go back to the pen? Let the niggers do us up? You too, up so fine? Even Odell? No sir, can't let that happen."

"Okay. Just so I have your assurance."

"You can count on me," said Lamar.

Richard watched as he melted into the darkness. He stood alone, breathing hard, in the brisk night, hearing the wind beat through the trees and now and then the squawk and rip of small things in the dark, fighting or dying. There was no moon; the stars rolled like wheat fields, torrents of them, high above, remote pinwheels of ancient fire. Richard wanted to weep but he could only obey: he counted in his head and when he reached the number three hundred, off he went.

As he approached the house he could see the old man sitting in his study, under some mounted game animals; a glass gun case stood against the wall; there was no old lady anywhere in sight, but he saw the blue glow of a television from an upstairs room.

He prayed there weren't grandkids or something in the house, or visiting relatives.

He knocked on the door. Maybe they'd be smart. Nobody just opened the door to strangers in the night these days. Maybe they'd be smart and call the sheriff, or get a gun and drive the interlopers away. He knocked again, praying for inaction.

The door opened wide.

"Why hello," the woman said.

"Er, hello. I'm, I'm an art teacher in Oklahoma City. My car broke down on the road. I was wondering if you could call the Triple A. I don't have to come in."

"And wait out there in the cold? Why, I wouldn't hear of it. That's the silliest thing I ever heard say. You come on in out of the chill and we'll get the tow truck on its way. Do you like coffee?''

Lamar slid in like a shadow of a cat and seemed to envelope her, muffling her cry. He had the shank hard against her throat, and Richard fixated on the way its blade pressed against her white, loose skin. She made a weeping sound, and in her desperation her eyes settled on Richard; they were widening in terror and begging, please, for mercy. Richard shuddered and looked away.

Two loud crashes boomed through the house, and Odell, for some bizarre reason without his shirt and with his hair wet and slicked back, broke in from the rear, an ax in his hand. He paused to howl at the ceiling or the sky beyond the roof, and Richard watched in abject fascination as the cry arose from him and his body shivered in rapture. All his demons were free and dancing in the room. He raced for the study where the old man looked up at him in utter befuddlement, then cowered from the blow he seemed about to receive from the immense half-naked man with the ax.

''The guns, Richard,'' ordered Lamar.

Richard ran to the gun case. Its glass stopped him. Inside, the gleaming treasures lay in repose. He could see green and yellow boxes of cartridges stacked neatly in the corner. He tried the handle, but the thing was locked. It baffled him, and then the bafflement departed as the glass seemed to explode out at him. Odell had just blasted it with the ax.

''Wook oub,'' said Odell, raising the ax in another mighty effort. Richard fell back as the ax smashed the door off the frame, and Odell greedily pulled a long-barreled gun from the rack and a box from the shelf, and began inserting red tubes into the weapon. With an oily *klak* he cycled it and turned.

"Dwan mub," he commanded, but the old man hadn't. He sat there shaking, literally stunned into shock from the way the universe had conspired in an instant to deconstruct his life.

Lamar had dumped the old woman, and came over to examine what lay before him.

"Goddamn," he said almost immediately. "Shotguns! Shotguns! You don't got no pistols? What the fuck is the matter with you, you old piece of shit!"

Angrily, he kicked the case. Then, grasping his fury, he took a shotgun off the rack and threaded shells into it. He pumped it, pointed it upwards, and fired.

The noise was terrific.

Richard had never been near a gun going off before in his life. The pain of it assaulted his ears. So loud! A satisfying rain of plaster cascaded down on Lamar, who smiled at this tiny victory over the world. Odell was dancing merrily around the room. Now and then he would smash something and holler. The two old people found each other at the couch, the woman weeping in the old buzzard's arms.

At last, Lamar went over to them.

"I thought you hunted, old fuck. *You!* I'm talking to you. You want me to gut the heart out of that old bitch? You talk to me, motherfucker."

The old man glared up at him.

"I gave up hunting deer last year. Sold all my centerfires. I—"

"You what?"

"I killed over one hundred deer, two elk, three bears, and a moose. It was enough."

"You fucking pussy, I want CENTERFIRE! I want OOOMPH! I want AUTOMATIC! I want a goddamn BE-RETTA! I want COLT! I want MAGNUM! You dicksuck-ing old puss, I wouldn't even fuck your scrawny ass, I'd give it to Richard. Richard, if he don't tell where the pistols are, fuck his ass. You hear me: Fuck him good up the ass and fuck his old lady up the ass.''

"Tell him, Bill," said the woman.

"I can't," said the old man.

"Tell him, Bill," said the woman.

"He'll just take them and go out and kill people in the world. He's going to kill us anyway. We're dead already. It don't matter none." He turned to Lamar. "You know, back in 1944, a lot of blond young men tried to kill me, in airplanes called Messerschmitts. But I bombed their factories and killed their wives and children and destroyed their filth. You're them, you prison scum. Go ahead, fuck my ass and fuck my old wife's ass. You can hurt me but you can't scare me.''

Lamar, for the first time in his life, seemed a little unsure.

"Richard, you hear that? A goddamn hero. Odell?''

"It's the Pyes," the old man told his wife. "On the news, the escapees. Just the worst trash. A sane society would have executed them both years back. Well, to hell with you, Lamar Pye and this simpleton and your little homosexual pal.''

"I'm not a homosexual," said Richard.

The old man spit on Richard.

Richard looked at the glob on his shirt. Then he looked at the old man. He was one of those scrawny old types, mostly leather and sinew, with furiously burning blue eyes. He looked like the sort of man who rose at four A.M. every morning and gave hell in buckets to any and all that had displeased him over his long life. He probably had a million dollars in the bank and believed he could take it to heaven with him. His children probably all secretly hated him, just as Richard had secretly hated his father. But like Richard, this man's children would never dare express their contempt directly.

"You goin' to let him do that?" said Lamar.

Why did he have to do that? thought Richard.

"You can't let a man do that. An old man with two shotguns on him, who thinks he's a hero. You got to break him down, boy."

"He's afraid," said the old man. "I can smell it on him. His underpants are brown and smelly. It happened in the Eighth Air Force all the time. Men like him, they never made their twenty-five missions. Your underpants—a mess, right?"

Richard swallowed. Yes, as a matter of fact, they were. He wasn't sure when it had happened but now he knew that it had. He swallowed again, wondering who he'd explain *this* to, then kicked the old man in the leg.

"Way to go, Richard. You show him. You be a goddamned man, Richard," shouted Lamar.

Everyone always talks, Lamar knew. That's the rule. But the old man had more grit than you find on the average yard, and Richard didn't have the stuff to get it out of him, even though he kicked him a batch of times as he lay curled on the floor in front of his weeping wife.

"Okay, Richard," Lamar finally said, not because he felt a pang of mercy for the square john but because Richard was truly disgusting him, his face all knit up like a girl's as he pranced his prissy way around him, kicking without a lot of force.

Richard looked at him, face twisted in emotion. Not rage, exactly; just some kind of terrible excitement. Shit, Lamar thought he looked like someone had stuck a pickle up his ass.

"Odell," Lamar commanded.

Odell turned the old man over on his back and twisted his arm backward and up like a corkscrew until the old man screamed. Meanwhile Lamar went looking for liquor. Could these people be Christian teetotalers? He had heard of such a thing but found it hard to imagine. The screams behind him were irritating.

He wandered into the pantry. Didn't quality usually keep booze in a pantry? Lamar looked around. He had never been in a house like this before. He wondered what it would be like living in a house like this. Pictures of a bunch of kids on the walls. He looked closely: it was like they were from Mars or something. All these kids and these pretty women and handsome boys who had to be the old man's daughters or sons or something. He wondered what it would be like to fuck a woman who looked like that? They didn't look like the *Penthouse* bitches, with the perfect round tits and the creamy skin. It looked fake, even if most evenings it got you off. These gals looked real, somehow, and sweet and tender. He imagined the fear in their eyes if he decided to fuck them. Lamar hadn't had true pussy in almost a decade. He'd almost forgotten what it would be like. Even now, he was a little unsure if he'd taste it before they finally got him.

There it was: brown bottles in a row, in a locked cabinet. He yanked the door open and a little piece of lock broke off. Some lock. Jack Daniel's Old No. 7, Tennessee drinking whiskey. Couldn't do better than that. He unscrewed the cap, took a swallow. Goddamn. Like wet smoke. Burns all the way down, your eyes tighten like fists and little tears come to them. Only way the world would ever get tears out of Lamar Pye. He took another quick swallow, then put back the bottle. Best not to let Odell know. Sober, Odell could be hard enough to handle. Drunk he could be death, and impossible. If Billy Cop came a-knocking, it wouldn't do any good to let Odell be drunk, because Lord knew that goddamned Richard boy would be no good in a fight with the law.

He wandered into the room with the television. The news was on. Some trashy-looking woman with an armful of babies was blubbering while two or three pretty girl reporters stood around and watched her melt down. She was blubbering about her poor husband Willard and what a good man he was. Lamar realized that was the wife of *his* Willard in the truck.

Goddamn, Willard, he thought. *You sure married yourself an ugly woman.* But he sort of wished he'd fucked her, ugly or not. He wanted to fuck *something,* that was for sure. Maybe he'd fuck the old man later.

Next his own picture came on, and somebody was talking about him, saying the authorities considered the escapees to be "armed and extremely dangerous." Wasn't *that* a mouthful?

The picture was the lineup shot from nine years ago when he had been picked up by OK City homicide after he and Odell had tapped Nicky Pusateri for the Pagans. Damnedest thing. You just could never tell. Shot that little prick square in the back of the head. Seen him go down, seen the blood squirt like tomato. Shot him again in the back and wrapped him in canvas and drove him twenty miles out and dumped him. And he was alive after all that?

He was, yes, and the dicks had come for Lamar, finding him stoned on amphetamines and living with a woman named Sally Two-Shoes, an Indian gal and sometime hooker who once in awhile would work a convenience store job with him and, though nobody ever found out about it, had killed her own father by drowning him in the toilet when he was drunk. He'd been making her blow him from the time she was ten on until she finally killed him, age fourteen. Anyway, they'd dragged Lamar into downtown OK City, some fancy building, and taken his pictures; he remembered one of the dicks smelled of garlic. Lamar looked at the picture again in the second before it vanished; he was wearing a golf shirt, the only one he'd ever had, with a little alligator on the pocket. Made him look like a pussy. Why'd he ever bought that shirt? His nose was squashed and his eyes dull and unfocused because he'd been sliding off the uppers; his lower lip hung open because his face was so relaxed on the drug downslope. His hair was long, though pulled tight behind him. He looked stupid. It had been his last instant of freedom.

Then some anchorwoman came on. She was pretty, like the farmer's daughters and the girl reporters with Willard's wife, maybe prettier. He wondered how it would be to fuck her, too. She was talking in a low, urgent voice about how dangerous these men were and how they should be avoided at all costs until the authorities finally caught up to them. She talked about the terrible obscenity tattooed on Lamar's knuckles, and she talked about how three men were already dead. Her face got all long and somber.

It somewhat tickled Lamar, the edge of breathy fear in her voice. He liked that a lot. He knew he scared square people. They looked into his eyes and they just saw pain and horror. That is, if they looked into his eyes, and they seldom did, or seldom had, even back in the world. You tattoo a F U C K and a Y O U ! on your knuckles, tends to chill the straights out.

"Lamar?"

It was Richard.

"Yeah?"

"We got 'em. It was a vault. The old lady gave us the combination."

"What happened to the old man?"

"He isn't breathing too well."

"He should have made it easy on hisself. Saved us the trouble. See what it got him? Oh well, fuck him if he can't take a joke."

They walked on downstairs, then into the basement. A shelf holding jelly jars set in the wall folded out on hinges to reveal an open Tredlock gun vault that stood about four feet tall and whose shelves appeared to display all the handguns known to man.

"Fifty-six, thirty-three, oh-eight," said Richard proudly. "I opened it myself."

Out of deference to Lamar, not even Odell had dipped inside. Lamar reached in and touched handguns, many of them.

"Turn on the goddamned light," he said.

The light came out.

Lamar examined the wares and at last discovered what it was he wanted. Yes, the man was a pistol shooter all right, and Lamar quickly seized what would be his prize. It was a .45 automatic with an extremely long slide and barrel, maybe eight inches. It had fancy sights mounted low to the slide. He looked to see that it was a Colt all right, but someone had added a new inscription under the Colt name that said CLARK CUSTOM GUNS, NEW IBERIA, LA.

"A bull's-eye gun?" asked Lamar.

"Go to hell," said the old man, crumpled on the floor, face swollen.

"I do believe I will, yes sir," said Lamar, "but it is a bull's-eye gun, ain't it?"

"Bill was state pistol champ, standing bull, rapid fire, three years in a row back in the seventies," said the woman.

"It'd be a treat to see him shoot one day," said Lamar, "but that ain't gonna happen."

Then he reached inside the safe and came out with something else: It was a big Colt .357 Magnum revolver with a four-inch barrel called a Python. He handed it to Richard.

"Here," he said. "You're a man now." Then he turned to the old lady.

"I bet you know how to cook real good. How'd you like to whomp up a real country breakfast? Eggs, bacon, juice, the works. I am hungry as hell and so are my friends, grandma."

"Don't help him a bit," said the old man.

"You are going to kill us," said the old lady.

"Yes ma'am, I probably will have to, not on account of not liking you but because that's the way things is. But could we eat first?"

"I suppose so," said the old woman.

"You're a fool, Mary," said the old man.

"Now Bill," said Lamar, "Mary's just trying to be a good neighbor."

CHAPTER 6

I must be some kind of trash, Bud thought, amazed at the speed with which he raced through his betrayals. It was so easy. It grew to be a habit, second nature. He could call Jen and bluff his way through a desolate little communication, subconsciously calculated to stay uncommunicative because the less he talked the less likely he'd screw up. Then he'd call Holly, and be so sweet and kind and decent, just that simple, that fast. Made him sick. But he could not stop doing it.

He was in the pay phone outside Jim's Diner in Ratliff City on Oklahoma 76, about halfway between Duncan and I-35 south to Dallas. Wasn't much here: the diner, a Sunoco, a Laundromat, and a convenience store. The diner was known for chili, but it was too early for chili: about ten in the morning, and they'd been on the road since six, part of a larger sweeping movement aimed at trying to intercept . . . intercept what? The inmates? Those boys hadn't been seen or heard from since the discovery of the truck with the body in it thirty-six hours ago.

The phone rang twice, then Jen picked it up.

"Hi, how are you? Thanks for the uniforms."

Jen, a slave always to her many jobs, had driven up to the Chickasha facility with five fresh uniforms in a plastic bag, plus underwear and socks, as Bud was running low off his first supply.

"Well," she said, "that's fine. We're all right here. So how are *you*?" Her voice was so Jen: far away, distant, with an undercurrent of some distress but nothing you could put your finger on.

"Fine. You know, it's beginning to get damn dreary, and nobody's got no idea in hell where these boys are. They're going to call off the roadblocks and roving patrols sometime soon, maybe as soon as tomorrow. It's pointless."

"It's terrible what they did to that poor vending service man," Jen said.

"Yes, it is, isn't it? They're bad boys. How are the kids?"

"Russ got his college board scores. They were so *high*. We should be proud of him."

"He takes after you. How's Jeff doing?"

"Oh, he's fine. He had a game last night, but it was close and he didn't get in. But he was in a good mood afterward. The boys went out for pizza and he went along."

"I should be there. This damn job. I'll be there next year."

"Oh, Bud?"

"What is it?" he said, glancing at his watch.

"Were you over near the Fort on Friday?"

Little signal of distress. Friday, yes. He'd been with Holly. In a motel room for a couple of hours. Place was called the Wigwam, a little down from the number four gate to Fort Sill, catering mainly to visiting military families. It was run by a retired city cop who let Bud have the room for free around midday.

Bud was surprised at how hard this hit him. He had never

had any trouble before. He looked up and saw poor Ted sitting at the counter over an untouched plate of eggs and a half-gone Coke, talking to the waitress.

"No, no, can't say that I was," he lied, trying to force some innocence into his voice and feeling himself fail miserably.

"Marge Sawyer *swears* she saw you pulling out of some parking lot. She honked, and you didn't see her. I only mention it because she wanted me to ask you if you knew that part of town, by the base, if you could recommend a good motel, something a little less expensive than the Holiday Inn, but in town, not at the airport. Her sister is—"

"No, Jen, wasn't me," he barked. "I don't know nothing about that part of town," he said, feeling the lies awkward in his mouth. "Look, I've got to get back on the road. Call you tonight if possible."

"Sure."

Bud hung up, feeling he had done badly and furious at himself for it; it was a bright morning, and he was surprised to find how hard he was breathing. Who the hell was Marge Sawyer? What had she seen? He'd been in uniform that day, too, so there could be no mistaking. Damn! It had been a foolish thing to do. Best to cut back for a while or something. . . .

He dropped another quarter and dialed the number. She picked up right away.

"Oh, Bud, it's been so long since you called. You said you'd call last night."

Now this always irritated Bud and in his present mood it struck a bad note. Sometimes just the managing of It got to be so damned troublesome that he needed a night off. There was always so much to remember: why he was late, what had happened, what route he'd taken home, all the things that go into running a deception. And sometimes it just wore him down.

"I couldn't get any time away from Ted. They got us running all over the damn place. I've only got a second."

"Well, how are you?" Holly wanted to know.

"Well, it's a hell of a lot more boring than just patrolling, I'll tell you that. But I think they're going to pull back after a while. This road stuff ain't panning out."

"Bud, you sound so irritated."

"I'm just tired, Holly."

"I miss you."

"Sweetie, I miss you too."

"The day they break it off—will I see you?"

"Well, I'll sure try," he said, feeling vaguely trapped. "I don't know if it's possible. I already missed one of my son's games and I want to get to the next one, in case he gets to play."

"Okay," she said in a tone that suggested it wasn't.

"I do miss you."

"I know you do."

"Talk to you soon."

He hung up, feeling sour as hell. Hadn't he just promised her that on the first day off, he'd see her? Great. He'd be exhausted, and what would the situation be with Ted, wouldn't he be off the same day? It was a mess. Sometimes Bud didn't know what the hell he'd do.

So after indulging the sourness for a few seconds, he headed back into the diner and slid in next to Ted.

"How is she?" Ted asked.

"Fine. Just fine. You call Holly?"

"Oh, Holly's okay, I suppose," Ted said. "Well, I reckon we should shove, huh?"

Bud shot a look at his watch. Ten-fifteen, yeah, they were due back on the road, just in case. He didn't like to be out of radio contact that long. Didn't realize he'd been on the phone for close to ten minutes. He took a last sip of coffee —lukewarm—and stood to peel some money off for the food. Not strictly necessary, but Bud knew that if you started eating for free—it was so easy—people soon stopped respecting you. He left a single for the girl, also irked that Ted never bothered to pitch in, at least with a tip.

"Oh, Bud," said Ted. "One thing. This girl here, she wanted to ask you something."

Bud turned to the woman, a middle-aged waitress, with the name Ruth on the nameplate of her uniform; she was vaguely familiar from previous stops, but he'd never struck up a relationship with her as he had with a few of the girls in other towns.

"Yes, Ruth?"

"Well, Sergeant, it's old Bill Stepford. He's stopped off for coffee each morning for the past ten years, every morning, nine o'clock sharp. He didn't show this morning. It sort of bothered me."

"I told her it was something for the Murray County sheriff's office," Ted said.

"Well, they're all out playing hero," Ruth said. "Sam Nicks hasn't set foot in this place since the jailbreak up at McAlester."

"Did you think about calling this farmer?" Bud asked.

"Yes sir, I did. The line was busy. Called four times and the line was busy."

"Maybe he's talking to somebody."

"Well, maybe he is. But I know Mr. Stepford and he is not the talking type."

"What about his wife?" Ted asked.

"Well, she's a mighty nice woman but she's not the sort to spend half an hour on the line either."

"Sounds like the phone is off the hook," said Bud.

"Bill Stepford hasn't missed coffee here in ten years. He came the last time we had heavy snow; drove his Wagoneer through the drifts. He likes our coffee."

Bud considered.

"Where is it?"

"Seven miles down the road. Then left, on County Road Six Seventy-nine. A mile, you'll see the mailbox. I'm afraid maybe he fell or something, can't get to the phone. People shouldn't live so isolated like that."

"Well," said Bud, "I'll call Dispatch and see if anything's going on they need us for. If not, maybe we'll take a spin by."

Lamar let Richard shower and sleep first, because Richard had driven while Lamar and Odell slept. So Richard sank into dreamless oblivion, a mercy. But when Lamar shook him awake at nine, he was still in the Stepfords' upstairs bedroom, still an escaped convict, still in the company of murderers.

Richard pulled on a pair of Bill Stepford's jeans and a blue workshirt and then settled in to do two things at once, under Lamar's instructions. He was to sit in the upstairs bedroom and keep watch, just in case. And he was to draw lions.

"Ah, now, Lamar? With everything that's going on?"

"Yes sir. I want it done, I want it perfect, so that when the time comes, we can move to the next step."

What next step?

Anyway, he now sat doodling, the original much-studied sketch before him. It was beginning to fade into gibberish, just a random blotch of lines. He wondered what Lamar saw in it to begin with. He knew it was insufferably banal: a lion, a woman, some sort of crazed Aryan fantasy, something out of the Hyperborean age. It matched exactly Lamar's arrested stage of development, but it had nothing to do with art; it was, rather, something out of that great unwashed fantasy life of the lumpen proletariat that expressed itself on the sides of vans or in comic books or boorish, bloody, boring movies. It was so coarse, untainted by subtlety or distinction.

Yet it had saved his life, he knew: It had in some way tamed Lamar's rage and redirected it, made Lamar see there was more to life than predation. And the drawing itself: There *was* something wildly savage and free in it that Lamar himself had responded to but which Richard had since been unable to capture, whether he stuck with lions or moved on to tigers and eagles. When he thought about it, it went away; you just couldn't do something like that offhandedly. It was a left-brain, right-brain thing. Lamar had understood and let Richard have a little bit of room on the issue. But now he was pressing him for results.

Fortunately, the farmer had a large selection of paper and pencils available. Working with a No. 2, Richard sat at the window, looking out dreamily, and tried to imagine some savage savannah where man and cat were the same creature, but woman was still woman. And on this plain, the strongest ruled, by tooth and claw and without mercy. And of these creatures, the most powerful and cunning was Lamar, Lamar the Lion, who wasn't merely a killer but also a shrewd and cunning king.

Richard's pencil tip flew across the page; he felt deeper into the concept of *lion* than ever before, as if he'd somehow entered the red zone, the mindset of the jungle, where you looked at other life-forms and one question entered your mind: What does it taste like?

He stopped. Hmmm, not bad.

Dreamily, he looked out the window. He tried to imagine

a plain dotted with zebra and giraffe and cape buffalo and little wily antelopes, and the ever-present hyenas.

And he almost saw it, too, though the illusion proved difficult to sustain when he noticed a black-and-white Oklahoma Highway Patrol cruiser rolling down the road toward the house.

Even though Bud was driving, he was still in his surly mood.

"Ted, you really ought to call Holly."

"Nah" was all Ted could say.

"She'll be worried," he said.

"The truth is, Bud," said Ted, "we just don't have much to talk about these days. I let her down, too. I can see in her eyes, I don't mean a thing to her. Goddamn, how I love her and there she is, and I can't reach her."

Bud swallowed uncomfortably. Something seemed to come up into his throat. Ted was truly miserable, stewing in his own pain.

"Now you and Jen, you have a perfect marriage. You're a team. She's a part of your career. She's happy with what you got. She never puts any pressure on you."

"Well, Ted, you know that appearances can be deceiving."

"Not yours, Bud."

"Ted . . . look, we're going to have to have a talk."

"A talk?"

"About some things you think I am that I am not. And about some other stuff as well."

"What?"

But they had arrived in the barnyard of the Stepford farm. The house was white clapboard, an assemblage of structures added as the farm prospered. The lawn was neat, and someone had planted a bright bed of flowers by the sidewalk. A huge oak tree towered over the house.

Bud and Ted climbed out. Bud adjusted his Ray-Bans and removed his Smokey hat from the wire rack behind his seat and pulled it on. He looked about. There was a fallow field, where the spring wheat had already been harvested and the earth turned. Copses of scrub oak showed here and there among the gentle rolls of the land, and far off, a blazing bright green field signaled the presence of alfalfa. There was a blue-stem pasture off to the right, and a few cattle grazed amid the barrels of hay.

"Looks okay to me," said Ted. "The goddamned phone is probably off the hook."

"Hello?" cried Bud. And then again.

There was no answer.

"Let's go up and knock and see what happens."

Richard ran downstairs. He knew he shouldn't scream but he wanted to. The panic billowed through him brightly. He wanted to crap again. His stomach ached as he raced thumpingly along.

"Lamar," he sobbed, "Lamar, Lamar, oh Lamar."

He plunged down the steps.

In the darkness of the basement, Odell was over by the workbench, sawing with a hacksaw. Richard looked and saw three long metal poles on the floor and three wooden boots or something.

Lamar looked over at him.

"Lamar," he gasped, "cops. State police."

Lamar just looked at him blankly. Then he said, "How many? A goddamned team? SWAT, what? Or just a one car?"

"I only saw one," said Richard. "Halfway up the drive-way. Be here in a minute."

Lamar nodded. He turned and looked at the Stepfords, who sat groggily on an old couch.

"You make a sound and you're dead. I mean that, sir, and I ain't a-fucking with you." His voice was level but intense.

Odell, meanwhile, had risen from his position and was busy threading ammunition into the shotguns that Richard now saw had been sawed off so that they were short and handy.

Lamar took one, threw some sort of lever with an oily clang.

"We're going upstairs. You tie these people up and I mean tight. Then you come up. You hear shooting, you come a-running, do you get that? And bring your gun."

"Hootin'," said Odell happily.

"Yes, Lamar," said Richard.

"Okay, Odell," said Lamar. "We goin' fry us some Smokey."

Lamar stuffed a dozen bright red-and-blue shells into his pockets and Odell followed. They raced up the steps.

Lamar watched them. A guy with some miles on him, and a kid. Standing in the sun, just looking the place over. The older one called out "Hello" and adjusted his duty belt. Then he got his Smokey hat out and set to fiddling with it. He wanted it just right, just set perfect on his head. Show-offy cocksucker. The kid looked somewhat grumpy, maybe tired. He wanted to get it over with.

Lamar knew they were cherry. He could smell it on them. They had no idea what they were walking into; if they had, they'd have had their pieces out and they'd be behind cover. He watched as they exchanged a few dry words, then made up their minds to come up to the house.

He could tell also that the young one had a vest on by the

unnatural smoothness of the way the cotton of his shirt clung to the Kevlar; the older one, though barrel-chested and big, was apparently without body armor, for there was more give in the material as he moved.

"Odell, you go out the back, around the side of the house on the left. You ain't gonna fire until I do. You wanna do the old guy first, same as me. He may have been in a scrape or two and maybe has been shot at. He probably won't panic so bad as the other. But main thing is, they can't reach the goddamn cruiser, because then they'll call it in, and in two minutes they got the goddamned backup in. We gotta take 'em out clean, you got that, sweetie?"

"Kwean," said Odell.

"You shoot for the head on the boy. Aim high, try and hit him in the face. The old boy, you can gutshoot him. He ain't wearing no vest."

Odell darted out the back, shotgun in hand.

Lamar moved up to the left of the window. They were too far for a shotgun. If this goddamned old farmer had had an assault rifle, he could have taken them both out with one fast semiauto string. He had four shells in his cut-down Browning auto, a pocketful of spares, and his goddamned long-slide .45, but he hated to shoot it out with a handgun. Too many ifs or maybes with a handgun.

The excitement in him was incredible. But so was the giddiness. He almost giggled. Bliss boomed through him. He tried to chill himself out, but goddamn, this was going to be *fun*!

When to fire? Fire when they knock on the door? Fire through the goddamned wood, blow 'em back? But maybe the buckshot didn't have enough power to get through the wood and would spend itself getting through it. No, best to let 'em get within ten feet and then pull down. Knock 'em down with the shotgun, then close and finish them off with the .45.

Ooooooeeeeeeee! Bar-b-cued Smokey!

They walked up toward the house. A large dragonfly flashed in the sun. Bud saw the flowers and the love of flowers the owners had put into them. Jen was like that, too. It seemed strange they hadn't come out to greet the policemen, as farm people were among the last in America to still show respect to the badge.

He had turned to Ted to remark on the stillness of it when Ted exploded.

Ted didn't actually explode; he was simply standing stricken in a sudden cloud of red mist and his throat had gone to pulsing colors and his eyes had widened with horror.

To Bud it seemed as if they had stepped through a glass door into another world and were suddenly ensnared in a medium of molasses or oil, something thick that dampened all sound and made their motions utterly painful and slow. There was no noise at all. Or if there was, Bud didn't hear it a bit. He felt the stings as though being attacked by a swarm of bees and had a sense that a leg had died on him.

And then the world flashed orange and he had no sense of anything, as if he'd been somehow snatched from time itself, and then he returned to earth a second later, surprised to find himself down on the ground. He had no memory of falling. Blood was everywhere. He looked at poor Ted, who was bleeding even more profusely at the throat and screaming soundlessly. A starburst had fractured the left lens of Ted's Ray-Bans; blood ran in a snaky little line down from the obscured eye. It all seemed to be happening so slowly, and he could make no sense of it at all, though the air seemed full of dust and insects, and then he realized they were taking shotgun fire from the left window and that he had been hit bad.

Boomy! Boomy! Boomy!
Gun go boomy-jerky, *shell outta poppy, gun go* boomy-jerky! *again.*
Ha! Ha!
Makey smoke, makey fire.
Bad 'uns fall down go hurt. Red on them. Look it, red!
Boomy *makey red.*
Mar go "Loady-shooty, loady-shooty" loud. Dell makey gun go boomy *again.*
Put in shell thing. Gun go klack! *then gun go* boomy!

Odell laughed.

Funny, so funny.

"I'M HIT, OH GOD!" screamed Ted, blowing through the soundlessness. Now there was noise everywhere, Bud's ears were ringing in pain and it was so loud he hurt. He had a coppery taste in his throat, as if he'd just had a penny sandwich. His lungs creaked and the rasp of Ted's breathing sounded louder than a buzz saw.

Bud didn't remember drawing the Smith, but he just had it there in his hand out of some miracle or something and he was pumping off rounds at the broken window, just squeezing and squeezing, and then another rake of pain ripped across his chest—Vest! Vest! he mourned—and he went down flat. The gun was lost. Then he had it again and brought it up and fired but came up with nothing but the sounds of hammer striking empty primer. He opened the gun and six shells fell out. He stared at it dumbly.

Speedloader. *Speedloader!*

Clumsily he grabbed at a speedloader from the pouch but his fingers were thick and greasy with blood. It fell from them and rolled in the dust, picking up grit where it was smeared with red.

"I'M HIT, OH GOD I'M HIT!" wailed Ted.

Cover, Bud was thinking, cover. The car was too far.

He rose and half-yanked Ted to the tree ten feet away. A large man ran at him and Bud lifted the Smith to fire and the man ducked. Bud couldn't figure out why the gun didn't fire. He looked. Oh yes. He hadn't reloaded. The speed-loader lay in the dust. He thought he had another in the pouch.

Reload, reload, he told himself, pulling the second speedloader out. He dropped it, too. Then he remembered Ted's gun and tried to get it out, but the security holster wouldn't permit the piece to be withdrawn. Ted shivered desperately beneath him. Blood pulsed out of a hole under his ear, and his whole face was spotted with blood. His legs were also bleeding.

"I can't see," he said. "Oh, Christ, Bud, I can't see."

"Be cool, be cool," Bud said, trying to make sense of it. He picked up his dropped speedloader and somehow got the tips of the six cartridges it held inserted in the chambers. He twisted the knob and the shells dropped into the gun. He slammed the cylinder shut and looked around for targets, but he could see nothing.

The car, he thought. Get to the radio, get backup, do it, do it *now*!

"Ted, I gotta run to the car."

"DON'T LEAVE ME, PLEASE, DON'T LEAVE ME!"

Richard tied the last knot too tight and felt the old man shiver in the cruelty of it. But he didn't care. He had other things to do. He looked at the two of them, trussed like pigs. Under other circumstances, a tragic scene. But not now.

He raced up the stairs to the kitchen. His thought now: *Get out of here.*

He would run to the barn and into the fields beyond. He simply would disappear while the shooting was going on. They would find him later. He would convince them: he had nothing to do with it.

But he was halfway through the kitchen when the first blast came, even louder than the one Lamar had fired last night. It was like being inside a kettledrum.

He dropped instantly, his face on the floor.

Boom! Boom! Boom!

It would not stop. The noise level just rose and rose and rose. He had no idea guns were so loud! He lay there on the floor and began to cry.

Please don't let me be hurt.

He tried to free himself from Ted and looked for targets. But smoke and dust hung in the air, illuminated by the sun. He blinked. Nothing made a lot of sense. Shotguns, two shotguns, that much he knew.

He thought he saw movement at a corner of the house and fired two-handed this time, fast, two shots, and when he rose to run to the car, a blast took his legs out from under him and blew him down. The gun skittered away. He couldn't see the gun. He tried to crawl.

"DON'T LEAVE ME, PLEASE," Ted yelled, grabbing at his ankle.

He crawled a bit further, until he looked up at Lamar Pye, standing over him.

"Well, howdy, Dad," said Lamar.

"Oh, Christ," said Bud.

"Yes sir, I was you, I'd make my peace too, Mr. Smokey."

"Fuck you," said Bud.

"Oh, ain't you a bull stud, though? Odell, come see what we have done bagged. Coupla Smokies." He turned back to Bud. "Liked that speed reload you done under fire. Right nice. Give this to you—you're a professional. You just got outsmarted. Odell, get that other boy's gun from him."

Odell Pye, amazingly big, his red hair tossed every which way, his face blotchy with pimples and freckles, walked over to where Ted cowered bleeding. He kicked him hard in the back. In pain, Ted spasmed outward, and Odell reached down and yanked his gun from him.

"Gun," said Odell, proudly, lifting Ted's Smith.

"That it is, Odell, that it is."

Lamar turned to Bud.

"Now, Dad, case you don't know it, your bacon is fried. I got no beef agin most cops, just other stiffs doing their jobs. But you Smokies shot and killed my old man many years ago. I wasn't even borned yet."

"Fuck you, Pye, and the horse you came in on. We'll get you, you watch."

"You watch, Trooper. I'm gonna cut a path across this state nobody won't never forget. A hunnert years from now, daddies'll scare their young kids to sleep with tales of mean old Lamar Pye, the he-lion of Oklahoma. Odell, put a shell into that cruiser's radio, and then check it for weapons."

Odell went to the car. Bud heard the report as he fired a shotgun shell into the radio. Then, a second later, he heard the trunk open.

"Eeene gun, eene gun," sang Odell, and Bud saw that he had shaken the case off Ted's AR-15.

Shit, he thought.

Then he thought, *Can I make it to my backup?* He had the Smith .38 around his ankle.

When Lamar turned, Bud lunged. He got to the gun, but he couldn't get the thumbsnap off clean because there was so much blood on his hand and his thumb kept slipping. Time he got it off, Lamar had leaned a big boot on his ankle, pinning it, and had reached down and removed the gun.

"Big boy like you, little lady thang like this? You ought to be ashamed."

He tossed the gun away.

"DON'T KILL ME! PLEASE DON'T KILL ME!" shouted Ted.

"Ted, shut up," yelled Bud.

"I don't think he can hear you," said Lamar. "I think he done lost his mind."

"He's just a kid. Let him be. He hasn't even been on long enough to make corporal. He's got a wife. He'll have kids sometime. Don't hurt him. Kill me. I'm an old man, I've had my kids."

Lamar's eyes widened in mock amazement.

"Tell you what," he said, "how 'bout if I kill *both* you and then you can argue in heaven over which one I *should* have killed." He thought his own joke was pretty funny. But then he turned to Odell.

"Odell, you go get that goddamned Richard and the old people. We are going to get out of here now, case anybody heard the ruckus. You get 'em loaded up."

"Yoppa, Mar," said Odell.

Lamar knelt down by Bud.

"You in much pain? I could do you now, save you some hurtin'."

"Fuck off, Pye."

"Sand. Smokey got sand. I like that in a man. Now I would say, though, your partner is sorta lacking in the ball department. He's whining like a baby. I hate babies."

"He's a kid, you prick."

"Still, gotta learn not to whine. Nobody likes a baby. How you onto us, anyhow?"

"It's on the net. There'll be sixty cruisers here in a minute."

"You goin' to face the Lord with a lie on your lips? Bible say that's a ticket to hell, friend. You'd best use this time to make your peace with God."

"Pye. Don't hurt the boy any more. And the old people. Let them go. You got me, you got your Smokey sergeant, that's enough game for one day."

"Say, you *are* a bull stud," said Lamar, "but I'm going to kill you anyway."

Bud tried not to shiver but he could not stop. He tried to make it stop hurting but it would not stop hurting. He looked. So much blood. He must have been hit a hundred times. He never guessed he had so much blood in him. It hurt to breathe, it hurt to think.

Lamar had gone somewhere. He was alone. He thought of Jen. Oh Christ, he'd been such a bad husband. All the things he'd never said or did. And at the end, all that time with Holly. Why? *Why wasn't I a good man? I only wanted to be good and it all came to this.* And he thought of his youngest son, Jeff. *Oh, Jeff, I wanted to be there for you so bad. I wanted to help you, show you things, and if you needed a little extra help, I wanted to give it to you. I never would have left you.* He missed his children.

"Bud," came a sob.

He rolled over through oceans of pain. He didn't know it could hurt so.

"Ted, just be calm."

"Bud, they're going to shoot us dead."

"They're just trying to scare us. They gotta get out of here fast and they know it. If they do us, our people will hunt them down and kill them and they know that. It's all bluff."

"No, it ain't. Bud, you'll make it. I won't. I'm dying no matter what. Bud, please. I miss Holly. I love her, oh Christ, I love her so. I'm sorry I wasn't the man—"

"Stop it, Ted."

"Bud, you take care of her. Promise me, please. You take care of her. You help her. Like you tried to help me."

"I—"

"PLEASE! OH GOD, I'm scared. PLEASE before I die."

"Ted, I—"

But Lamar was back. A car pulled up, a Jeep Wagoneer. Bud saw the two grim old people sitting ramrod stiff in the back. They were next. A twerpy-looking white boy was driving—that goddamned Richard Peed. Lamar and Odell walked over.

Lamar said, "You made your peace with the Lord yet, Trooper?"

"Eat shit," said Bud.

Lamar walked over to Ted. Ted had folded into a fetal position half on his belly and his side, and was weeping softly. Lamar bent over him with the .45 and shot him in the back of the head. His hair jumped a little as the bullet tore into it. Then he turned to Bud. But the .45 was empty, and its slide had locked back.

He handed the gun to Odell and brought his shotgun to bear. The range was about twenty-five feet.

"You shoulda worn your vest, Sarge," said Lamar merrily.

Bud crumpled against the buckshot and heard no noise:

He was in the center of an explosion. Red everywhere, the smell of dirt and smoke in his nose, the sense of heat and the thousand things that tore into him. He felt his soul depart his body.

CHAPTER 7

They traveled in silence for the longest time, Odell behind the wheel, beaming with bliss, a wary Lamar next to him, and Richard and the rigid Stepfords in the back seat. At one point, Mrs. Stepford whispered something to her husband.

"Excuse me," he said, "Missus has to go weewee."

Lamar said, "I'm sorry, ma'am, but I have to ask you to squeeze it in a mite longer. We have to make some tracks."

"What the hell difference does it make?" said Mr. Stepford. "You're going to kill us same as you done them law enforcement boys."

"Just cooperate, okay, old man? I got to concentrate on where I'm going."

They drove onward, over country roads, right at the speed limit but never breaking any laws. They heard no sirens, and the radio announced no discoveries of police bodies. They saw no helicopters.

"Okay," said Lamar, looking at a map, "you want to go on straighty-straight. No turnee. Y'all keep your eyes open for Cox City, where we're going to go left on 21 to Bray. He can't read the signs but he can drive straight and turn when I tell him."

"Where are we going, Lamar?" asked Richard.

"Richard, I ain't ready to talk to you yet. Got to figure this out yet and what I'm going to do with you. You just be quiet."

"Did I do anything wrong?"

But Lamar just glared ahead. Finally, past Empire City, Lamar took off his hat. It was a wide, white Stetson, once Mr. Stepford's finest Sunday-go-to-meeting hat. He made a show of examining the small pinfeather in the band, but it was clear he had made a decision. He pirouetted around in the seat to face the three in the back.

"Now Richard," he finally said with a good deal of weariness, "I want to know—where the hell were you during the fight?"

"Ah," said Richard, "ah, I went through the kitchen after Odell. I was going to circle around from the *other* direction, see. Only it was over before I got there."

"Weren't not," said Mr. Stepford. "I could hear him. He was lying on the goddamned kitchen floor. He was crying."

"I believe you'd make a better outlaw than this poor Richard boy here, don't you, Mr. Stepford?"

"Believe I would, Lamar, though I don't run with no trash like you boys."

"Well, anyway," said Lamar, "Richard, what the hell am I going to do with you? You got to do more than just *art.*"

"Lamar, you know this isn't my cup of tea."

"It sure ain't. But if I can't trust you to back me up in a scrape, what the hell good are you? We are in Scrape City from here on out."

"Lamar, I don't even know how to shoot the g—"

Lamar's arm flashed back, and he slapped Richard hard with the hat across the face. It didn't hurt so much as shock Richard, who looked at Lamar with utter dismay. This merely made Lamar more angry, and he commenced to beat heavily on Richard with the hat, slapping it at him. Richard cowered, covering himself with his arms.

"That used to be a fine hat," said Stepford.

At last Lamar settled down. He turned back to the front, breathing heavily. His anger had mottled his face red; his lungs wheezed and ached in his chest. He said to Odell, "Pull over. Anywhere's fine, this big field."

Odell slowed the old Wagoneer down, let it slew off the gravel shoulder a bit, then eased it across the drainage ditch and into a field. He let the smooth V-eight perk for a few moments, then, satisfied, he turned the key and let it go silent.

The road, a narrow black ribbon, cut across the wide flatness of cotton and peanut fields. No cars were anywhere in sight. The sky was huge, piled with clouds like castles. Some scrub oaks lay a quarter mile to one side.

"Okay, folks," he said. "Time to get out."

"Don't do this, Lamar," said Mr. Stepford. "You are scum but you can't do this to us. You have come to admire my wife's cooking and my fine collection of guns, which served you well in the fracas."

"I have to do what I have to do, old man. You too, Richard. You got to come, too."

"Oh, God, Lamar," said Richard.

"Stop your sniveling, Richard," said Mrs. Stepford. "Lamar, do what you will but shut this boy up. He is giving me a headache. But can I pee first? I've been holding it in very tight."

"Yes, ma'am. Odell will watch, because it don't mean nothing at all to him. The rest of you, turn round, give the lady some privacy."

They did as he commanded. Richard saw the trees far

off. It wasn't fair. He had *tried*. He had wanted so hard to do what was expected of him.

"Lamar, please."

"Shut up, Richard. You all set, Mrs. Stepford? Thank you ma'am. This way."

He walked them into the field. It was near twilight. The sun was setting in an orange smear. It looked like a Constable sun to Richard. Utter serenity lay across the land. It was the exact opposite of the pathetic fallacy: Nature was being ironic, damn her exquisiteness. They wandered across the field. Richard felt as if he were an ant on a pool table. The horizon around them was remorselessly flat. They came, after a time, to a fold in the land and stepped down into a gang of scrub oak trees abutting a messy little creek. It was utterly private.

"Okay," said Lamar. "This will do. Have y'all made your peace with God?"

"You piece of shit, Lamar," said Stepford.

"Don't make it hard on yourself, old man. It don't have to hurt a damned bit. Don't run or nothing; there's only pain in it."

"Hold me, Bill," said the old woman.

"You are a goddamned beautiful woman, Mary," said Bill Stepford to his wife. He was crying a little. "You gave me fifty great years and you never complained a bit. Mary, I wasn't a decent husband. I had an affair. I had many affairs. The sharecropper's daughter, Maggie? Minnie Purvis, in town. Al Jefferson's niece, the secretary. Mary, I am so very sorry."

"It's all right. I knew about them."

She turned to Lamar. "This man flew fifty missions over Germany in the war. He was wounded twice and won the Distinguished Flying Cross, though he says it's nothing. He came back and built a farm up from fallow ground and was the Grange president for twelve years. He raised four sons and two daughters and gave work to over a hundred itinerant laborers and their families. He paid for their medical while they was here and for three of their children to go to college and he never asked for nothing. He is a good man. You have no right to end his life in this field.''

''He is a good man,'' said Lamar, ''and I don't have no right at all, except that I have the gun and that gives me the right.''

He turned to Richard.

''Here,'' he said, handing him the trooper's silver revolver. ''This belonged to that dead cop. That old boy was mean as cat shit right up to the end. Maybe some of that grit will rub off on you. Shoot them. Both. In the head. Or I will kill you.'' Then he raised the long-slide automatic, thumbing off the safety, and leveled the muzzle at Richard.

Richard swallowed.

''He don't have the guts,'' said Stepford.

''Well, you just give him the chance,'' said Lamar. ''Go on, Richard. Show me you are a man. Do some men's work.''

Richard turned. The old people were on their knees. Mr. Stepford held Mrs. Stepford, who had begun to cry. Richard felt queasy as hell. Here was the naked thing its own self. Put the muzzle to the head and pull the trigger. Be over in a second. But he *didn't* have the guts. It was too horrible. Would their heads blow up? Would it squirt? Would it be gory? Wouldn't there be blood everywhere? He turned and faced Lamar's gun and saw his own death in Lamar's blank eyes.

''Oh, shit,'' he said. He remembered the classic Yale experiment where most typical Americans routinely pumped up the juice and tortured some poor fool, because somebody told them to. Well, this was different. His life was on the line.

He turned and pressed the gun against Mrs. Stepford's neck and, closing his eyes, pulled the trigger.

Nothing happened except a click. He pulled it again.

"It's broken," he said.

"Richard, you are so dumb," said Lamar. "Get your ass back to the car."

Richard scampered back.

"See," he said, "he do have the guts to do it. He just too dumb to know the gun weren't loaded. Sorry to put you folks out. Had to test the boy. He ain't much, but I don't guess you'll be signing up, Mr. Stepford, so I'll have to make do."

"Lamar, you like to scared Mary to death."

"Couldn't be helped. Got to do what I got to do. That simple. You get in my way on a job, old man, I'll shoot you dead. But you have sand, that I admit. You took all I had to hand out and I respect that. Believe it or not, you'd last on the yard, and that poor boy would die if I hadn't saved him. Now you all stay here tonight. It won't get cold. Come morning, you amble over to the road. We'll be long gone by then. You'll be back home tomorrow."

"Lamar," said Mary Stepford, "you are a bad man and they will kill you, far sooner than you plan on. But maybe it'll be fast, on account of what mercy you showed today."

"Thank you," said Lamar. "That may be the nicest thing anybody said to me. Sorry we had to steal from you and take your guns. But I have to do what I have to do."

"Goodbye, Lamar," said Mary.

Lamar turned and walked back to the car.

Bill watched him go.

"Mary, you are such a fool. That man is pure white scum. He'll be dead before sunrise tomorrow or the day after and a lot of folks will go with him. Can't believe the softness in your heart for such a scoundrel.''

"Well, Bill Stepford," she said, "he's everything you say, and worse, but he's one thing you never were, as I have known and lived with for many a year. He's true to his own.''

They drove south, then west, in the setting sun, through farmland and small, dull towns. Finally Richard said, "Thank you, Lamar.''

"Thank you, Richard. Odell, Richard proved he was a man. He can pull the trigger.''

"Dell poppy-poppy," said Odell with a smile.

"That means Odell is happy, Richard. You have made that poor soul happy. You are part of the family.''

"Thank you, Lamar.''

"Now, we got to find us a place to hunker up and work out our next move.''

"Lamar?''

"I hope you like to camp, Richard. Me and Odell spent more than a few nights under the cold stars. It ain't a problem. Can't check into a hotel and don't want to go running with the biker gangs, because Johnny Cop has them so snitched out you can't spit amongst 'em without hitting a badge or a microphone. I don't feel like kicking down no doors, at least not for a bit, too much to worry about. We'll try and lay about a time in the backlands.''

Richard only had one gift. It wasn't much, but he had been hording it for this moment, when he at last felt he'd passed a test.

"Lamar?''

"What?''

"I think I may have a place to stay," he said.

CHAPTER
8

He felt his lips first. It was as if they were caked in mud or scab or something. Experimentally, he tried to move them and felt them crack apart, breaking into plates of dry skin. There was no moisture in his mouth.

He heard the drip-drip-drip of something. He could not move. His body was hardly there. He seemed unable to focus or remember anything except orange flashes, flowers, the buzz of insects. Then he remembered Lamar leaning over Ted and the way Ted's hair puffed from the muzzle blast. He remembered curling. He remembered the shotgun shell tearing into him. He remembered the pain.

Jen!

Jeff!

Russ!

Lost, they were all lost. He felt like his own father, that handsome, rigid man, glossied up in funeral parlor makeup, asleep in his coffin, redder and pinker in death than he'd ever been in life.

But there was light and maybe, now that he concentrated, sound. It was as if he were swimming up from underwater, a long, long way toward the surface. He just barely broke it and the smell of something came to his nose . . . bourbon.

Lt. C. D. Henderson of the OSBI was looking at him through specs. The lieutenant fell in and out of focus. Now he was an old man, now a pure jangle of blur. Finally he cranked into some kind of stability.

"He's coming to," the lieutenant said, as if into a megaphone. The words reverberated in Bud's skull.

Jen appeared. He tried to reach out of death for her, but he was ensnared in a web. She appeared grief-stricken, her face grave and swollen. He had not seen such feeling on that impassive face in so very long. Jeff swirled into view, intense and troubled. Russ, even Russ who never went anywhere with them anymore: Russ looked drained of anger and distance, and Bud could see the child in him still under the intensity of his stare.

"Oh, Bud, don't you dare die on me," Jen said.

He couldn't talk.

"Dad," Jeff said. Jeff was crying. "Oh, God, Daddy, you made it, we're so damned lucky."

He saw the plasma bag suspended over one bandaged arm and another bag dripping clear fluid over the other. He lay swaddled in bandages. He felt something attacking his penis and squirmed, thinking of rats. Then he remembered from other visits to emergency wards: a catheter. He was so thirsty.

"Jeff," he said, finally.

Jeff kissed him on the forehead. He wished he could reach out and stroke his son's arm or something, but he couldn't move. Now and then a shot of pain would cut at him.

Russ reached over and just touched him on the arm.

Bud nodded and blinked at his oldest son.

"He's coming out," a young man in a hospital uniform

said, and Bud saw his nameplate, which read Dr. Something or other. When had doctors gotten so young?

He looked back to Jen. He felt a tear forming in his eye. He saw young Jeff, so fair and pure, and Russ with all his complicated brains and hopes and hair, and recalled again the bullet blowing into poor Ted's skull.

Why did I do so poorly? Caught me without a thought in my head. Came in and took me down. Took us down. Lamar Pye blew us away.

"You're going to be all right, Sergeant Pewtie," said the doctor. "The blood loss is the main thing. Another hour and you'd have bled to death. That old guy was tough, I'll say."

Bud's eyes must have radiated confusion, because Jen explained.

"Old Bill Stepford. He hiked thirteen miles through the dark until he came to a farm, and called the police. They got there by midnight. They'd been looking everywhere but had no idea what had happened. You almost bled to death. That was three days ago."

"T-T-T-Ted?" he managed.

"Don't you worry 'bout Ted," said C. D. Henderson. "He ain't in no pain where he is now."

He had to know one last thing, even as the effort of asking it seemed to drain him of energy and will.

"Why?"

"Why," said C.D., "because that damned Lamar is scum, that's why."

Bud shook his head imperceptibly.

"Why . . . am . . . I . . . alive?"

"'Cause you ain't a dove, that's why," said C.D. "Old man Stepford was a dove hunter come the fall. Only shells Lamar could find was light birdshot. Numbers eight and nine. A surgical team had you on the table over four hours,

Bud. Dug close to a thousand pieces of steel shot out of your hide. But not none of them life-threatening and there ain't going to be no lead poisoning neither. Lamar popped you with maybe five, six shells from a sawed-off barrel. He must have thought he'd blown your heart and guts out from all that blood. Hah, goddamned good thing you left your goddamned vest off! But anyway he'd sawed that barrel off to a nub and the shot pattern opened up and nothing got inside your chest cavity or to your spine and nervous system or your brain. Tell you what, though. You ain't goin' through no metal detector no more, Bud.''

Bud slept until he swam up again to brightness. This time he focused onto the face of Col. W. D. Supenski, superintendent of the Highway Patrol. The colonel was another version of Bud: husky and remote with the public, with one of those pouchy faces that looked like feed sacks left out for a decade on a fence post, he'd been a Marine fighter ace in the Vietnam war all those years back and, in the company of those he trusted—other white men who carried guns and believed in the abstraction of Authority—could be quite a folksy old charmer.

''Well, damn, Bud,'' he said, ''not even old Lamar Pye could put you out of commission!'' The colonel had small, dark eyes that were capable of three expressions: blankness; sick, consuming fury; and genuine delight. It was the latter force that beamed through them today. ''Though I must say, I've seen turkeys hanging in the barn that looked a sight better.''

Bud offered a feeble smile. No one in his family was in evidence.

''Been talking to Jen, Bud. She's a fine woman. You are a lucky, lucky man there, Bud.''

Bud nodded.

"Bud, it's my great pleasure to tell you that the Department of Public Safety and the Oklahoma Highway Patrol has decided to confer on you the highest duty award it is within our power to give, the Medal of Valor."

Bud swallowed.

"We found six spent cases from your .357, Bud, and your empty speedloader. Severely wounded and under fire from two sides by murderous killers, you were able to draw and engage the enemy and even reload. And maybe it was the fear you put in the Pye boys that made 'em release the Stepfords three hours later. Maybe you saved those lives, too. And if your damned partner hadn't done the baby-goo on you, you boys might have even brought the Pyes down."

"Sir," Bud said, "Ted tried his damnedest."

"I'm sure he did, Bud. But the fact is, you returned fire and he didn't. We found him on his belly with his hands over his head and his legs drawn up like a little baby. He just lay there and they came and shot him. He didn't fire a bullet! Bud, the truth is, we get paid to stand up to boys like that. That's what the people want. Now, Ted's going to get a posthumous award. The Oklahoma Highway Patrol Star of Bravery. His name goes on the big plaque at Department of Public Safety in Oklahoma City. And a funeral! Bud, we're going to have troopers from all over America coming in. Because our community hangs together in times like these."

"He should get the best medal," Bud said. "Not that medals mean a damned thing."

"Bud, it don't mean much now and I know how you feel. I lost more than a few wingmen. But in years to come, that medal will mean more and more, especially to your boys. I know. I been there."

"Yes sir," said Bud. "Now what about the Pyes? Did we pick them up yet?"

"Fact is, the damned Pye boys have dropped off the earth. Don't know where they are. We got OSBI and FBI and troopers and sheriffs and MPs all over the state digging for 'em. Even the goddamned media is cooperating, though it's a first. We'll get 'em."

Bud nodded, but he didn't agree. Lamar might be savage and crazed, but he wasn't dumb. He had that inmate cunning, always had an angle to play.

"Now Bud, you just rest. Take your time in recovering, and I've already talked to Jen. You just let yourself mend. You don't never have to go back in a cruiser again. If you want that lieutenancy that you turned down so many times, it's yours. You could get paid for the job you already do, which is running a troop, if Captain James is telling the truth. Bud, you'd get a captaincy eventually, and your own troop. Or, we could bring you up to headquarters to run the firearms training section. You'd like that, wouldn't you Bud? Be a fine cap on a fine career!"

Bud smiled meekly, knowing he didn't have to say a thing.

The next time he came awake, it was the pain that awakened him. The drugs had worn off. How he stung! He felt like a horde of bees had worked him over. Every little twist and jiggle and the bees got back to work. This wasn't going to be no piece of cake.

He was desperately thirsty. Jen poured him a glass of water, and he drank it greedily. He had the sense it was another day or so later, and that it was night.

"How's Holly?" he finally said.

"Oh, that girl's taking it fine. Sometimes it doesn't hit them for a bit. She'll have some rough days ahead. I was over there last night. Donna James and Sally McGinley and a few of the others had brought hot dishes. It was very nice.

She seemed all right, I suppose. She was very happy for all the support and everyone agreed it was best she hadn't had kids yet. She'll remarry, there'll be plenty of time for that. They're going to give Ted a medal, one of the highest. The funeral will be something very special.''

"How was she . . . toward you?''

"Toward me? Why, Bud, whatever do you mean?''

"I got her husband killed, that's what I mean. I like to have shot that boy myself from the way I handled things.''

"You stop that, Bud. No one has said such a thing, or even thought it, I would know. You-all ran into pure black evil, that's all there is to it.''

But Bud didn't think so. What percentage of his awareness had he lost in his little snit about almost getting caught? It came back to him; *that's* what he'd been thinking about on the drive from the road to the farmhouse. Had he missed something? Car tracks, signs of disturbance, any of the little things, the signals a policeman has to be aware of, that might keep him alive? Had he gone out back, where they must have stashed Willard Jones's stolen car? No, not Bud. Goddamn Bud was just sawing away on some other bullshit, about getting himself caught with his pants down. Open the door, and let in Mr. Lamar Pye, thank you very much. And Lamar did what Lamar would do, because that was Lamar: you only had to look at those glaring eyes or read the jacket about the long list of felonies and killings to know what Lamar was about.

A black vapor seemed to blow through his mind.

"I want to go to the funeral,'' he finally said. "I have to do something for Ted.''

"Bud, they say—''

"I WANT TO GO!'' he yelled in a violent husband's voice that meant he wanted no discussion.

"It's tomorrow,'' Jen said.

"Go get a doctor, goddammit, Jen, do it!"

"Bud!"

"I have to go to that thing. It's the last and only chance I'll have to do right by him. That's all there is to it."

It was sunny, a fabulous day in April, and the oaks looked full and majestic against the flat and dusty plains of the Lawton Veteran's Cemetery. The breeze rattled the leaves—so much shimmering green, all of it stirred by the persistent wind, that Oklahoma wind that seemed to wash over everything—amid the gray stones that stood over men who'd died because a bitch called duty had said so. Far off to the northwest stood Mount Scott, hardly a mountain but still the commanding elevation in the Wichitas: It was an ancient, dry old hill, bleak and stony.

Bud was so sunk into himself now he could hardly focus. The beauty of the place and the death of the place; he responded to it in an especially bitter way. Maybe it was the drugs. They had to keep him stoked to the gills or the pain would begin to build. But Bud was the sort of man, as Jen would tell you, who, when he sets his mind on a thing, that thing comes to pass. So Bud sat in the wheelchair as Jen pushed him along. He wore his dress hat, his dress uniform, and Ray-Bans because his eyes were hollow and blood-rimmed; seven small bandages were visible on his face and neck; under his shirt a single huge wrapping protected his hundreds of wounds, and on his legs still more of the smaller patches. He could walk if he had to, a slow step at a time, but for now this was all right.

What he felt more than anything was fatigue. Not pain, not anger, not regret: a ton of liquid lethargy. The air weighed too heavily upon his body. He wanted to sleep but he couldn't sleep. He had no words for anybody. The glasses, sealing his eyes off, helped, but he had the enormous urge to just lie down and go to sleep. Nothing seemed worth two cents anywhere in the world.

But he knew he had to be here somehow.

Jen and Jeff pushed him across the flatness. Up ahead, they could see a little draw where the last ceremony was beginning. Troopers from all fifty states and police representatives from nearly as many cities around the country had arrived. When these things happened it was amazing how many cops wanted to be part of it, to come by and say, there, brother, it's all right. It could just as easily have been me. You did your best.

"Bud, you all right?" Jen asked.

He'd snapped at her twice as they were getting him dressed. He knew he was behaving badly in front of his son.

"Yes, I am fine," he said. "I'm ready to go dancing, goddammit."

"Dad," said Jeff.

"I'm sorry, Jen," he said. "Ain't fit to sleep with the dogs today."

That goddamned Lamar Pye running around free as a bird and poor Ted is going into the ground. Wasn't right. Wasn't no kind of right.

Now the anger seethed through him. He could live with the pain, but the anger was something else entirely. Could he live with that? He didn't know.

Up ahead, he could see TV vans parked and handsome people in the artificial brightness of the camera lights standing apart from the milling crowd of law enforcement types. That irked him, too. He'd been watching the TV news. Seemed like Lamar and Odell Pye had become famous and poor old Ted was second-string. There had been long interviews with "miracle survivors" Bill and Mary Stepford and a hundred shots of the most famous oak tree in Oklahoma, the one behind which he and Ted had cowered while

Lamar and Odell had fired and advanced on them. There was footage of shotgun shells and pistol cases littering the ground, a night shot of the caravan of vehicles at the farm, the blue-and-red eggbeaters filling the darkness with their urgency, the medevac chopper rising to haul bloody Bud Pewtie to Comanche Memorial Shocktrauma, even a shot of poor shot-up Bud on the trundle being wheeled in from the roof to the emergency room. He looked dead as hell, face white, partially covered by a bloody sheet, one shoe off and one shoe on.

Jen pushed him through the crowd, which magically melted and stilled. Now and then a low "Howdy, Bud" rose, and Bud nodded to acknowledge. As the last of the crowd parted, Jen slid him into the front row where the big shots sat, Colonel Supenski in his dress blues, a man from the Governor's Mansion standing in for a governor who couldn't make it, two old people who had to be Ted's grieving parents, Captain James, and at the end of the row, Holly.

If he had been seeing her for the first time, he'd have fallen in love with her all over again. She looked still and grave and almost numb; but her skin had blossomed somehow, as if it were dewy with moisture; she seemed as pale as a white rose, here eyes focused on nothing as she just sat there in a kind of solemn haze.

Told you I'd see you on the day we got off it, he thought. *Another one of my damned lies.*

She felt him looking at her, and she smiled.

The smile blew him away.

He loved her smile. One of the best parts of their intimacy was the way they laughed so hard at each other's strange jokes. They shared some kind of wavelength or something.

Holly rose and came over and smiled bravely at Jen and knelt down and touched his hand.

"How are you, old trooper?" she said.

"Holly, I tried so hard. Just couldn't save him. They got us cold."

"It's okay, Bud."

She rose and gave Jen a hug and then hugged Jeff before returning to her seat.

Bud had been through too many before. The details were all familiar, and only the tiniest, most meaningless deviations set this one apart from the others. A trooper honor guard consisting of one man each from Oklahoma, Arkansas, Texas, New Mexico, Colorado, and Missouri walked the casket from the hearse to the bier and set it down, and only one man was out of step by the end of the trek instead of the usual two. The casket was heavy, but they always were: just dead weight, after all. The elaborate business of the flag folding proceeded awkwardly because the team was newly united; but eventually they got it crushed into the tricorn shape, only stars showing, and the team leader presented it to Holly with a little salute.

Twenty yards off, the seven-man firing team fired three volleys, for a total of twenty-one; the volleys were ragged as they always were, and, in the vast space, the gunfire thin.

The worst moment was always taps. It didn't matter if the bugler played it well or poorly, in tune or out; there was something in the mournful ache of the music, and how it spoke of men dying before their time for something they only vaguely understood and being only vaguely appreciated by the people on whose behalf they died, that made it hurt so much. Bud bit back a tear, feeling the blackness in him rise and rise yet again. He saw the puff of hair as the slug went in and Lamar unbending from the task with the blank eyes of a carpenter or a stonemason.

No words were said, beside an invocation by the minister. And then it was over, that fast. Holly was swept up and embraced and borne out. The troopers and cops began to file to their cars.

"Okay, Bud?" Jen wanted to know. "Or do you want to stay a bit."

"No, let's get out of here."

Four days later, Bud was released from the hospital. At home, he lay there feeling slightly liberated. But in a bit the black vapor settled over him again, almost like a blanket that he could pull tight. Someone had warned him of this: post-stress syndrome, a bitch to get through, feelings of worthlessness and failure and bone-grinding fatigue. All right, so: I got it but good.

He chased Jen out and she slept in the living room. She never saw him cry; nobody had ever seen him cry and goddamned if he would start now with that shit. But he had a night when he cried and another night when he locked himself in the toilet and threw up bad. The doctor dropped by twice a day, and there was a long session with Colonel Supenski, a highway patrol shooting investigation team, and homicide investigators from the Murray County Sheriff's Department and the county prosecutor's office. Bud told it all to them, except his surliness over the near slip of being caught by Jen; they went over it doggedly, who was where when the shots came, this and that, like a slow-mo replay in a football game. Would Bud testify before a grand jury in order to get a true bill against Lamar? Bet your ass he would!

He tried not to think of Holly, but at night that came over him, too: the flash of the gun, the softness of her skin, the ugly powder burn melted into Ted's skull, the tautness of her nipples, the grin on Lamar's face as he pivoted with the shotgun, the smoothness inside her thighs. One became the other: flash and explode, orangeness, pain, ecstasy, all of it crammed together. He yearned to call her. But he couldn't.

On the fourth day, it was at last time to rise. He got himself up and slung on blue jeans, a starched white shirt with a point collar, a good pair of Tony Lama boots, brown with a black shaft. He threw a bolo tie, with a horse's head on the clasp, around the shirt neck, tightened it up. He slid a Colt Commander with a Shooting Star magazine crammed with eight hollowtips into his waistband over his kidney, then pulled on a sports coat.

He lumbered down the steps, at first feeling woozy. But then he got the hang of it.

"Jen, I'll be out a bit. Then I'll stop at the hospital. Back before dark."

She came from the kitchen and intercepted him at the front door. Her face was gray and remote and, as always, somewhat impassive, except for the glare in her eyes.

"You can hardly walk. Just what do you think you're doing, Mister?"

"I feel I have to say something to that farmer."

"Write him a letter or give him a call. That's why they invented the telephone."

"Without this old boy's gumption, I'm in the ground and you're the one they're bringing the hot dishes to."

"Send him a card. Bud, you still have steel in you. Suppose something breaks free and you start bleeding again. You could bleed to death."

"If I was meant to bleed to death, I'd have done it with a thousand steel balls in me, not in my truck driving out to the country."

"Do you have a gun?"

"The Commander."

"Good. I don't want you out in the world without some protection."

"Didn't do much good the last time," he said, "but the theory sounds promising."

Bud went to his truck, a blue Ford F250, climbed in, and stuck the key into the column switch, then paused. Christ, would there always be somebody pulling on him? Would it ever end?

Looking carefully left and right, he eased out the clutch and backed into the highway, then threw a bit of gravel as he accelerated. In seconds he came to a larger road and slipped into traffic behind a huge cattle carrier.

Bud worked his way through the gears in the heavy-duty four-speed, tugging the stick firmly, his feet light on the accelerator and clutch pedal. He loved the goddamned truck, he truly did.

But Bud didn't drive straight out to the Stepfords'. With no conscious thought at all, he stopped at a convenience store and went to the pay phone. He dropped the quarter and dialed the number. It was just like the last time, in front of the diner, just that simple.

In time she answered.

"Howdy," he said.

"Thank *God* you called," Holly whispered. "Oh, Bud, I can't talk now. The minister is here. He thinks he's helping. Oh, lord, seeing you would help."

"I been home and couldn't call, you know. I've got something to do anyway. Can you meet me in Elgin, that diner, Ralph's, I think it is, say about two this afternoon?"

"I'll be there."

Bud hung up and returned to the truck. The drive to the Stepfords' passed without incident. On the way he drove by the diner where the waitress had mentioned Bill Stepford's absence: Why hadn't that set bells ringing?

Reason was, a policeman will knock on a thousand doors in a career, maybe a hundred thousand. Maybe a thousand policemen knocking on a hundred thousand doors over a twenty-year span will produce one Lamar Pye, waiting in the window with a semiauto shotgun, ready to blow them to hell and gone. The numbers say: Go ahead, knock on the door. Lamar was just the road accident that happens to other people and makes life interesting.

Bud now came to the mailbox and the road into the farm. He turned, headed down it. The same line of oak trees, the same just-turned wheat fields, the same eventual arrival at the house itself, a white clapboard structure with new rooms added every decade or so; the porch, the barn, the feeding pens, the mud, the hay. It all looked the same, except now the yard was much crisscrossed with tire tracks from the multitude of emergency and police vehicles.

And the tree. Bud looked at what for two or three days had been the most famous tree in Oklahoma and North Texas, where he and Ted had sought cover and from which he had fled to the cruiser to call for backup, not making it.

Bud parked where he'd parked before, the obvious place. It was now as it was then: still, green, just a farm. He had a bad moment where he didn't want to get out. Am I ruined now? he wondered. No real fear for twenty-five years, but then I've never been hit in twenty-five years. Now, has this thing ruined me? Am I afraid to make the stop or knock on the door? His breath came in little spurts.

He opened the truck door, hearing the buzz of cicada as he had that day. He smelled alfalfa and animal shit, as on any farm. He stood for a moment, looking around. It could have been that day, same bright weather and warmth, same time. But then his knee began to hurt because there was a tiny ball of steel under the kneecap that the surgeons hadn't had time to get out. Maybe they'd go back and get it, maybe Bud could live with it. And as he thought about that one, in a hundred other places, his body began to sing. The Percodan was wearing off; he checked his watch, it was an hour till the next dosage.

Shit, he thought. It wasn't a bad dream. It all happened.

He closed the door and headed to the house, but halfway up, as before, he was intercepted by a man with a shotgun.

"Now, hold on, mister, this ain't a tourist attraction. You got business you see my lawyer, but otherwise you clear on out."

Bill Stepford was spry and peppery as a cat, even with half of his face swollen like a blue-green grapefruit. He didn't exactly point the gun at Bud but just sort of clung tightly to it, as a man who's gone without water may cling to a canteen even after his rescue. His blue eyes, one round, one flat, both fiery, burned into Bud and a Y of veins stood out on his forehead.

"Mr. Stepford, I ain't here to sell or buy a damn thing, I came to offer up my thanks."

"Goddamn yes! Mary, come out! Look what's showed up! It's that Bud Pewtie, the man too tough to die. Up and about in six days—my lord, son, you must be made of pure gristle."

"No, sir, I'm made of skin and bones, just like you, and maybe you saw some of the same kind of blood on the ground."

"I surely did. Thought you were a goner."

"I was till you walked halfway across Oklahoma and saved my hash. That's what I came on by for."

"Bud, dammit, it wasn't nothing. I'm an old coot who walks ten miles a day. If I hadn't gone two miles in the wrong direction to start, I might have gotten there earlier."

"Don't think it would have made much difference, sir. I

had another few hours of life left any way you cut it, and poor Ted was already in the barn.''

''Bud, you come on in and have some coffee and tell me all about your adventures.''

''Ain't much,'' said Bud, following. ''Got a thousand holes in me and maybe a hundred of them little tiny balls no probe could get out. None of 'em went too deep. They just cut the Jesus out of me, that's all. I'm damned glad you hunt doves and not deer with those deer slugs.''

''Bud, I have a case of Winchester deer slugs under my workbench. Old Lamar just never found them! Don't that beat the monkey!''

They headed inside, laughing like old pals.

Mary Stepford, looking pale and leathery, rose from the sofa to greet them. ''Well, Mr. Pewtie, I swear, I never thought you'd be coming by for coffee.''

''I didn't either, ma'am. I thought my coffee-drinking days were over.''

''Well, you are a sight for these sore eyes,'' the old woman said, and pulled him close and gave him a down-home hug.

''I came by to thank you-all. A letter or a call didn't seem right, after what you did. You were the heroes.''

''A bad boy like Lamar don't leave you no choice, Bud. You got to be at your best or you're finished.''

''You'll get him, Bud.''

''Ma'am, I have to confess, the last thing I want to do is run into the Pyes again. Scared me then, scare me now. Maybe if I'd had a second, just a second, to get my bearings. But it happened so fast.''

''That's scum for you,'' said Bill. ''They know the advantage of surprise—works for 'em every damn time, just as it did against me.''

They had a nice little visit, and Bud kept it light, because the old woman seemed a little shaky, though old Bill Stepford was billowing brimstone and hellfire most of the time. He didn't really want to take them back through it. What was the point, really?

When it came time for Bud to leave and the old man walked him back to his truck, only then did the conversation meander back to the three convicts. Stepford ran salty profiles of each one by Bud.

When Bud heard how useless Richard was, he wondered why Lamar hadn't dumped him.

"Maybe it's the lions," Stepford said.

Bud had read all the police reports; he'd talked to colleagues just that morning to get the latest. But this was new.

"Lions?" he said.

"Yes sir. He drew pictures of lions for Lamar. Don't ask me why. Silliest damn things."

"You wouldn't, say, have them pictures?"

"Sure do, Bud. Care for a look?"

"Yes sir," said Bud.

He was thinking, *Lions?*

CHAPTER 9

No one ever said Lamar was afraid of work. On the first day on the farm, he rose early and drove the Stepfords' Wagoneer into the barn, into an empty stall. He removed the battery. Then, with a pitchfork, he climbed to the hayloft and laid into the pile up there and threw it to the floor of the barn. Then he forked the hay around the vehicle until it could not be seen. No one would ever stumble on it, and no one could look at the huge pile of hay filling one of the empty stalls and suspect that a stolen car was hidden under it.

The next morning, he chopped wood. Around ten, Odell came out and joined him, and they split all of her logs into firewood in a heroic fourteen-hour stint. The next day, they decided to clear land where she said she wanted eventually to plant a garden, out beyond the barn. Although it had been merely the most banal passing suggestion, for nearly a week Lamar and Odell dug the prairie thatch out and fought their way down to red dirt, which they then leveled and raked and graded, digging at least a hundred large rocks and a thousand small ones out of the earth. Then they cut down a dozen of the scrub oaks and some dead mesquite, reduced the wood to kindling, and dug out the stumps, maybe the hardest of their labors, for the trees had been joined to the earth stubbornly, like the partnership in an ancient marriage, and it took enormous investments of sweat and will to break them apart. The sun was bright and harsh, and the wind snapped across the dry prairie. Far off, the scuts of the Wichitas stood out, the only feature on the otherwise featureless horizon.

"Look at them," said Ruta Beth. "Lord, how they work. They work like my daddy worked."

"They're basically elemental men of the earth," Richard said grandly, though this insight was lost on Ruta Beth.

She simply looked at him through guared little slits of eyes, nothing showing on her grim face, and said, "Richard, sometimes you say the craziest things."

A major disappointment: He had not impressed Ruta Beth at all. She took one look at poor, pitiful Richard and abandoned him before the relationship had even begun; it was Lamar, beaming with testosterone and sweat, who drew her like a beacon.

Ruta Beth Tull was twenty-eight years old and sinewy as a wild dog. She usually wore Sears jeans, a thin, cheap wool sweater over a faded blouse, heavy farm boots, and a black hairband, which pulled her dark cascades of hair into a rope behind her head. She had chalky skin and mean little eyes, with which she constantly scanned the world for threat or aggression, never relaxing, never giving, always on alert. Her fingernails were chewed to grimy nubs, and she was always hugging herself in a slightly unseemly way. But her grimness hid a romantic streak once directed at Richard and in a second's passing redirected toward Lamar.

When she had seen Richard's picture in the paper during his trial for criminal assault against his mother, she had cut it out. She wrote him a letter that went out in the next batch of correspondence, among other missives—to President Clinton, the governor, Meryl Streep, Hillary Clinton, Robin Quivers of *The Howard Stern Show,* Nancy Reagan, Ronald Reagan, Barbara Bush, two of Charle Manson's female followers she'd seen in a TV interview, and Reba McEntire—on a variety of noteworthy subjects. She had never before gotten an answer, except the routine "Thank you so very much" from the Clintons, which she didn't count as a real answer. But in the case of Richard, her answer showed up three months later, at eleven P.M., spattered with blood, along with Lamar Pye, and his damaged cousin.

The document that initiated this unlikely course of events was the strangest, looniest letter Richard had ever read; it even shocked him a bit.

"Dere Mr. Peed," it began,

> though you cannot know me, at the same time we are One. I believe in another life, in many other lives, we must have been boy and girl friends. We must have offended the Gods with the purity of our passion and so they cursed us and sent us too wondering through time, always close enough to know the other's presence, the other's sorrow, but never close enough too touch, too hold, too kiss, too have secshual untercoarse.
>
> As did you, I lost my beloved parents in a tragedy. It wasn't easy, but now I have made peace with the sorrowful passing of Mother and Daddy. They frequently talk to me from heaven, which is a very nice place. It's like a Howard Johnson's, where someone come to change the sheets every day. It has a very nice salad bar.
>
> Mr. Peed, I miss you, though I have never seen eyes on you. I have stared at your picture so hard in the

Daily Oklahoman I have almost wiped it off the page. Mr. Peed, I believe we could have a wonderful life together if only we could meet. Thank you for your attention.

Yours fondly,
Miss Ruta B. Tull
Route 54
Odette, Oklahoma.

When he showed it to Lamar, Lamar read the first paragraph, silently moving his lips across each word, and said, "Richard, I can't make hide nor hair out of it. Is she crazy?"

"I think so, Lamar. Crazy as hell. But . . . she likes me. She lives in the country. Her parents are dead. I'm thinking maybe it would be a place to put up."

"Hmmmm," said Lamar. "Well, suck my cock, why the hell not? Better'n shittin' in a wheat field, where we'll catch cold and our noses run with snot."

They found the farm lurking behind a solitary mailbox inscribed with the name TULL on Route 54. It was in a desolate sector of Kiowa county, about thirty miles west of Lawton, halfway to Altus. It felt like the true West, all right, prairie for grazing mostly, some fields heroically turned for wheat, but generally the feeling of wide-openness in every direction except due east, where the mountains lay. The highways transected Kiowa like lines in a geometry problem, and off of the asphalt now and then a ribbon of red dirt would run, disappearing in subtle folds of the terrain. The farm lay at the end of a mile of such narrow red dirt road and when you stood in its front yard, your back turned to the two-story clapboard house, rotting and dim, and facing outward, you felt as if you were among the last men on earth. Just flat grass, distant mountains, and the snapping wind as far as the eyes could see.

Ruta Beth asked no questions. She took one look at the trio and knew who they were and why they were there. It was the message from God she had been expecting these long, lonely years. It never occurred to her to be frightened. She smiled at Richard and nodded knowingly to the astonished Lamar but went first to Odell.

"You poor thing," she said, "you look famished. You come on in. I don't have much but what I've got I'm willing to share."

"Odell likes cereal, ma'am," said Lamar. "It's his favorite thing."

"What do he like?"

"Er, he likes that Honey Nut Cheerios a lot. He likes your sugary ones. He don't like the 'healthy' ones, you know, with the nuts and all."

"I have Corn Flakes."

"Ah, he'll *eat* 'em. But he ain't crazy about 'em."

"I like cereals, too. I have some others."

"Cap'n Crunch?"

"No, Mr. Pye. I don't have no Cap'n Crunch. How about Special K?"

"Ain't that just like Wheaties? Odell don't like Wheaties. He did, long as there was sugar on it, till they put that Michael Jordan on the box. Where we come from, we hate the niggers. I know we're supposed to love the niggers these days, but you try and love our niggers up at McAlester and they just laugh and cut your throat. Killed me a big nigger, that's what started this whole goddamned ball rolling."

"I do have some Frosted Mini-Wheats."

"Frosted Mini-Wheats! Odell, you hear that? Frosted Mini-Wheats! This gal has Frosted Mini-Wheats!"

"Weeny-eets! Weeny-eets!" Odell began to chant, his vague features united in a rapturous passion.

"You come along then, Odell," she said, and took the big man inside.

Lamar turned to Richard.

"Your gal's pretty goddamned sweet, if you ask me. You better make her happy or I'll crack your skull."

That's when Richard knew he was lost.

Lamar was thinking about painting the house. It was a mottled gray, peeling and sad. He wanted it to be cheery, blinding white, the white of happy white folks on a rich farm, with lots of kids. He had a brief rare little brush with fantasy: all of them there, Ruta Beth and Richard and Odell and Lamar, all of them happy in that house. But even as he drew some warmth from it, he knew it would never happen. Goddamn Johnny Cop had seen to that. If Johnny Cop hadn't a-shot his daddy, lo those many years ago, he'd never be in this mess, with all these worries, all these things to think about. And now he was getting hot again.

Still, he could paint the house. That would be his next project. He could scrape the old dead paint off, take a week or so, then sand down to new wood, another week. Take maybe two weeks to give the place another coat. Odell could do some of the work, although Odell's tiny mind had never had much in the way of skill. Odell could dig or hoe or plow all day long, seven days a week, but he couldn't do anything that involved thinking. He just didn't understand.

"Odell, now, think we gonna knock off for the day," Lamar said. It was six-thirty P.M. of the third day of the second week. They'd finished reroofing the barn, and they'd restrung about a mile of fence between Ruta Beth's and the McGillavery's property, because the McGillavery's cows kept breaking into Ruta's far field and that meant the

McGillavery boys would come looking for them, and that would be trouble.

He and Odell walked back to the house.

"Odell, go wash," he said. "Wash-wash, for dinner."

"Din," Odell said and went merrily off.

He knew he'd find Ruta Beth out back, working at her wheel. It amazed him what she could do. Just the lump of clay, the pumping of her foot, the spinning of the wheel, and some kind of miraculous thing occurred. Goddamn! He loved to watch it.

And there she was, hunched over the spinning wheel, her hands actually sunk into the blurred muck, her face intense and furious. The muck seemed to be spinning itself into something thin and graceful today, like a candleholder that he remembered his mama had before his mama died.

"Amazin' what you can do," he said.

She almost never blinked; she had this funny way of just looking at something until she'd sucked it dry. It amazed him that she wasn't afraid of him, a mankiller like him, with F U C K Y O U ! tattooed on his knuckles, who made the quality nervous if he were in the same goddamned county.

"Mr. Pye," she said, "it ain't nothing, really. You could do it."

"Me, nah. I'd mess it up. But go on. Love to watch you."

She worked intently for another few minutes. Then she said, "What will you do? Them cops won't never stop looking. You have to move on."

"I know. I hate to go. Ain't ever seen Odell so happy. It's where he should be. Can't hurt nobody, can't get in no trouble, no liquor, no niggers or hacks trying to take from him. He could be happy here."

"You love him. Everybody says you are the meanest man there is, but you love him."

"He's all I got. We go way back."

"It's so beautiful. But they will get you. Stories like yours never have happy endings."

"This here place is my happy ending."

"I swear, I don't see no bad in you."

"But bad is what I am. I guess I was borned to it, on account of what happened to my daddy. I never once looked back. Only thing I's ever any good at."

"You could have been a farmer."

"Then somebody come and try and walk on you. You can't let that happen. So you stop 'em, and next thing, you're on the run. That's how it started. Goddamned Uncle Jack kept Odell in the barn. Kept him chained. Beat him. His own son. Beat that boy. He got thirty dollars a month from the county to keep that boy on account of his being so sick in the brain and he didn't spend a goddamned penny of it on Odell. Only reason he took me in is because the state paid him twenty-two dollars a month on me, so as to get me out of their reform school. He was brother to my daddy Jim, who was killed dead by state troopers over in Arkansas, and when my mama Edna Sue died and they put me in their reform school and I give them so goddamn much trouble, 'cause people was always trying to back you down, and I just got it in my fool head nobody was going to back me down, anyway, they sent me to my uncle and his wife Camilla, and I was just shit to him, shit that brought in a Social Services check.

"One day he beat Odell so goddamned bad I thought the boy would die. Because Odell had shat up his pants. They had so much trouble teaching Odell about the bathroom. Anyway, I reckoned to stop it. Caught Uncle Jack along the Perkinsville Road, drunk as usual on Odell's money. Ain't done nothing in my life that made me feel so good as when I put the blade into that mean old bastard. And it's been like that ever since, me watching out for Odell, him for me, we was all we had in the goddamned world. And it wasn't so bad, we'd made our place, until goddamned Junior Jefferson pulled his stunt.''

It was as complete an accounting of his life as he'd ever given to anybody.

''You've had such a hard time.''

''The House is full of men with hard lives. We're just like them, that's all.''

''It's a sad story. Mr. Pye, I honestly believe if you'd have caught a break somewhere along the line, you could have been a *great* man.''

''I don't know why you'd say such a thing. I'm just a piece of scum.''

''But what would you do if you could do anything?''

Lamar thought. The question had never been put to him before.

''I'd like to invent a ray,'' he said. ''You know, like a beam of light. And everything you shine it on, you make it . . . *fair.* You shine it and there's a lot of money and nobody's sick or angry or nothing, you just make people *happy.* That's what I'd do. A happy ray. I'd shine it in all the prisons and all the shithole, jerkwater towns. I'd shine it on Odell and he could talk and his mouth would be mended up. I'd even shine it on the niggers, yes, goddammit, I would, and they would change their evil ways.''

She beheld him gravely.

''That is the sweetest thing I ever did hear.''

''Well, it won't never happen,'' said Lamar.

''You're like that ray. You give people hope. You watch. They'll believe in you like in Jesus or Mr. Elvis Presley. They know you stand for freedom.''

She touched his knee.

"I thought you loved that Richard. He showed me that letter."

"I guess I did. Don't know why I thought so much of poor Richard. He ain't but a ninny. I doubt he has hair on his privates. What is it you want? I'll give you everything you want."

"No woman ever said that to me. So sometimes I'd take it."

"I want you to have it. I so bad want to give it to you. I'll be your true first, Mr. Pye," she said shyly, "and you'll be my first, too."

Richard could tell he'd fucked her. It had really only been a matter of time. A woman as nuts as Ruta Beth would almost certainly end up fucking a crazy fuck like Lamar.

Anyway, when they came in from the barn, loosey goosey and giggly, they both smelled of cunt. It was, to Richard, a low, rank odor. His mother smelled like that sometimes, after one of her "friends" had visited, when he was a little boy and he'd been made to play in the garden.

But now Lamar was happy as a goddamned head of household who's just made the mortgage. Even Odell picked it up. He looked up from his cereal bowl and smiled brightly, flecks of Frosted Mini-Wheats clinging to his lips and yellow teeth. He was happy.

It's like a family, my God, thought Richard. It was some terrible parody of happiness: Lamar the daddy and Ruta Beth the mommy and Odell and Richard the two boys. It was the normal life he'd never had.

It was such a good time, the little family in the kitchen of the farmhouse, laughing. Some demented Norman Rockwell could have painted the picture and put it on the cover of *The Saturday Evening Post,* Richard thought, Lamar with his ponytail and tattooed knuckles and scrawny Ruta Beth with her chalky Addams Family skin and her inbred farm face; and Odell, eternal boy-man, with a tunnel for a mouth and a mop of reddish hair and two tiny eyes. And, of course, him, too, Richard, who'd blinded his mother one day in a fit of rage because the parafascist right-wing *Daily Oklahoman* had refused to review his exhibit, "Richard Peed: Artist in Transition," at the Merton Gallery on Dwight Street.

They even did errands, like any family. It turned out that Ruta Beth had no paper anywhere in her house, no writing implements, nothing. She didn't even have any magazines, newspapers, or books. So of course she had to go out and get tablets of paper and pencils for Richard to continue his lions with, as that was his most important contribution. And she also had to drive all the way to Murf's Guns in Duncan to buy double-ought buckshot for the shotguns, when they learned from the TV that goddamned salty old state cop had somehow managed to survive because he'd been hit with birdshot.

But Lamar wasn't mad, he was so mellow in his new life.

"Goddamn, was he a tough old boy!" he hooted. "He was a right tough old buzzard but birdshot didn't get him done! Won't he have something to tell his grandkids!"

The heavier shells were important for another reason.

"Only one last thing to figure," said Lamar. "That's the place where we going to do our next job."

Richard, smiling, wasn't sure what Lamar meant by job.

"You know. To rob. We're robbers, Richard. Don't you get that? It's our work. And the way I work, them shotgun shells going to come in handy!"

CHAPTER 10

He pulled into the Elgin diner. Erect and brave in sunglasses, she sat in a window booth. She looked pale even through the distorted reflection of the interstate on the surface of the glass. She was not dressed in black but in a neat little sleeveless polka-dot dress. The freckles on her arms matched the pattern of the dress. And when she saw him, her face lit up. She waved her hand tentatively. He waved back.

Oh, lord, he thought, here it is.

He got out of the truck, reached back and tucked the Commander, which had slipped a bit, back behind his kidney. He'd taken a Percodan half an hour early, after leaving the Stepfords, so the pain had gone down somewhat. Still, he was moving like an old man, a step at a time, as if the air itself sat on his body with a special kind of violence. He was nearly fifty; he felt a hundred and fifty. A geezer, full of melancholy and black thoughts. His legs ached, his body seemed cut from old stone as he climbed the steps.

He entered and her smile lit the place. Goddamn, how the young woman could smile. Was it all young women or just this one? He began to feel a little woozy. As he approached, she rose and took his hand and gave him a quick kiss.

"Well now Bud, who painted you the color of dead roses? Oh, my poor, poor baby."

"Well, you know how to perk a fellow up, don't you? I've felt better, that's for sure."

"Are you in pain?"

"Oh, nothing I can't handle with only the slightest help from a million milligrams of heroin every twenty minutes or so."

"You'll joke when the devil comes 'round with his bill, Bud."

"Take my women, take my money, take my life, but don't take my sense of humor, Mister."

"When that colonel came to tell me about Ted, it took him an *hour* before he got around to you. That was the worst, Bud, my Bud. I had to sit there playing the grieving widow just crazy to know about you, Bud. Oh, Bud, happiest day of my life they told me you were going to make it. I had to keep crying when all's I wanted was to laugh because they said you were going to make it."

"Holly, damn, you look good."

"Oh, Bud. Oh, Bud."

"Holly, I'm so very sorry about Ted. No man deserves to die like that. He wasn't a bad boy. I just fouled up. I wish to hell I could do it over."

"Well, you never can, can you?"

"How are you holding up?"

"Bud, I'm fine, now that the funeral is over and poor Ted's mother and dad have gone home. I don't have to play the sobbing wife no more."

"You know, the patrol can arrange for a doctor, or somebody to help you. You know, someone to talk to you."

"Bud, you're the only person I want to talk to."

"And the insurance. What it is, it ain't a fortune, but it's damn comforting. There's no horrible financial thing crushing down on you."

"It's fine, Bud. It'll get me through more than a few years, and they said they'd try and help me get a job."

"Great."

"Bud, you're not facing this, are you?"

"I don't know."

"Bud, I don't want to talk about me. I want to talk about *us*."

Bud looked out through the goddamned window to green Oklahoma. A hundred yards away he could see the interstate and the cars flashing down it. Where he'd made a living for so long.

"Bud, we can have everything now. I'm sorry Ted got killed but it wasn't your fault and it wasn't my fault, it was Lamar Pye's fault. Now we can be together. It's one less difficulty. It's time, Bud. You know it as well as I know it."

"Holly, I—" Then he ran out of gas.

"Don't you want to be with me?"

"Lord, yes."

"Then, Bud, why not? Why can't you just do it."

"Holly, you should know he loved you very much. What happened to him, he just lost his nerve and it was eating him up. He thought less of himself, not you. He deserves a little time before we up and move in and start sleeping together for the whole world to see."

"You never cared too much what the world thought."

"Yeah, maybe. And there's the other thing."

"What's that?"

"Lamar."

"Lamar?" Holly said. "Oh, yeah. *Lamar.* Now what the hell you think that means?"

"It don't feel right with him still out there."

"Bud."

"Holly, I said I'd take care of you for my partner. That was the last thing he asked before Lamar come over with the gun. And I will. I swear to you, I will. But I got to take care of my partner first."

"Ted's dead, Bud, there's no care to be taken. And nothing with Lamar Pye is going to bring him back."

"Well," Bud said, without much more to offer.

"Is that it, Bud? Lamar? You're going to go up against Lamar? The whole goddamned state of Oklahoma can't find Lamar and you're going to find him?"

As usual, he didn't know what he meant.

"I don't know. What I mean is, nothing feels right with Lamar on the loose. Wouldn't necessarily have to be me gets him. Frankly, the last thing I want is to run into Lamar. It ain't *personal*."

"The hell it ain't."

"Holly, I just . . ."

"So you aren't going to touch me?"

"Did I say that?"

"Seems like what you meant."

"I swear to you, at that moment when Lamar meant to finish me, what was in my heart was the thought I'd never been with you fair, in the open, the two of us, at a restaurant, a barbecue, you know, a damn couple. Last thing on my mind as I went under."

Was it true? It felt true about now. But he wasn't sure. He really didn't remember.

"Damn, Bud, you kill me."

"Well, that's my job."

"You know that place two exits back. The Do Si Do Motel?"

"Yes."

"Got us a room, Bud. Wanted to celebrate being alive."

Bud looked at his watch. He was due at the hospital by three and it was already near two. But what the hell. It was only a hospital.

Their differences—was it a woman-man thing or a Bud-Holly thing?—had to do with being naked. She didn't mind it. She sort of liked it, in fact, and could be so damned casual about it. Bud hated it; just that feeling of vulnerability, of being wide open to assault, of being a fat man whose nakedness revealed his idiocy. So it was that after they had made love, he had to pull the sheets up around his loins. In secret and terrible fact, he yearned always when they were done to dress instantly; but he also knew that the moments afterward were the most hallowed to her, were in some sense the point of the exercise, where her oneness with him was at its most intense, and so he could never deny her them.

"Goddamn, Bud," she said. "Lamar may have filled you with lead, but he sure didn't take your manhood. You had plenty left for me."

Why did she think him that good a lover? In the beginning he'd been a mighty engine, able to climb the mountain two or three times in a single afternoon. It was the incredible joy of freedom, of a new, other life. But the beginning was long past, and it seemed to him at least that his mighty engine only just got up the hill these days. But he figured that what she saw was what she wanted to see: that buck from the first weeks. He knew he'd never be that again, or at any rate, not with her. It saddened him, but he never quite had the guts to put it into words.

"You sure he didn't shoot you with love potion instead of lead?"

He laughed. She could be so damned girlish. Her breasts showed: they were little things but beautiful; he loved their weight, their heft, their round perfection and pink tips and the way they jiggled ever so slightly when she laughed.

"It was steel he shot me with," he said. "Steel shot. Another lucky break. The infection rate on steel is much lower than lead. But that ain't luck at all, compared to having you."

"You didn't start bleeding."

"No."

The bandages held; no telltale red spots marked the opening of the tiny wounds.

"It must have felt like being hugged by a stamp collection," he said.

"Oh, Bud, you are so funny! First time I saw you, I thought, oh my, it's John Wayne himself, but then you got me to laughing and I saw how much better you were than John Wayne. Or anybody."

Her absurdly high vision of him! How could he say no to a woman who thought so highly of him? He came the closest to being the man she thought he was and believed him to be when he was with her; and no other place in his life.

"I wish I could stay here forever," he said suddenly.

"No, Bud," she said. "It ain't good enough. We deserve a house and maybe our own kids. Or to travel. A real life. We were meant for it. We were supposed to meet, I believe that in my heart."

"I believe you're right," he said, exactly what he didn't want to say. It amazed him: Somehow he always did the exact opposite of what he set out to do. He was turned inside out. But not by her. She was just Holly, as usual. He was turned inside out by It, the thing, the two of them.

"Well, sweetie, ought to be heading back. I'm late."

"You go. Bud, just promise me. This Lamar thing? You're not going to let it grow into some huge obsession.

Some mission, where you got to get your revenge? It ain't worth it. It would just get you killed.''

"It ain't anything like that. I just want to be part of the team that brings him down, that's all. A part of his end, the way I was a part of his beginning.''

The doctor was angry because Bud was so late, and he seemed to wish he could find something seriously wrong with Bud and throw him back in a hospital room out of sheer meanness. But Bud's wounds resolutely refused to break and bleed; it was as if he had sealed himself up again.

"Your colonel called. He said he'd tried to reach you at home. I don't think he was happy.''

"Well, I didn't get in any trouble today, so he shouldn't be too angry.''

"What you did, Sergeant, was you got laid.''

Bud looked at him in surprise.

"Sir, I—''

"No, I know it, I can tell it. Physiological signs. I don't know what you've got going, Sergeant, but I wouldn't press it.''

"You ain't going to—''

"No, it's your business. Just don't try and go too far too fast. You could get hurt again. And this time permanently. Now take your Percodan.''

And when he got home, there was only more trouble. It was Jeff's game night, and Bud had promised he'd go. He was late and Jen had gone on without him. He gobbled a sandwich and almost called Holly, since he was alone in the house and she was back now, too. But he thought the better of it and instead raced across town to the Lawton Cougars field, where the JV team was playing its home Thursday night game under the lights.

Bud found Jen sitting high in the bleachers.

"Hi," he muttered.

"Where *were* you? The colonel called and then they called from the hospital and everything."

"Ah, you know. Got to jawing with that farmer and next thing you knew I was all out of time."

Her stony, isolated silence was rebuke enough; he knew from the sullen set of her body and the sealed-off look on her face that she was angry and hurt.

"Please don't get so mad. I was late. I'm here. Now how's Jeff? Is he in?"

"No, he's on the bench. He never starts, Bud, you should know that. Not this year."

Bud looked and saw his youngest son, appearing small and wan, sitting in the theatrically bright bath of lights, at the end of the bench. Jeff was an outfielder, who could run down any ball and would even thrust himself brutally against a wall to make a catch if he had to; but his batting was something of a family tragedy. It had just all but disappeared. He'd hit .432 his freshman year and been a star; and now, as a sophomore, had moved up to varsity. But then the slump had begun; it just sucked the life out of the boy, and the harder he tried, the worse he did. He was stuck on the JV team and couldn't even get into the lineup.

Bud checked the scoreboard: It was seven to two, the Altus Cardinals leading the hapless Cougars, top of the fourth. It seemed that Jeff didn't move; it was as if he were enchanted, in a bubble; the game flowed around him, players ran or swaggered by, yelling and hooting, but Jeff was frozen in some far-off place, as if in another world, lost in concentration.

"How do you feel?" she said.

"It's not bad," he said. "You know, at the end of the drug cycle the pain is bad and at the beginning it's okay. It just slides back and forth."

"I'm sorry I snapped at you, Bud. I just got so scared when they told me you'd been hit. Finally after all these years. And I expect you to be moody. After what you been through, it's a marvel you can even face the world."

A Cougar got on second and another walked. The few fans, mostly dads and moms, began a desultory clapping. But the boy on second was thrown out trying to steal, and the next boy hit into a double play.

"Jeff could hit this guy," Bud said bitterly, "I *know* he could."

"You're so angry, Bud," said Jen. "I can't say I blame you, what you went through, seeing poor Ted, your own near miss. It's so horrible. But I can't stand to see you eaten up like this. Can't the department get someone for you to talk to?"

"Stop it," he said brusquely. "I don't need to talk to nobody. I just need to get back to work. The whole thing will feel better when we get this creep locked up. That's all."

Now a Cougar dropped a fly, and then another one threw to the wrong base. In a second, the score had jumped to nine to two. But Bud was secretly pleased. It meant that Jeff's chances at hitting were better.

And, indeed, in the eighth, with two down and nobody on, Jeff was sent to the plate. Bud watched the younster unlimber from the bench, stretch and twist, try to shake off the cramps in his neck. Then he placed the batting helmet on his head and went to the batter's box.

Bud tracked him as he went, his face set in the taut mask of a warrior, his eyes squinting as if to crush every last mote of concentration onto his immediate problem. He entered the box, took three almost ritualized hip pivots, dragging the bat through the zone as if to arrange himself like a machine for the proper setting by which to engage the ball.

In the bright fake light, he looked so lean and strong, so poised, so perfect. Bud realized his heart must have been yammering and his knees shaking, but from the distance Jeff could have been a Cal Ripken or a George Brett, a natural hitter.

Oh please let him get a hit, he requested of the universe. *Some mercy for my son. Let him do well, or not so bad. Do not let him fail. I've failed enough for both of us; please show him mercy.*

The pitcher, a tall and whippy black kid, wound and delivered, and Jeff took a called strike. The ball popped sharply into the catcher's glove, dust rising from the impact like a gunshot. Bud thought again: The bullet hits, Ted's hair flies, and Ted is gone. He shook his own head, as if to clear the troubling thoughts from alighting anywhere, and dialed back into reality to check as Jeff took what was apparently the second of two balls.

"This should be his pitch," he said to Jen.

The pitcher fired and Jeff, overeager, swung wretchedly. He looked like a crippled stork, and the ball ticked weakly off into foul territory to the third-base side.

"Damn," Bud said. "He should have *parked* that one in the wheat."

He thought: *Oh, Christ, I would give my life for my son to do well.*

On the fifth pitch, Bud thought the pitcher uncoiled with a particularly venomous spasm, almost snakelike in the strike of his arm, and the ball swept toward Jeff in high theatrical light just as Jeff himself seemed to unscrew from the hips up, shoulders following hips, arms following shoulders, bat following arms. The whole thing was liquid somehow, punctuated by the sharpest crack Bud had ever heard, much louder and more decisive than the shots Lamar had launched at him. The ball rose, the noise of the desultory crowd rose, Bud himself rose, screaming "Yes, yes, YES!" and the ball sailed outward.

Go you bastard, GO! Bud willed it, oh *please*.

He saw the left fielder crouching at the fence, and as the ball descended, the boy leaped and it seemed he had it zeroed. But felt despair rise like a black tide into his heart, but the leap wasn't high enough by three feet and the ball bounded away in the darkness.

"Oh, God," Bud said, grabbing Jen's arm, "he hit a home run! Jeff, Jeff, WAY TO GO!" He was crying, literally, as his son trundled sheepishly around the bases to be greeted at home by some of his fellow players.

"God," he said to Jen, "I'm so damned happy."

"Bud," she said, "my God, you're bleeding."

CHAPTER
11

Odell sat with the AR-15 in his lap and a red wig on his head. He had tits. He was wearing lipstick and a blue fur-trimmed coat from the year 1958, the year that Ruta Beth's daddy had bought it for Ruta Beth's mother at Dillon's Department Store in Oklahoma City. He didn't look much like a woman. He looked like a gigantic transvestite with an assault rifle, if you looked close.

But who would look close?

He sat benignly in the back seat of Ruta Beth's little Toyota twelve miles beyond the Red River on the outskirts of Wichita Falls, Texas, just off Interstate 44 on its long pull from Oklahoma City. Sitting next to him was Richard, also with tits (tennis balls taped inside the dress), also with a wig (black), and a red hat with feathers curling down as well, all of it having at one time belonged to Beulah Tull. Ruta Beth had done the makeup, though Richard thought she'd gone a bit overboard on the rouge. In the mirror, he'd looked like some kind of corpse. If Odell didn't seem to mind, Richard certainly did, but of course he would say nothing.

In jeans and sunglasses, his ponytail tucked out of sight

under the brim of Bill Stepford's Stetson, Lamar sat, chewing on a long stalk of wheat. Next to his right leg, also out of sight, was the cut-down Browning A-5 12-gauge, though it was not loaded with birdshot but double-ought buck shells. He had the long-slide .45 in the waistband in the small of his back. And next to him, in the driver's seat, with Bud's Mossberg, sat Ruta Beth herself, also in a cowboy hat.

"That's it," said Lamar. "What we come this piece to see. That's it, our ticket to tomorrow."

But Richard didn't get it.

"I don't see anything," he said.

"Use your *mag-i-nation,*" said Lamar.

They were parked at a Denny's Restaurant, just off the interstate ramp. The sign said Maurine Street. Its lot jammed with cars, the restaurant sat on a small podium of land like the king of everywhere, the remnants of a crowd visible through the double-glass doors out front and the windows that circled it like a bright necklace. At the entrance to the parking lot stood a proud art moderne sign, turquoise and red; at night, it would blaze like a beacon up to the interstate.

"I just see . . . a *Denny's,*" said Richard.

"Ennys," Odell said and giggled.

"Is there a problem here, Aunt Lucy?" said Lamar. "Aunt Lucy, you trying to take command of the outfit? You got a better idea?"

"But . . . wouldn't a bank be better? It would certainly be more dignified."

"Di-fied," said Odell, rocking ever so slightly.

"Well now, let me explain," said Lamar. "You got to keep up with the times. Bank robbing ain't what it used to be. A, they keep the big money in the vault, with a timelock, so you only got what loose money's up front, sometimes less'n a hundred or so bucks. B, you got the goddamned cameras all over the place. Aunt Lucy, are you listening?''

''Lamar, I'm sure you're right.''

''Then you got silent alarms, you got money packs rigged to explode and cover you with red dye that don't wash off for a week, you got private security services, sometimes you got guards. A bank can be a pickle.''

''I see.''

''Now, a Denny's, in a little asswipe Texas city on a late Sunday afternoon? Let me tell you what you got. You got the big old breakfast money from about a thousand Texas Baptists. Them Baptists, they like to go to church and pray all morning, then stroll on down to Denny's for breakfast. They shovel down the goddamn homefries and pancakes and eggs and bacon and syrup and butter and coffee like hogs at a trough. They bloat up and begin to belch and pick their teeth. Whole goddamn families. It makes 'em feel close to the Lord, don't ask me why. So 'round about four, you got maybe ten, twelve thousand in small bills in the manager's safe. You got no cameras. You got no guards. You got no heroes. You got nothing but a staff of assholes what hates their goddamned jobs and ain't about to die for no Denny, whosoever the motherfuck he may be.''

''Enny,'' said Odell, cheerfully.

''Daddy, I swear, you know *everything*,'' said Ruta Beth. ''You are so smart.''

''Now if you like, Aunt Lucy, we'll drop you off and you can rob a bank while we do this here Texas Denny's.''

''No, Lamar,'' said Richard.

''Thank you, Aunt Lucy. Ain't you the sweetest thang. All right, darlin', let's go for a little drive through the neighborhood, then park and you and me head in for a lookiesee. We'll leave the two ladies in the back.''

"Yes, Daddy," she said.

Ruta Beth pulled the car out, turned right into a residential area, turned and turned again, passing by small white houses, well tended, with green lawns. Squares' houses, and now and then a square could be glimpsed, hosing down a midsized car, pushing a mower, just bullshitting with another square.

Richard looked at them, seeing a lost world flee by. Once he'd had such contempt! The people! Fools and jerks, parvenus and philistines, without a brain in their head, nothing to sustain them but delusions like . . . baseball . . . family . . . work. Yet now their dreariness broke his heart; it looked so comforting.

"Git that long, sad look off your beautiful puss, there, Aunt Lucy," said Lamar. "You git to looking that sad and I wonder if you ain't about to make a break on us."

"Lamar, I was thinking no such thing."

"Yeah, I heard that before. He acts up, Odell, you conk him good."

Eventually Ruta Beth swung around and they pulled into the Denny's parking lot.

"Okay, you gals stay put for a bit. Odell, you tuck that big piece away case anybody looks in. We're going to check the place out."

Richard watched Lamar get out of the car, stop, and so casually stretch himself as he pulled on a jean jacket over the .45. Then he put his arm around Ruta Beth, and just as casually as a couple of high school kids on a date, the two of them sauntered into Denny's.

Richard sat back, trying to relax. He felt absurd in the getup. And he was bored. But he couldn't get out of the car, because in the open, the fraudulence of his disguise would be obvious. He looked over at Odell, who grinned at him with empty, happy eyes. Looking into Odell's eyes could make you insane: they were guileless and remote, far removed from concepts such as cause and effect or right and wrong. He was simply a gigantic baby, who needed to be fed and wiped. Lamar brushed his teeth every night, talking to him in that sing-songy voice, baby talk and giggles. Yet in Odell there was a kind of innocence. He wasn't evil. He had no choice at all in the matter; he'd probably have been better off in the prison, where at least he was feared and respected, which meant he was left alone; or in a home somewhere, if there'd been money to put him in a home where they could study the strange gaps in his mind that left him mute and empty, yet curiously able to perform small hand-eye tasks like driving or shooting. Left to his own ways and shielded from temptation, he probably wouldn't hurt a flea.

Richard turned from Odell and found himself looking into the blank sunglasses of a deputy sheriff.

Lamar sat at the counter, sipping coffee. He looked like any middle-aged cowpoke, Texas style. Behind his shades, his eyes scoped the place out. It was done in green-and-brown zigzags, low-intensity colors to soothe people. He checked for entrances: the main one in the front right-hand corner of the building and, around to the side, an emergency exit, painted over. The windows gave a good view of the parking lot, however. His eyes went back to the counter, followed it to the register, which he saw was some kind of computer type deal. He figured when he went to the john, he could carefully check the register and see if there was a silent-alarm button or wire near the cash drawer, rare but not so rare it shouldn't be checked out. Hell, who knew, in goddamned Texas there might be a sawed-off or a six-gun slung under the register. This damned state had guns everywhere! There was a mirror on the wall, too, probably okay, but he made himself a note to check it out. You put the point of a pencil up against it; if there was a gap between the pencil and its reflection you were okay, but if they touched, it was a one-way job, which would mean a watcher or maybe even a shooter on the other side.

The kitchen, as usual, was behind the counter, with a long Dutch window through which to slide the plates. Now it held two cooks; on Sunday, at least four, maybe six. All of them black. Would they make a fuss to save the bossman his insured money? Probably not, certainly not older guys. But a young buck, like the niggers on the yard, busting with come and wanting to show how dead tough they were? Hmmmm. Would bear watching.

He pivoted slightly to study the layout of the tables. Only one dining room, that was fine, but what wasn't was the dogleg as the greedy bastards that ran the place had set six booths in the hallway that led to the bathrooms and the manager's office as a no-smoking zone. Be hard for one man to cover both the main room, with its fifty or so tables, and the hallway, ninety degrees to the right. The register man could probably cover both; or he himself, as he took the manager back to his office, could cover the hallway. But where would he put his tail gunner? Best place would be in a window booth halfway down. That way, the tail gunner could watch for heroes in the crowd, and take them out if he had to, and also keep an eye tuned to the lot for cops. And there was that back way out, which pleased Lamar if it came to shooting. You never went into guns; you always went away from them, flanked them and dealt with them.

And then the problem with a goddamned wheelman. With only four players on the crew, and one of them shaky as hell and another a cherry, and the room big, there was no way he could have the wheelman out and running. Needed the crew inside, all of them, even dickhead Richard. Didn't like that at all. Have to park right there at the entrance and run in; *but* a cop driving by might see the car, engine running, doors opened, empty. That's the sort of thing that set them off. Have to run a test on the patrol runs. How often does Johnny Cop come a-moseying by? And only three days till Sunday. Best to wait until *next* Sunday. But Richard would crack, Odell would get dangerously bored, and who knew what might go down with Ruta Beth here?

He looked over to Ruta Beth, who had turned.

"Shit," she said, "a cop."

The deputy tapped on the window. He was just a boy, really, mid-twenties, with cornsilk hair and eyes that were too far apart behind the aviator's shades. Actually, he looked a bit mean and surly, and he stared right at poor Richard. He gestured.

Richard just stared at him stupidly, his mind utterly blank with panic. In fact, he wet his pants; the warm urine cascaded over his crotch under the dress. He blinked back tears. Behind him, Richard could feel Odell tense and see one of his hands disappear as it slid under the blanket where the AR-15 lay. The buttstock of the rifle was in plain sight; if the cop looked at it and could get beyond the idea of the absurdity of an assault rifle in the back of an old Toyota with two old ladies, he'd have them cold.

Richard began to gibber. Strange noises came from his throat. "Ayah, ayah, ayah," he began to chant through utterly dry lips. His mouth felt like a hole full of sand. Impatiently the cop repeated the strange gesture, and then tapped on the window.

"Wahl wn-duh," said Odell.

More gibberish. Then it cleared magically in Richard's head: Roll down the window.

His trembling fingers flew to the crank and he wound it

down, feeling an idiot's smile splay across his face. He was beyond panic, he was in some place where butterflies of pure fright flitted and danced.

"Howdy, ma'am," said the young cop.

Mouth agape, Richard nodded moronically.

"It's such a hot day, I was somewhat worried to see y'all sealed up like that. A dog can die in an hour locked in a car, yes, ma'am, seen it myself. You going to need some air."

It was pure nonsense to Richard. Why didn't the cop notice his whiskers, his thickish shoulders, the black hair on his arms, the broadness of his hands, or the goddamned rifle butt sticking out of the blanket between the two?

"Ya'll from out of town? Oklahoma. Down here visiting?"

Richard's tongue seemed to constrict; he wasn't sure what he was about to spit out.

"Aunt Lucy! Oh, Aunt Lucy, don't you git upset."

He looked over and saw Ruta Beth flying down the steps toward him and Lamar hanging back but eyeing the situation carefully.

She ran to Richard and began to strke his hand gently, saying to the cop, "You know, Aunt Lucy was as perky as a bumblebee until the stroke. Now she just sits in the rocker all day long with Mrs. Jackson and they rock and rock and rock. On Thursdays, we like to take them for a long drive. Only chance they ever git to be off the farm."

The young cop stepped back, looking from Ruta Beth to Richard and back again, never once considering Lamar.

"Thursday's Bill's day off," Ruta Beth continued. "He works at the Chalmers plant up in Oklahoma City. Lord, he's a kind soul. My first, Jack Williams, Jr., why that man wouldn't do a thing if it weren't to his own advantage." She turned dramatically. "Bill, honey, it's okay. You can go back and get the ice cream."

Lamar nodded, and headed back inside.

"They *love* ice cream," Ruta Beth continued to the young officer. "But, lord, you can't take 'em *inside*. They just can't handle it, all the hustle and bustle. So we leave 'em in the car, git a quick Dr. Pepper, then bring 'em their ice cream. It's the best part of the week."

"Okay, ma'am," said the young officer. "Just checking. The old lady evidently rolled up the window—"

"Aunt Lucy, you bad girl!"

"And I tried to make 'em see how quick they could run out of air on a hot day. Seen it happen to dogs all the time. Mama comes back from the grocery with her two kids and Fido's done bought the ranch in the back seat. Terrible way for kids to learn about dying."

"Well, I will *talk* to Aunt Lucy, you can believe me. She's just *got* to learn."

"Be seeing y'all. Hope you come back to Wichita Falls."

"Well, I certainly hope we do, too."

The cop passed Lamar, now emerging with two ice-cream sodas in paper cups, and tipped his hat. Lamar smiled and came around and climbed in.

"Here you go, Aunt Lucy," he said loudly, and made a show of handing the cup to Richard, but at the last moment pulled it away.

"Aww," said Richard.

"You blanket-head, Richard," he hissed as he slid in. "Goddamn, you couldn't think of *nothing* but to look at him like you swallowed a goddamned fish?"

"I'm not an actor, Lamar."

"No, you ain't," he said, then, turning, "Honey, you saved our goddamned bacon on that one. You done just great. I think you got a future in this shit."

"Lamar," said Richard, "can I have my soda?"

"No, you may not," said Lamar. "Odell gets one soda because he sat cool as a cucumber with a smile on his face, just like I told him, and Ruta Beth gets the other one, because she handled that Johnny Cop slicker'n motor oil. You don't get nothing, Richard. Another second and I'd have had to pop that boy and we're on the run again, for nothing, you dummy. Shit." He gave Ruta Beth a kiss as they pulled out.

"Thank you, Daddy," she said.

"Wich-ud weewee," said Odell.

"What's that, Odell?" said Lamar. "Honey, did you understand him?"

"He's saying Richard went weewee," said Ruta Beth.

"Oh, Aunt Lucy," said Lamar, "you are *such* a baby!"

CHAPTER
12

Nothing panics you like your own blood, but by the time he'd gotten to the hospital, Bud had figured out that he probably wasn't going to die that night. And he didn't: Stitches underneath his arm had popped when he leaped to celebrate Jeff's home run, but the loss was minimum, though the young emergency room doctor wouldn't release him and so he spent another night in the hospital despite his considerable moanings and groanings about it.

"He complains like that all the time," Jen told them. "It's his idea of fun."

But the next morning, Colonel Supenski himself showed up, with lion eyes and not a lot of old-boy fellowship.

"Bud, you are ragging on me something fierce."

"Yessir," said Bud, glumly.

"Now, I want you to consider doctor's orders *my* orders. You can't go roaming about doing God knows what. It's not a vacation. You're still on duty and your duty is to recover, and return to active duty."

"Yessir," said Bud.

"Bud, I can see in your eyes, something's eating at you.

I know how being shot can make a man call into value a lot of the things he holds dear. I want you to—''

Bud fixed the colonel with a glare.

"What are you saying, Colonel?"

"There's talk, Bud."

"Talk? Talk about what?"

"Bud, as I understand it, somebody's wife saw you and Ted's widow at a diner in Elgin. It didn't seem right."

"Whose business is it?"

"It shouldn't be nobody's business, Bud. But that isn't the point. What should and what is are different as night and day. The truth is, if you wear the badge and walk the walk, you have to live a life that not only *is* free of taint, but *looks* free of taint. It isn't pretty, and it sure isn't fair, but it's what it is and that's the fact, and I know you know same as I do. Now all's I want from you is recovery time. Do you understand?''

Bud took a deep breath. Never in his long career had he ever argued with authority. It wasn't his way. If you enforce rules, you live by rules, that was that. But this time, for whatever reason, maybe just his prickly orneriness or some deeper sense that the universe was now ever so slightly unhinged, he said, "What's going on between Mrs. Pepper and myself is just nobody's damned business but hers and mine and maybe my wife's. That's all there is to it.''

The colonel looked at him hard.

"Bud, a dee-vorce, a scandal, it could cost you *so* much. Believe me, I know. I went through one in the Marine Corps fourteen years ago and it took me forever to get back on my feet. I never ever got the love back of my middle daughter and I will die regretting that. All for a younger woman I thought I loved who is now married to a general. So I know, Bud. I've been there. Plus, Bud, I got the patrol to think over. You up and marry the widow of the man you

were partnered with who got killed when you were along
. . . might git some folks talking. Next thing you know,
you got those news boys looking for dirt. It's a hard thing."

"Yes sir," said Bud. "I hear you. But what I should tell
you is Ted's dying words. He asked me to look after
Holly."

"Okay, Bud, I believe you. Now you just get better and
ever damn body going to be fine."

They let Bud go that afternoon, but before he drove
home, he called Holly.

"Hi."

"Oh, Bud, tell me, it wasn't nothing?"

"No, just some stitches broke, some minor local bleeding, that's all."

"Oh, that's great. And they're going to let you out?"

"I am out."

"Oh, Bud, can I meet you?"

"Holly, that's just it. People are beginning to talk. The
colonel said something."

There was a long silence on the line.

"Holly, the last thing either you or I need is some huge
mess over who's with who."

"So what are you saying, Bud?"

"Well, I don't know."

Bud thought about how simple it all became without
Holly. It was as if all the weight that had accrued on his
neck and shoulders over the last few months suddenly took
flight and vanished. He saw the future before him as a kind
of sentimentalized postcard, golden and pure. Yet even as
he could not bear the thought of hurting Jen, neither could
he bear the thought of hurting Holly.

"Bud, do you want it to be over?"

"No, Holly, of course not. I couldn't live without you," he said.

"Bud, I couldn't live without your bad jokes."

"We just have to be careful for a time is all. This settles down, we get it all straightened out."

"When will I see you?"

"Well, I got a grand day planned for us tomorrow. I want to go through Lamar's prison stuff. Everyone else has, why shouldn't I? Anyway, that's a long drive up to McAlester. I could meet you, say, in Duncan, at eleven, we could drive on up, get lunch, I'd go into the house for an hour or two and then we'd come on back and have dinner on the way."

"Oh, Bud, don't that sound like the prom itself!"

Bud drove on home then, and got there just as Jeff had returned from practice. Jen was back late and, behind, seemed to be manufacturing some despair over the dinner that she felt she had to prepare. The issue was: chicken or fish. Neither sounded like much to Bud.

"Goddamn," he said, "we got some celebrating to do. This boy hit a home run, I just got out of the hospital, and you worked too late to put in one more minute here. Let's go out to dinner. I need meat, red meat, freshly killed. The Meers Store. Any objections?"

"Dad, it's so expensive for hamburgers."

"Whatever. Let's go. We can put it on the card."

"Bud, we haven't paid that yet."

"Well, it ain't overdue so it won't bounce. Come on, Jen, let's give this boy a thrill, like the one he gave us last night."

"Dad," Jeff said in a voice dense with mock despair over his father's shameless corniness.

"Now come on, people, time's a-wasting. Maybe even Russ would join us, if he ain't snooty these days."

"I have a paper due tomorrow," Russ called down from upstairs.

Honors history. Russ looked like a goddamn beatnik, but he got straight As and was a good boy, even if he rarely spoke one word in a language his father understood.

"We shouldn't leave Russ," said Jen.

Bud bounded up the stairs, the ache in his legs vanished in his explosion of enthusiasm. It was suddenly overwhelmingly important that Russ be there, that they all be together.

His oldest son's room was a strange jungle to him; the junk-addict rock star in the poster, all the narrow little paperback books without pictures on the covers by people Bud had never heard of—Camus, Sartre, Nietzsche, Mailer, Dostoyevsky, names like that—magazines with words rather than pictures on their covers, too, a whole universe that just puzzled Bud, who'd had to drop out of Oklahoma State his freshman year when his father had died of cirrhosis in an Air Force hospital, and had gone into the Air Force himself for four years the next week.

"Now, what's this about a paper? It can't wait?"

"Dad, if I screw up this thing, Foster won't give me a rec to Princeton, like he said he would."

"Your brother did so well."

"I know. That's terrific, I'm really happy for him. But, this *paper*."

"Sure, I understand," said Bud, who of course didn't. Russ was a thin boy, more bone and muscle than flesh, who wore his hair troublingly long. Bud tried never to look at his left earlobe, where something glittered; and he didn't approve of the way the boy dressed almost purely in black except for a battered leather coat of the sort the pilots had worn when Bud was an air policeman those many years ago.

Russ had just charted his own course through life. He

loved his folks and never gave them a lick of trouble, but he wanted a wider, more passionate world. Read all the time, was trying to read himself out of Oklahoma.

"It's okay, Dad," said Jeff, who had come up the stairs after Bud. "He's a brain, he's got to study."

He didn't say it angrily; he and Russ never competed directly, and ran in completely different circles in high school. It was all right, it was cool.

But Bud felt a flash of anger: he loved it so when his boys were together and he could hover over them as he had when they were children, perhaps most fascinated at his own sense of kingship than out of any sense of giving them something, too. It was a selfish thing, Jen had told him: The boys had to be who they were, not his little servants, there to reflect his glory. He didn't quite agree, but everywhere he saw the signs: authority breaking down, both on the road and in the home. It was a losing battle, no sense at all of even fighting it. The day of the father as master was ending, closing out. He knew that and could get through it, he told himself. But he missed that sense of lordship that used to come with paying the mortgage.

"Okay, no problem, we'll bring you something."

"Thanks, Dad," said Russ.

They left shortly, and drove through the dark. Nobody said much on the way over. There wasn't much traffic as they took Cache Road through the built-up strip abutting Fort Sill and then got to plain flat highway west of Lawton. Twenty miles out of town they turned and drove up through the Wichita National Wildlife refuge, where buffaloes could actually be seen. The mountains rose around them like humps of stone. The Meers Store was an old mining-company store whose quaintness some clever people had preserved; now it served huge hamburgers made from authentic longhorn beef, said to be low on cholesterol, high on flavor. It was one of those down-homey joints, known for good beef, cold beer, and flirty waitresses. Full of junky posters and deer that nobody in living memory had killed. It didn't take long to find a table, and in just a bit more time, Bud was draining a Budweiser and waiting for a big hamburger, his favorite.

"Jeff, you should be so proud. I thought I'd bust a gut when you hit that ball. I *did* bust a gut."

Jeff gave a strange, self-conscious shrug.

"You did so well, Jeff," said Jen. "We're so proud."

"Well, one lucky swing doesn't make a season."

"No, but it just might start you off on a path to success. I feel you have the talent to be a major league player, if that's what you want bad enough."

"Probably not, dad."

"He should still plan to go to college, Bud," said Jen.

"Sure, sure, I ain't saying he shouldn't. But he should also be damned proud. What pitch you hit?"

"Dad, I don't even remember. I just decided I'd swing. Truth is, I'd pretty much given up. Didn't think I could hit him. The ball was just smoke. That guy was good. He's pitched a couple of no-hitters this year. He's only a sophomore. They say he'll go pro before he graduates. But he threw it where I could hit it. God, it felt so good."

"Well, sir, it looked good, too."

Bud sat back. He ordered another beer when the girl brought the food. Delicious, as anticipated.

It was dark in the place, and as he ate, he could see people, but not their faces. They could have been anyone, he thought, and thought of all the hundreds of times he'd come across grotesque things on the road, where out of nowhere scum hit innocent people and took their money and sometimes their lives. The people just couldn't do a thing about it, except hope for mercy, that's how sudden and ugly it could come.

His family sat in the light; who was in the dark? Who waited?

Was it a Lamar Pye, death just waiting to happen? And who would protect them? He, Bud? He was sworn to be off with his young woman, having the kind of adventure he'd never had when he was a young man and was so lucky to get to now.

But who would save them from the Lamars?

He looked at them. Jen was telling Jeff about a new jacket she thought he ought to get for his college interviews. Jeff was saying that Russ didn't get a jacket but didn't *need* one, he was such a brain. They were intent on their conversation, and Bud wanted to hug them both and hold them from the darkness.

He met her at eleven and they set off for McAlester. Why? Everybody—FBI, OSBI, U.S. marshals, Department of Corrections police, Pittsburg county sheriff's department, Oklahoma City homicide—had gone through the squalid collection of convicts' possessions, such as they were. These were the very best professional investigators in the state; what could Bud find that they couldn't?

Bud knew the answer: nothing. Anyway, he wasn't really even an investigator, having spent most of his career on the road, where things happened fast and furious and you handled a hundred decisions and situations a day, but no penetrations into mystery or playing a dozen varying accounts off against each other or cultivating a network of informants. But still Bud somehow wanted to know Lamar in a way that reading his jacket could not provide. He wanted to touch the things that Lamar had touched and cherished, and see what Lamar felt about life.

"I don't know how you can put your hands on those things. What do you expect to get out of it?" Holly asked, just as Jen had that morning. Jen had said it was a sick obsession; Holly, however grudgingly, accepted it.

"I don't know," he said. "Don't the Indians believe if a man holds a thing dear some of his soul rubs off on it? But Lamar don't have a soul. Maybe his evil rubbed off on his stuff. I want to see what's left in it."

"Bud, that's crazy."

"Well, maybe it is. But I'm going to go nuts if I just sit around that house and take Percodans. It'll be a nice trip."

They took Oklahoma 7 east from Duncan toward the small penitentiary city 125 miles away. It was a bright summer's day, and on either side of the highway, the farmland spilled away, the neat fields broken up by stands of trees or low hills, all of them decorated with the rhythmic pumping of the oil wells, which somehow looked like giant insects at their feeding, up, pause, and then greedily down again. Now and then, they'd blow by some hopeful rural town, usually with pennants flapping and gas station signs climbing heroically into the sky and a small civilization of fast-food joints.

Bud loved it: highway America. Always different, always the same. He loved the snap of the wheat in the wind and the small tidy places and the neatly furrowed fields and the high blue sky and the green everywhere. It had given him such a thrill to roll down that ribbon of concrete in his unit, aerials whipping, lord of it all, and all who looked on him knew that he was the man that counted.

He looked over at Holly. She was such a pretty young thing. He didn't believe he'd ever seen a person in whom the features were so perfectly formed. Why did she like him so?

She looked over and smiled. She had nearly perfect teeth.

"What are you thinking, Bud?"

"I'm wondering how come of all the men in the world you picked me. You could have had any of them."

"Well, I could not have, and you know it. I picked you because you were the kindest and the strongest and the bravest and the best. Who wouldn't pick such a man?"

He shook his head. The absurdity of the praise almost irritated him; he remembered the fear, the sense of worthlessness he'd felt when Lamar brought the shotgun to bear for the last moment, just before pulling the trigger. Whatever his virtues, they were valueless that day.

The cloud that passed through his mind must have shown in his eyes.

"Bud," she said, "can't you let it go? The thing with Lamar, Ted's death, that horrible thing. It's over. The others will get him, sooner or later."

"It's forgotten. Okay? I swear it."

"Oh, Bud," she said with a sigh, "you are such a wonderful liar."

That seemed to let the tension escape, and they drove the rest of the way in a buoyant mood; he flirted and she laughed. They listened to the radio. There was an oldies station in Oklahoma City that they picked up, KOMA, and Bud knew more of the songs than Holly did. They made jokes about the troopers parked by the roadside or occasionally cruising down the other side of the highway strip. It was light and pleasant.

In under two hours they came to the small city of McAlester, and from the highway they could see the city's only remaining industry—its prison. From Oklahoma 1 as they headed in, it looked somehow magical, like a Moorish city or a Camelot: the high, white, fortresslike walls shining in the sun. It looked so cheerful, so promising, but it was such a fantasy. No cheer in that place, and goddamned little promise.

"Here we go," said Bud, turning off Route 1 for the two-mile spin up West Street, until it delivered them into the prison itself. Was it his imagination, or did he feel a sense of dread and evil as they approached, as if the air, somehow, had gotten heavy?

McAlester State Penitentiary was everything you thought of when you heard the word "prison." The walls were huge and blank and festooned with cruel razor wire, and up close the fraudulence of the whitewash revealed itself, because you could see the ancient bricks mortared into place in the millions and you knew that under the bright paint they were dingy, as though soaked in woe.

"So much bad comes out of a place like that, it makes you wonder," said Bud, as he turned off West Street onto Prison Boulevard, in the shadow of the vast south wall itself. "The convicts call 'em gladiator schools. It's where a young kid with a wild streak learns how to be a burglar, a buttfucker, a cop killer, and how never to feel nothing about what he's done. You don't want to know what goes on inside a place like that. You can't begin to imagine it. But I'll tell you this: Nothing good ever came out of an American prison. I'd drench 'em in napalm and turn every last boy inside into ashes and black bones, and start over."

"The newspapers would scream," Holly pointed out.

"They would until they watched the crime rate fall."

Bud pulled into a slot marked LAW ENFORCEMENT just shy of the admin building that crouched under the walls and turned his truck engine off. Lamar and Odell and Richard: They'd come this way. He remembered from the newspapers that first day after the escape: the arrows pointing to a second-floor grated window in the admin section of Cellblock A out back, where that poor boy had parked his truck and they had climbed into it and waited for him to come to his death. Then they'd driven out the gates, turned left, turned left again, and come down this merry little street with the cheery visitor's center, the warden's big house like a mansion, even a tacky little museum, before turning down West Street and heading out into the world.

"Open that glove box," he said.

She did and saw a small black gun.

"That's a Beretta 84 .380," he said. "Thirteen shots. Safety's on. Anything happens—"

"Bud—"

"I know it's silly and not a thing will happen. But you know how my mind works. Anyhow, you take that gun and push the safety down with your thumb. Then all you have to do is pull the trigger thirteen times. That should make him *really* mad, so after that, you slug him with it."

"Bud, you are so strange. Do you really think there's going to be *another* prison break?"

"No. But like the man says, if you want peace, prepare for war. I'll be back in an hour, okay?"

"Yes sir, it's not a problem."

"You sure?"

"Yes sir. I brought a paperback book along to read."

"Good."

They were expecting Bud, but if he anticipated any personal apology for the things that McAlester had unleashed, he got none: only professional courtesy, distant and cool but not rude. He checked his Colt Commander with an assistant warden, who took him into a bleak little office. There in three battered cardboard boxes were all that remained in the Big Mac of Lamar Pye, his cousin Odell, and Richard Peed.

"No letters," said the assistant warden. "Lamar and Odell haven't gotten letters in years. Nobody cared about them or even knew about them. Until they broke out, they didn't exist."

Bud nodded.

"I don't know what you're looking for," said the assistant warden, "but if you think you're going to find it there, I think you'll be disappointed. How long do you want?"

"Oh, an hour or so?"

"That's fine, Sergeant. Take your time. No rush. No one's going anywhere."

Bud sat down and pulled over Odell's box. It was mostly clothes, neatly laundered blue jeans and plaid shirts, a few prison denims of the sort that were no longer strictly mandatory. The underwear, all clean. No porn. He seemed not to have a sexual bone in his body. A model airplane, poorly assembled. Some kind of World War II ship, with glue smeared all over it. A shank, cut from a shoehorn, wickedly vicious. And, finally, a cigar box, just as a small boy in a fabled boyhood would have, a Huck Finn.

Bud opened the thing: first off, he saw a faded picture of a farm woman, taken, judging from her hair, some time in the sixties. She had that severe, Depression-era look, no meat at all on her sinewy features, narrow eyes that expected no mercy from the world. Her taut mouth held a tension of sorts. She was hunched in a cheap coat, though the sun was shining. The picture was blurry, but in the background he saw white clapboard, a farmhouse perhaps. He turned the picture over. ODELL'S MAMA CAMILLA, ANADARKO, OKLAH 1967 it said, in bold, childish letters, though the writing could not have been Odell's since the man was hopelessly retarded and illiterate.

Next out came a coloring book. Bud opened it. Some-

time early sixties, badly done, the crayon strokes violent
and mixed, paying no attention to the lines. The book was
drawn from a Walt Disney cartoon movie called *Sleeping
Beauty,* full of thin, beautiful blond people. An act of cruelty, Bud thought, to give such a thing to a hulking, damaged boy like Odell, with the hole in his face and the nothingness in his mind: He could just look and wonder at what
he could not have, ever. A woman's flowery hand had written "Odell's favorite book" inside the cover, and paging
through, Bud finally came upon what must have been
Odell's favorite page. It was a dragon, rearing up fero-
ciously, about to strike a handsome knight with a sword.
Alone, it was not touched by a crayon; the image held too
much power for young Odell to defile.

That was it. So little for a human life, even an Odell
Pye's. He pulled the next box over, finding it heavy. It had
to be Richard's, because the heaviness soon revealed itself
to be books. Richard was a reader: *In the Belly of the Beast,
In Cold Blood, The Pound Era, Thus Spake Zarathustra* by
somebody whose name Bud could not even figure out how
to pronounce. The books looked a little like Russ's, which
somehow irritated him. Paging through them, Bud found
lines highlighted in yellow marker. It was all gibberish,
mostly about violence.

> Thus speaks the red judge, "Why did this criminal
> murder? He wanted to rob." But I say unto you: his
> soul wanted blood, not robbery: he thirsted after the
> bliss of the knife. His poor reason, however, did not
> comprehend this madness and persuaded him: "What
> matters blood?" it asked; "don't you want at least to
> commit a robbery with it? To take revenge?" And he
> listened to his poor reason; its speech lay upon him

like lead; so he robbed when he murdered. He did not
want to be ashamed of his madness.

Crazy stuff. What the hell could it mean?

He guessed Richard was trying to figure out what he was
doing in here. Too bad, Richard boy. You made your decision, now you got to take the consequences.

Bud put the little book down and went through a few
heavy and glossy paperback books on art, mostly painting,
again nothing pornographic. Some art supplies—sheaves of
drawing and tracing paper, a small box with pencils, chalk,
chunks of charcoal for sketching, but no sketches. No
weapons, just shaving gear, all neat, and a toothbrush, the
toothpaste neatly rolled up. A comb, a Bic razor, some
Colgate shaving cream, soap in a plastic box. It all gave
Bud the creeps for some reason, and he soon tired of Richard and his intellectual vanities.

He pulled the last box over. PYE, L., it said on the outside.
The clothes were neat in a professional convict's way:
jeans, a jean jacket, even a pair of cowboy boots, much
polished, much worn. A stack of magazines: *Guns &
Ammo, Shooting Times, Gun World,* and a profusion of
stroke books. Bud paged through them: *Penthouse* and
Playboy and a few more obscure ones that seemed to show
women in stockings or women bent over, spreading their
asses, exposing their tuliplike assholes or leaning back and
ramming plastic or rubber dildoes into amazingly prehen-
sile vaginas. Again, Bud felt slimy, as if Lamar were
drawing him in, making him party to Lamar's own inner
horror. He set the magazines down, found a well-thumbed
copy of *The Picture History of the Third Reich.* He found
something called *The Turner Diaries* and another called
The Last Clarion for the White Race. Aryan brotherhood
shit.

At last he came to an album of sorts. He pulled it out. LAMAR'S BOOK, it said in blocky letters, the same letters he recognized from the back of the picture of Odell's mama. He opened it up, encountering a crumbling yellow news clipping from the *Arkansas Gazette* of August 1955.

HERO TROOPER SLAYS TWO BEFORE DYING, the headline read, and Bud made out the murky one-column shot of a man identified as "Trooper Sergeant Swagger."

A State Trooper Sergeant shot and killed two suspected murderers on Route 71 north of Fort Smith yesterday afternoon, before dying himself of gunshot wounds inflicted by the two men.

Dead were Sergeant Earl Lee Swagger, 45, of Polk County, a Marine Congressional Medal of Honor winner in the Pacific in World War II; and Jim M. Pye, 27, of Fort Smith and his cousin Buford "Bub" Pye, 21, also of Fort Smith.

State Police give this account of the event:

Yesterday morning two men answering the descriptions of Jim M. Pye and Buford Pye robbed an A&P in downtown Fort Smith, shooting two employees. They escaped in a white 1954 Ford. Authorities immediately began roadblock procedures, but the two assailants evaded the roadblocks.

They were spotted by Sergeant Swagger on Route 71; he gave pursuit and managed to drive the vehicle off the road near Winslow. Attempting to arrest the men, he was shot in the lower chest and stomach.

As the two men made their getaway on foot, Sergeant Swagger shot and killed Buford Pye. Then, he trailed Jim Pye for nearly three hundred yards into the corn fields where he exchanged shots again with his assailant.

Pye was hit in the eye and the stomach and was found dead at the spot.

Sergeant Swagger returned to the car to await medical attention but bled to death before help could arrive.

He leaves a wife, Erla June, and a 9-year-old son, Bob Lee.

Wow, thought Bud. *They knew how to build a lawman in those days.*

Wonder if I'd have the guts for that action?

Rather than contemplate so melancholy a topic, Bud gave the page a turn. Next was a report card, from the Arkansas State Reformatory Middle School, dated June 1962. Lamar got a bunch of 3s and 4s in his subjects—As and Bs, that was—but some educator had written:

Lamar shows great potential when his classes interest him, but his tendency for getting in fights or disruptive behavior threatens his academic achievement. He must learn impulse control. Additionally, he sexually assaulted two younger boys; he clearly has overly mature aggressive tendencies as well as serious resentment of authority. He had better be given therapy quickly before he develops serious personality pathologies.

Of course he wasn't; of course he did.

The next page, another news clipping, from the Anadarko *Call-Bulletin* of January 1970:

FARMER FOUND SLAIN ON PERKINSVILLE ROAD.

The story simply related how a farmer named Jackson Pye—the third worthless Pye brother, Bud concluded—had been stabbed to death by a mysterious assailant as he walked home along a country road from a nearby tavern.

There were no witnesses. The report also said he was survived by his son Odell.

Another page: CONVENIENCE STORE ROBBERIES CONTINUE.

Another: LOCAL MAN ARRESTED ON RAPE CHARGES.

Another: BAIL DENIED TO VIOLENT OFFENDER PYE.

Another: PYE ESCAPES FROM COUNTY LOCK-UP.

Bud riffled through the pages: the raw verbs of crime headlines yelled up at him from the seventies, and the crimes, mostly robbery and theft, now and then a murder and a sentencing. Lamar had become the compleat career criminal, master of a dozen violent trades, his acts marked by brazenness, violence, and a certain nutty courage. Lamar had balls, no doubt about it.

PYES CONVICTED IN PUSATERI KILLING read the last one, an account of how Lamar and Odell shot a motorcycle gang snitch in the head and dumped him, how he miraculously survived to identify them before dying.

SENTENCE FIFTEEN YEARS TO LIFE FOR EACH KILLER COUSIN.

The album was Lamar's life, what he was proud of, his résumé. What would you do with such a man? How could he possibly be reclaimed? He came from criminal stock, he evinced antisocial behavior from an early age, was unnaturally aggressive, and took to the lifestyle of the professional criminal with extraordinary ease. He was born to be a criminal, that was all.

Bud put the book down. There was nothing at all here, except a warning for any and all who dared mess with Lamar Pye without backup and lots of firepower. Put him in your sights and blow him away, that's all.

He glanced at his watch.

He'd been at it three hours! Jesus Christ! And Holly was still waiting outside.

He reached for the pile of slick magazines to reinsert in the box, but by their very slickness, they fell to the floor, skidding and opening. Bud cursed and bent to retrieve them and then noticed something strange. Across the rolling mountainous breasts of the Penthouse Pet of August 1991, there was inscribed some sort of figure. It wasn't a drawing, but the impression of a drawing that had been done on a paper laid across it.

Bud picked it up, tried to find some angle of light that would reveal its secret. That didn't work; the image kept collapsing as the light changed. It occurred to him to do a tracing. He remembered that Richard had some light paper in the art supplies in his box and he quickly got it out. He laid the paper across Miss August, only slightly obscuring the thrust of her tits, the pronglike tightness of her nipples; with a piece of charcoal, he delicately rubbed the paper, just enough pressure to leave the charcoal everywhere except in the grooves, where it sank under pressure.

When he was done, he looked at what he had brought out: It was the image of a lion.

CHAPTER 13

Mar go bye-bye wif Rutie-girl.

Dell go barn, see moocow. Plus Wi-chud. Moocow nicey-nice. Soft. Smell toasty. Eyeballs browny like poop. Big eyeballs. So still. Eyeballs so brown. Touchy moocow, moocow go "Mooooooooooooo," Wi-chud go "Nonononono!"

Wichud girl!

Wichud girly-girl, like Rutie-girl!

Wichud always Boo-hoo, like girly. Wichud baby thing.

Then . . . Rutie-girl back. No Mar. Where Mar? Mar go? Mar go away far?

WHERE MAR?

WHERE MAR?

Dell feel bad. Dell hurt. Dell scarey-scare.

WHERE MAR?

"Mar be here," Rutie-girl.

Wi-chud. Where Mar?

Rutie-girl, where Mar?

Wi-chud go "Me no know," nicey Dell.

Dell go boo-hoo. No Mar. Dell go boo-hoo. Dell want Mar. Dell red. Red inside. Red Red Red Red.

WHERE MAR! DELL WANT MAR!

Wi-chud, you tellum or Dell go BONKY on head, Wi-chud.

Wi-chud, crybaby girly, "No No Dell, No Hurty."

GO BONKY Wi-chud. GO BONKY!

Then . . . Mar!

Mar new car!

Car whitey!

Dell be so happy-happy.

"New car, new car," Dell.

"Yes, it is, Odell, and now we're going to repaint it," said Lamar, as he climbed from the dusty vehicle. "Richard, you're a painter, ain't you? Time to pull your weight, son. Let's get this sucker repainted."

But Richard looked like somebody had just squeezed all the air out of him. He was the color of dead petunias.

"What's wrong, boy?"

"Odell hit me! Twice!"

"I don't see no blood. If he *really* hit you, you'd be bleeding."

"But he *hurt* me."

"Odell, no bonky Richard. Richard nicey nice. Odell, go me sorry."

Odell's face lit in contrition. Genuine pain seemed to briefly shine from his eyes.

"Dell baddy bad," he said.

"See, he apologizes, Richard. Okay? Does that take care of it?"

"Ah," said Richard, "I suppose."

"Lamar, the baby has been upset at your absence," said Ruta Beth. "I wonder if we could control him if you weren't here."

"Don't you fret that, hon," said Lamar. "Now come on. We got work to do."

But Richard wondered. For just a second there, it looked as if Odell was going to lose it. His dull eyes inflated in fear and rage, and it was as if his whole chest swelled. He had grabbed Richard and slapped him hard atop the head twice. Richard had felt like a rag doll. The fear/hate of losing Lamar had turned Odell briefly psychopathic and frightening.

It scared the shit out of Richard. In one of his "moods," Odell could hurt anyone. He shuddered at the thought: Odell, alone in the world, without Lamar.

"Come on, boy, get to work," commanded Lamar.

They spent the afternoon with cans of spray paint and Richard tried to lose himself in the work. He was surprised how much he enjoyed the simple task: It was freedom from lions, it was freedom from fear, it was freedom from Odell's whimsy or the utter domination of Lamar. After a frenzy of taping over the trim, he sprayed the bright orange paint on the car in smooth, circular motions, almost as if it were an airbrush, amazed at how quickly the car picked up its new color and how good he was at it. He was much better than Lamar, a lot better than Ruta Beth, and completely better than Odell, who simply could not get the concept of smoothness and just hammered a spot onto a single sector of the car so clumsily that even Lamar saw the hopelessness of it and gave him another job. And pretty soon they had it: a nice orange car.

The next day, Friday, Lamar said to him, "Okay, Richard, you come with me today. We goin' pick up our second car."

"A second car?"

"Yes sir. It will surprise you how a dumb Okabilly like me got this sucker planned out, Richard. We actually going to use three cars. Yep. You got to plan it right if you want to stay ahead of Johnny Cop. Them boys got their computers and their helicopters and their what-all. Gittin' harder and harder to do an honest day's stealing. But I think I got em buffaloed on this one, yes I do. Hey, boy, you're a-running with the big dogs now. Ain't it a toot?''

"Yes sir,'' said Richard.

As they were pulling out of the farmyard in Ruta Beth's Toyota, she came out and gave Lamar a little peck on the cheek.

"You be careful, hon.''

"I will. And you take good care of Odell. You watch him. He can wander off.''

"Don't you worry about Odell. Me 'n' him going to have a good time. I'm going to work and he's going to spin the wheel for me.''

"Good. He feels useful then.''

"Richard, you mind Daddy. He knows what he's do-ing.''

"Yes ma'am,'' said Richard.

"Don't be late, honey.''

"We won't be.''

"You want the roast beef tonight?''

"That'd be super,'' Lamar said.

They pulled out. Lamar was happy.

"Damn,'' he said. "She's the best goddamn girl a man could find. I'm a lucky man, Richard. Yes I am.''

They drove the mile down the red dirt road, turned left on 54, then, a few miles down, west on 62, toward Altus. The highway was flat across a flat land under a high west-ern sky and a blaze of sun unfiltered by the thin clouds. The mountains jutted from the plains and the wind snapped across the earth. Now and then a tractor would slow traffic down or they'd meander through some one-horse town, a brick bank and hardware store, a strip mall with an auto parts place and a Laundromat, the inevitable 7-Eleven.

"See," said Lamar amiably, "trouble with those god-damned Seven-'Levens is that ever goddamned hour the manager sets a certain amount of the cash in the timelock vault. Through a little chute up top. So at any given time you can't get but what the store's taken in in the past hour. Ain't hardly worth the goddamn trouble."

He knew so much!

He knew how stores were organized, what kind of vaults they had, how police patrol shifts worked, how city and state cops differed in their investigative approaches, how to operate any kind of gun or machine, how to get into or out of anything, how to rewire or deactivate electronic security devices. It was as if he had burrowed into the very structure of the universe and knew all of its useful secrets.

"Now, Richard, I do want to talk to you 'bout Sunday."

Sunday! Richard didn't want to think about Sunday. He had just willed it out of his mind.

"You tell me what your job is."

"I'm your tail gunner."

"That's it. Now, what's a tail gunner do?"

"He pretends to be a victim of the robbery. He doesn't pull a gun or anything. He's just with the squares, his hands up, everything. But he's watching in case there's some hero or undercover cop."

"You never know about undercover cops."

"Or some cowboy. Lots of cowboys in Texas."

"Now, Richard, what are you looking for?"

"Man with a gun."

"And what might the signs be?"

"Ah—" Richard struggled to remember. "He'll have a coat on, no matter how hot it is. And he'll be very conscious of the coat. He'll always be adjusting it, you know, pulling it tight to keep it from falling open. You really think we may run into a man with a gun? Remember when that crazy guy went into Luby's? There were a hundred people in there and not one of them had a gun.''

''We may not be so lucky. You going to see a bulge?''

''A bulge. Maybe a—''

''No, Richard, goddamn, don't you remember nothing? These new holsters are real slick in holding the piece in tight to the body. In the old days, you could always see a bulge. It's all changed now with this here ballistic nylon, plus all the cops wearing flat autos instead of rounded wheelguns. You probably be up against a boy with a Beretta or a Glock or a SIG. Rangers carry SIGs, Texas highway patrol, Berettas. You got to read his body. Got that?''

''Yes, sir,'' said Richard disconsolately, feeling very much like a teenage boy who had disappointed his father.

''And what else?''

''Ah—what else?''

''What else.''

''I don't know—''

''You dumbhead. It may be a bitch! Yeah, used to be damn few women working police and fewer by God of them packing guns. Now you got a goddamn one-in-five chance it'll be a woman. Now if there's an undercover or plainclothes or off-duty cop in there, you got one chance in five it's a woman. Could be a woman with kids, woman at a table with her daddy or her old man, could be a nigger woman, a Mex, anything. You read the goddamned body, look for the way they carry their hands, the way they don't swing about fast because it might cause the coat to fluff up, you got that?''

''Yes sir.''

''And if you see it and she goes for it when the job is coming down, Richard, what's your assignment?''

"I have to shoot."

"Yes sir, like I told you; gun out front, you look at the sights, you LOOK AT THE SIGHTS, and you fire fast, three times. You put her down, Richard, or she gonna put us down. You think you can't do it? Think on this: I get hit, Odell may go hog wild with that AR. He could make that goddamned Luby's thing look like Sunday school. You want that on your conscience?"

"No sir."

"No sir. Quick in, quick out, nobody gets hurt, we go home rich."

They were in downtown Altus now, driving through the dusty streets. It was a low old town, with no buildings over three stories, lots of closed-up storefronts, a general store, a courthouse and city hall that looked as if plush times had passed by many a year ago, the usual statue of Will Rogers, who never met a man he didn't like, a few benches. But Lamar didn't go for it.

"Too open. Pull 'round the other side of town, we'll find something with a bit more privacy."

They cut through what passed for the Altus suburbs, little houses swaddled under wilted trees, and soon enough hit the commercial strip, U.S. 283 running north.

"Yeah, this is more like it. Pull in there."

Richard pulled into a strip mall crowded with cars. Food Lion was the big draw; there was also a yogurt shop, a county library, a Rexall, a movie complex with five tiny ratty little theaters, and a sporting goods store.

"Ooo, movies, ain't that a treat. Pull in here, Richard."

"We're going to the movies?"

"No, Richard, we are not going to the movies. Richard, sometimes I wish I'd left you in that goddamn cell for the niggers. They'da been more happy, I'da been more happy, and hell, boy, maybe *you'da* been more happy."

They sat in silence. In awhile a car pulled in, and a father and son got out and went up to the box office. The father bought two tickets and they went in.

"Now ain't that a gift. See, Richard, he'll be in there two hours. When he comes out, it'll take him at least a half an hour to figure out that he didn't forget where he parked his car, but that somebody stole it. It'll take the cops, even in a hick burg like this, another fifteen, twenty minutes to come on by to write the goddamned report. By that time, we'll have that sucker wearing a different color and new plates."

Slowly, Richard drove over to the car, but Lamar said, "We got some time, you just cruise a bit. We got a last thing to talk about."

Oh, Christ, thought Richard.

"You got one other job."

"What is it, Lamar?"

"Now, say something goes wrong. I catch some shit. I don't make it out. Or I get hit bad and die in the car, bleed to death maybe. The law is closing in, it's all gone down, it's turned to yellow cat shit."

"Lamar!"

"It could happen. This is risky business, sometimes the craziest things fuck you up. You listening? You can see it in your *mag-i-nation?*"

All too easily. Richard felt like crying.

"I saved your ass from the niggers, I got you out, I got you this new life. Richard, if they catch you, you can tell them you was forced in all of this. Richard, you might even be a hero in all this, you could tell them all the bad things we done. The Stepfords will say you didn't do nothing, that goddamn lucky-ass John Wayne–looking Smokey sergeant will say you didn't shoot nobody. Hell, they'll make a movie with what's his fucking name, Richard Gere, that the one, he's playing you. But you owe me one thing, Richard.''

"Yes, Lamar.''

"You still got that Smokey's gun? You ain't lost it or nothing?''

"No, Lamar. I have it. It's back at Ruta Beth's under the mattress I sleep on.'' He hated it. It was a big silver thing, hard and slightly greasy. He was supposed to dry-fire it a hundred times a night to develop strength in his hands, but he could never pull the trigger more than twenty-five times before it hurt too much.

"Oh, you don't have it now? Great, Richard. Well, never mind. If it goes to the skunks on us, Richard, and old Lamar's been turned to meat by some state cop with a shotgun full of Number Four, you wait till Odell's head is turned, then you put that gun muzzle behind his ear and you pull the trigger. That's the sweetest thing could happen to Odell if I'm not here.''

"I-I—I thought you *loved* Odell.''

"I do. Too much to want to have to think about what would happen to him if I weren't there to watch out for the boy. Who would care for him? Who would explain things to him? There ain't no mercy in this world for a big old baby who's listened to his evil cousin, done harm and can't talk for himself. Who would brush his teeth? Who would make sure he eats? Sometimes, he don't even know enough to eat at all. He's the sorriest soul on earth, truth is. They'd make him into some kind of geek show if I'm dead and they catch him, then they send him to some hole without me to figure out what's going on and to make the way for him. Couldn't have that, Richard. No way. So you got to do what I tell you.''

"Yes, Lamar.''

"I knew I could trust you, Richard. Okay, drop me here."

Richard pulled over and Lamar slipped out, took a quick look-see in each direction, then smooth and unruffled as could be, just bent to the car door and slipped a long, flat piece of metal down the window shaft. With a few swift diddles—backward, while looking around with the softest and most relaxed expression on his face—he popped the lock and jumped behind the wheel. In a second, he had it started. He backed out, pulled by Richard with a smile, and headed off on his way.

CHAPTER
14

On Saturday, Bud went to the new Lawton public library just down from the new police station and looked at art books and books on Africa. Lions. What the hell was this thing about lions?

Was it just lions? Or was it another theme—the lion in art? Of the latter, there wasn't much. He only came across one painter who could be called a lion artist, a Frenchman named Rousseau who painted the goofiest things Bud had ever seen. The stuff was called primitive. The most famous showed a lion licking a sleeping black man under a spooky moon. Bud gazed on the picture, trying to figure it out. It actually kind of shook him: it was like looking into someone else's dreams—it had that clear, serene quality to it, almost childish. It seemed somehow smug that its meanings were sealed off to normal folk like himself. It gave him the goddamn willies.

The other famous lion painting, also by Rousseau, actually wasn't primarily about lions at all; instead it was about a woman on a chaise lounge in the jungle. She had the same spooky calmness. In one corner of the picture, a lion and a tiger, almost lovers, gazed from the dense green trees. It also had that childish quality, but there was nothing in it that seemed to have to do with Lamar Pye or Richard Peed, because they were so peaceable and in a way, so unnatural. To Lamar, nature was savage; this kind of wussy lion would strike Lamar as a kind of sacrilege somehow.

But then Bud noted a small drawing in an art history book jammed with paintings of important men and battles. Was it a lion? It was a cat, but could it be a lion? He looked close at the caption, more foreign gibberish with one recognizable key word: *"Lion tourné vers la gauche, la tête levée, 1854,"* it read. The artist was another French guy, a Eugène Delacroix.

This Eugène appeared to know a bit more about lions than his poor countryman Rousseau. There was nothing phony or movie-like about it and this lion couldn't have come out of any dream. It was a big beast, somehow shivering in the delight of its own existence, its head corkscrewed slightly to the left so that you couldn't see the famous lion profile or much of the familiar mane. The beast seemed to be stretching itself on some plain somewhere. But Eugène must have feared lions and known what they could do, in a way the dreamer Rousseau never could: Eugène somehow got its throbbing power, the bunched muscles under the skin, the sense of sheer grace and coiled energy stored in it, its animal purity. But the eyes, especially, seemed to have some secret meaning: They were jet-black arrowheads set in the narrow skull, animal eyes, devoid of mercy or curiosity, merely intent on feeding whatever instincts happened to play across the lion brain. Odd how much emotion a few lines inked on a piece of paper one hundred odd-years ago could stir.

Bud shivered himself, though not with delight. He felt the power of the predator, the instinctive killer. Maybe *this* is what Richard was trying to bring out.

But that was all he came up with, and so he put the art books aside, and turned to the lion as animal, gazing for hours at lion photography from a variety of texts. This got him even less. Lions, for all their vaunted majesty, were just big cats. In their slouchy poses, their silkiness, their slope-bellied laziness, he saw a cat one of the boys had once had, a yellow tabby thing hung with the name Mischief, who'd laid around the house all day watching the human beings with total disinterest, seeming as harmless as a slightly animated pillow. But every once in awhile, he'd bring in a tiny lung or heart or something, as an offering, as if to a god. As if he, Bud, master of the house, were the god. Whatever, it worked; the cat lived with them in perfect harmony for eleven years before finally dying comfortably of old age. Bud had always liked its split personality: that it could be the complete tabby by day, then slip out at night and revert to savagery, rending some small creature down to its organs.

But this got Bud nowhere except into a blinding headache. He called Holly and had a brief but entirely pleasant chat, as he told her all about the lions of the Lawton library, and she laughed at the image of the big old boy who looked like John Wayne looking at books on lions and how the mamas must have thought he was crazy or something. She said he was damned lucky they didn't call the police.

Then he said, "Uh, I was thinking, I might drop by tomorrow."

"You was, was you?" she said, in flirty fake astonishment. "Well, whatever gave you *that* idea?"

"Oh, a little fellow."

"Well, if you come, you best bring him along."

"About noon?"

"Yes sir," she said.

When he got home, everybody seemed happy. He even

felt happy, though he had to gobble a Percodan to keep from hurting. It seemed that all was at peace in the strange realm he called his empire; he didn't have to mollify any of his far-flung, rebellious provinces. He had a few beers, a light supper, and went to bed before either of the two boys got home from dates or parties or whatever. He dreamed of lions.

On Sunday, Bud rose and, feeling he hadn't been paying enough attention to Jen and feeling also guilty over what he had planned for noon, went to the nine A.M. service with her and Jeff. Russ, of course, the intellectual, had stopped going to church in the eighth grade.

So Russ slept, because he'd been out late the night before on some fool thing. At least he hadn't come back with another earring. Bud put his anger aside or in the little place where he stored it, and drove across town with Jen and Jeff in Jen's station wagon.

Jen had taken to going to the Methodist Church though, like Bud, she'd been christened a Baptist. Her father, a prosperous farmer up near Tulsa, had always referred, sneeringly, to Methodists as Baptists who forgot where they came from, and although Jen stuck with her father on pretty near everything, she'd decided to give Methodism a shot, and it stuck. The Methodists had a preacher named Webb Fellowes whom she liked a great deal because he always gave a damned entertaining sermon: for a younger man, he seemed to be quite wise and respectful, and he was funny. Today he told an amusing story about a rich Texas oilman who annually gave 15 percent to the church and quite a sight more when the parishioners decided to build a new building. Afterward, this Texan was asked if he belonged to the church. "Hell no," he said, "the church belongs to me!" Bud saw what Webb Fellowes was getting at: It wasn't a thing about how much you gave in dollars, but how much you gave in your heart.

If that's the case, he thought, I ain't much of a Christian, especially because as soon as the service is over and Jen and Jeff and I go to get some breakfast, I'm going to go break a commandment.

After the service, they walked down the line that got them to the minister, and he was well up on things.

"Hear you hit a dinger, son," he called out heartily, clapping Jeff on the arm.

"Yes sir, I did," said Jeff.

"That ball's still climbing," said Jen.

"No ma'am, it just barely made it over the centerfielder's mitt," Jeff said, "But it was a home run nevertheless."

"Well, Mrs. Pewtie, you've got every right to be proud."

"And every right to be thankful," she said, and took Bud's arm and brought him a little closer.

"How're you doing, Sergeant?" asked Webb Fellowes.

"Well," said Bud, "they tell me I won't be going through any metal detectors without setting off every alarm between here and Kansas City, but I feel pretty good."

The minister laughed.

"The Lord looks after those who know He's there," he said.

Bud smiled enthusiastically at the young minister and at the absurdity of the statement. What a crock, he thought as he pumped Fellowes' strong hand, the Lord don't look after nothing. He just sets the goddamned Lamar Pyes of the world loose, and hell comes for a meal nearly every place that boy hangs his hat.

Afterward, the family went to the Denny's on Cache Road near the Holiday Inn and had a nice big breakfast, though Bud, who hated to wait in lines, grew restless while waiting to be seated and began to get somewhat angry. But there was no point to that. Then he remembered that once he'd had lunch with Holly in this place, but it hadn't gone well because he was so frightened of being seen by somebody. He tried to put all that out of his mind.

Bud had what they called their Grand Slam, three scrambled eggs, homefries, bacon, and a pancake.

"Bud, I swear, you leave some food for the people still in that line," Jen said, in her abstract way.

"I don't know why, but I am damned hungry."

"You haven't been eating since it happened."

"Lamar Pye took my appetite, that's for sure. But I do believe he gave it back to me today." He shoveled down a forkful of homefries. They were a significant weakness of his.

"Dad," Jeff said, "I wanted to head out to the batting cages on sixty-one. I don't want to lose what it is I got. Can you drive me out?"

"Sure," Bud said, trying to keep a little stab of disappointment off his face, his plan with Holly just washed up. "When do you want to go?"

"Oh, anytime. Figure we'd get home and change and then go."

"Sounds good," he said, feeling like a heel for what he was about to do. "Oh, say, I'll tell you. I was going to log in some range time today. I think I may invest in one of those nine-millimeters. I don't never want to try and speedload under fire again. Sixteen shots'll beat six any day of the week. The Lawton boys carry these Glocks and I thought I might head over to their range and see if I could talk one of them into letting me run a box of ammo through to see how I like it. Though Jed Wheelright had a Beretta I liked a lot. So, whyn't you relax a bit after you get home, let the food settle, and I'll go on. Be back in an hour or so. Then we'll go hit.''

''Bud, you know you get to talking guns with those boys at that range you won't be home till well after nightfall.''

It irked him that she knew him so well.

''No, I swear it. Just fifty rounds in the Q target, just to see if I can hit a goddamned thing with a nine, much less a Glock, and then I'm home.''

''Believe that when I see it,'' Jen said.

''Sure, Dad. I have some reading to do anyhow.''

When they got home, Bud changed into jeans and a loose-fitting golf shirt that wouldn't rub against the bandages that still criss-crossed his wounds, and took his midday's ration of Percodans.

''I'm going now,'' he called, but there was only sullen silence from Jen.

But of course Bud didn't drive to the range. Instead he drove to Holly's trailer in Sherwood Village, parked around back, and feeling self-conscious as hell, slid up to the door. As he knocked on it, he took a glance at his watch.

Now that's a terrible sign, he thought. Every time you *start* by looking at your watch, it ain't going to be a good thing at all.

But she opened the door in a short white robe, and her perfect, thin, long legs got him to forgetting about the time and for an hour or so, they were the only two people in the world.

''God, Bud, you sure you ain't eighteen?''

''You make me believe I could be, that's for sure.''

''I'da hated to know you when you were eighteen. You'da *killed* me, I guarantee it.''

''You were one, then. And I don't think I knew the difference between my pecker and my carburetor. Didn't until you began showing me three months ago.''

He lay back, trying to suck all the pleasure out of the moment. The room was sunny and bright, her spare bedroom, because Bud still felt queer about making love to Holly in a room where she and Ted had been, though that spot was but ten feet away from where he now lay, through a thin tin wall.

"Goddamn, I feel good," he said. "Nobody ever made me feel as good as you do."

"You ain't so bad in the how-good-it-feels department yourself, Mr. Pewtie," she said. "But Bud—"

He lay there a bit, watching the shadows play on the ceiling.

"Bud, I want to know just one thing. Are you at least working on it? By that I mean, *thinking* about it. There's work to be done. We got to find a place. You ought to talk to Jen and the boys. You ought to talk to a *lawyer*. There's much to be done. It can't just happen, up and sudden."

Bud faced the ceiling. Everything she said was true.

"Holly, this ain't the time."

"But it's never the time."

"I told Jeff I'd drive him out sixty-one to the hitting cages."

Now she sighed.

"Okay, Bud, go to the hitting cages with Jeff. But you have to *do* something. Soon. It ain't fair to nobody."

It wasn't so bad after that was said. He dressed, she joked with him and wouldn't sulk or act victimized, and she gave him a good fare-thee-well, so he could go off and be with his son without the cloud of a bad secret scene hanging over him.

About a mile from home, he pulled into a strip mall parking lot and opened the lockbox in the rear of the pickup. He took out his shooting bag, where he kept his muffs and shooting glasses and assorted tools, and picked

up a small brown bottle of Shooter's Choice bore solvent.
He squirted it on his hands and worked it in, like a hand
cream, because the odor was so totally associated with firearms in his house. The act itself disgusted him. It was so
common and low.

You have become cheap, he told himself.

Then he locked it back up and drove home. He checked
his watch. He was only half an hour late. He prayed that
Jeff hadn't lost interest or gone off with friends.

"I'm home," he yelled, coming in the door. "Sorry I'm
late. Jeff, let's go."

"Okay, Dad," Jeff called.

"Russ, we're going to hit at the cages. You want to
come?"

"Nah, thanks, Dad. It's okay."

Jeff came bounding down the steps in cutoffs, a collar-
less jersey shirt, and his Nikes. He looked ropey as a cowboy, a string bean of a boy, all sinew and muscle and rangi-
ness.

"Okay, let's go."

"Y'all be home by dinner," Jen called from the kitchen.

Now again Bud was happy. Nobody was in any pain
anywhere. Once again he'd gotten away with it. Nobody
suspected a thing, and even Holly seemed content. The
edge he might fall off of wasn't so close, at least for a little
while.

He and Jeff drove out Route 61 to Mick's Driving Range
and Batting Cages, a down-home entertainment center that
had seen better days but for which each had conceived a
deep affection.

"How was the Glock, Dad?" Jeff suddenly asked.

"What?" Oh. The Glock. The *Glock.* Now he had to lie
to his son, flat out, something he hated to do.

"It shoots well. Just like a revolver, you pull the trigger

and off she goes, no cocking or anything. They got the safety in the trigger, little latch you pull automatically when you pull down. But I don't know. Didn't have much feel to it. Not like my Smith.''

''Could you trade grips?''

''No, the whole damn frame is one piece of plastic. Technically speaking, it doesn't have grips. They do have this little rubber sleeve you can pull over it, I hear, give it a palm swell and finger grooves. But I think I like the Beretta nine-millimeter best. It feels just like that Beretta .380 I have.''

''I heard that Beretta nine's a good gun. The GIs carry it.''

''That they do,'' said Bud. ''Problem is, it costs about one hundred dollars more than the Glocks do. That's why the cops all like the Glocks. You can own one for about four-fifty. A Beretta run you five-fifty, six. Hell, my .380 was nearly five.''

''Dad, you ought to buy the gun you like. If you ever have to use it again, it'd be better to have one you liked rather than one you got a good deal on.''

Bud nodded. The boy was right. At least someone in the family was thinking straight.

Mick's Driving Range and Batting Cages was set on a rolling chunk of green Oklahoma farmland that overlooked the surrounding countryside, and now and then, when the artillery students were firing over at Fort Sill just to the north, you could hear the rolling booms of the big 155s as they detonated against far mountainsides. The road ran on a crest, the highest point in the county, and from the complex you could see for miles. It was a windy day, and Mick's was always festooned with pennants, like some kind of extravagant musical comedy, and the pennants snapped and fluttered in the wind.

The driving range was full up with golfers driving their little pills out onto the green like tracer bullets, but for some reason the batting cages had never quite caught on. Jeff had no problem finding an empty one.

"Dad, you going to hit?"

"Nah, I'll just watch. I'd pop stitches if I swung the bat too hard. We don't need that. You need some money?"

"Yes sir, I do."

Bud handed over a ten-dollar bill and took a seat on the bench as Jeff got change and fed the tokens into the machine.

He stood easily at the plate as the mechanical device ninety feet away issued what sounded like a reptilian clank as it came to life. Then, with a shiver, its arm lashed out, and it dispatched a ball. Jeff just leaned into it and sent it sailing with a satisfying crack.

Jeff was hot. He was in the zone. He was really seeing it. Bud just sat there and watched him and enjoyed each second of it: the snap as the arm uncoiled and sent a ball whistling inward, Jeff's seemingly slow stroke, the inevitable contact, and the rise of the ball, a white dot that screamed toward orbit then fell disconsolately to earth.

"Man, you are really whacking that ball today," Bud called.

"Yes sir," said Jeff. "I am out of the slump."

When Jeff used up the first ten dollars, Bud gave him another, and then, when that was gone, offered still another.

"Dad, you don't have to."

"It's okay. It's so great to see you out of your slump."

"Nah, it's fine. I feel good."

Jeff and Bud headed back to the truck.

"What are you doing different? Can you tell?"

"It's the head. I was leading with my chin and it was throwing the whole swing off. That, plus pressing. So I just concentrate on keeping my head still, *watching* the ball, and swinging through. It's working.''

''Was it set on fast?''

''Absolutely, Dad. From the start.''

''Well, if I were a scout, I'd give you a hundred-thousand-dollar signing bonus, on the spot.''

''I'd settle for a Coke.''

''It's a deal.''

They got Cokes at the machine, nodded to gruff old Mick, and headed home as the twilight passed on toward darkness.

''You mind if I see if anything's on the radio, Dad?''

''Nah, go ahead,'' said Bud.

Jeff fiddled with the stations, looking for KOKY, out of Oklahoma City, the big rock station, but as he slid through the sounds he cut across some urgent chatter that signified catastrophe, built around the last two syllables of the word ''robbery.''

''Wait, stop,'' said Bud, but they couldn't get a clear signal. It must have been some Texas ghost signal or something.

But Bud grew concerned, in his way, and said, ''Switch to the AM. That news station.''

''Dad, you said—''

''Jeff.''

''Okay, okay.''

Jeff switched bands to get to KTOK, and they heard the weather, a network feed out of Washington, with headline summaries of notable local stories.

''See, it's—''

''Shhh,'' commanded Bud, for he'd heard the announcer launch into another story.

''Authorities in Wichita Falls, Texas, have issued an all-points bulletin for three escaped convicts in connection with a bloody shoot-out and robbery at a Denny's Restaurant this afternoon. Six persons are dead, including four law enforcement officers, in an armed robbery that netted an undetermined amount of cash. Oklahoma convicts Lamar James Pye, his cousin Odell Warren Pye, and Richard Franklin Peed escaped from the McAlester State Penitentiary in Oklahoma April second. They killed a prison guard, an Oklahoma highway patrolman and a bakery goods driver —and kidnapped an elderly couple—before dropping out of sight four weeks ago. Police say today's armed robbery and shoot-out in Wichita Falls shows that they are armed and dangerous and at large in the North Texas-South Oklahoma region.''

CHAPTER 15

The eggs lay before Richard. They seemed curdled and dissociative as if they were losing their very sense of eggness; they were disintegrating untouched before his eyes. Next to them, a small mountain range of homefries dried out as if in preparation for an ice age. Altogether, it hardly looked like food anymore. His coffee had grown tepid and rancid.

He glanced about, consumed with that same queasy feeling he'd had in the car before Lamar and Odell had gone crashing in on the Stepfords. Everywhere he saw families, couples, a few lone Air Force personnel just sitting there eating their food. They had no idea what visitation was about to come crashing down upon them. In just minutes, Lamar, Odell, and Ruta Beth would be upon them, to take the money and threaten them with violence.

"Coffee?"

He looked up into the eyes of a waitress.

"Ah, no," he said.

"You okay? You hardly touched your food."

"No, I'm fine, I'm okay."

"You want me to take it?"

"No," he said. "Not yet."

"That's a real pretty picture."

"Huh? Oh! Thanks."

He'd been doodling. Lions, of course, as per his master's wishes. He dreamed of lions. They pounced and lunged through his deepest thoughts. He just couldn't get the neck right, though.

Somehow the waitress dissolved. He wished he could quiet his rapping heart. His knees were shaking. The big minute hand drew nearer and nearer to four, when everything would start happening, depending on what police call signals Lamar monitored on his new Radio Shack scanner in the car.

"Could be a bit before four, could be a bit after. Depends," Lamar had said, dropping him off half an hour before.

He swallowed. The gun in his waistband hurt. It was a huge thing, and of course they didn't have a holster for it. He just had wedged it in, though Lamar had done some magical thing with a string, running a little loop down into his pants, tied at either end on his belt, forming a kind of truss that held the gun from slipping further.

He took a last look around, trying to remember.

Men in coats, like the one he wore? No, only a cowboy over there or farmworker or something, in a jeans jacket too short to conceal a handgun. A woman undercover cop? No possibility. That was the thing about Denny's, it was the American melting pot at its best, every stripe and shape of American you could imagine, but in here today were only doughy middle-aged types, with their mamas, and a couple of Air Force enlisted women, Wichita Falls being a big Air Force town. Air Force people flew airplanes, right? They didn't have guns. They could bomb, they couldn't shoot. In the kitchen, from what he could see, was just a mess of black men, in their forties, working up a sweat and laughing to beat the devil all the time: certainly not off-duty policemen.

That left the manager, a fat boy with pimples in his early twenties, with the eyes of a squirrel and a perpetual grimace of near hysteria. He'd be the one Lamar took in back to open the safe. He'd be the one Lamar had said he could break in a minute, never you mind how. He stole a look at the young man, who was officious and neurotic at once, now shooing two waitresses off to fill water glasses or pour more coffee, now rushing back to get on the cooks, now working the register. What a world of pain awaited that boy. Richard felt indecent, exposed to so much imminent hurt and yet so unable to stop anything.

I'm like a falcon, he thought. It was a metaphor that had come to him when Lamar had driven off in the station wagon. There he had it, his freedom. He could just drive away, nothing held him, he had a car, he could go and go and go. Instead, ten minutes later, he headed back to the farm. That was the falcon part. Falcons are trained by their masters to believe there's a tether holding them to the master's wrist. The master manages this by keeping the falcon on his wrist with a tether until the falcon finally falls asleep. Once he falls asleep, he's convinced, but sometimes it can go for days, man and falcon just trying to outlast the other until sleep. With him, it had taken about ten minutes. Some willpower! Now he believed that no matter where he went, he was tethered to Lamar, until Lamar set him free. And Lamar would never set him free.

He shook his head, took a last look. Then he felt the pressure of eyes upon him and, turning to look out the window that his table sat next to, saw the station wagon pull into the lot.

The car paused, waited for another to clear out of the lot

and pull into traffic. He took a last look around. He hadn't thought the room would be so full. It was supposed to be between lunch and dinner. These damn Texans. They couldn't do anything but by their own rules.

The car pulled up and into a disabled-only parking place. He saw Lamar, in his cowboy hat, and Odell, rocking gently in the back seat, and Ruta Beth, all staring at him. Richard took the handkerchief out of his pocket and waved it gently. That was the signal. He watched as Lamar slid off his hat and pulled the ski mask down. Ski masks seemed to magically appear on Ruta Beth and Odell. The doors were opening. In long raincoats to conceal their weapons they were out of the station wagon. It was happening.

Just then, as he looked back toward the cash register, Richard saw the Texas highway patrolman come out of the men's room, drying his hands.

Lamar listened to the scanner, set on 460.225MHz, the police car-to-car frequency, as they approached the restaurant. Its messages and strange half-language of ten-codes and regional jargon crackled sporadically.

"Ah, Dispatch, this is R-Victor-twenty-four, I am ten–twenty-four on the Remington Street accident."

"Ten–four, R-Victor-twenty-four, ah, ten–nineteen the station."

"Ten–four, Dispatch. I have a ten–fifty-five in custody."

"Copy that, R-Victor-twenty-four, you want Breathalyzer?"

"That's a big ten–seventy-four, Dispatch, he can't hardly walk none. Video would be nice."

"Ten–four, R-Victor-twenty-four."

"Dispatch, this is R-Victor-eleven, I am ten–seventy-six the domestic situation on Wilson Boulevard, can you ten–forty-three?"

"Yes, R-Victor-twenty-four, suspect is a black male, about twenty-five, over three hundred pounds, with a knife. Be careful, Charlie."

"Great. Thanks Dispatch, you always give me the good ones."

"Ten–four, Charlie. Let me know when you're ten–twenty-three."

And on it went.

"Them boys got themselves just a quiet Sunday afternoon. A few drunk niggers, that's all. Hoo boy, what they got a-coming."

Lamar waited for a car to clear, then pulled into the restaurant parking lot. Carefully he navigated his way to the entrance and pulled up in front of it, sliding into the open spot marked for a wheelchair.

"Lamar, I'm pretty scared," said Ruta Beth.

"Sweetie, you gonna be just fine. Odell, you a-ready?"

"Eddy," said Odell placidly.

"Okay, boys and girls, let's kick ass and get paid," he said, pulling his ski mask down.

Each burst from his door. Lamar went first, low and crab-like, almost a scuttle, but not a run because there were four steps to climb to get up into the restaurant, but also because when you ran you were out of control and control was the heart of the job.

Armed robbery was about it and nothing else: you made your statement in the first second and drew your lines—you were in charge. If anybody stepped over the line, man, woman, boy, girl, baby, you had to hurt them bad. No exceptions, no mercy: You broke their bones, you broke their spirits, you took their money, and you left them crying and shaking. They could not get it in their skulls that any way but yours existed. If you had to kill them, you just did it, cold and sudden, and went on with business.

Lamar was through the door first, his heart steady as a rock, his eyes darting like swallows, and in the first second he saw the cop. The cop saw him; a little something passed between them, and the cop took a half a backward step as if to say, Whoa, Partner, let me think on this one, but by then Lamar had the shotgun out and the cop knew he was finished and was determined to go out like a man. He was fast; in his life he'd probably dreamed such a thing a thousand times, for it was one of the risks of the job. His right hand flew to his automatic.

Meanwhile, in a fraction of the same second and equally without a conscious thought, and without a twitch of curiosity—though he did note the cop's unexplained presence, and meant to deal with it later—Lamar raised the cutdown Browning A-5 from under his coat and blew a double-ought into that surprised old boy. Texas Highway Patrol still had those old-timey thirties uniforms, gray shirt, red collar and epaulets, and they carried SIGs, and this boy was meat before he even touched his own gun. The double-ought erupted into nine .32 slugs traveling at over a thousand miles an hour and took his life from him and sent him knocko backward against the wall between the two restrooms, to the left of the manager's office. He slid down the wall, leaving a webbing of gore upon it, for the pellets, or some of them, passed on through, and his life's blood spurted from his ruptured heart as he fell.

What Lamar didn't know was that he had just called in on his radio jack, which ran up from the transmitter on his duty belt and was affixed to his lapel. Fourteen miles away in the basement dispatch room of the Iowa Park barrack, a dispatcher heard what she recognized immediately as the amplified sound of a firearms report. She began frantically to call in the men on her network and in two minutes made contact with fourteen of them. The fifteenth had just called in going-out-of-service (10-7) at Denny's for his twenty-minute break. Getting no reply, she calmly began to broadcast: "All units, all units, I have a possible ten–thirty-three at the Denny's off 287, there at Maurine Street, can somebody please verify. Possible Signal thirteen." Signal thirteen meant "Officer down, assistance required immediately."

Lamar knew none of this, of course. He turned from his murder to face what he did expect, utter incredulity. Everywhere he looked he saw slack mouths and gaping eyes as the echo of the shotgun blast seemed to rattle around in the still air and the gun smoke drifted into layers. Then the stupidity broke like glass into fear: Lamar could almost feel it shatter through the room. A child began to cry; moms squirmed to draw their children in to them, and dads put out their hands to calm the older kids, though their faces drained of blood as the great possibility of death dawned on them. The airmen at the far table were sheet white, almost pissing in their fancy blue uniforms. The gun smoke spread through the room like vapor. It was incredibly quiet except for the sudden clickety-click as the spent 12-gauge shell hit the floor and rolled.

Quickly Ruta Beth had pulled Bud's Mossberg from under her coat and vaulted the counter to chill out the nigger boys behind the Dutch door and the two waitresses behind the counter. Odell had the AR-15—two feet of black plastic Colt assault rifle—and waved it toward the seated citizens, who immediately melted under its threat. Though it was a semiautomatic, Lamar knew its power for crowd control was awesome, for anyone who'd watched TV would assume it was a machine gun.

"Y'all stay seated and we won't hurt you none. We come for Denny's money, not yours," Lamar yelled in a loud, unhurried, almost country-and-western voice. Witnesses would later say he sounded friendly-like, sort of like Travis Tritt or Randy Travis.

His eyes caught on Richard at his window table. The boy looked almost as scared as the square johns.

Then he pivoted his attention to the short, pimply boy at the register. He closed quickly, put the 12-gauge at the youngster's chin.

The boy's mouth was working dryly. He looked like a fish Lamar had caught during one of his infrequent stays in society. His jaw seemed to twitch as he sucked for air.

"Don't hurt me," he said.

"I will kill you if you don't gimme what I want."

The boy's fingers flew to the computer register and he punched a key and it flew open.

"Take it, sir. Take it all."

"That's smalltime shit, boy. In back. The safe. You open it or by God, you'll wish you had."

Using the gun as a prod, Lamar pushed him along. They stepped over the dead cop, whose eyes had glazed like marbles. He lay in a satiny pool of his own blood, legs akimbo, head bent in an unnatural way, both hands almost delicately relaxed. He looked like a fallen angel. Lamar dipped down and with one hand removed the SIG from a safety holster. Lamar knew how to bypass the fake thumb-break and find the real one further down the strap. It was a P220, in .45. That made him happy. He liked .45s. He slid this one into his back waistband, right next to the holstered long-slide Clark Colt.

In the office the safe was a small Sergant & Greenleaf model, an eight-digit multiple-tumbler combination variant, sunk in the wall behind the manager's grimy desk. He pushed the boy over to it.

"It's a time lock," the boy lied badly.

"Do you think I'm dumb, sonny?" Lamar asked. This

was the dicey part. He really only had but a minute to break the boy down. It's funny the reservoirs of courage and sheer cussed orneriness you find in the most common people. Maybe the boy would be a surprise hero, giving up his life to save Denny a few grand. It bothered Lamar that he was so young. An older man would roll over in a second, having the wisdom of witnessed pain in his time and knowing nothing was worth a squalid death in the back of a cheap restaurant.

Lamar walked around behind the boy and suddenly smashed him with the shotgun, driving him to the earth. The shudder of the blow resounded satisfyingly through the weapon. The boy, leaking blood, lay on the floor, dazed. When his senses returned, his eyes bulged with animal fear. Lamar bent and, with one quick movement, he trapped the boy's little finger in the fulcrum of his fist.

He broke the little finger.

The boy yowled in pain. He began to weep. He blubbered and was attempting to request mercy when Lamar stilled him by thrusting the shotgun muzzle into his larynx.

"I ain't got no time. You open the safe or I'll break all your fingers. You won't never play the piano again. Then I'll gut-shoot you to die slowly. You think I won't? You want to try me? I will as sure as rain."

He stood back. The boy regained some composure and crawled to his feet. Snot ran down his swollen face. He applied himself to the combination lock and had it opened in a second.

"You shouldn't have lied to me," Lamar said, like a stern father. He fired once into the boy's chest, blowing him out of the way. He wasn't sure why he'd done it. It just was there for the doing, and without a conscious decision having been reached, he did it.

From the floor, the boy gurgled and mewled and began to

address a speech to someone named Andy, but Lamar paid no heed. He stepped over the fallen boy and leaned inside the safe. Pay dirt! Fourth of July! A little stab of elation jerked through him. Swiftly enough, he pulled the locked cash bags off the shelf, knowing they could be easily enough cut open later, and dumped them into a laundry bag he had purchased that very morning. He took a last look around, noted nothing, and stepped out into the restaurant proper.

It was as if he'd never left: It was like a still photo called *the Robbery*. Ruta Beth and Odell held the public and dispirited staff at bay. A couple of the waitresses were weeping, one almost hysterically. The square johns just looked up in horror, afraid to disobey, afraid to do anything, afraid to exist. No heroes in this crowd, no sirree. It was going swell. Plus, he'd got to whack a Smokey!

"Okay, boys and girls, time to—"

The sound of a siren rose, and then another.

It froze them. Lamar turned, Ruta Beth turned, even Odell turned. Watching them, Richard turned, too.

Oh no!

He felt the panic flap through him, and though he struggled to control it, he could not. His mind was full of spiders and firecrackers. A squad car, its flashbar pumping electric light into the bright air and its siren howling like a wounded animal, sped toward them, followed by another and another. He knew he had to get out of there. The police would kill him! He jumped to his feet blindly, and then confronted his next most devastating horror. A woman had risen from the table across the aisle with a small automatic pistol in her hand. She was aiming at Lamar. Richard's hand flew to his gun, but he couldn't get it out. He screamed as loud as he could.

The woman fired.

The bullet missed.

She fired again, and missed again, as Ruta Beth fired. Her double-ought buck, delivered from a range of about twelve feet, drove into the woman, punching her backward into another booth, containing old people, who like atoms liberated in a chain reaction began to race toward the exit. Plates and glasses spilled to the floor and coffee spewed across the tables.

Lamar screamed, "The cops are coming. They going to shoot y'all dead." He raised his shotgun and fired two fast blasts into the ceiling.

It was too much, the noise, the death, the seething gun smoke. Someone threw a chair through one of the big windows and then through another one, and the square johns, like rats on a ship, began to pour out into the parking lot, leaping the three-foot drop to the earth just as the first two cars pulled up. A cop emerged from each, shotgun ready, but could find no targets in the human tide that gushed from the restaurant.

Quickly Lamar threw his shotgun away and handed the money bag to Odell, taking the AR.

"I'll cover, you git yourself out." He grabbed Odell and gave him a kiss on the mouth, then turned to Ruta Beth.

"You saved my bacon, hon. You did just fine."

"Lamar, you have to—"

"Don't you worry about me none. Now git. Take old Richard, too."

He quickly went to the doorway and fired three swift shots at the only cop he could see. The gun had a liquid jerk to it as it fired, but it came back on target quickly; the officer sat down sadly. Then Lamar swept over to the other target and fired twice at it, smearing the windshield with a quicksilver of fractures.

"Wi-chud," yelled Odell, picking Richard off the floor. The bigger man half-carried him through the broken window. There was glass everywhere, the sounds of gunfire, a general sense of panic loose upon the face of the planet, and Richard's own immense fear. He looked back and saw Lamar like some crazily heroic mythic sergeant from some war movie firing away, blazing like Rambo at the police. Then he was in the car.

Odell punched it and the car backed savagely, hitting something and knocking it down with a terrific clatter, then roared ahead, seemed almost to tip as it lurched on two wheels into the street and then, in a burst of sheer acceleration, really whooshed down the road. But just as quickly it slowed to almost a halt, took a severe turn, and began ambling along at a content pace.

Richard sat up; they were in some quiet suburb, an undisturbed fifties world of small frame houses, overhanging trees, and green-filtered sunlight. Behind them, the turbulent sounds of sirens rose and rose and rose.

"Mar," keened Odell. "Mar."

"That's okay honey," said Ruta Beth, who'd taken the mask off to shake out her long hair. "Daddy can take care of himself."

Lamar dropped the mag out and slammed a new one in. He pulled back the bolt, a weird kind of plunger deal atop the weapon, and let it fly forward. He looked over the sights and could see nobody. Two cop cars were parked aslant at each entrance to the parking lot, and he knew he'd hit one of the cops and the other had shown no signs of fight, having retreated behind his car, where he was bet-your-ass on the horn, calling in reinforcements.

Lamar licked his lips, which were dry as sand.

Well, goddamn, boy, he told himself, *you done got yourself in some damned pickle.*

He took off his ski mask and threw it away. If he was going out, he was going out as Lamar Pye, bad man and legend, the white boy with the biggest dick in the whole Mac. He shucked the raincoat, a great relief, as the goddamned thing was hot.

He fired five quick shots at the gas tank of one of the cop cars, hoping he'd get an explosion, but it never happened. Instead a couple of poorly aimed shots came his way.

He fired quickly, emptying the magazine to drive them down, then slid back from the door and crawled low over glass until he reached the kitchen. A black teenager cowered against the sinks, crying.

"Don't hurt me none, sir," the boy sobbed.

"Shut up. You ain't been hurt. *I'm* the one they's tryin' to hurt." He almost shot the boy, but what would that prove? It might do him some good back in the joint if he let a nigger live where he'd killed a passel of whites.

He rose and ran to the rear delivery entrance and opened it. Two cops fired shotguns at him, but he ducked inside in the second before the buckshot arrived to spall the door.

You got to bring the fight to them, he told himself. *Cops ain't used to that. They used to men folding up, but here I got to go at them and go at them hard, or they going to get my white boy's ass for good and only.*

He went to the back wall, where, high up, there was a window. He could never get through it, but he could get a good, clean shot at one of the officers.

But as he was about to fire, he noticed what he had climbed up on. It was the sink, and next to it was the garbage chute. He kicked the flap that covered the chute and discovered a ramp about eighteen inches wide leading at a sharp angle into darkness, though he thought he saw a glimmer of light.

Fuck this, he thought. *They got me covered if I stay here.*

He dumped the AR and wedged himself into the chute. A sickening stench rose to his nose, the stench of decayed food, grease, decomposition. He thought for a second he wasn't going to make it, that his ass would hang him up, and the cops would come find him half in, half out. But he slid down with astonishing speed, was launched airborne into lightness, had a strange sensation of liberation, and then found himself amid fetid food and packaging in a Dumpster. He rolled out of it, wishing he had the AR. But he still had two .45s. He looked about quickly, finding himself in a well in the rear right side of the restaurant. Lamar stepped upward and found himself slightly flanking the two cops who had the back cover. He saw the Texas Highway Patrol car parked out back, too; now he got it. The first patrolman had come in and parked at the rear, entered through the rear, and gone in to wash his hands. That's how come Richard hadn't seen him.

He shook his head. From out front came the crackle of shots and the sounds of sirens as yet more reinforcements arrived. Time to kick ass, he thought and ran toward the police car.

It was simple murder, the best kind. The guys never knew he was on their left. He just ran at them, a gun in each hand, and when they looked up it was too late to do anything. It seemed to happen in slow motion; it had an incredible clarity to it, like a football replay on the TV. He watched as the one half rose to bring his shotgun to bear, but the man seemed to be climbing through molasses or motor oil, his eyes big as eggs, his fingers scrambling at his gun like some kind of honky-tonk piano player as he tried to find the trigger. Lamar's first shot hit him in the throat.

The Adam's apple seemed to explode as if rigged by demo-
litions experts, and the blood spurted from it in a dark red
spray. The other took more killing. As he spun away into
the fetal position, Lamar shot him twice, only to discover
he had a vest on, so he leaned in close and shot him in the
head. He watched the hair fly—why was this familiar?—
and the dust or mist rise as the body went into that complete stillness that was sheer animal death. He stood over
them and emptied his magazines into them, feeling for just
a moment the most powerful king on the face of the earth.

Lookame, lookame! he thought, exultantly.

He threw both handguns and one of the police shotguns
into the back of the cruiser, slid in, found the key, and
started the car. Another cop car came around the corner,
and Lamar gunned straight at it until it swerved. He banged
it hard, shattering glass. Then he backed and turned to face
the fence that kept him in. It was a Cyclone. Lamar knew it
to be weakest dead center between poles, and so that's
where he aimed the car, punching it.

The big Crown Victoria smashed the fence, slowed, then
blasted through vegetation; something lashed and shattered
the windshield. But in a second burst of energy the car
bashed through, seemed to drop a bit, then landed in a
backyard. Lamar pushed the accelerator down, smashed
over a patio—driving lawn chairs this way and that and
sending a picnic table full of hamburgers and deviled eggs
flipping crazily through the air—crunched a hedge, and
peeled across front lawn until he hit street, took a hard
right, and really leaned into it. Behind him, he heard the
sound of sirens.

CHAPTER
16

Bud got there by ten P.M., and the crime scene was still a damn county fair. He'd listened all the way in on the radio. The identification had come quickly enough through elemental police work: The serial number of the recovered AR-15 was checked against the National Criminal Information Center computer files, which promptly revealed it to have been Ted's, taken at the Stepford farm. Within minutes, a faxed bulletin from Oklahoma authorities with Lamar's mug on it was shown to the busboy who'd gotten a good look at Lamar; he ID'd him immediately. So by six P.M., the APB for Lamar, Odell, and Richard and an unknown fourth gang member had been issued.

But so far, there'd been no arrests, although the brass had ordered a full roll-out of all North Texas and Southern Oklahoma law enforcement units, including air-ground search teams with infrared capacity, canine units, and horseback Rangers moving across the range and farmland south of Wichita Falls. The Rangers set up roadblocks on all the major roads and at the three bridges over the Red River fifteen miles north of the city, and established patrols up and down the riverbanks.

Bud parked down Maurine Street a bit and made his way back to the scene. Gawkers, of course, were out in the hundreds; the roadway was jammed with pickups, lots of teenagers and young roughnecks. It had a carnylike feel to it, which Bud had noticed before at big accidents on I-44, and which always made him a little angry. Someone was hooting "Goddamn, ol' Lamar Pye got clean away" to the beeps of horns. Bud spat in disgust, but it didn't surprise him that, to some, Lamar might be a hero for his wild ways and unwillingness to take any crap from anybody. That's what was poisoning America, he thought.

He approached the barrier of yellow crime-scene tape that had been run from pylon to pylon around the perimeter of the Denny's. A batch of TV camera crews were off to one side, sending their feeds back to the big cities. At least half the official vehicles in Texas filled the parking lot, and inside the shattered restaurant, evidence technicians probed and collected and representatives from the region's police agencies stood around talking, issuing bulletins, putting out information on the radio net and what-have-you.

"Hold on there, sir," said a Texas highway patrolman as Bud ducked under the tape. "You can't cross that line."

Bud flashed his ID folio.

"Oh, sorry, Sarge. You Oklahoma boys are all over this one."

"These are our boys," said Bud. "Killed one of our troopers a few weeks back. We want 'em bad."

"I know that. I was at that young man's funeral and it was a sad one. Well, if we catch 'em in Texas, we'll be glad to send y'all the bodies. They dropped four officers and two citizens. That Lamar, he's a goddamned piece of work."

"That he is, Trooper. Who's in charge?"

"Our Colonel Benteen running the show, like he usually does. Some Rangers trying to horn in, as usual."

"We got the same problem with our damned OSBI boys."

"Well, I think you got your OSBI down here some place and your own colonel, the Polish one?"

"Supenski. Yep. And that Lt. C. D. Henderson, of the OSBI?"

"That's the one. That boy's a drinker, you can smell it on him. Anyway, you'll find 'em inside. Good luck."

"Thank you, Trooper."

Bud walked on, passing between vehicles and knots of men sipping coffee and talking in low, intense voices, and at last entered the restaurant.

It looked like the last building left standing in a battle-ground. Its windows all shattered, its walls pocked with bullet holes, shards of glass and window frame everywhere, tables tossed this way and that. And, of course, the chalk outlines of bodies long removed. Bud saw two, one against a far wall, between the men's and the women's rooms, and another deeper in the restaurant itself. Great pools of gummy blood marked each spot. Each death spot had the quality of magic to it, somehow: no officer or technician would come within ten feet.

"There's a third in the manager's office. That Lamar, he blew away a twenty-three-year-old trainee manager after breaking one of his fingers to get him to open the safe. Bud, what the hell are you doing here?"

It was Colonel Supenski.

"Well, I couldn't stay away."

"No, I suppose you couldn't. Goddamn this Lamar, he's a full-toot son of a bitch. He must be crazy."

"He ain't crazy," Lt. C. D. Henderson said. "He just likes the buzz it gives him when he pops a feller. It's like sniffin' human glue. 'Lo, Sergeant Pewtie." He fixed Bud with a squinty look from behind his specs. *How could he be so* old *and still be a lieutenant,* Bud wondered. Then he sniffed the familiar vapor of bourbon cut by the breath mints that didn't quite hide it, and he knew.

"Lieutenant," he nodded.

"Goddamn," said Lt. Henderson, "he's a smart one. The Texas boys found the car Lamar's gang made its getaway in five miles down the road. He didn't just steal one car, he stole *two,* damn his soul, so eyewitness IDs and tag numbers of the getaway car ain't worth piss. And there won't be any prints on it, you watch."

"Who was the woman he shot?"

"Well, the witnesses say this other feller shot her. We don't know who this guy is. Whoever, he blew away this citizen, a Mrs. Rhonda McCoy, of Wichita Falls. Mrs. McCoy was a probation officer for the State of Texas and had a concealed-carry permit. She tried to do her duty. She was so overmatched it wasn't even funny. Died in front of her parents, and her husband and her two kids. Jesus."

Bud looked at the carnage.

"He got out through a goddamned garbage chute. Scum in, scum out. Don't that just fit the bill? Go on, Bud, take a look. Around back."

Bud walked through the restaurant and cut into the kitchen. A number of men stood around the chute. There, on the counter, tagged and bagged in a big cellophane evidence bag but unmoved, was Ted's AR-15. He went over and looked at it. It was a black and glistening thing, plastic and parkerized metal. Had a modern look to it, like some sort of a gun from space.

"He got it from a goddamned state trooper in Oklahoma," one of the Texas cops said. "Killed him for it."

"I know. I was there," said Bud.

"You're Pewtie."

"Yes, I am."

"You must be made out of steel to come out of something like that. They say you're the toughest cop in Oklahoma."

"Right now I don't feel so tough," Bud said.

If I'da been minding my business, he thought, *maybe this didn't have to happen.*

He walked on back through the kitchen to an open door. In the rear he saw two bodies on the parking lot, evidently the last to be removed, and another fleet of cops standing around, some taking notes. Beyond, the Cyclone fence was smashed down, and a path of sheer destruction indicated Lamar's escape route.

"Hey, Pewtie, we had twenty cops here and we was overmatched. You shouldn't feel so bad."

"Catch that boy in my sights the next time, and I'll pull down and lie to the shooting board about it," Bud said.

"We all feel that way," said the Texas cop, "except we don't got shooting boards in Texas."

Bud walked back through the rubble of the restaurant, trying not to step on anything.

"You don't have to go so dainty there, Sarge," an evidence technician in white plastic gloves said, "we pretty much done bagging."

"I feel like I'm in a goddamned war zone," Bud said.

"Were you in 'Nam?"

"No, no, I wasn't."

"Well, it reminds me of a place called Hue after Tet. Bad shit, I'll tell you," said the tech. "They got coffee over there, you want some."

"Thanks," said Bud, and turned, wondering, *What the hell am I doing here? Why did I come? What's it prove?*

He shook his head, isolated amid the clutter, sure he was stupidly in the way, and then he saw the lion.

Bud stood stock still, looking about to make sure nobody

had noticed it, and wondered whether or not to call out. To call out what? Hey, come look at this?

It was on the floor, covered in glass splinters, more or less shoved aside amid other papers by the evidence techs as they pawed through the rubble looking for clues. It was so odd how it had just hooked on the tiniest corner of his vision as he scoped the room, wondering what the hell to do.

He went onto one knee and very gently pushed two crumpled placemats aside, as well as a dozen assorted pieces of glass, to reveal more of a third and what upon it had caught his eye.

Yes, another lion, drawn absently, presumably by Richard as he waited for the raid. Richard must have been used as recon and then tail gunner, though all agreed it was the new gang member who'd done the shooting.

"Hey, techie," he called.

The technician came back.

"You got something there, Sarge?"

"You got prints already?"

"Yep, we got 'em and fed 'em into the FBI fingerprint lab. Amazing how fast that goddamn computer works."

"You get a make?"

"We already made both Pyes and the Peed guy, no sweat. As for the fourth member, we grilled witnesses but nobody can remember him touching anything. We got the shell he ejected—maybe a latent will turn up on that."

"Okay, I got a feeling this belongs to Richard Peed. He's the artist."

The man looked at it closely.

"I don't see no oil spots. Pal, I doubt seriously we could get a print off that. Getting prints off paper is tough. You need some kind of hard, glossy surface, glass, linoleum, Formica."

"That's what I thought. You want to bag this sucker?"

"Yeah, I ought to."

"But, could I get an impression of it, a Xerox or something?"

"There's a Xerox machine in the manager's office."

"So you won't scream if I go Xerox it and then bring it back?"

"Don't mean a thing to me, Oklahoma. What you want it for?"

"I got a thing about lions."

Bud picked up the placemat, which was emblazoned with the Denny's crest and some connect-the-dots games and riddles ("What's black and white and red all over?—A newspaper") for kids, and walked into the manager's office. A flung spray of dried brown blood against the wall, savage and shapeless, almost a map of the explosion of the charge through flesh, signified the spot where Lamar had killed the young manager, and the tape outline on the floor marked his fall. In the other corner, undisturbed, was a copying machine, and routinely, Bud pumped out a facsimile of the placemat, which he folded and put in his pocket. Then he walked back to the tech, who trapped the thing in an evidence bag and ziplocked it shut, pausing only to fill out a slip.

"Say, Bud?"

It was C. D. Henderson.

"Yeah, Lieutenant?"

"Bud, you want a drink? I got a pint, be happy to give you a shot. Helps clarify the mind, they say."

"No thank you, Lieutenant. It'd put me out cold."

"Anyway, they tell me you're a pretty smart boy. Always top of your class, outstanding arrest records, a rep for writing good reports."

"I'm just a highway jockey, Lieutenant. You boys are the detectives."

"You don't have something going?"

"Sorry, I don't—"

"You're not working some angle on Lamar no one else has cottoned to?"

The odor of the bourbon was overwhelming.

"As I said, I'm not an investigator. You boys are the investigators."

"Yes sir, that's what it says, and I know you Smokies don't like it a bit. But a smart boy like you . . . experienced hand, good operator. I don't know, Bud. Seen you digging through evidence, and then running off to make a photocopy. Looks mite peculiar," he finished up, squinting at Bud through shrewd old country eyes.

"Ain't doing nothing. Come to see what this goddamn Lamar done. That's all there is to it, Lieutenant."

"'Cause I know how it would please a stud boy like you to get another crack at Lamar."

"I ain't going up against Lamar, no way. He got the best of me once and I don't doubt but that he would again. He's too much hombre for me. If I should get a lead on Lamar, I'd call the marines, the FBI, and state cops from here to Maryland and back."

"Yeah, but would you call the OSBI?"

"Hey, this ain't a turf thing."

"Yeah, I hear that ever damn time one of you Smokies tries to bump me off my own investigation. Now we might get some good leads out of all this physical evidence. I want to be there when it goes down, you hear me?"

"Yes I do, Lieutenant. Loud and clear."

"Good man, Bud. You and me, we're old salts, we can get along. You git something, you call old C.D. I want in on it. Ten-four, Trooper?"

"Copy that," said Bud.

CHAPTER 17

The water was cold. He couldn't make it another second. He would die. He could feel his lips chattering and his body growing numb. It was so cold.

"I can't make it, Ruta Beth," Richard said.

"Shut your mouth, you damned fool," she spat back. "You lie there like a goddamned man or I'll have Odell hold your head underwater for a few minutes."

"But it's hopeless. He isn't coming."

"Daddy will come," Ruta Beth said. "Goddammit, Daddy can take care of himself and he will come. Isn't that right, Odell?"

"Will cwuh," said Odell, also chattering.

The three of them crouched in a patch of reeds, the cold water of the Red River running up to their necks. They were in a desolate spot, about ten miles outside Burkburnett, between the Burkburnett and the Vernon bridges over the river. A hundred yards of strong black current lay between them and the promised land of Oklahoma, but the rush of the water was so strong, Richard knew he'd never swim it; it would suck him down and drown him. There was no mercy at all in the night. The wind whistled and rattled through the reeds; in the dark he could just see riverbank and mud flat. And enemies were everywhere.

A few hours back, a Department of Texas Safety four-by-four with two squint-eyed Rangers had come lurching down the riverbank, punching its way over fallen logs, skimming into the low tide where necessary, its spotlight playing in the brush for signs of the robbers. But it had passed by, at one point only fifteen feet from them, and gone on down the line. It would be back.

Then, about an hour later, there were lights on the Oklahoma side, as presumably a duplicate of the same mission unfolded over there. But the trucks weren't the problem. The problem was the helicopters.

They came in fast. They came low, and their noise seemed to explode from nowhere as they roared along the river about a hundred feet up, two, three times an hour. These hunters really wanted to kill something. Once, Richard had caught a glimpse of the observer hanging out of the cabin door, a squat man with huge binoculars, a cowboy hat, some kind of mouth microphone and the meanest-looking, fanciest black plastic rifle Richard had ever seen. It looked like a ray gun. He was a boy who meant business; he wanted to drop a bad man before the night was over.

"Can't we wait on the bank?" Richard now moaned through his chattering teeth. "Won't be another helicopter by for an hour."

"You're the biggest fool I ever met, Richard," said Ruta Beth. "Didn't Daddy tell you 'bout infer-red? With that infer-red stuff, they can see you in the dark by the heat of your body. That's what they're doing—hunting you by your heat. Them boys get a reading on heat from three bodies hiding in the grass, goddamn if they won't have a whole company of Rangers here in 'bout a minute."

How did Lamar know so much? Lamar knew everything.

But Lamar was dead.

"He'd have been here by now if he was going to make it," Richard said. "We are going to freeze to death and that will be that."

"Daddy is too goddamned smart for any Johnny Cop." She was even beginning to talk like him. "Now Richard, please shut up or Odell will have to discipline you."

"Yes, Ruta Beth," Richard said.

"Wi-chud," came Odell's glottal spasm.

"Odell, I heard, no bonky, please!"

But Odell didn't want to hurt Richard. Instead he gathered him up and hugged him. It was the strangest thing; Odell's arms just drew Richard in, and his great body seemed to absorb Richard. There was nothing sexual in it at all, for the sex part of Odell's brain lay happily dormant; but it was all tenderness.

Wi-chud makey makey good. Wi-chud no cold. Wi-chud, like, makey warm.

Odell's love bloomed like a hothouse flower: Richard felt the heat radiating from the big body, and in the embrace, the purity of survival. *Odell! What a strange boy! What planet do you come from?*

The warmth saved Richard. It reached out and plucked him from the frozen loneliness of his exile and gave him a life. He yearned to lose himself in it. He knew now he could get through anything.

The hours passed. Six more times the helicopter roared by. At last the dawn began to nudge its way across the sky.

"Ruta Beth?"

"Yes?"

"What do we do if he doesn't show?"

"Nothing. Wait some more."

"But they'll catch us."

Ruta Beth had no response. It was true. The car they had arrived in was deposited under a camouflaged tarpaulin in some trees but a mile or so away, at the end of a farm road near an abandoned farmhouse. In daylight, its shabby fraudulence would be uncovered swiftly enough. Spotted by the chopper, it would draw hundreds of cops within minutes; they'd fan out with bloodhounds, find the trail, follow the little party to the river's edge, and find it cowering there.

Across the river, Ruta Beth's Toyota had been artfully hidden. It, too, would be discovered in daylight. The only real chance was to get across the river in darkness, pull away in the Toyota, which as yet had no criminal charges against it, and head by back roads to Ruta Beth's farm.

In the slow progress of light, Richard at last saw Ruta Beth's stony face. She was a true believer in the cult of Lamar, but even now he could see that her hope was vanishing.

"He'll be here," she said. "Know he will."

Waiting for Lamar. It was like some existential play written by a perverted Frenchman high on keef and boy-love. But instead of snappy patter and ironic reflections on fate, the three principals merely huddled in the water, wrinkled as prunes, waiting for the sun to rise and betray them.

At least, thought Richard, it would be over soon.

A fish bit him. He started at the impulse of pain fighting through his numbness, but the fish bit him again. Not bit him—goosed him, almost comically, squeezing his balls playfully.

"Odell?"

But Odell's passive face indicated no measurable mental activity.

What the—

"Goddamn," said Richard. "He has come."

Lamar broke the water like a seal, shivered in great animal fury, and snorted merrily, "Hah! Shoulda seen you jump, boy!"

At that moment, Richard loved him.

"Lamar! Lamar!" spouted Ruta Beth.

"Mar! Mar! MARRRRRR!" aped Odell.

"Now folks, hold it down! It ain't party time yet. I got to git you out of here."

"Where you been, Daddy?"

"In some damn john's garage. I managed to git me out by cop car, dumped that, cut crosstown and ended up hunkered down in this garage, waiting for the lights to go down so's I could jump-start the car and come a-calling on y'all. You got the money?"

"You bet we do, Lamar," said Ruta Beth. "Come, give me a hug and a kiss, honey."

"Believe I will," said Lamar, and as Odell watched happily, the two swarmed toward each other in the grayness for a big sloppy kiss.

Only Richard thought to wonder: How many did he kill to get out?

But, disengaging himself from Ruta Beth, Lamar announced, "Now, it's time to move. Where's that goddamned canvas sack, honey?"

"Up on the bank, Daddy. You want me to git it?"

"I do."

He turned to Richard. "You look cold as a corpse, boy. You chattering?"

"I-i-t's so *cold,* Lamar," Richard said.

"Hell, in three hours Ruta Beth'll have you eating biscuits by the fire."

Ruta Beth pulled the big canvas sack close to Lamar.

"Great, babe," he said, and reached in to pull out a coil

of thin, waxy rope. Richard could just barely make it out in the gray light.

"You swim, Richard?"

"Yes," said Richard.

"Good. Now I want you to swim across and slip-knot this to a tree good and strong so that these folks can pull themselves across."

"I-I—" gulped Richard.

He looked. The torrent of the Red was strong, swollen with rain; it thundered along and in the gray light was beginning to show the source of its name; it looked like a river of blood, rushing out of a sucking chest wound, pausing only here and there to generate eddies of bubbles where the current curled on itself and lashed downward. Now and then a stick or piece of vegetation would come shooting along. It was the river of death, that's all. Out there, Richard would surrender, his limbs pummeled by the long night's cold; he would be sucked down, then shipped downstream, a bloated, leaky corpse.

"Haw!" barked Lamar. "Had you there, son! *I'll* swim the goddamned river. You help me git the rope set around a branch here, so it don't get away. Then you go across hand by hand. You got that? Ruta Beth, you follow. Odell?"

"Yes, Daddy."

"Wop," said Odell.

With that, Lamar and Odell unleashed the rope and got it secured around the stout trunk of a green willow that grew crookedly out of the bank. Lamar tied some strange superknot that only a bosun's mate or an Eagle Scout would know.

"Okay, Odell, you hang on to these bad boys," and he pulled two handguns from under the water. Odell took them eagerly.

"Wish me luck," said Lamar. "Wish to hell I hadn't

a-skipped all them swimming lessons back at the country club.''

He threw himself into the water like a child at the beach and in several long strokes was gone. It was almost five minutes before they saw him scuttle out at the other end, slither up the bank, and secure the other end of the rope to another limb. He gave the signal.

''Okay, boys,'' said Ruta Beth, ''Daddy's calling. Odell, can you go first?''

''Go,'' said Odell.

Odell began to pull himself across the river, hand over hand along the rope that ran just under the water's now pinkish surface. With his great strength he went quickly, even though he carried the money sack.

''Now you, Richard.''

''No, Ruta Beth. You go.''

''Suit yourself, but don't mess around, Richard. The law gonna come soon and we can't wait. And if they git you, no matter how much you fear Lamar, you will betray him. We both know that.''

She fixed him with a burning glare. Her small country face, so severe in the gray light, had the aspect of a Botticelli nude's, so reduced was it to planes and angles. It was as if she were putting the evil eye on him, some furious hex thing, so that he could not escape his fate. Then off she went, and being light and farm-strong, pulled herself along without apparent effort, until he lost her in the rush of the water.

Now it was Richard's turn. Tentatively he pulled himself out. The current was so much stronger than he anticipated. When the river deepened so that he could no longer stand, it scared him. He almost froze on the spot. But then he got his nerve back up and launched himself farther. With each pull on the rope, his anxiety increased. The rope was deeper, his face was farther in the water, it was so cold, the current was so strong. At one point the rope seemed to sink a good two feet beneath the surface and it was all he could do to keep his head above the water, sucking in half a lungful of air now and then. From his vantage point he could see nothing —no land, no sky, only the glinting surface of the water, as if the universe had become nothing but water. The idea of it terrorized him.

Yet he pulled on. Then he opened his mouth too early and caught a swallow that rocketed down him. The cough racked up through him, seizing his body, but still he clung to the rope. *Just a little farther,* he thought. He managed to get two more pulls on the rope in before surfacing for air. *I must be nearly there,* he thought.

But he made the mistake of turning to look at the far shore, which he assumed must be but a few feet away; he could barely see it. He wasn't even halfway.

The depression of it hit him like a sledgehammer.

Give it up, he said. *Give it up.*

But he fought on, blindly. It was a long, groping night walk; the world resolved itself into the roar of the water and the exhaustion in his arms. He ached to surrender. At one point, he did, and ordered his hands to release him. But they would not. He found it in himself to go another few pulls and then another. A good, sweet lungful of air got him over his worst despair. Onward, he pulled.

It was going to take forever. But at the next sighting, he was astounded at how close the shore was. And with a mighty pull, he got himself into the shallow waters. He saw them in the brush a few feet back from the river's edge. His feet touched. He let go of the damned rope. He stood to raise himself and wave.

And then the current had him.

* * *

"Richard," said Lamar, almost conversationally. Richard was so close, he was coming out of the water, then he just seemed to sit down and the water scooted him along. His face had a silly half-smile, as if he couldn't believe what was happening, as if this were some damned joke.

"Richard," said Lamar, irritated. "Git your ass out of—"

But he was gone. The water had him, and as Lamar watched, the silly look melted into one of sheer terror and weakness. Richard panicked, began to flap, lost control, and was out of sight in seconds.

"Wi-chud," said Odell.

"That boy's gone," said Ruta Beth. "Water took him."

Lamar just watched. He felt something like disappointment. Then he was angry. Goddamned stupid Richard, come all this way, and—

"Shit," he said.

"Lamar, it's over. Let it be," said Ruta Beth. "Let it be."

Richard sank. The world turned dark and liquid. There was no light down here. Weakly he kicked and waved against his fate, but there was no mercy at all, anywhere. He fought for air, but the water beat its way into his lungs. He gobbled for air, but there was only water. He closed his eyes in the gray light.

He thought of his mother.

Mother, he wanted to cry.

His mother was a beautiful woman. She drove his father away with all her "friends." They were a rich, aristocratic crowd from Tulsa, third-generation oil money long removed from the smell and sweat of the fields, and his father preferred the old boy network of kick-ass riggers and up-from-penury scalawags like himself, who'd made their fortunes on guts and nerve. All these puffy people, all of his mother's friends with their Eastern pretensions, they finally drove the poor man away, though Richard didn't think there'd ever been a divorce.

Richard's mother told him he could be an artist. She took him to art lessons so early and surrounded him with artistic people. He went to Europe when he was six, nine, eleven, and fourteen. It wasn't her fault he turned out so disappointingly. She had done everything she could.

Somehow, things were always set against Richard. She would arrange for "introductions" to various prominent men in the East when they traveled there, but the men were always disappointed in him. He had a gift but not a great one, that was clear, and he was so much less interesting than Mother, he was a wretched conversationalist, he didn't have her buoyant charm, her vividness, her confidence. And she told him that, not in subtle ways, but baldly and to his face.

"Richard, you could do so much better if you weren't so meek. You will not inherit the earth that way, I promise you. You have to learn to project. People don't find your self-doubts attractive at all. Reach out, open up."

But the more she pushed him, the more he sealed up. It was as if he was blossoming inward, becoming more retarded and pitiful and self-conscious and crippled with terror. He was afraid of everything!

On the day it happened, he returned home and found her with a friend. Eventually the friend left, and she came downstairs and mixed herself a drink, still beautiful at sixty-one, and asked him how the newspaperman had liked the exhibition.

"Uh," said Richard, aching with dread, "Mother, he didn't show."

"He what?"

"He didn't show. Mother, I don't know what happened, maybe he got lost."

"Richard, I have over four thousand dollars invested in that exhibition! What do you mean, he didn't show?"

He stood there, thirty years old, quavering like a child. He hated her almost as much as he hated himself.

"Call him," she said.

"I did. He wasn't there."

"Call him *again*."

"Mother."

"Call him, Richard, call him *now*. You silly little fool. You cannot let people simply *walk* on you. It's why you always end up with nothing and why I always have to bail you out. I pay for everything, Richard. You get everything for free."

He made the call.

The man was there.

"Uh, Mr. Peed, sorry, I told you I'd come by if I could. But the art critic thing is only part of my job; I also have to read all the Sunday feature copy and we got a little behind and I just couldn't make it. It's not *The New York Times,* you know. It's just the *Daily Oklahoman.*"

He hung up.

"Call him again," his mother said.

He was never sure, not then, not in the immediate aftermath, not in the months of meditation, why it happened the way it did when it happened. Why that day, that minute? It could have been any other day, any other minute.

It was the maid who called the police.

He tried to make them see, he wasn't trying to *blind* her. He was really trying to kill her. But the knife was short—it was a butter knife, quite blunt—and somehow she had proven so much stronger than he thought; she'd gotten down beneath him so he couldn't reach her heart. After the first pitiful blow, she'd sort of curled up, so he had to unpeel her, but she was very strong. The only place he could stab her was the face. The eyes? Well, the eyes *are* on the face, aren't they? It wasn't his fault.

Richard suddenly broke the surface of the water. He was way out in the river. The trees were hurtling by. It was much lighter.

A flood of sweet oxygen poured into his lungs. He smiled, but the water sucked him down again.

Richard yielded to death.

It embraced him and he embraced it. He felt its strong arms pull him in, smother him. There was no pain at all, only a persistent tugging that broke through the numbness in his body. He had a last dream of Lamar, of all things: pitiful, crude, powerful, violent Lamar. Odd that he should think of Lamar here at the end.

Lamar had him up on the surface. Richard choked on air.

"Calm down, goddammit, Richard," screamed Lamar, "don't fight me."

He was upside down in somebody's strong arms. The sky was bright and blue, the clouds rushed by. A helicopter should have come, but it didn't. Nothing came. The roaring had ceased. He felt as if he were in one of the swimming pools of his boyhood and wanted to spit a gurgle of water to see if he could make Mother laugh.

He felt the ground, and in his exhaustion looked up to see that Odell had him and was pulling him ashore.

Lamar came out of the rushing red water a second later, beautiful in the gray dawn, soaked and muscular, his hair wet, his denim clothes plastered to him, his face grave with effort and pain.

He smiled at Richard.

"You are a peck of trouble, Richard, I swear."

"C'mon, boys," said Ruta Beth. "Let's git before god-damned Johnny Cop shows."

CHAPTER 18

No one knew how to run a crime scene anymore, the old man lamented. It was stunning they got any evidence at all these days. These sloppy damn kids, rough and eager as untrained young dogs. No one had even erected a windbreak.

"Can't you do a little something about the breeze, son?" he gently corrected. A young OSBI agent began to look around for something out of which to construct a barrier to prevent more wind erosion, but he was so clumsy in his efforts, C.D. worried that he'd do more harm than good.

The old man hawked a gob of phlegm out of his dry old throat and squatted in the dust. The wind whipped through the scrub oaks and, two hundred yards away, the angry red torrent of the river surged along toward Arkansas. It was high this time of year, full of the melted snows of the winter, and treacherous; other times of the year, it'd dry to a trickle. Had Lamar calculated on that, too? Was he *that* smart?

"It could be nothing," said a young Ranger captain named Tippahoe, offered up by the great state of Texas as his opposite number.

"It could be our goddamn break," said Lt. Henderson.

"I musta run a thousand tire tracks and I ain't come up with diddly, 'less it's to tie a specific vehicle to a specific location. Don't know what good the goddamned track is without the vehicle."

"Well, son, maybe you're right and maybe you ain't. Believe I'll just play the hand out, as it's the only one the Good Lord deemed fit to deal me." He turned from the obstreperous Texas Ranger to a foolish-looking young Oklahoma highway patrolman lurking nearby with a walkie-talkie. "You got any word yet on those evidence technicians?"

"Sir, they's coming. Tied up in traffic outside of Oklahoma City."

"They can't chopper 'em in?"

"Sir, all the choppers tied up in trauma delivery."

"Okay, tell you what. You tell them Lieutenant Henderson says to call Colonel McClutcheon, the operations officer of the Four Hundred and First Aviation Battalion at Fort Sill. See if he can free up a Huey and get those boys in here before the glaciers arrive from Canada. Colonel Robert M. McClutcheon. He owes me a thing or two."

"Yes, sir, I'll *tell* 'em, but—"

"That's all, son."

The small party was standing under a gloomy sky in the wasteland of scrub and low vegetation that was part of the Red River basin, on the Oklahoma side. A half mile or so away, on the Texas side, a Texas policeman had located a stolen Volvo in a ditch. This discovery had led to another: a stolen Camaro, once white, now painted orange and covered in a camouflaged tarpaulin. They were currently being dusted for prints by Ranger technicians, but C.D. knew what the prints would show: These were the various getaway vehicles stolen by Lamar Pye and his crew members.

There might be a print of the fourth member of the gang, but C.D. doubted it. Lamar was too smart.

But those discoveries, in turn, had yielded this tiny little scrap of hope on the Oklahoma riverbank. Here, in the dirt, a very, very good track off still another vehicle. C.D. appreciated the orderly way Lamar's mind had worked, how cleverly he'd planned it out, stashing the legal vehicle at the end of the train of stolen ones so that as they made their final fallback to their hideout, they'd do so in a car that couldn't, of itself, attract attention and whose plates would run legal if checked. Such a smart boy.

C.D. turned and made as if to mosey off just a bit in search of new evidence. But of course he slipped the brown paper bag from his left inside pocket, unscrewed the lid, and took a fast swig. I. W. Harper, seven years old, like the smoke off a prairie fire. He went to wooziness, then came back out, feeling calmer and more in charge. He screwed the lid back on, lightly, and slipped the pint into his pocket.

He turned back and had that odd feeling that everyone had been staring at him but had just that second looked away so as not to embarrass him. Everyone, that is, except for young Captain Tippahoe, whose face was knitted up with contempt and impatience.

And where were you, Tippahoe, when I shot it out with Luke Sweetwater and Indian Joe Brown in 1957? Where were you when I took six inches of blade in the stomach from crazy Sally Pogue and only saved my life with a .45 fired as she was getting up to my throat? What about the time I faced down two hundred citizens of Gem City and saved the lives of two innocent nigger brothers that I knew hadn't raped Mrs. McLintock in 1966? Where were you, Tippahoe?

But Tippahoe didn't know and wouldn't care. He just

stepped back, took off his hat, and ran his hand through expensively trimmed hair and acted vaguely superior.

C.D. looked down at the little trace of ridges and grooves in the dust. It seemed to lose a bit of its distinction even as he watched, as a gust of wind took another quarter inch off the top.

Where are them damn boys, he wondered. He wouldn't let the Rangers do it. He only trusted his own OSBI team. He wanted another drink.

"I hope it lasts," said Tippahoe. "And I hope it ain't a goddamned wild goose chase. We sure don't do things like this in Texas. What you gonna do, Lieutenant, track down all the cars in Oklahoma?"

"Oh, I may have a card or two up my old sleeve," said C.D. and hawked another gob of phlegm into the wind.

He looked back at the track in the dust, which seemed to lose another millimeter of distinction. Was it the second piece of evidence, he wondered?

The agent sent to build the windbreak was now struggling with sticks and a blanket. It looked hopeless.

Come on, boys, he thought. *Come on.*

"Lieutenant?"

"Yes, son?"

"They're telling me the army's going to detail a chopper to pick your team up in Oklahoma City."

"Well, praise the Lord and pass the bourbon, son."

Bud was changing the oil on his truck when Jen came out and told him the colonel was on the phone. It was Tuesday afternoon, about two. He'd gotten back from Wichita Falls the night before last, not even bothering to call Holly.

Then he had slept late, had had bad nightmares, awakening in a foul mood, no good to man or beast, wife, son, or girlfriend. He had laid low the whole day, grouchy and forlorn, like an old cougar in its cave.

Now he was trying to make himself something human again.

He wiped Valvoline off his hands and went in the house. "Sir?"

"Bud, I figure if you're well enough to go bouncing out to Wichita Falls on your lonesome, you might be well enough to do some real work. Am I right?"

"Yes, you are."

"No uniform necessary, Bud. You can go in plain-clothes. I'd carry, though."

"I always carry, Colonel."

"You use your truck. Write the mileage, we'll reimburse."

"Got it."

The colonel then explained what had happened.

Around ten yesterday morning, two Rangers had discovered the abandoned Camaro and the Volvo that Lamar had stolen on the Texas side of the Red River. A print team lifted some good latents, which were quickly made as Lamar, Odell, and Richard's. Also discovered was a hundred yards of green No. 7 rigger's rope, which could have been bought in any hardware store between Dallas–Ft. Worth and Oklahoma City. It had been stretched across the river. The team had evidently used it to get across.

"Don't that beat all, Bud? That Lamar, he's a goddamned genius. We got the bridges covered and helicopters with infrared, and he *still* beats us. Bud, he's smarter than that even. The shell that was ejected from the shotgun that killed that lady probation officer? There was a print on it. Lamar's! He loaded his buddy's gun, because he knew we already had his prints!"

"He's a goddamned smart boy, all right," said Bud, wondering where he fit into the operation.

"Well, maybe Lamar done slipped up just a bit," said the colonel. "On our side of the river, we found tracks of the car they had stashed to take them out of there. Old C. D. Henderson threw a goddamned red-ass tantrum and got them to make a cast. We faxed the tread to the FBI and we got a make just like that: It's the pattern for a Goodyear 5400-B, a low-end nonreinforced radial made entirely for Japanese cars with sixty-inch wheelbases and six-inch tire wells. Goddamn if that old drunken coot didn't hit a jackpot. Only three varieties of car can wear it—your Hyundai Excel, your Toyota Tercel, and your Nissan Sentra, from the years 1991 on. Moreover, two of the companies changed their design last year. So it can only be three model years of the Hyundais and the Toyotas and four model years of the Sentras. The last getaway job's got to be one of those, you follow?"

"Got you," said Bud.

"We shook out about forty-two hundred cars registered in South Oklahoma that can wear that set of tires, Bud. About two hundred of them are registered to people with felony convictions. We're fixin' to raid on them, just to be sure, because C.D. is dang sure they'll run to kind."

"I could—"

"No, Bud. Your raid days are over. We're going door-to-door on the other four thousand. It's going to take a heap of manhours, Bud. It ain't the glory route, that's for sure. I got five other ex-detectives and retired patrolmen working the job. You get the address, you find the car, you lookiesee the tires and if you get the right set of tires on the right car, you call in the license number and we see what we shake out. Maybe we stake out, maybe we raid, depending. Bud, you can imagine, there's a lot of goddamned public pressure on this one. That's why we're working so damned hard.''

"Yes sir.''

The colonel told him the Joint States Task Force was headquartered at the old City Hall Annex near the police station in downtown Lawton, where he'd show up to get his list, and Bud said he'd leave right away. The colonel said he appreciated it, but he knew he could count on Bud.

"Oh, and Bud?''

"Yes sir?''

"That other matter?''

Bud didn't say a thing.

"Bud, you still there?''

"Yes sir.''

"That other matter. That's in hand, ain't it, Bud? Ain't going to be no big scandal, a heroic patrol officer caught in a love nest with his partner's widow, nothing like that?''

"No sir,'' Bud said.

"Good. Knowed I could count on you, Bud.''

Bud went back outside. He tossed the empty oil bottles and the used filter into the trash can, and poured the used oil into a couple of Zerex containers. Then he picked up the two Craftsman wrenches he'd used and tossed them onto the clutter of his workbench. He felt a flash of shame: he could find time to sneak away and fuck Holly a couple of times a week, but he couldn't take time to clean up after himself at home.

He went back inside and showered and changed into a good pair of Levi's, his best Tony Lamas, and a white shirt. He went down to the gun safe, took out the Colt Commander and pinched the slide back to make sure it was loaded, then snapped on the safety and slipped it into an inside-the-pants holster, which he then inserted into the waist of the jeans and hooked on his belt. He had two extra magazines in a belt mount next to the Colt. Last, he put the Beretta .380 with the thirteen-shot double-stack clip inside his shirt behind his belt buckle. It would hurt like hell after a while, but let it. Better to have too many guns than not enough.

"Bud?"

"Yeah?"

"You come here a second now."

Now what the hell did she want?

"Jen, I don't have time. I have to—"

"You come here."

That was Jen's no-nonsense voice. Shit! She sounded loaded for big game. Was he going to have one of those bitter explosions, where her sense of isolation from him and his lack of passion for her lashed out at him? It seemed to happen all the time.

"Jen, this is no goddamn time—" he started to bellow as he walked into the kitchen, but what stopped him short was finding her and Jeff looking like they'd just swallowed a whole flock of canaries.

"Bud, what have they got you doing?" asked Jen.

"They got me knocking on doors as part of some combined state task force, that's all. It won't be nothing, that I guarantee you. Now what's going on?" he said.

"Remember, Dad. I was asking you about the 9-millimeters?"

"Yes, I do." Bud remembered his lies to Jeff in the car on Sunday.

"Well, sir," said Jen, "maybe this'll help with Lamar, just in case. I called my mother and asked for a loan."

"Jen!"

"Six hundred dollars against my share of the farm profits this year. And so Jeff and I went down to Southwest Pawn and Gun this morning. This here's to get you out of that low mood. And so you don't have to use those speedloaders anymore.''

She held out a blue plastic box, and Bud knew in a second his wife and son had just given him a big Beretta 9-mm automatic. A sense of shame hit him. He swallowed, felt himself blushing.

''Jen, that's so . . . nice.''

''Dad, I got you this. It's a shoulder holster for the Beretta,'' said Jeff, holding out a plastic package with the name Bianchi on it. ''Now you go anywhere, you go in style.''

''Jeez,'' said Bud. ''I sure as hell don't know what I did to deserve y'all.''

Eagerly, they helped Bud mount up. With a box of 115-grain silver-tips that Miss Edna at Southwest had thrown in to aid the cause of law and order, Bud soon had the new Beretta stoked with seventeen rounds and had another magazine of sixteen on the counter. It was a black brute of a pistol, a kind of inflated version of the .380 inside his shirt. It fit his hand like a handshake from a brother, and when he brought it up to a Weaver grip, he found its sight picture clear and vivid.

Next issue was getting into the X design of the rig, not the easiest thing, but eventually, with everyone helping, they got it done. The spare magazine went in a pouch that hung under the other arm, as a kind of counterbalance to the heavy automatic. When he slipped on his sports coat, it would be hard to see he had become a three-gun man. But the thing felt like a brassiere, or how he imagined a brassiere would feel. The gun hung underneath, tight in its holster but loose enough to slap him if he turned quickly; a quick grab presented it neatly enough, but it was a move he'd have to work on, until it was smooth as silk.

Goddamn, he figured, counting it up, no wonder I'm

walking slow these days. Got fifty-eight rounds of ammo stowed on me. That ought to be enough for anybody.

Bud went back to the safe and took out an old .30-30 carbine he'd hunted deer with as a young man. It always helped to have a long gun along; you never could tell. With a box of twenty .30-30 softpoints, he walked to the truck and put the long gun in its case behind the seat. Jen brought out his sports coat, a light tan cotton thing, and his hat, a white Stetson. He pulled on his Ray-Bans.

"You look like a Texas Ranger," she said.

"You'd best hope not. They're the meanest boys that ever walked the planet. Oh, wait, forgot something."

But she had it. His briefcase. Full of Richard's lions.

"Your damn lions."

"While I'm looking for this tire, I'll do some thinking about the lions. Maybe I can figure what he's got going."

There was an awkward moment and then he embraced Jen.

"Thank you," he said. "It was damned sweet of you."

But she pushed him away, brusquely, as if the gift was what any woman would give her husband.

"You run a hundred rounds or so through that, Bud. You know they jam more in the first fifty rounds than they do in all the others."

"I will, hon."

"That gun ain't supposed to jam ever," Jeff said. "I read all about it in *Guns & Ammo.*"

He gave her another hug.

"Go on, get out of here. Earn us some money so we can feed these damn boys," she said, turning.

Bud drove away, into Lawton, but not yet toward downtown, instead veering east into the first strip mall that boasted a pay phone. Quickly he dialed Holly's number.

The phone rang and rang and rang.

Where was she? Probably met someone. Good for her.

He was about to hang up when, at least fifteen or so rings into it, the phone came off the hook and he heard her tired voice.

"Hello?"

"Are you all right? Were you sleeping? I was worried."

No answer, only her heavy breathing.

Then finally she said, "You were going to call two nights ago. I was up all night waiting."

"Holly, I went to Wichita Falls, the robbery? You hear?" She had not. He told her.

"So you couldn't call? In all that, you couldn't call just once?"

"Holly, I'm sorry. There was no time down there and by the time I got back, it was really late. I just—I didn't think."

"And you didn't call yesterday."

He was contrite.

"No. I had a bad night. I'm sorry, I didn't do nothing yesterday."

"Bud, look what you're doing to me."

"Holly, this business has come up again. They want me to do some work for them."

He explained briefly what would happen, how he was going back on duty, searching for cars with a certain set of tires over the southern half of the state.

The Beretta was so heavy under his arm.

"Bud, you make all these promises, then you sort of fade. You like the sex great, but when it comes to making plans, then you fade. You're not there. You're off somewhere."

"I'm sorry, Holly. Is there anything I can do?"

"Yes, dammit. I have to move. I can't stand this place.

We have to find some new place. Will you look for it with me?''

It seemed excruciating to him. It would be horrible. He hated the new-marrieds aspect of it—checking for shelves and views—and he felt so indecent. But he said, ''Of course I will. *Sure* I will.''

''Oh, Bud,'' she cried. ''I knew you would. Oh, Bud, I knew you would.''

''Now, sweetie, I got to go.''

''When will I see you?''

''Soon, I swear. We'll start looking soon.''

''Oh Bud, I love you so much!''

Feeling relieved, Bud drove over to the City Hall Annex, an old office building, hastily reconfigured to its new purpose. On the first floor, in a wide-open bank of rooms, a few Texas Rangers hung around. There was a phone bank and a slew of operators, and a radio receiver, just like at the highway patrol shop, and a filing cabinet, as well as the by-now regular complement of computer terminals with civilian clerks. And who seemed to be running the show but his old friend Lt. C. D. Henderson of the OSBI, who looked spryer than Bud had ever seen him. For once, the whiff of booze didn't cling to him. A smile even came across the creased old face.

''Howdy there, Bud. They told me you was coming back on as an emergency investigator.''

''Yes sir, I am,'' said Bud. ''Figure I can pound on doors as well as anyone.''

''Well, there's many a door needs pounding. Bud, we've already got 'bout six men out there, but with close to four thousand names, the more the better.''

''So where'm I heading?''

''Well, let's see, many of 'em are in Lawton, where

we've sent most of our men, and another hotbed is way out in Ardmore. But let's work you in from the country side. You won't get as much done, since there's some space between ranches, and you may get sick of looking at cattle, but it's got to be done."

"Great," said Bud.

He was issued a stack of computer printouts bearing addresses and car registration data for Tillman, Jackson, and Cotton counties, in the southeast sector of the state, about two hours' ride. He was told he'd probably end up heading out to Greer and Harmon and Kiowa counties, too, in the next few days.

"Your truck got a two-way?"

"No sir, it don't."

"Okay, we'll issue a Motorola portable unit, you won't have no problem. It'll be pre-set to our net, forty-four point nine. You ten–twenty-three each stop and ten–twenty-four afterward, just in case. We always want to know where you're at. I hope you ain't lucky again."

"I hope I ain't either."

"You got it, right? You just tell 'em we're doing a criminal investigation involving a motor vehicle and investigating is *elimination* and we want to check them off the list. You find the car, then you check the tires. If you get the right tires on the right kind of car, then you call it in, wait for what the computer kicks out, and sit by until we decide to raid or stake out. That's all. If you should bump into anybody nasty, you do not want to be in it without backup. You're even more on your lonesome now."

"I get that. I'm looking at cars and tires, not to make arrests. I told you, I don't want to cross with old Lamar again."

"We got a heavy-duty SWAT team—Rangers, troopers, and an OSBI supervisor sitting out at Fort Sill airfield, with army pilots. Anybody gets in a jam, we can have twenty men there in a few minutes.''

''Sounds good to me.''

''Ten-four, Bud.''

Bud picked up his radio unit and a map, and headed back to the truck. It took him a few seconds in the cab to get the electronic gear set up. Then it crackled to life.

''Dispatch, this is six-oh-five, I am ten-seven, outward bound to Tillman county.''

''Ten-four, six-oh-five.''

Bud took 44 south of town, followed its straight shot south to the toll plaza at Oklahoma 5, then got off to follow 5 into Tillman's vast and empty flatness. It took him about two hours to find his first stop.

''Dispatch, this six-oh-five, I am ten–twenty-three at Loveland, Route 5, the Del Rio farm, looking for a 1991 Red Tercel, that's license plate Oklahoma One-fiver-niner-niner-Roger-Mike.''

''Ten-four, six-oh-five.''

Bud got out at a decaying farmhouse and began what would become his routine for the next two days. He knocked on the door, showed his badge ID, introduced himself, and went into his song and dance. It was amazing how cooperative people could be. Most Americans just love to help the police.

''Why, sure, Officer, it cain't be me or mine,'' they'd say, or some variation thereof.

In Loveland, a gnarled Hispanic grandfather took him out back and showed him the car; it hadn't been driven in a year, and rested in rotten splendor atop a quartet of cinder blocks. And so it went: Sometimes the cars were clean, sometimes beat-up. Sometimes they'd been recently sold, and the name of the buyer or the dealership was gladly provided. Sometimes Bud had to wait for a man to come home from the plant or the bar; sometimes it was a boy, returning from town or chores or the Dairy Queen. But sooner or later, the car would turn up, he'd examine it, steal a look at the tires, and pass on it.

Twice, in the first two days, he found the right set of Goodyear radials on the right car, itself no crime. One was down near Cookietown in Cotton County, owned by the town's Southern States Grain and Seed branch manager, a florid redhead with blemishy skin and a belly as large as the outdoors. It seemed unlikely, but maybe the man's son or brother or something had some connection with . . . Bud called it in, but the computer produced no evidence of previous criminal activities associated with Mr. Fuerman or his wife, no other family members in existence according to records. Then, on the Cherokee reservation near Polk Lake in Tillman, he came across a run-down one-story government tract house, half its shingles flapping in the dry wind, and as he walked to it, he felt a hundred eyes on him. Cops always have a feeling for such a thing but don't let it go too far, or it just plain flat ruins them. Bud conquered the little whisper of fear and knocked on the door to find a woman with a face that looked as if it had aged in lava for a century or two, as if she had worn away all her teeth gnawing on bones. Finally, after he explained in English what he wanted, she said for him to go out back. He found the thing, a beat-to-shit Hyundai Excel, once yellow, now nearly rusted out. And only one of the tires was a Goodyear 5400-B, and it was as bald as a rock. Maybe that one and only that one had been the track the detectives had picked up near the Red.

He felt the eyes on him again and looked up at the house, wondering if even now Lamar Pye weren't squinting over a gunsight at him. But he quelled the feeling, walked back to his truck, and called it in. Half an hour later, the response came: The car, registered to a Sonny Red Bear, could not be linked to criminal activities, and no trace of criminal records, either local or federal, could be found for either Sonny Red Bear or any of his family. Just then the door burst open, and Bud saw what had scurried so mysteriously behind the doors of the little house: It was a mess of kids, squalling and seething, led to the car by a handsome woman. The children crammed in any which way, and she got in and drove off.

Bud played a hunch.

"Dispatch, can you ten–forty-three the name Red Bear for a State of Oklahoma daycare license?"

"Got you, six-oh-five."

He waited and then it came back that, yes, one Carla Red Bear had applied to the state for just such a daycare license, though its issuance was pending.

"You got a violation to report there, six-oh-five?"

Bud paused. Was a time, yes, he'd report any violation. The law was rigid and unshaded and it was meant not to be violated, whether the issue was speed limit or murder. And he was a rigid man. Or at least he used to be. But today he wasn't out here for any business other than Lamar Pye. He'd cut the Red Bears some slack and maybe it would come back to him in some way.

"Naw, Dispatch, just curious. I'm ten–twenty-four here, and out."

"Got you, six-oh-five."

Other than that, there was no excitement as Bud prowled the byways of the third, then the fourth, then the fifth county over the next few days in search of the three car models in their appropriate years. He threw himself into the hunt so because he knew that it represented an escape from It.

And so it was finally, on the sixth day, a Tuesday of the

following week, when he was nearing the end of his list, that he reached an address on a rural route near Altus, in Kiowa County.

He paused at the entrance to the road in, and ten–twenty-threed his location. It was a barren part of Oklahoma, and the raw wind whistled across the rolling prairie. He could see the house a mile in, clapboard, old and peely, with its constellation of attendant lesser structures. Behind, the mountains stuck out of the earth, and here and there snaggy mesquite trees clawed at the sky or a parcel of scrub oaks nestled like drinking buffalo around a creek. He headed in, checking once again to make sure of the registration of the car, a Toyota Tercel, and the name of the owner: Tull, Ruta Beth.

CHAPTER
19

Lamar would never admit defeat or even disappointment. Still, $4,567.87 wasn't exactly a huge sum, given what they'd had to go through to get it.

"Now, maybe it ain't a lot," he said, "but it ain't a little either. Not by a damn sight. Why, there's lots of places to go, lots of places to see, on almost five thousand dollars."

But the truth was, Ruta Beth had over nine thousand dollars inherited from her beloved late mother and daddy already in a bank account, which she was willing to just fork over to Lamar.

"Ruta Beth, that wouldn't be right. You just don't give money to a person, even though you love him."

"It would be right if I said so," she said.

"Well, maybe come a rainy day, that money'll help out. In fact, maybe we'll borrow against it, though I can't but guess they'd have the serial numbers recorded."

"That would make Mother and Daddy happy," Ruta Beth said.

Lamar smiled. Still, he was secretly upset. A night or two after the robbery, when the little family was gathered around the TV at the news hour, watching for the latest on their own celebrity, a flashy black man came on and said, "Some are calling the Pyes the boldest gang to come out of Oklahoma since the thirties, when Pretty Boy Floyd roared out of the Cookson hills and lit up America with his desperado ways. But what Pretty Boy had in style and substance, this gang makes up for in sheer firepower. And dumb luck. They are the gang that *could* shoot straight but couldn't think straight—the horrifying face of modern crime."

Lamar brooded silently on this for a bit, until his anger at last came welling out during the weather. He suddenly started bellowing like an enraged father.

"All this goddamn shit about Pretty Boy Floyd and Bonnie and Clyde and Johnny Dillinger and how great they were! It's shit, I tell you. What we done, we done *better'n* them old boys, by a goddamn cocksucking mile." His outburst quieted them all, even Odell, who was working on a big bowl of Frosted Mini-Wheats. Lamar seemed to have it back under control, but a vein on his head suddenly began to throb. And then Lamar got tooting again.

"In them days," he said earnestly, looking at Richard, "in them days, the police didn't have nothing. The radios had a range of about ten feet, when they worked, fingerprints was brand spanking new and had to be hand-catalogued by clerks, there weren't no computers, the cars was slow, they didn't have no Magnum pistols, your biggest gun was your .44 Special, they didn't have no helicopters, no infrared, no fax, no nothing. Hell, the FBI in them days was nothing but another gang, with machine guns and BARs. Nobody did hard time in a joint where all the niggers was uppity. Why hell, *any* goddamned body could have been a desperado. Now look what we got to contend with. Look what we went through to get a lousy five grand. I'm telling you, no Charlie Floyd, no Bonnie Parker, no goddamned Johnny Dillinger could have pulled off what we pulled off.

We don't get no credit. They're saying we were just god-damned lucky. Well sir, lot more to it than luck, by god-damn God. Yes sir. Yes sir.''

He sat there, seething.

''You should write that boy a letter, Lamar,'' said Ruta Beth.

''No ma'am. Another way of how come our type is better than them old-timey ones. The cops been using that trick for years. Go on the radio or the TV and disrespect an honest job of thieving, so that the thief goes and gits himself all smoked up, and pulls a rash job or sends a letter or something. No sir, what we have is self-control. I guarantee you. We are goddamned serious.''

Then he got up and went outside. They heard the Toyota start up and leave the farm.

''Daddy is upset,'' said Ruta Beth.

''Set,'' said Odell.

''He has a right to be upset,'' said Richard. ''I wish I had a surprise or something to give him so that he would feel better.''

It was a wonderful idea!

''A surprise!'' exclaimed Ruta Beth in joy. ''Odell, has anyone done give Daddy a surprise?''

Odell's face went slack as he contemplated this problem. For minutes his eyes registered NO OCCUPANCY, but at last he found a kernel of information to impart, took a deep breath and tried to find the way into speech. His face mottled with effort. The suspense grew. He looked like he might explode. But finally, he said, ''No prise!''

''Whooee,'' squealed Ruta Beth. ''Let's give him a surprise then.''

''A cake,'' said Richard, who had himself always fanta-sized about a surprise party when he was a child.

''We ain't got no cake,'' said Ruta Beth.

"Gake, gake," said Odell.

In Odell's mind there was a memory of cake, too. He remembered:

> *Way back old time. Mama sing. Mama kiss. Cake! Softee sweet, on fire. "Happy birthyday to you, happy birthyday to you-oo, happy birthyday to Odell, happy birthyday to you." Mama so nice. Cakey good! So long ago!*

"You hush now, Odell honey, there ain't no cake. We'll make do with something. Come on."

The merry band went into the kitchen. They opened the cabinets and, indeed, could find no cake. But Odell did quickly spot a can of store-bought vanilla frosting. He liked to spread it on bread.

"Fros! *FROS!*" he said urgently, pointing, his whole face turning red in the effort.

"Oh, Dell, honey, that's *wonderful*," said Ruta Beth.

Odell smiled.

"You could put that on something," said Richard. "It wouldn't be a cake. But it would be sort of a cake."

"Well, I'd like to have a real cake," said Ruta Beth. "It's a damned shame we ain't got no cake."

"Could you bake one?"

"No time."

But Odell was not through yet. He began jumping up and down with excitement and pointing. His face lit with frustration as he tried to find the words to present what was clearly the most complex thought his brain had ever attempted to generate. His eyes rolled. His tongue fought in his mouth for fluidity.

He was putting two pictures together in his mind.

Ed + Fros = Cake.

How could he get them to understand?

"Ed," he was saying, knowing that somehow it was wrong. The harder he tried, the more angry at himself he got. Sometimes he wanted to rip out his own eyes and tongue for being so different. The pressure rose as he tried to form the word!

"Ed. ED!"

"Ed?" said Richard. "Ruta Beth, do you know what he's trying to say?"

"No idea," she said. "Odell, honey, you go slow and try and say all the letters."

Odell made an effort to calm himself. When he at last seized control of his own voice, he spat out the word "Bed."

Bed? thought Richard.

"Bread," shouted Ruta Beth. "Yes, Richard, he's saying *bread*."

The excitement was intolerable. Richard felt it himself. Yes. What was a cake but bread with sugar? Well . . . why not put some sugar on a nice loaf of bread, then cover it with frosting. Wouldn't that be sort of like a cake?

"We can do it!" he shouted, exalted. "We can do it."

Odell smiled rapturously as Ruta Beth kissed him and "Wi-chud" gave him a manly clap on the shoulder.

Eagerly, they set to work. Richard's artistic talents came to the fore. One problem was that, shed of its wrapper, the loaf of bread kept separating into slices. It was Richard's brainstorm to pierce it with uncooked spaghetti strands to provide a kind of internal discipline that would hold it together. Odell didn't have the patience to spread the frosting, but it turned out that Richard didn't either, even with his art training. It fell to Ruta Beth. With her eyes squinted and her tiny face knitted up like an angry fist, she dabbed the frosting on the sugary bread a dollop at a time. When she was finally done, by God it did look like a cake!

"Gake! Gake!" shouted Odell.

He began to sing, "Py birfee, a-py birfee."

"We need candles," said Richard. "Candles would really make it work."

"Suppose it ain't his birthday? Or suppose he's one of them that don't like to be 'minded of his age?" Ruta Beth asked darkly.

But Richard held firm. "No, it *should* have candles," he said. "I think we can take it on principle that Lamar is the sort of man who'd see the necessity for the ceremony."

His will held sway. They had no birthday candles, of course, but they did find some candles kept in case the power went out. Richard cut them up and wedged them, like carrot stumps, into the frosting. When they were done, it looked pretty much like a cake. But something was missing.

Richard tried to guess what. It just looked sort of disappointing. The frosting was white, somewhat unevenly applied, but mainly it was that the shape of the loaf of bread wasn't obscured enough. It just looked like a loaf of bread smeared with frosting.

"We can do better than *that*," he said.

Then he knew.

"It needs . . . a lion!"

Everybody agreed that this was a wonderful idea. Richard set to work. Quickly he located supplies: peanut butter to etch the face, two raisins for eyes, smashed bits of Frito to form the mane. Steadily he worked, as the other two hovered over him in the small, warm kitchen. At first it was chaos. But Richard had invested so much over the weeks in lions that he was able to bring the shape out from nothingness, just seem to demand that it emerge from the swirls of peanut butter. And the liquidity of the peanut butter as a medium was interesting: somehow it was more naturally akin to the texture of muscle that he had had so much trouble getting into his drawings. The body-form just seemed to define itself out of the glop, powerful and radiant, vibrant with predatory muscularity. It pleased him.

Slowly, like a Mediterranean mosaicist adding his last few tiles, he built the Fritos into a mane. Then he added the two raisins. They were too big. It looked stupid. Then he saw a half-opened package of Oreo cookies; Odell liked to pry the Oreos apart and lick the frosting off. He took a cookie out, broke it into bits, and found two of approximately the right size that looked like eyes. Carefully, he placed this last detail where it belonged.

"Wi-on! Wi-on!" shouted Odell.

"Lordy be," said Ruta Beth. "It do look a lot like a lion."

Just then, they heard the car pull into the yard. Lamar parked near the barn, then ambled toward the house.

"Git ready for a su-prise!" called Ruta Beth.

Lamar climbed to the porch, opened the door, and stared at the candles glowing in the dark.

"Now what the hell—"

"SURPRISE," shouted Ruta Beth, Richard, and Odell simultaneously, leaping from the corners of the kitchen at Lamar in the split second after Ruta Beth had turned on the lights.

For the first time in his life, Lamar stood agape. His mouth fell open. He looked at them dancing merrily in the kitchen and at the thing they had made for him.

Then he started to cry.

"That's the goddamned prettiest thing I ever saw," he said. "Oh my, oh my, oh my, how you have made me proud today. That's the goddamned best surprise a man could get! And a lion on it! Richard, boy, I know your work, that's you! Oh, it's so goddamned nice!"

"Gake! Gake!" shouted Odell.

"Well, let's up and have us a piece," said Lamar.

"Lamar, it ain't a real cake. It may not taste like much," said Ruta Beth.

"Well, damn, I'd say it's as real as a cake could get, Ruta Beth." He bent to cut it, but Odell yelled "Kwan-dul, kwandul."

"Candle," said Richard. "He is saying, Blow out the candle. Make a wish."

Obediently, Lamar blew out the candle.

"What'd you wish for?" Ruta Beth wanted to know.

"For us always to be this happy," he said. He cut the cake into four pieces, the knife in his big fists, the F U C K and the Y O U ! blazing off his knuckles, and passed the pieces out, for the birthday boy always hands out the cake. And if they sort of closed their eyes and let the sugary bread run in with the frosting, it did taste like real cake. There wasn't but a dime's worth of difference between the two of them.

So it was that Lamar woke strangely happy the next morning. He had started scraping the house for its new coat of paint, but somehow he didn't feel like it. They all needed to chill after the rush of the robbery. It would be a good day to take it easy. He wanted to check the far field, which Ruta Beth said her daddy had once dreamed of planting with alfalfa, but he wasn't quite sure if he wanted to plan that far ahead. It would be a shame to start something so ambitious and then have to let it go for one reason or another. Odell was up watching the early morning cartoons on the TV, which he never missed, and Ruta Beth was messing around in the kitchen. Richard was still sleeping, of course.

So Lamar went out to the creek that ran between Ruta Beth's and the McGillavery's place. He was trying to think of another job. A job that would light up Oklahoma like the goddamned Fourth of July. But it was hard with this crew. They'd just managed to skip by on the Denny's and had been lucky, as that goddamned TV nigger had said; suppose that damned woman had hit him, instead of missing? It was probably Richard's scream that made her miss. Richard wasn't much good at nothing, but the scream had helped probably more than it had hurt. Lamar didn't like to think how close he'd come to buying the ranch, even with a little .380. Goddamn, old Ruta Beth had been faster than Odell on the return fire. Wasn't she a peach?

But—what kind of a new job were they capable of? You needed a really hard crew to bring off something fancy. Richard could drive, he and Odell could handle the heavy stuff, and Ruta Beth could tail-gun. That was about all that was available. He now saw that going in without leaving someone in the car was a big mistake. Almost got them all killed. So he tried to think of something they could do. Another Denny's? Nah. Maybe a grocery market or the big PX at Fort Sill. Or what about something that nobody had ever done—say, a whole mall? Wouldn't that be something: the whole goddamned thing! Or a rodeo? Had anyone ever robbed a rodeo? What about one of them casinos the Indians had built on their tribal property. Or a high-stakes bingo game?

Lamar sat back, dreaming of the glory of it all, mightily pleased. So much was possible. Two months ago he'd been just another con in the grim hole of the Mac with nothing to look forward to except trying to hold on to what he had. Now look: He had a family! He had a family! He hadn't worked it out just yet, but if they could do two or three more scores, big ones, then maybe they could lie low. Maybe buy a camper and go to Florida or something. Lamar had never seen Florida. He had an image of beaches and water and palm trees. He could imagine Odell splashing in the water and Richard drawing and Ruta Beth just staring at him in that hard way she had, as if she were trying to suck his soul out of him through her eyes. How that girl could stare! Anyhow, he imagined them happy, happy always.

Come the middle of the afternoon, he got to feeling thirsty and thought how nice one of those ice-cold Coca-Colas Ruta Beth kept in the fridge would taste, and so he decided to head on in. He was a man very much at peace with himself and ready to face the world when he rounded the corner of the barn and saw a truck coming down the driveway toward the house.

Bud pulled up in front of the house. He heard no dogs barking; strange, because most of these farm places had dogs. But the Stepfords never did, either. Bud felt a little buzz from somewhere, he wasn't sure where. It was like that time a week or so ago on the reservation; just a sense of being watched.

He picked up the mike.

"Dispatch, I am ten–twenty-three the Tull Farm, off 54 east of Altus."

"That's ten-four, six-oh-five, we have you."

"Listen here, Dispatch, got me a feeling. Want you to run the name Tull through records real fast, see if anything kicks out."

"Ten-four, six-oh-five. You hang in there."

"Ten-four."

Bud sat for a minute or two in the heat. Usually, you pulled into a farmyard, the Mrs. came out to see what was going on, or one of the hands leaned out of the barn or something. But it was just quiet. He could hear the slow tick of the truck cooling. An old farmhouse lay before him and beyond, in the emptiness, the Wichitas, standing out like boulders. The wind snapped; sunflowers along the red dirt road bobbed and weaved in its force. A cicada began to saw away like a lumberjack.

He looked back at the house. These people hadn't given up: someone had commenced scraping to prepare the wood for new paint, though the job was at rest now. Still, it spoke of hope for the future. Looking around, he saw the fields were fallow, but they didn't look grown out. Hard work: hard as hell. Bud had worked farms when he was a young man, between classes at Oklahoma U. before he had to drop out, and he'd hated it. There was no harder way to make a living than to pull it out of the earth with your own two hands.

"Six-oh-five?"

"Ten-four, Dispatch."

"Ah, we have nothing on Tull in our records. I did do a cross-check and it seems some years back a Mr. and Mrs. Tull, that address, were killed, but there's nothing in the records to indicate adjudication in the case."

Maybe that was it. The feeling of death, heavy in the air; the way it sinks into the wood. A farm couple, murdered. Nothing in the records to suggest the culprit had been caught. Seemed eerily familiar, but he couldn't place it.

"Okay, thanks, Dispatch. I'm going in. Wait for my ten–twenty-four."

"Wilco, six-oh-five. Good hunting."

Bud touched his three guns: the big new Beretta under his arm, the Colt on his right kidney, and the little Beretta .380 inside his shirt. Okay, he thought, time to go.

Lamar watched the man climb out of the truck. He knew he was a cop from the long time he'd spent on a radio in the cab. Now the man got out, looked around, set his hat just right, yet still paused, checking. Cautious bastard.

Lamar had sunk into the high grass. He didn't move a muscle. Then the cop came around the truck, still looking, and by God, Lamar thought he'd fall through the earth itself. It was that goddamned trooper sergeant, the one he thought he'd smoked at the Stepfords, big as life!

Pewtie, that was it. Pewtie. Oh, ain't you a tough bastard your own self? Pewtie was big and had that flat cop face, weathered and serene, that just drank in every damn thing. Lamar had seen that goddamned face a hundred times.

But now it was time to think. What's he doing here? What's he up to? Is it a raid? Goddamn no, there'd be SWAT people and FBI and choppers and OSBI hot dogs all over the goddamned place. This Pewtie was here on his own.

Lamar wished he had a gun on him and told himself he'd never again be without one. He thought of his two .45s upstairs in the bedroom, freshly cleaned, each with a magazine of glinting shells in it. But he also knew if he'd had a gun, he'd have drawn and fired and, no matter what, Pewtie's 10-23 would have brought the boys here soon enough.

Then he thought of a new problem. What happens if he sees poor Odell? He'll know him in an instant. He'll draw and shoot and poor baby Odell will just go down, spitting blood out with his Frosted Mini-Wheats. Or Richard? He would recognize Richard, too, for he'd have that cop gift for memorizing a face off a bulletin, able to pull it up at a moment's notice.

We are fucked, he thought. If he sees them two, we are fucked. If I kill him now, if I can, then maybe we're not fucked so fast, but we are fucked.

Best thing that could happen?

Ruta Beth.

Come on, Ruta Beth honey. You got to get us out of this.

* * *

Bud looked around one more damned time. He could see nothing in the yard that seemed the slightest bit out of place. He decided just to get the goddamned thing over with.

He walked toward the house. A ladder leaned against it, and Bud could see the line where the paint scraping had halted. Whoever did the work knew what he was doing; the old paint was scraped off down to bare wood slicker than a whistle. Maybe they did it with a machine or something, but it just looked like hard work to him, the old-fashioned kind. No job for a slacker, that was for sure.

He climbed up on the porch. From inside he heard the sounds of the television, a cartoon show for children. That was good, too. Kids meant family meant probably not escaped-convict armed robbers and killers. Now he was feeling pretty good. He knocked on the door.

He heard some rustling inside, but he wasn't sure what it was. At last, the door opened and a chalky-faced young woman stared at him. Her wide eyes were dark as coal, and she wore her dark hair pulled back in a long ponytail. She was in jeans and a nondescript print blouse, sleeves pushed up. She fixed a glare on him, which might have been fear and might have been hate.

"Miss Tull?"

"Yes I am," she said. "If you're here to sell me something, I don't need nothing."

"No ma'am," he said, and took out his ID folio with its golden State of Oklahoma shield. "My name's Russell Pewtie; I'm an investigator for the state highway patrol."

"I ain't done nothing wrong," she said.

"I'm not saying you have, ma'am. It's just that we're investigating a crime and we may have a lead in a tire-tread mark so we know what kind of car it is. Your car fits the profile. I just want to take a look at it so I can cross you off my list and get on to the serious business.''

"Ah—" she said. Was it a look of panic in her eyes? Bud began to pick up a sense of disturbance.

"Ma'am, if you'd like to call the family lawyer and have him come on out or something?"

"I don't have no family lawyer."

"Well, ma'am, I'd be happy to wait until you called someone. If you like, I can give you the number of Legal Aid and they can either supply or recommend a lawyer. But no charges are pending against you, Miss Tull. We just want to account for these cars so by process of elimination we come down to ones we can't explain. Those are probably our boys.''

"Okay. Sure, it's—sorry, I'm just not used to policemen.''

"I understand. Wouldn't be natural if you were, ma'am.''

She stepped outside. In a flash glimpse, he saw a kitchen and through a hall and two doors, the blue TV glow.

"Your son, ma'am?"

"What? Oh, the TV? No, I just like to leave it on. It keeps me company.''

"You live alone?"

"I do. Since Mother and Daddy died, I've been here by myself.''

"I see. You're having some work done?"

"Yes. Got tired of looking at the old dead paint. Hired some men to clean it up and paint it. But then they got another job, so they ran off to do it. Said they'll be back, but you know how hard it is to find quality work these days.''

It seemed to hang together, but Bud was wondering: *Why is she so nervous?*

* * *

Lamar watched as the trooper ID'd himself to Ruta Beth and began to gull her into something.

Would she be smart enough? Would she make some stupid mistake? Goddamn, how could they have tracked him? He had been so careful, he had thought it out a step at a time, sometimes staying up all night just worrying his way through it. What could he have done wrong?

He looked this way and that. Odell must be still camped in front of the tube: if you didn't give that boy an order, he'd be content to sit there like a bump on a log from June till November. Richard was the goddamned problem. Richard could bumble in at any moment and start to cry. The cop would recognize him, it would all fall apart.

It came down to this: Lamar *hated* the idea that the trooper sergeant he'd caught so flatfooted a month and a half ago would be the one to bring him down. He saw the stories now, for he knew how they thought: The newspapers and the TV would turn it all personal, they'd make this lucky motherfucker into the greatest goddamned detective since Dick Motherfucking Tracy! He, Lamar, would be the goat!

Lamar's anger ruptured like a boiler exploding. He felt his muscles begin to tense and the blood begin to sing in his ears.

Be careful, he told himself. *You get mad, you make a goddamned mistake.*

He tried to clear his mind in order to figure out choices. Maybe he could double around, get into the house by the back way, get to a gun, and just blow the fucker away. But . . . that would take minutes. It might come apart before then, and he'd be stuck in the fields out back, while Bud Pewtie blew away Odell and Richard and called for backup.

What would Pewtie do? Would he go in the house or was he after something else?

Suddenly, Ruta Beth stepped outside, closing the door after her, and the two of them began the long walk to the barn.

Lamar slithered backward, a snake, then plunged into the darkness of the barn and began to look about for some kind of weapon. Then he saw it: the ax he'd used to split logs. He had it up in a second, and slid into a pool of darkness inside the door, dead still, not hardly breathing. The ax had killing weight to it. If he got just the smallest break, he'd be on Pewtie like the night. One swipe and it would be over.

"This must be that shoot-out in Texas," she said. "It's so terrible what them men did. Why do people have to be so cruel?"

"Ma'am, I've been a police officer for nearly twenty-five years, and the truth is, I don't know. Four thousand dollars. Couldn't buy nothing with that."

But as he was talking, Bud was looking all about. Something still didn't sit right with him. Her nerves, the idea of leaving a television on just to hear it. Why not a radio?

"I keep it out back by my wheel," she said.

"Beg pardon?"

"Wheel. I am by profession a potter. I turn clay on a wheel. Then I paint it and glaze it and bake it in a kiln. I can make pret' near anything by now. Then I go to craft shows on the weekend. It isn't much, but it's a living."

"Well, that's nice. Funny, I met all kinds but I don't believe I met a potter before."

"I'd be pleased to give you a pot, Mr. Pewtie."

"Well, that's kind of you, ma'am. I think I'll just get it checked off and be out of your way."

"Gits kind of lonesome out here, that's why I'm talking up such a storm."

"I can appreciate it."

They walked through the barn and out back to her work area. Her potter's wheel stood under a lean-to, the coal-fired kiln next to it, and on her bench were several cans of paint and her pots. They blazed with color. She seemed to be doing some imitation Indian thing with them, but they were better than any pottery he'd seen in the reservation shops. The colors were jagged, almost savage, and stood off the ocher like blood pouring from a wound.

"My," he said, impressed, "you are a hell of a potter. Those things are beautiful."

"Why, thank you, Officer," she said modestly.

And then he turned to the car.

Lamar watched as she boldly led him toward the barn. *Beautiful, sweetie, beautiful,* he was thinking.

He could have pounced at any second, and in his mind he thrilled at the prospect of it. That was what he was addicted to: the hot fun of the violence. He saw himself really getting his weight into it and bringing that blade whanging down into the trooper's bull neck. What a wound it would open! The meat would splay open, red and pulsing, maybe a sliver of bone would show. There'd be more goddamned blood than you could shake a stick at. Pewtie would turn, stunned, unbelieving, and his eyes would lock onto Lamar's and beg for mercy, and he'd weakly raise his hands, but Lamar, with his great iron-pumper's strength, would bring the ax down again and again in a rain of killing blows. It excited Lamar. He wanted to do it so bad!

They paused to gab a bit at her workbench, and the cop said something that Lamar didn't catch. But when the cop started to examine the car, Lamar slid through the darkness and got almost within spitting distance. He could lunge out now at any instant and take the man down. His hand tightened and loosened on the ax shaft and he tried to control his excitement and think through the red rage that clouded his brain so that he could figure out the right thing. Hell, maybe he should just do it and to hell with it.

But he waited.

"Hah," said Bud.

He stood up, a little disappointed. The old, once-red Tercel lay blistering in the sun. Its plaid interior had faded, and was anyway jammed with blankets. Spots of rust flaked the left rear fender, and the rear bumper also looked rotted out a bit.

Then he leaned back again, looking at the escutcheon on the old tire. Slowly he walked around, one by one, looking at them.

Nope! Goddammit, nope.

The tires were old, all right, but they were Bridgestones, not Goodyears.

For some reason, he'd just had a suspicion this one might be the one, the woman's nervousness, the isolation, the anomalies of the TV and the hard male work put into the place.

"Well, thanks very much, Miss Tull. I see I can scratch your name off the list. No ma'am, I don't believe you shot up any Denny's restaurants lately."

"Not in this lifetime, at any rate," she said with a little laugh.

Bud disengaged abruptly from the situation. It was of no more interest to him.

"Well, I'll be getting out of your hair now. Have to get over to Granite."

"Sure, Mr. Pewtie. Now, I can't interest you in one of them pots?"

Bud looked back. One of them really did leap out at him: ocher glaze, black diagonals, and a bright orange sunburst, like the end of a world.

"Could you sell me one?"

"I get fifteen dollars for the small ones and twenty-five for the big ones."

Ouch! Not cheap.

"But I'll tell you what. Your choice, ten bucks."

"Hell, that's a bargain if ever I heard of one."

Fortunately the pot he chose wasn't a big one, so he forked over the ten without feeling terribly greedy. He didn't as a rule like to take little extras with the badge but hell . . . once in a while didn't hurt a thing.

She fetched the pot, brought it to him, and the two of them walked back through the barn to his truck.

"Come on back," she said. "I enjoy visitors."

"Thanks, Miss Tull. Good luck to you."

He got in.

Now if they were just lucky a little bit longer. If Odell or Richard didn't come walking out of the house.

Lamar watched from the pool of shadow behind the barn door. His heart was thumping. Pewtie was too far away to get with the ax now. It was in the hands of God.

He diddled with the car a bit, picked up his radio, and called in what Lamar assumed was his 10-24—task completed—and then with majestic leisure started the truck. It took him another minute to back out of the yard and then three more minutes to pull down the dirt road to the macadam, take a left, and then disappear.

There seemed to be a long pause in the day. Lamar found that he was doused with sweat. Unlike the race out of

Denny's he didn't feel exhilaration; he just felt the total numbing meltdown of shock that attends survivors of near-death experiences. He didn't like it a bit.

He looked up. Ruta Beth came out of the house, almost in a daze. She cupped her hands as if she were about to call to him.

"No," he said, loud, but not a shout. "Don't call. Don't look left or right. Just mosey into the barn, in case."

At that moment Odell opened the door, looked out in confusion.

"Odell, stay where you are. No, wait—and make sure the shotguns is loaded. Keep Richard in the house."

Odell nodded and ducked back in.

Eventually, Ruta Beth came on over.

"You was in the barn the whole time."

"I was. One silly move out of that boy and I'd have cut him open with this ax."

"He had two guns. I saw them both. One under his coat, the other in his belt."

"Probably had more, goddamn," said Lamar. "That boy was loaded for bear. The car. It was the car he wanted to see, honey?"

"Yes it was, Daddy."

"Tell me 'xactly what he asked. 'Xactly. I have to know the words."

Numbly, Ruta Beth reiterated Bud's explanation.

"I see," said Lamar, concentrating mightily. "He said he had to 'check it off.' They still use that old one?"

"That's what he said, Daddy."

"Now, honey, you think real hard. Tell me the whole talk. Not just what he said, but what you said. I have to know if you said something that gave too much away and a sly old dog like him might sniff it out."

Laboriously, she recreated the conversation, now and

then prodded by Lamar's insistent probing. It went on for ten minutes. But then she said, "I tried hard, Lamar. I didn't do nothing on purpose."

"Honey, you done great. See, he caught us in a mistake. We should have stories prepared. Last thing you ever want to do is try and be making stuff up as you go along. Trip up too easy. No ma'am, got to have your story straight up front, got to have it worked out and tested, that's how you do that kind of work. Goddamn, Ruta Beth, I must say, you got to be some kind of *natural* at that kind of work."

"Have you figured it out? Why he was here?"

Lamar thought a little harder, and then he had it.

"Tires," he said. "That was soft dust this side of the Red. Sure enough we left tracks in it. They must have got a good tire print and the F-fucking-B-I done 'em the models of cars them tires could fit. So they're just wading through the DMV listings, hoping to turn up the right car with the right tires and the right fucking boys. They're so goddamn worried, they even got old Bud Pewtie, his hide so full of buckshot still he can't hardly walk, out doing shitbird work."

He was laughing now. He saw the joke in it.

Ruta Beth stared at him in horror.

"But Lamar," she said. "They was right. I got them tires two years ago when they was marked down because the tire place said Goodyear had discontinued the line and they just wanted to reduce inventory."

"Not *them* tires, no ma'am. Night of the party, I went out, remember? Goddamn, I got to thinking about the ways we could slip up and only one I hadn't covered was the goddamn tires. I swapped 'em with Bridgestones I lifted off a Hyundai Excel. Hah! Old Bud Pewtie thinks he's so goddamn smart. He ain't as smart as no Lamar Pye."

CHAPTER
20

On the final day, Bud tried to make it last longer. He dawdled, he examined each car with microscopic attention, he wouldn't disengage from conversations, he just let it drift. But still it ended. He pulled down the driveway of a farm all the way over near Healdton in Jefferson County. The sun was a huge pink balloon sinking through wavering atmospheric phenomenon, and the twilight was still and windless. He looked each way as he pulled onto the road, and saw the black band of the highway stretching in a straight shot toward a blank horizon.

Okay, that's it.

"Dispatch, six-oh-five, do you copy?"

"Six-oh-five, over. What's your situation?"

"Ten–twenty-four on the O'Brian location."

"Nothing to report, Bud?"

"No, Dispatch. Nada, zilch, negative. Anybody get anything?"

"That's a big negative, six-oh-five. Lots of disappointment at this end. Best git yourself home now, Bud."

"Thanks, Dispatch. Ten-four and out."

Bud clicked the radio off. In two weeks he'd gotten to

know Dispatch a little, a retired Tillman deputy sheriff, another good old boy like himself, steady and salty. In a sense he wanted to please Dispatch as much as himself or Lt. C. D. Henderson or Colonel Supenski. But it wasn't to be. The joint task force, in two weeks, had called on close to four thousand addresses in the Southern Oklahoma region, and located close to four thousand Toyota Tercels, Hyundai Excels, and Nissan Sentras in the proper model years. Of these, over eight hundred had worn the Goodyear tires; each owner had been investigated and either cleared or interviewed at length. Some fourteen were put under surveillance, which had itself yielded nothing. Meanwhile, joint Highway Patrol–OSBI raiding teams had entered the domiciles of close to two hundred former or currently wanted felons who owned the proper car. Again, nothing, although the lieutenant himself said they'd served warrants on and apprehended over twenty-eight fugitives from justice in the process.

Bud himself had been to over 230 domiciles in the past two weeks, working twelve, fourteen, and sometimes sixteen hours a day, roaming the back country roads of the southernmost five counties. Some nights he hadn't even come home but had checked into truck-stop motels for a few hours' ragged sleep, and one night he'd just climbed into a sleeping bag and slept under the shelter of the open tailgate. Oddly, it had been his best sleep.

He tried to think it all over as he headed back to Lawton, to turn in the radio and see what the hell to do next, if there was a next. Goddamn Lamar, smart as a whip. All them brains spent on defeating the law, and completely unyoked to any moral compass. He could have been a doctor, a goddamned lawyer, with brains like that. But he spent all that time just figuring out one thing: how to get away with it. He wasn't your ''criminal genius,'' like the movies had it, sleek and cosmopolitan with a taste for fine wine, and maybe his IQ wasn't the kind that tests could measure. But he was a smart boy.

Tiredly, he turned on the AM radio to KTOK, the Oklahoma City all-news station, and listened to the numb recitation of the world and the region's events, from what the president had done on down to what happened in the Oklahoma City council that day.

And soon enough, he got the bad news.

"In Lawton, highway patrol and OSBI authorities today called off a statewide dragnet for the car they believed was used by escaped convict Lamar Pye and his gang in the May 16 robbery and shooting spree in Wichita Falls, Texas, which left four law enforcement officers and two civilians dead."

We'll just have to wait for you to strike again, Lamar, Bud thought. *And this time, I know you'll make a goddamned splash and a half.*

"In a related development, Lawton school officials revealed today that a Lamar Pye 'cult' appears to be growing and gaining strength in Lawton high schools, elevating the escaped convict and armed robber into a folk hero. At Lawton West last night, vandals defaced the school gym with 'Long Live Lamar' and 'Go Lamar' graffiti. Superintendent Will C. Long said—" The superintendent's voice came on the air: "It's a symptom of the moral limbo in which all too many of our children are raised that some of them would consider a Lamar Pye a hero."

Shit!

That really got to Bud!

It was like these goddamned kids today. They thought it was funny or cool when somebody stood over a poor policeman and blew his brains out or caught him coming out of the men's room with his hands wet and blew him away with a blast of double-ought.

The news put Bud in a black funk, a near rage. It made him wish he was a drinking man still, and he felt like pulling over to the next bar he found and chasing his anger away.

Instead, he drove on as the darkness increased, changing to a C-W station, whose jangly rhythms soothed him some. And then he knew he had to call Holly again. It just came like that and he didn't bother to fight it at all.

He found a pay phone by a convenience store the other side of Oil City. He had to call collect because he didn't have enough change.

"Well, howdy, stranger," she said. "I thought you'd dropped off the earth."

"Been looking at three-year-old Toyotas, just like a real detective. How are you?"

"Bud, I'm okay. How're you?"

"Honey, I'm outta Toyotas, that's how I am, and I'm missing you something kind of bad."

"A likely story."

"Only the truth."

"You ain't had sex in awhile. That's what it is."

"No ma'am, that ain't what it is. I miss Holly. She's a peach. Now I don't think I'm gonna be doing a thing tomorrow. You and me were going to look at places."

"Oh, Bud. I thought you'd forgot."

"No ma'am. Be over 'round ten."

"Bud, I was looking through the want ads. I found a house to rent. I want you to see it so bad."

"Ten o'clock?"

"Oh, Bud, I love you so much!"

Now why did I go do that, he said to himself when he hung up. *Back in It all over again.*

* * *

Bud woke the next morning to a dilemma: since he was only going house hunting with Holly, did he need his three guns? The answer seemed clear but wasn't. It might seem to be "No." But if he didn't put the guns on, then Jen would surely know he wasn't headed off on police business. Still, the prospect of walking into strangers' houses with a smile on his face and three automatic pistols on him wasn't pleasing either.

That's how it was. In this business you were always thinking, figuring angles, trying to work your way two or three jumps ahead. You always had your lies prepared up front because you didn't want to improvise under pressure, where you'd surely start contradicting yourself and anyone with half a brain could unravel your tale. It was like living in enemy territory all the time.

Goddamn, turning me into Lamar Pye, he thought as, after his shower, he put himself into the rigmarole of slipping into the holsters, loading the guns and magazines, every last thing, including the little Beretta .380, which felt as if, over the days, it was going to wear a hole in his belly.

"I may give up on this goddamned .380," he called to Jen as he slipped the gun into an open button and down behind his belt at just the right angle so that it didn't give him too much difficulty.

But she didn't answer. Grim again.

"Okay," he called, "I'm going."

She came around the corner and fixed him with a glare.

"Anyways, where you off to? I thought they called the search off."

"Well, they did," he said—sliding into his lie, not looking quite at her. That was what a good liar could do: look you straight in the eyes and sell you the Tallahatchie Bridge. Not Bud; he sort of let his vision dawdle into the middle distance—"but I got some paperwork to do, and I don't want that damned lieutenant thinking any the less of me. I can't do a thing to impress him. I'll just mosey down to the Annex, check some things, diddle around, be back by mid-afternoon."

"I don't see why you have to go today. You've been gone for the best part of two weeks."

"I have a *job* to do," he said. "Let me do my *job,* all right?"

She reacted as if she'd been slapped, which in a way she had, as well as lied to straight up. With a bitter expression, she retreated, and then said, "Russ hears today. If the news is good, you should be here for him and we should take him out to celebrate."

"Would he go out with us, though? He just sits up there reading."

"We have to try."

"Should I go up and say good luck to him?"

"He's sleeping. Jeff's gone but Russell doesn't have classes until ten today."

"Okay. I'm sorry I yelled at you. This thing has me down."

"It certainly does," Jen said, numbly.

"I'll see you."

He gave her a brief kiss, and went out and climbed into his truck.

He drove, by a roundabout way, to Holly's.

He parked and went in. It was just that simple. One woman, and then the other, without so much as a how-do-you-do.

"Oh, don't you look like a stud, Bud. Bet I know what you want!"

"Holly, I got all these goddamned guns on me. Getting out of 'em is harder than getting out of my boots."

"Well, I guess you'd rather play with them than me, Bud," she teased, but he answered in earnest.

"I just put on this shoulder holster. It's a pain to get out of and back on adjusted just right."

"Okay, Bud. Have it your way. You may never get another chance."

But she was dressed herself and only teasing him. She looked so damned cute today he could hardly stop himself from wanting her. Who wouldn't want such an attractive young woman with all that spunk and that way she had of poking fun at everything? When he was with her, every other damned thing seemed to go away. It just felt so normal.

They stopped for coffee at an out-of-the-way place and then drove on to the first of her addresses, a small place in a nicely kept neighborhood on Sixteenth Street, a block or so down from Lee Boulevard near the south side of town. The lady who owned it was waiting for them, a wispy, white-haired old bat. She took up with Holly right away, all but ignoring Bud, as though she sensed his true irrelevance to what lay before them and started gossiping with Holly like a daughter.

Bud awkwardly put his big hand with his wedding ring on it behind him, in a back pocket that pulled his jacket back, and walked up the walk behind the two ladies, feeling left out but also so strange. He now had to face it, the part of It that had left him acutely uncomfortable all these late weeks. It was this "house-hunting" thing. Why had he agreed to it, except out of stupidity and sloth? It felt like such a violation. Actually going into another home, looking at it and imagining a life in it, while a few miles away a wife and sons went about their business, completely unaware of the betrayal that was being planned coldly against them by their sworn protector.

Bud shook his head. He climbed the porch, looked at the blooming dark void that lay before him, into which the ladies had disappeared, then swallowed and followed.

A young family had lived here, he saw in an instant. The place stank of young kids—the way they piss, the way they smear their food on everything, their warmth, their noise, their considerable odors. It was now empty, but on the cheap carpeting were the stains of baby food and spilled milk and weewee. Here and there on the walls was a smear of pudding or a dried stalk of broccoli.

"See what a nice sunroom," the lady was saying. "The Holloways said they used it as a family room."

Bud looked at the small, windowed-in back porch, which smelled of mildew.

"Who lived here?" he asked suddenly.

"Sergeant Holloway and his family. He was transferred to Germany and Rose and the boys went with him, though I don't think she was too happy about it."

"Be good for kids to see a foreign country, though," Bud said. "Mine never did."

But he was thinking: another sergeant's home. Some goddamned fool for duty, giving his whatever to some bigger outfit, doing well enough but not truly well.

He looked around, sensing the other sergeant.

"Was he an artilleryman, ma'am?" he asked, wanting just one more detail somehow.

"No, I believe he was a military policeman, though with an artillery battalion. The whole battalion deployed to Germany."

Bud nodded, looked around. Another cop!

He listened as the two women clambered up the steps. When they were gone to the upstairs, he poked a head in the kitchen. It was small, colored yellow, with flowers on the wallpaper, and all the appliances looked scratchy and sticky. The linoleum was worn where the kitchen table had been, and a bulletin board was literally riddled with hundreds of puncture marks where various family documents must have been hung. He had one in his kitchen, too.

He sat there, imagining the shouts of children, maybe the bustling of the woman in the kitchen, trying to make a good meal without a lot to work with. And where would the sergeant be? Yes, in the living room, plunked down on the sofa, watching the goddamned football game. How many times had such a drama played out in his own house? And now and then Jen would come out and yell, "You boys be quiet, your daddy's watching the football game" or "Your daddy's trying to sleep." Had she hated him for it? Had she resented it? You saw things like that all the time: the woman just finally saying to hell with it and sinking a butcher knife in the husband's chest, or getting out the deer rifle and nailing a .30-30 through him, or soaking him in hot grease. Had Jen ever wanted to do that?

He thought of Jen as she'd been when he'd met her, all those years ago. The prettiest woman he'd ever seen, and when she'd returned a few of his shy smiles, he'd hardly known what to do. She'd stood by her man, too. She waited for him his first two long years in the air force and married him then, spending the first two years of marriage in a tiny apartment on his sergeant's salary outside the Pope AFB in North Carolina, where he'd finished up as an air policeman. She'd gone with him when he went back to school, and when he decided to join the troopers instead of staying the course, feeling too old among all those kids, she'd said fine, and made do with a trainee's salary, and then a Trooper First Class's salary, the long years at a corporal's salary when, even though he'd passed the sergeant's exam, others with seniority or connections got the job. She'd had the kids and done the crap work, and gradually took over everything he didn't like doing, like the checkbook, the taxes, the PTA meetings. She always managed a part-time job. She never made a big point over how much more money her daddy had than he was able to make, and if she was disappointed in the life that Bud had built for them all those years rolling up and down Oklahoma's highways, she never let it show. She'd worked like hell out of commitment to a man and some idea of a family. Was it her fault she'd put on weight and the years had drained her face of joy and her conversation of everything except a sullen, sometimes bitter, irony?

Suddenly an overwhelming melancholy came over Bud. He couldn't take it anymore: the teeming, swarming sense of family in the old house. The sense of a sergeant, his wife, the children, no money, and the struggle to hold it all together in some way. He turned and went out to the front porch, where a beat-up sofa sat, like a throne from which to view the neighborhood. He put himself down on the arm and took in great draughts of air. That helped somewhat. For a second there, he'd felt like he was going to puke. He wondered if he wasn't coming down with something, and ran a hand across his brow only to have it come away damp.

All your systems breaking down, you old fool, he told himself.

He had a sudden urge to just bolt. Just get the hell out of there. To hell with Holly and this nonsense about the house. Nothing would make him feel sweeter than to put some distance between himself and Holly and the damned old biddy and run on back to Jen. If he confessed, got it off his chest, maybe he could get his marriage and his family back. *Do it. Do it* now*!*

But he didn't do that either. He sat there for a time, looking up and down the quiet street: trees, small homes, a few kids out and about.

"Bud? Bud, honey? Could you come up here?"

Bud turned and went upstairs, where three small bedrooms and a john lay off the short hall.

"Bud, Mrs. Ryan says we could knock down one of these walls and make the two littler bedrooms into one big one."

Now why would they want to do that? If his boys came, he'd want them to have a place to stay and some room, even if it was small.

"You could turn it into your office, honey," she said.

"Yeah," he said.

"My fiancé is a highway patrol officer," Holly explained to the woman.

"I'm glad you're a law officer. I seen that gun on your backside. I thought maybe you were that awful Lamar Pye."

"I'm no Lamar Pye," he said, "though I've spent considerable time looking for him."

"He's a terrible man," said the woman. "My daughter lives in Wichita Falls and I've eaten many Sunday breakfasts in that restaurant. I think it's terrible what he did. I hope you-all catch up to him and kill him dead. I'd hate to see him go to court and some fool decide he was the true victim in all this."

"We'll get him," Bud said.

"Bud, honey, Mrs. Ryan says she'd let us have the house for only three-fifty a month. We could move in right away. It would be so wonderful. It's a nice quiet neighborhood."

Bud smiled, and said, "Holly, we've only begun looking. Don't you think you ought to see some other places?"

"Yes, honey," said Mrs. Ryan. "Your fiancé is right. You should see a lot of places, so you don't feel you've rented in a panic. I've seen too much of that."

"You don't have any other prospects?"

"No, I don't, honey. You take your time."

"Don't we have other houses to see today, honey?"

"Yes. Okay, I'll call you later in the week, Mrs. Ryan. Thank you so very much."

They walked to the truck and got in.

"Now, let's see," Holly said. "I think this next one—"

"Holly, can we just hold off on this? We saw a house today, it was fine, don't we want to think this thing through a bit?"

"Bud!"

"I just—I don't know, Holly, it just suddenly didn't feel right to me. You could move into that house by Friday. And what then? I might not be ready for—well, I don't know."

"Bud!"

"And Holly—my God, that woman was talking about Lamar Pye, who shot and killed your husband. Blew his brains out. And you didn't even blink an eye. You just went ahead with your question about if the house was available. This boy killed your husband, damned near killed me, and killed a mess of poor folks. You got to have some response. You can't be human and not."

"Well, aren't you Mr. High and Mighty? I didn't notice you getting solemn about Mr. Lamar Pye the last time you had me every which way from Sunday. You didn't give a *damn* about Lamar Pye then, or about Ted Pepper either."

"Holly, I'm only saying—"

"Bud, I *have* to get out of that trailer."

"I'm sorry, Holly."

Her face knit up in a small flinch of pain.

"Oh, Bud, I just want a house of my own. Please. You don't have to move in. Just help me move. Please."

"Holly."

"Please. I ain't saying you have to move in. But—you'll have a place."

"Holly."

"Just say yes, Bud. Just on this one thing. Think of the fun we'd have up there." Fun was her word for sex.

"Oh, Holly—if it makes you happy."

She squealed in delight and gave him a big kiss. Then she ran off to tell Mrs. Ryan.

After a lunch, he dropped Holly off and drove quickly to the Annex so that he could see it and feel it and know what was going on and in that way his lies to Jen about having spent the day there would be that much more authentic. He entered to find it all but empty. Dispatch manned the radio unit, but there was no traffic. A few clerks sat at their computer terminals listlessly, but none of the Ranger types were around.

"Any news?" Bud asked Dispatch.

"Not a thing, Bud. We going to have to wait for old Lamar to strike again, that's all, and hope we get luckier."

"I wonder how many he'll kill this time," Bud said.

"Bud, Bud, get your goddamn ass in here," came a scream from the inner office.

"What the hell is going on?" said Bud.

"You don't have to go in there, Bud. In fact, probably best not to. I ain't seen him so bad."

"Then I'm—"

"Bud, come in! Get in here, damn you!"

The words were slurred and desperate.

"Shit," said Bud, and headed in to discover the office a disaster, with paper, computer printouts, books everywhere. A paper cup sat before Lt. Henderson on the desk, and Bud could see that it was half full of amber fluid.

The old cop stared at him. He had one of those wrinkled prune faces under a thatch of hair, but now it was rosy with the power of bourbon. He reeked. His chin seemed to want to pitch forward as he fought for a bitter consciousness and blinked back the darkness.

"Bud, have a drink with me. Just one. Do both of us a world of good," he said, adding a sloppy and uncharacteristic smile.

"Can't say no to that," said Bud, and watched as the older man poured a couple of fingers' worth into another paper cup he pulled from his desk.

Bud tasted the whiskey. Fire and memory and buzz, all at once.

"That's a good drinking whiskey, Lieutenant."

"Bud, I think they're going to let me go."

"Lieutenant, I am sorry."

"Goddamn their black fucking hides. I give 'em close on forty years. Now I come up dry and it's enough to push old C.D. out the goddamned door."

"I'm sorry, Lieutenant."

"Sorry ain't got but piss to do with it," said the old man, pouring himself another shot and draining it with a gasp.

"It was my idea. Took a mess of convincing. All that overtime. Cost the state about five hundred thousand dollars but I told my boss and yours—and they told the governor—that it'd get 'em Lamar Pye."

"But it didn't."

The old detective stared into the grim space.

"What the hell did I do wrong? What did I miss?"

"Lieutenant, I'm not a detective. I'm a road cop, that's all."

"Dammit, Bud, there aren't any more detectives. I'm the last one. Your metro boys, your young Feebs, your Treasury agents or ATF boys—they're not detectives, not any of them. They're clerks. They do crime scene or they tap wire or they interview witnesses and take notes. But they don't do no goddamned detective work, not a one of them.''

The old man's head lolled forward and his lower lip hung loose. He seemed to breathe heavily through his mouth, and once again fought for consciousness. His eyes closed, but then like a lizard's peeped open again.

''You listen to my thought on this problem and tell me what I done wrong. Here's how I broke this sucker down. They always run to their own kind. They do. That's the first principle, sure as summer heat. No place he could go but into the criminal community. He's got to be somewhere, among folks who'd give him aid. We got the biker groups nailed, he ain't there. And we got the goddamned car-tire type. So, if we cross-reference, we come up with close to two hundred possibilities. He has to be there. *Has* to be. What did I miss?''

''Lieutenant, I don't know.''

''Did I miss a category? Felons, known informants, fences, criminal lawyers, anybody in the culture. What category could I have missed? What other category is there? That's what I believe I'm missing. I'm missing a category. Bud, you got any categories?''

''Lieutenant, as I said: This ain't my line of work.''

''See with Freddy Dupont, the missing category was *secondary experience*. That is, reading. That's what done it. So I'm missing a category, goddammit.''

''Lieutenant, I wish I had an idea.''

''See, it's points. You need two points to draw a line. One point: criminal community. Another point: the car-tire track. But . . . goddammit, nothing. I need a third point. Goddamn, a third point! A third category. Another drink, Bud?''

''Lieutenant, I got to get on home. I got a boy hearing about college today.''

"The baseball player?"

"No sir. The student."

"A ball player and a student. It sounds like a fine family, Bud."

"It is," said Bud.

The lieutenant took another hit from his paper cup, and the whiskey seemed to bring a tear to his old eyes, or maybe it was just that something blew into them. Anyway, he said, "Nope, never had kids myself. Just never had the damned time." Then suddenly he lit up and for a second his melancholy seemed to evaporate.

"Say, Bud," he said, "one of these days why don't you bring them boys over? Love to meet 'em. Bring 'em over to the house and we'll sit 'em down and give 'em their first drink. Best a boy learns to drink with his daddy and not out behind the woodshed. I won't have much to do hanging around the house. I'd like that, Bud."

Bud knew it was the drink talking, just as when he said, "That sounds like a damn fine idea, Lieutenant," he knew he'd never do it. It would be horrible: His two sons, who were already from different planets than their old fart of a father, locked in some strange little house with this bitter old coot who was from still another planet. It would never happen. Besides, he didn't think the old man really wanted it to happen either.

He checked his watch. It was nearly four. Damn, he was late.

"I ought to be going now, Lieutenant."

"You go, Bud. You done good work, all my boys done good work. I'd rise to shake your hand, but I pissed up my pants a few minutes ago and I'm too embarrassed to move."

"Oh, Lieutenant, I—"

"Don't pay it no nevermind," said the lieutenant. He

poured himself another drink, emptying the bottle, and threw the bottle into the wastebasket, where it shattered. Then he looked up and seemed surprised to see Bud still there.

"Go on, get out, get about your life!" he commanded darkly, and Bud hurried out.

"Bud," said Dispatch, "your wife called when you were in with the lieutenant. She wants you to call."

Thank God he was here when she called!

He found a phone.

"Sweetie, it's me."

"Bud, Russ got in. They're going to give him a full scholarship. He's going off to Princeton University!"

"All right! Hey, isn't that great!" Bud said. A surge of joy leaped in him. Something was turning out in his life!

"He'll have so many chances. He'll meet so many people. A whole new world will open for him!"

"That's great. I'll be home in a little bit and we'll go out, if that's what he wants."

"He said he would. He wants to see some friends later, but he'll go out."

"On my way!"

Russ deserved it. He'd worked hard at his studies and he was a very bright boy, the school counselors had told them.

It was in this mood that, as Bud drove home, he passed a large gray structure on Gore Boulevard, which he had passed perhaps five hundred times before; but for the first time, he noticed the lions.

CHAPTER 21

It was the fucking neck.

The key to the lion lay in its neck. Somehow, in the density of muscle and bone, in the knots of hair, in the fucking shortness of the structure, there lay the secret to that amazing regality, that kingly magnificence.

Yet Richard could not free it, not, that is, with a pencil or a crayon or any conventional drawing implement.

Lord how he had tried. Like popcorn puffs, his crumpled-up failures lay scattered about him in the upstairs room of Ruta Beth's farmhouse. He felt a killing headache. He could not get it: his beasts all had a strange tightness to them. He drew them in his sleep, he drew them in the air with an empty hand, he drew them in his mind, he drew them on paper, and he had never quite brought it off.

In fact, if he thought about it, his best lion had been done in the liquid medium of peanut butter. It was the image he'd crafted on the mock cake: something in the wet fluency of the material and the ease of its manipulation and the lack of pressure or expectation had freed him to really achieve the pure essence of lionhood. And his first dumb drawing in the Mac and maybe a doodle here and there, on a placemat, in the margins of a book or magazine, those, too, had had the freedom he needed.

You think too much, he thought. What had Conrad said? "Thinking is the great enemy of perfection." Boy had he gotten *that* one right!

Richard stood, yawned, trying to shake the tension from his back and neck and the weariness from his wrist. Lamar and Odell were out in the fields on some absurd agricultural project, Ruta Beth was behind the barn working at her fucking wheel. He was alone.

Of course it would help if Lamar had told him the point of the lion. Did he want a formal portrait? What was his thing about the lion, where would it go, what would it become? If he knew that, then maybe it would be better or easier. But Lamar wasn't saying; he was too sly. It was as if in some preliterate, instinctual way, Lamar knew it was wisest not to disclose this information. He wanted Richard to struggle and build the lion out of that struggle, rather than providing for him a neat little dedicated, purpose-built image. He was a tyrannical patron!

So: the lion.

What is the essence of the beast?

He was a hunter. He *hunted.* He roamed the savannah, took down the helpless, and stole their meat. He hunted to live.

But no—he also killed to live. The hunting wasn't the point, the hunting was only the rationale. Something in the lion loved to close in, enjoy the fear and the pain of the quarry, and experience that sublime moment when its spastic struggle ceased and its eyes went blank, and, bathed in the black torrents of its own blood, it passed into limp death. What a Godlike moment, what a sense of cosmic power, how thrilling!

Richard tried to find that impulse in himself. No such

luck. Knock-knock, who's there? Only us lambs. He shivered, disgusted. Such a thing did not exist for him. That's why it was hopeless.

He stood and restlessness stirred in his limbs. He suddenly ached for freedom. He needed to move. He began to roam through the upper story; not much, three bedrooms and a bathroom that Ruta Beth kept immaculate, especially with, as she put it, "three big, strong boys in the house." The toilet seat was down.

He wandered into the room Ruta Beth and Lamar shared. Again, it was farm- and convict-neat, the sign of people used to living to very high standards of imposed discipline. Yet you could look at it for a hundred years and never divine from its clues that a Lamar Pye, killer and robber and buttfucker, had taken up occupancy.

It titillated him a bit to be in Lamar's private space. The blood rushed to his head. He knew how the Angel Lucifer must have felt when he wandered into God's bedroom before his exile. For just a second he tried to imagine what it would be like to be Lamar, the Lion: to look upon all living things as prey, and to know with blood-boiling confidence that you had the magic power to drive them to the earth and rip their bloody hearts from them, to taste the hot blood and feel the weakening of their quivers as they slid into death.

He had to laugh. *Yeah, right.* The feeling was hopelessly counterfeit. It didn't belong to him. *Who are you trying to kid,* he wondered.

Then Richard noticed something: It was an envelope, manila, on the closet shelf hidden behind shoeboxes. It struck him as odd, for nowhere else in Ruta Beth's strange little house was there a hidden treasure.

Feeling just a little daring, Richard snatched the envelope, saw that it was stamped "Kiowa County Prosecutor's Office, March 15, 1983."

Now what the—

He opened the flap and reached inside.

There were two of them, green with age, in frozen copper postures of the hunt. Bud pulled to the side of the road and looked up at the building and saw what it was: the Harry J. Phillips Fine Arts Society.

Bud paused for a second, as an intriguing thought whispered through his mind. He glanced at his watch. Had some time. He decided, what the hell.

He got out, reached behind the seat, and removed his briefcase. Setting his Stetson right, he climbed the low concrete steps, pausing for a second to look at one of the lions close up. All the power and glory of its musculature stood capured in the art; the piece was an homage to the power of the lion, and even Bud felt a little thrill at looking at it.

He went inside, where it was dark and had the feeling of a cathedral, hushed and almost religious. A uniformed guard watched him come.

"Closing time is five P.M., sir," the guard said.

Bud flashed his badge.

"Looking for the head man. Who'd that be and how'd I find him?"

"Dr. Dickstein. He's the curator. Admin offices, down on the left."

"Thanks."

Bud walked down the corridor. He looked at the paintings. They made him feel insignificant. A few made no sense at all; others seemed like photographs of explosions. Now and then one would throw up an image so arresting it stopped him in his boots. But in time, he made it to the office of the curator and stepped inside to find a young man in shirtsleeves and wire glasses sitting at a computer terminal. He was one of those wiry boys, with great coils of hair, like electrified springs. He looked a little like Russ, Bud couldn't help thinking.

"Ah, excuse me."

"Can I help you?"

Bud pulled his badge.

"Sergeant Bud Pewtie, Oklahoma Highway Patrol. I'm looking for Dr. Dickstein. He in there?"

"Er, no. *I'm* Dr. Dickstein. Dave Dickstein. Sergeant, what can I do for you?"

God, they were growing them young these days! Bud immediately felt he'd screwed up, not getting that the guy who ran such a place could be so young.

"Sir, I was hoping you could give us some help."

"Well—" said the young man, some ambivalence leaking into his tone.

"You may have heard, we had three convicts break out of McAlester State Penitentiary a couple of months ago. Now they've set to armed robbery and they killed four policemen and two citizens a few weeks back."

"The TV's full of it."

"Sir, it seems that one of them was an artist. He studied art back East in Baltimore."

"Yes. I still don't—"

"Well, I have some of his drawings here. It turns out he likes to draw lions. Lions."

The young man looked Bud over intently.

"Sir, I'm no art expert," said Bud, "and the truth is I couldn't tell one joker artist from another. I can't even remember which one sawed off his ear. But I thought I might find an expert and have him look at the drawings. Maybe he'd see something I wouldn't. Maybe there's a meaning in them I just can't grasp. And somehow, maybe, I don't know, it would lead me another step of the way."

"Well," said Dr. Dickstein, "I did my Ph.D. on Renaissance nudes. That doesn't have much to do with lions. But I'd be happy to look at them. Did you see our lions, by the way, Sergeant?''

''Yes, sir, I did. That's what brought me in here.''

''Replicas of the lions outside the Chicago Art Institute. The lion has been a theme in romantic art for a thousand years. It usually represents male sexuality, particularly in the Romantic tradition.''

''These boys ain't so romantic.''

''No, I don't suppose they are,'' Dr. Dickstein said.

Richard slid out the photograph. He stared at it with some incomprehension; its details were exact and knowable but they had been arranged into a pattern that made no sense at all. He saw a bedroom slipper, a bedroom, a bed, two sleeping forms, a nice nightdress, a bathrobe.

Then he realized that the room in the photograph was the room he was at that moment in. And that the bed was the bed that still lay between the two windows, which Ruta Beth and Lamar now so placidly shared. In fact, the photographer had been standing almost exactly where Richard now stood, except that he had been perhaps three or four feet closer to the foot of the bed than Richard now was.

Involuntarily, Richard took the steps over the hardwood floor until he stood in the exact spot. He looked at the bed, which was ever so neatly made, so tidy, with a white bedspread with little rows of red roses on it. He looked at the wall above the bed, white and blank and formless.

He looked back in the picture. It was the same, except that the two people in the bed weren't sleeping, they were dead. Someone had fired something heavy—even Richard knew enough to suspect a shotgun—into them as they slept. The shells had destroyed their faces and skulls, and the inside of their heads, like fractured melons, lay open for all the world to see. Jackson Pollock at his most amphetamine-crazed had contaminated the wall: flung spray, spatter, gobbets of flesh, patches of skin, a whole death catalog of the contents of the human head displayed on that far wall, which was now so tidily cleaned up and repainted.

Richard felt woozy. Ruta Beth's parents, obviously; the tragedy she had so glumly and vaguely referred to in her letter was a murder. Someone had broken in and blown Mother and Daddy away. Ruta Beth had probably discovered them like this; that explained her weirdness, her craziness, her strange devotion to a man like Lamar who, whatever else, could protect her.

But . . . she stayed in the same house?

She slept in the same bed?

Richard shivered.

He looked back at the picture. Blood, blood everywhere, a carnivore's feast of blood, the triumph of the lion over its prey.

Something in him seemed to twitch or stir. He noticed that—good heavens!—he was getting an erection.

Quickly, he put the photograph back in the envelope and the envelope back where he had found it. He returned to his desk. The blood sang in his ears.

The lion. The lion.

His pencil flew across the page.

Bud opened his briefcase and spread the three drawings out on Dr. Dickstein's desk: the crude tracing he'd found among Lamar's prison effects, the drawing from the Stepfords, and the doodles on the placemat at the Denny's crime scene.

"He studied at a place called the Baltimore Institute. Is that good?"

"The Maryland Institute. It's a fine school," said Dickstein. "You know, this is very unusual. If you study the lives of artists, indeed you find violent and maladjusted men. But almost always their rage is directed at the self. The ear, you know, Van Gogh, that sort of thing. It's rare that they express their hostility to the world at large. I suppose they're too narcissistic."

"We ain't sure how much he's in command. He was celled with a tough lifer con, an armed robber by profession. Very powerful criminal personality. We think Richard just got sucked up in it. Lamar has a way of getting people to do what he wants. He's the real monster."

The young art doctor stared at the three drawings for a bit.

"This one isn't in his hand?"

"No. It was in an impression I found in a magazine that was in Lamar's possession in the pen."

"It's traced. The line is heavy, crude, and dead."

"I believe that's right. Never saw the original. It was etched in a *Penthouse*. The light caught it right and I brought it out myself."

"Yes. But clearly the original drawing is Richard's."

"Yes sir."

"Yes. I see commonality. And this, this one, it's the one he worked on the hardest."

"Yes sir. At the Stepfords'. They told me Lamar *ordered* Richard upstairs, to draw while looking out."

"So it was an assignment?"

"Yes sir."

"It represents . . . Lamar's view of himself?"

"Yes sir."

"Very roman—look, Sergeant, you don't have to call me sir. Dave would be fine. Everybody around here calls me Dave."

"Dave it is, then."

"Good. Anyway . . . it represents Lamar's view of himself. Men who think they're lions see themselves as powerful, kingly, sexually provocative, very romantic in their own eyes. Incredible unself-consious vanity. Typical criminal personality, I'd bet."

"Sounds pretty familiar."

"Yes, I thought it might. And . . . it doesn't quite work. I think you see in the second lion something studied, perhaps too 'cute.' The first one is much cruder, but it's much better. Richard is trying to do too much in Number Two. He has conflicting impulses. It's very Renaissance, actually, very Italian. He's trying to please his patron, the powerful lord who doesn't know much about art except what he likes, and yet his own subversive interests keep breaking through. His talent is betraying him. He knows that the subject matter is beneath him. He sees through it, so he really can't force himself above the level of the commercial hack. He despises the material. It's so coarse: Viking—primordial warrior stuff, the killer elite at play in the fields of the Lord. Hmmm. What is it Arendt says about the banality of evil? This is it in spades, and Richard knows that. He doesn't like drawing it but of course he hasn't the guts to say no. What would happen if he said no?"

"You don't want to know."

"I'll trust you on that one."

"Is he any good? As an artist?"

"Well . . . there's something here, I don't know. He has technical skills, yes. And he doesn't want to do it, but he is doing it and that tension makes it somehow interesting."

"How about the third one?"

"Ah—lots of vigor, dash, panache. Done off-handed. With his left brain. Something else was on his mind."

"He did it just before the robbery. They had him as

lookout. If he'd have done his job right, maybe all them people wouldn't have died."

"You don't like him, do you, Sergeant?"

Bud thought a moment.

"No, not really. He had choices. Lamar and Odell, they never had no choices. They were born to be trash. They learned at the toe end of somebody's boot. Richard could have done anything. What happened to him didn't have to happen. He was smart enough for it not to have happened. That's what I despise about him. He's not even a good goddamned criminal. Lamar's a great criminal. Lamar's a pro. This poor pup, he's just what the convicts call a fuckboy."

"I can see how prison would be somewhat hard on him," said Dr. Dickstein.

"And that's it?"

"Well—yes."

"Thanks then. You've been some help."

The museum director's eyes knitted up then, and he seemed to really throw himself at the three drawings.

At last he said, "You know—I don't know, there's one other thing."

"Yes sir?"

"It probably doesn't mean a thing."

"Maybe not. But tell me anyway."

"What I see here is a process of—" he paused, groping for a word. "What I see is a process of purification, somehow. He's honing, reducing it, concentrating it, trying to simplify it. He's trying to reduce it to pure essence of lion for Lamar."

Bud looked carefully at the drawings. From Number Two to Number Three it was true: same lion, same posture, but somehow simple, less fretwork to it, the lines bolder, the suggestion more powerful.

"Why?" he asked.

"Well, he's getting close to cartoon almost, one could say. Or emblem. He's reducing it to emblem or trademark. I don't know. But there's definitely a lot of work, a lot of practice, a lot of method gone into it. Now, he's nervous before the crime, he's not thinking, it's just come welling up. And he gets this one, which is by far the best. Whatever he's reducing it to, he's almost there. Lamar will see that."

Bud looked at the drawing. He was trying to figure out what it could be. Was Lamar going to put a trademark on his crimes?

"I don't know," said the doctor. "It looks like something I once saw, but . . . Is there a visual tradition in criminal culture? Possibly it has to do with graffiti or hex signs or some such, some unique signature, some proclamation of deviance that says to the world, 'I am the bad man'?"

He paused.

It looked like something to Bud, too.

Then he remembered the mottling of blue stains on Lamar's arms as Lamar bent to put a bullet into poor Ted and the F U C K and the Y O U ! Lamar wore on his knuckles.

It appeared to Bud perfectly formed and beautiful.

"It's a tattoo," Bud said, astounded at his own insight. "Richard is designing a tattoo for Lamar!"

CHAPTER 22

"A tattoo?" said Richard.

"Goddamn right," said Lamar. *"That's* what you been workin' on! And now, by God, you done it!"

What lay before them on Ruta Beth's coffee table was Richard's best and final lion, a beast so pure and fierce it leaped off the paper at you to tear your throat out. It sang of blood. Next to it was a beautiful young blond woman, tawny and silky and adoring, her arm around the king, lost in his mane. It was like a Nazi wet dream.

"I want to proudly wear that on my chest. I want a *artist* to put it there, in a nice parlor. Not no convict thing, like this here trashy shit on my skin now."

"Lamar. I'm sure a good one could. I mean, I saw tattoos in McAlester I wouldn't have believed. Evidently it's gotten quite sophisticated. It's not crude anymore. The artists are quite free with line and color."

Lamar carefully unbuttoned his shirt and shucked it off. Though he hadn't been working out regularly as in the Mac, his body was still sleek with muscle. On his pneumatic arms, the fading blue ink of prison tattoos that had lost their vitality spilled like stains. But on his hands, the F U C K and the Y O U ! still told the world who he was.

"See," he said, "it's like it was meant to be. I never had nothing on my chest. I done that all on my arms and hands and back when I was young and stupid or young and drunk or high on crystal or all three. But here, I'd like that lion, just as bold as bold can be."

"Daddy," said Ruta Beth, "that would be cool. That would be the coolest thing."

"I think it would be, too," said Lamar. "See, I've always seen myself as a lion and this here thing is what would make it so. Baby Odell, what do you think? Do you think Lamar would look cool with a lion on his chest? You know, a real roaring lion, like the one Richard here been practicing to draw."

Odell's damaged mind grappled with the concept and at last grasped it. *Picture. On. Skin. Lion.* Grrrrrrrr. *Scary. Pretty.*

"Too! Too!" he said, so excited he sprayed Frosted Mini-Wheats and milk with each syllable.

"He wants one, Lamar, that's what the boy's saying," said Ruta Beth. "Can he get one?"

"Well, sure. Maybe not when I do it, because somebody'll have to stand guard. But later we'll get him a right nice one. Odell, what you like your tattoo to be?"

But Odell did not want a lion. He wanted something else.

"Doggy! Mar, me doggy. Doggy Dell. Yoppayoppa?"

"Yes sir, Baby Odell, we'll get you the goddamnedest best doggy ever there was. Right, Richard. You could design a doggy just like you done a lion, Richard, couldn't you?"

"Of course, Lamar."

"Daddy, I want one, too."

"Of course, honey."

"I want a picture of my mother and daddy. On my back. And a raven. I want it on my right shoulder blade."

"Bet Richard could do that too, huh, Richard?"

"Ah—yes."

Actually, Richard thought he was going to faint. Ever since he was a boy Richard had hated needles. What was tattooing, as he understood it, but ordeal by needle? Just sitting there, the tattoo artist would puncture and puncture and puncture, injecting a small permanent blot of color under the skin, until some hideous banality like a skull and cross-bones or a battleship or F U C K and Y O U ! was formed. He knew he couldn't get through it.

But he also knew this is why he was here. In some way, his skill with the pen had jiggered something deep and yearning in Lamar. It had drawn Lamar to him, made him important, even magical, to Lamar. It had, he supposed, saved his life.

"Richard, I want your help."

"Help?"

"Be the foreman. Son, you worked so hard on the drawing and now I would say it's perfect. I want you to work with the skin artist and get it exactly that way. I don't want no slipups!" His mood turned briefly dark. He pulled the muscle of his biceps until they could see where drops of blood, once red but now faded pink, dripped off a tattooed slash in his arm, opened by a dagger. It was a trompe l'oeil of some earnestness but not much skill. However, what infuriated Lamar was the third drop from the wound.

"See that one? Look, see it?"

They all crowded around.

"Yes sir, Daddy," said Ruta Beth. "What's wrong?"

"See how it goes *out*. All the others go *in*. That's what's wrong."

But Richard realized it wasn't a mistake. The tattoo artist, whoever he was, was trying to make the spurts of blood slightly more authentic by varying their configuration and modulating their placement in the stream, knowing instinctively that irregularity meant realism. If he'd done it the way Lamar had assumed he'd do it, it would somehow be deader. It was the endless battle between the patron and the artist for control of the work! It was the Pope versus Michelangelo!

"I suppose I'd have to do some research. I'd have to find a guy with the skill. You can't just walk in on these things. I'd have to see samples of his work. I think they have magazines full of tattoos. You could find a guy from them. And then we could—"

"No, no," said Lamar, "that would take too long. He does something this fancy, I'll be laid up for a month while it heals. Longer I wait, longer it's going to be. Want it done now, tonight."

"But Lamar, I—"

"The Fort! Don't you get that?"

"The Fort?"

"Fort Sill. Outside the Fort, on that Fort Sill Boulevard."

"Tattoo parlors?"

"You got that right. We go tonight, we check 'em out, if you find a boy who can do what I want, then we do it tonight. We lay up, 'bout a month. I figure another job. We pull it off, then by God it's Mexico and a vacation!"

"A vacation," said Ruta Beth. "Oh, Daddy, you think of everything."

It happened rarely enough anymore, because everybody had such different schedules and agendas, but it happened tonight, and Bud was a happy man.

They were all there, his wife and his two sons, gathered around a dinner table in the Mahogany Room of Martin's,

Lawton's finest restaurant for forty years. And the place still knew how to put out a pretty good plate of roast beef, its specialty, though tonight Jen had decided to have some fish thing and Russ, though the honoree, had chosen a plate of linguini with pepper sauce.

But he was happy, Bud was. They sat there eating, Bud shoveling down the forkfuls of reddish meat that always so delighted him. The boys looked great. Russ, the object of all attention, had slicked up his act a bit: He wore a white shirt buttoned at the top and a pair of black jeans over his black boots, and his long hair smoothed backward. The earring was still a little one. Jeff, in a blazer and tie, looked a little more like Bud's idea of a Princeton student.

"We are so proud of you, Russ," said Jen.

"See, what's so great isn't just that Russ is smart," said Bud. "The world is full of smart people. Lamar Pye, he's smart. He's smart as hell. But Russ *works*. That's what's rare. The world is full of people who think they're just too damn smart to work."

Russ was modest through all this but seemed to be enjoying it. Only Jeff was unusually quiet, although he also had good news: He had been moved up to varsity.

"Well," said Bud, "they say a man is rich to the degree his sons make him proud—"

"Who says that, Dad?" said Russ, teasing the old man.

"Well, I don't know who exactly it was, maybe a Russian, maybe a Greek, and maybe I just made it up, but if it's true, then I'm the goddamned richest man in Oklahoma tonight."

"Well, Dad," said Russ, "maybe I'll flunk out."

"You won't flunk out. No man who works as hard as you has a thing to worry about. Then you go on and go to work doing what you want and you have sons who'll make you just as proud as you two make me."

"You-all listen to your daddy," said Jen. "He's speaking the truth. You boys have been a great thing for us, made us so happy. Not a lick of trouble between the two of you, thank the Lord."

Bud had more roast beef.

"Bud, do you think we should order some champagne?" said Jen. "I think these boys are man enough."

"Mom," said Jeff, "that stuff costs eighty dollars a bottle."

"Well, Jeff," said Bud, "your brother has just saved us about a hundred thousand dollars, so I think we can spend eighty bucks."

"Jeff, the domestic is forty-two fifty," Jen said.

"You can buy it in a liquor store for about fourteen dollars a bottle," Jeff added.

Bud called the waiter over and ordered a bottle of champagne, slightly shamed by Jeff into choosing the domestic one. When it came, he ordered it poured for the whole family.

Then, dramatically, he said, "And here's to Russ and all the hard work he's done."

They all lifted their sparkling glasses and drank; but Bud only let the stuff touch his lips and did not swallow.

"Here, let me pour some more," he said, giving each a half glass more, until it was all gone.

The boys and Jen finished the champagne and then it was time to go. Bud looked at his watch: about ten. He called for the check and paid it with his Visa card without wincing, though it was about forty dollars more than he had expected. Still, except for Jeff's strange sullenness, it had been a wonderful evening.

Is it the last? he wondered.

Am I about to do some fool thing and move into a little house near the airport with a young woman?

* * *

. ''Bud?''

''What?''

''You were talking to yourself.''

''I must be going crazy.''

They drove in Jen's station wagon through Lawton's quiet streets and pulled in the driveway about ten-thirty.

''Dad, do you mind if I go over to Nick Sisley's?'' asked Russ. ''He's having a party.''

''No, fine, but don't be home late. Isn't that right, Jen?''

''That's fine.''

''How about you, Jeff? You have any plans?''

''I think I'll go over to Charlie's,'' he said.

When the boys had disappeared, she said to Bud, ''And I see you're going out, too.''

''Oh?''

''You didn't drink any champagne.''

''I may go. Have to make some phone calls first.''

''Bud, what's going on?''

''Oh, got me just the tiniest idea that might lead us to Lamar. Probably nothing. Just want to check it out.''

''Tonight? Can't it wait?''

''Jen, it's nothing. I'm just going over to the Tribal Police Department over at the Comanche complex. I just want to ask some questions, is all.''

She fixed him with her harshest stare, as if she'd never heard of such a thing in her life. Then disillusionment crept across her features and, utterly defeated, she went upstairs. He heard her wheezing disappointment. He watched her go, feeling as though he ought to say something. But no words arrived at his lips, and she just turned into the bedroom and closed the door.

* * *

Lawton was two towns. It was a church-going, tree-shaded small Oklahoma city, with wooden houses nestled on streets that Andy Hardy would have been proud to call home, where every third block sported a park or a school or a church, a town where all life coagulated toward the Central Mall and the county seat for Comanche county. And it was a soldier's town, jammed up with pawn shops and girlie bars and porn stores, from Fort Sill Boulevard around to Cache Road and out Cache Road for a mile or two.

The Fort Sill Boulevard strip, just beyond Gate No. 3, was hopping tonight. Cars jammed its narrow way and it blazed with neon. Young artillerymen, freed from the day's duty of delivering their 155-mm packages into the mountains, their ears booming still, their heads aswarm with the computations necessary to send the shell in the right direction, wandered in packs up and down it, looking for diversion. This usually involved fleshly appetites, and there were places on the strip where for an honest hundred bucks a man could get a good drunk with a good blow job thrown in for good measure; in others, two hundred could be spent with no blow job to be had anywhere on the premises. You had to know where you went.

But among the girlie joints, and the Mailbox USAs and the porn shops and the pawn shops, there was to be found now and then a tattoo joint: Skin Fantasy was the title of one; the Flesh House, another; Skin Art still another; Little Burma Art House, the Rainbow Biceps, and on and on.

It was crowded, as it always was in the hours approaching midnight, and the Toyota crawled along through the traffic.

"You sure this is safe?" said Richard.

"Sure it is," said Lamar. "Down here it's mostly MPs, looking for drunken soldiers. The city boys stay clear. Besides, this car's been checked by the great Bud Pewtie himself and passed with flying colors. There's nothing in the system on the car.''

Ruta Beth drove through the traffic very carefully, nudging an inch ahead at a time. Nobody paid them any attention; mostly it was cars full of soldiers looking for a place to light.

"How's that look, Richard?" Lamar asked.

The place was called Tat-2's, with a gaudy neon sign on it, and underneath it said "Best in the West" and under that, "Trained By the Great Sailor Jerry Collins of Honolulu, complete to Liner and Shading Machines. Custom work available. Bikers welcome."

"Hey, that looks like the kind of place, huh, Richard?" said Lamar.

"It looks promising."

"Well, go check it out, son."

Gulping, Richard got out of the car and went into the small shop. Two semihuman forms lounged behind a counter, and on the walls were hundreds and hundreds of little designs. Of the two, the one that appeared to be the woman watched him most closely; the other was completely zoned. The odor of disinfectant hung in the air.

"Ah, hello," said Richard.

The woman looked at him up and down, squint-eyed. She must have weighed 350 pounds and wore a cutoff biker denim shirt; her huge arms bulged from them and were inked from top to bottom in webbed darkness, with jots of color here and there. When she lifted her face to him, he saw the tattooing extended from her shirt up her neck to her chin. He turned and looked at the other morose character; he was equally gaudy, but what Richard first took to be skin disease was actually a rather elaborate spiderweb that covered half his face. He wore a leather vest, exposing a whole blue museum on every square inch of his cellulite, but the best touch was the gold pin that pierced his nipple.

An involuntary shiver glided through Richard.

"Hep, sport?"

Hep?

Help, she meant.

"Ah, yeah," he said, trying to sound tough. "Was thinking of a piece. Chest. Multicolored. Private design."

"Custom-like, you mean?"

"Yes, ma'am."

"Don't do much custom. More a West Coast thang. Movie stars. These goddamn soldier boys just want 'I Luv Mama' pricked on."

"Ah, it's not for me. For a friend. Let me show you the design."

Richard walked over to the counter and unfolded the lion, rampant, and the beautiful woman, and the castle.

"Shee-it," said the woman. "Rufe, you touch that?"

Rufe came out of his stupor, bending to see.

"Glory," he finally said. "That's a two-thousand-dollar custom tattoo. Take me best part of a week."

"Could you get it?" Richard asked. "The subtlety. The line running down from his mane to his body to his paws, the way it captures his tension and strength. The neck. Look how coiled and alive the neck is. Also, the loft in the woman's breasts. See how elastic and alive they are? We don't want tracing. We don't want a dead line. We want something *vibrant*! Can you do it?"

"Sure he could. You could do it, cun't you, Rufe?"

But Rufe bent over and studied very carefully.

Then he said, "Jamie, show him. The crucifixion."

She turned and bent and pulled her blue denim shirt up. What Richard saw on her broad back was indeed the crucifixion, only it was a handsome biker being crucified, etched there in the flesh in vivid blues and reds, surrounded by state troopers in the roles of Roman centurions.

Richard could hardly keep a straight face.

"Pretty goddamned great, ain't it?" said the woman.

"It's a goddamned masterpiece," said Rufe.

"It's something," said Richard, meaning it differently than Rufe and the woman took it, but as he looked at it carefully, he saw that it wasn't quite what he had in mind. What the piece had in drama and detail it certainly lacked in subtlety of line. The figures all had a stiffness through them, and they all stood at the same angle; the faces were identical. It was like a drawing by a sick, crazy boy, high on amphetamines and inner sadomasochistic fantasies of penetration and blood but lacking entirely any grace or sense of life.

"It's just not what we're interested in, sorry," he said.

"I'd do it for fifteen hundred," Rufe said. "Just like that picture you showed me, every last line and detail. Ain't nobody can do work like that around here but me."

If he's the best, thought Richard.

"Okay, well, maybe so," said Richard. "Still, it's a little . . . you won't be offended?"

"Tell me. I'm a man. I can take it."

"It's a bit stiff. The person on whom you'd be working . . . he wouldn't want it stiff. It would upset him and when he gets upset, things happen. Take it from me. You don't need this job."

"Okay. Your money, your skin."

"Who's the best? The very best. It's worth twenty bucks for the time it'll save me."

He pushed the bill across the counter.

"Well," said Rufe, "truth is, the big action's dried up and left Lawton. It's mostly a West Coast thing. But—well, there's one guy left around here. He don't work much. But,

I have to say, he's a goddamn genius. Done it his whole life.''

''What's his name?''

''Jimmy Ky. He's a good fella. Born in Saigon. Started in the Orient, where it's an art. See the spider on my face. Had that done in sixty-five in Tokyo by the great Horimono.'' He leaned forward. ''See how much lighter it is; them boys got the touch, I must admit. Jimmy Ky studied under Horimono. He's got the touch himself. *If* he'll work on you.''

''Oh, he'll work on this guy. Where's his place?''

It was Bingo Night.

HIGH STAKES BINGO! the sign said, lighting up the night sky. The Bingo Palace was the largest and most vivid building in the Comanche Tribal Complex off Highway 65, where an obliging U.S. government had constructed a quartet of sleek structures for people who cared very little for such things.

The parking lot was jammed, and in the windows of the Palace, Bud could see a full house of farmers and city folks bending over their cards while gaudily costumed ''squaws'' and ''braves'' walked among them, selling new cards, Cokes, bags of peanuts, and the like.

''Okay, folks,'' came a voice booming over the PA that even Bud could hear out in the dark, ''we have an I-6? I-6, everybody! And remember: You win on two cards, you win four times the jackpot!''

But Bud turned from that spectacle and instead walked through the dark to a lower building a hundred yards away. He tried not to notice the high, unkempt grass or the beer cans and coke bottles that lay in it, and he tried not to notice the graffiti defacing the nice new buildings.

Comanches. Once dog soldiers, the most feared of the

Plains Indians, a magnificent people, ride a week on pemmican, fight and win a major cavalry engagement against numerically superior and better-equipped foes, then ride another week on pemmican. Now they tended their gambling franchise and watched their customs crumble as their young people were lured away to the cities. Bud shook his head.

He reached his destination, which bore the designation COMANCHE TRIBAL POLICE, and slipped into what could have been any small-town cop shop, a dingy, government-green holding room with a sergeant behind a desk and two or three patrolmen lounging at their desks. All of them wore jeans and baseball hats and carried SIG-Sauers in shoulder holsters. They were lean, tough young men, none too friendly.

"Howdy," he said to the sergeant. "Name's Pewtie, Oklahoma highway patrol." He showed the badge. "I'm looking for a lieutenant called Jack Antelope Runs. He around?"

"Oh, you state boys, you always come by when you got a crime to solve and you can't solve it. Gotta be an Indian, don't it?" said the sergeant.

"As a matter of fact, it don't," said Bud. "It's gotta be a piece of white trash mankiller that makes the average brave look like your Minnie Mouse. But I got a matter Jack might be able to help me on."

"That's all right, Sarge," said Antelope Runs from an office, "don't you give Bud no hard time. For a dirty white boy, he's not as bad as some I could name. Howdy, Bud."

"Jack, ain't you looking swell these days?"

Jack Antelope Runs had a cascade of raven black hair running fiercely free and was wearing a little bolo tie that made the thickness of his neck and the boldness of his face seem even more exaggerated. He was a huge man, approximately 240 pounds, and his eyes beamed black fire.

"Come on in, Bud. Glad you still walking among the palefaces, brother, and not with the wind spirits."

"Well, old goddamned Lamar Pye tried to show me the way to the wind, I'll tell you."

Bud walked in and sat down.

"So what's it all about, Bud? Is this a Lamar thang?"

"Yes it is."

"I figured a Gary Cooper boy like you'd take it personal."

"Now, Jack, it isn't that way, no sir. I just had an idea I wanted to talk to you about."

"So, talk, brother, talk."

"I seem to remember a circular some months back. Isn't there a big Indian gang making a move to take over narco from the bikers? Seems I been bulletinized on that item a few times in the past few months."

"They call themselves N-D-N-Z," said Jack. "Mean and nasty boys, yes sir. Started up in prison. You put our brothers in white prisons and sure enough they going to start up their own gang, to stand against the niggers and the Mexicans and the white boys."

"It's another thing we're guilty of, yes it is," said Bud.

"It ain't strictly a Comanche thing, though some of our young men have done the dying. But it's run mainly by Cherokees. You might talk to Larry Eagletalon at the Cherokee tribal complex. He's—"

"Now, actually, I ain't interested in the gang."

"Except you think maybe Lamar might be profiting from native American hospitality in some jerky tribal backwater?"

"No, it's not even that. One of the hallmarks of N-D-N-Z, as I recall, is a really and truly fine ceremonial tattoo around the left biceps? No? Yes?"

"Why, yes it is."

"Now, sir, I got me a funny feeling whoever's doing that work is a real fine tattoo boy. Maybe the best in these parts."

"The N-D-N-Z braves wouldn't have any less. That's what cocaine money buys these days. Fast cars, white women, bold tattoos."

"Yes sir. Now, suppose Lamar wanted such a fine tattoo. Where'd he go? To those goddamned scum joints on Fort Sill Boulevard? Catch hepatitis B in them places."

"It don't sound like a Lamar, but you never can tell."

"But he wants *the best*. And isn't the boy doing this work *the best*?"

"So it's said."

"Where'd such a boy be found?"

"Hmmm," said Jack Antelope Runs.

"I just want to check it out. See if Lamar's been around. Maybe that's another step. Maybe we stake out. Lamar shows up, our SWAT boys are there, and Lamar goes into the body bag. No one has to know any information came from the Comanche Tribal Police."

"Bud, for a white boy, maybe you ain't so dumb."

"I'm just a working cop."

Antelope Runs thought a minute, and then finally said, "You know what happens to me if I start giving up Indian secrets to white men? The N-D-N-Z boys leave me in a ditch and nobody comes to my funeral and nobody takes care of my widow and my seven little kids."

"I hear what you're saying."

"I'll ask around, but that's all I can give you. Understand?"

"I guess I do, Jack. I just hope Lamar doesn't decide to stick up your high stakes bingo game next. He could send a lot of boys to wander among the wind spirits."

"I hear you, yes I do. But it's a white-red thing. I can't change that. You can't change that."

"Okay, I see I been wasting your time."

"Here Bud. Give you a card. Let me write my home phone in case something comes up and you have to get in touch."

"It ain't—"

But Jack Antelope Runs scrawled something and handed it over to Bud, who took it and sullenly walked out.

He felt the laughter of the boys in the squad room as he left. Another white boy bites the dust.

In the parking lot he heard, "N-2. N-2. Last call, N-2."

He got into his car, feeling old. Another wasted trip.

Then he looked on the card, and at Jack Antelope Run's writing.

It said: Jimmy Ky. Rt. 62, Indiahoma.

It looked deserted. The neon was out, but if you pulled up you could see that, if lit, the sign would have read— under three or four Chinese letters—TATTOO KEY. You'd have to know where to look, though. The parking lot was deserted and the place was way out on Route 62, near In- diahoma. It was a clapboard shack by the roadside, across from a deserted gas station.

"Nobody's home," said Richard. "We'll have to come back."

"I think tonight's the night. Come on, Richard. Y'all wait here while we take us a lookiesee."

Lamar got out, and bent to check his .45. Richard heard mysterious clickings. Then Lamar walked up to the door and knocked hard.

Time passed. The wind whistled through the high grass out back. Above, the stars seemed to fizzle and pop like silent fireworks—the sky was the record of a huge explosion. Violence was everywhere, or at least the hint of it. There wasn't a sound to be heard anywhere in the universe except for the persistence of the wind.

Eventually definite shuckings and shiftings were heard, and deep inside the house a light came on. The door opened a crack.

"Go away," somebody whispered. "We closed."

The door slammed shut, but Lamar caught it perfectly with the flat of his foot, his full force behind it, and knocked it back open. In reddish light there stood a scrawny Asian, about sixty. He looked mottled, as if suffering from some skin disease.

"You Jimmy Ky?" Lamar demanded.

"Jimmy Ky no here no more. He go away. Go far away. I Jimmy Ky's father."

"My ass," said Lamar. "You're Jimmy Ky. Got a goddamn proposition for you."

Lamar stepped inside and Richard followed.

"I heard you the best," said Lamar. "Well, I want the best."

The Asian looked at him, betraying no fear. Richard now saw that the mottling on his face was tattooing, but of a sort he'd never imagined: It was lustrous, dark, vivid, incredibly detailed, and ominous. The old man was dark blue and red, his face gone in a kaleidoscope.

"You do that yourself?"

"My master Horimono."

"Well it's pretty goddamned good. You that good?"

Lamar's aggression filled the air; he was like the lion confronting a goat. But the goat was strangely unafraid; the old man just looked at Lamar without much emotional investment.

"I his apprentice still," he finally said.

"Show him, Richard."

Richard gave him the drawing of the lion. Jimmy Ky looked at it for a long moment.

"It's shit," he said. "Why you want this trash? Go town. Lots of people in town do this trash."

"No, no," said Richard, "that's just from your Asian perspective. This is done from the *Western* perspective, and it's stylized in a different method. It has to look *Western,* it can't have that exotic—"

"I can do. Best! Make it roar. But it trash," said Jimmy Ky, bluntly.

"It ain't trash," said Lamar. "Look at the way he got the fire and the pride of that lion. Look at that bull neck. That's a goddamned piece of art. We got money."

"How much?"

"How much you need?"

"Ah, for that, forty-five hundred dollars. You wan, you pay."

"Four thousand bucks! Ain't no tattoo worth that kind of money."

Jimmy Ky looked at him shrewdly.

"How bad you want it, mister? You no want it, you go away now. I go back to sleep."

"Goddamn," said Lamar. "Seems like a robbery."

"Gotta pay for the best," said the old man.

"Shit," said Lamar. "How long?"

"Maybe twelve hours. Start now, be done tomorrow afternoon. Then you go lie down for about a week. Get drunk. Infection set in, lots of pain. You got want it. For every color, you suffer. Fever, sweats, lots of agony. No fun at all. How bad you want it?"

"Shit," said Lamar. "I can get through any goddamned thing."

He turned to Richard. "You and Ruta Beth, you park across the street at that gas station, out of sight. You stay there as backup. You tell Odell to come on in. He's working shotgun. Got that?''

''Yes, Lamar.''

''Okay, old man. Let's get to work. You make me a lion, okay.''

''Hokay, Joe. Can do.''

The old man actually seemed happy.

Bud missed it the first time. There were no lights on. It was just a deserted clapboard shack on the way to Indiahoma on a bleak stretch of highway. But when he'd gone on into Indiahoma, he realized he'd gone too far. He turned around and headed back. He seemed to course through inky darkness. The roast beef in his stomach hadn't settled yet. He was half a minute from pulling that goddamned .380 out from under his belt buckle where it had grown into a massive problem. What on earth did he need *three* guns for? Two was enough for any man.

But then he saw it, standing stark against the bleak prairie under some runty trees. He pulled halfway into the parking lot, gave it a once over. It seemed completely quiet and abandoned. There were no cars in the parking lot, and he could see a neon sign that wasn't on. But up near the edge of one window, he could make out just a sliver of light.

What the hell, he thought, feeling ridiculous. *I've come this far, I may as well go all the way so the evening won't be a total loss.*

Richard looked at Ruta Beth in the low light. He could hear her breathe, see the darkness in her eyes. He actually felt pity move through him. Imagine, a child like that coming upon the murder of her parents.

''How are you doing, Ruta Beth?'' he asked.

She fixed him with a narrow glare.

"What the hell do you care?"

He felt her pain. "Ruta Beth, I know how hard life can be sometimes. I was thinking how if you ever needed anyone to *talk* to, why, I'd be ready and will—"

She recoiled.

"You ain't got no romance in mind?"

"Ah, Ruta Beth, why—"

She drew back her little fist, knotted into a clot.

"You put your hands on me, Richard, and I swear, you will be sucking teeth for a *month*. And that before Lamar gits done with you!"

"Ruta Beth, I only meant—"

"Shut up," she hissed. A truck pulled into the parking lot across the way.

A man in it waited for a second, then got out and just stood there.

"Can you see?"

"Big guy, cowboy hat, that's all."

"A cop?"

"I don't know. Not in uniform. Do they have plain-clothes detectives way the hell out here?"

"I don't know," said Richard, who had no idea.

"I doubt it," said Ruta Beth, to herself mainly, since she expected no sensible answer from Richard. "Maybe if he come from the city. But he come from the other direction, from Indiahoma. He's probably some big goddamn brave, in a big truck the government bought for him, just out for a cruise. A chief or some such shit."

"Why would he stop here?"

"Maybe he knows Jimmy Ky."

"He ain't a cop," said Ruta Beth. "How could a cop have found this place. Coincidences like this don't happen in the universe. Not no how."

They watched as the big man went up toward the house.

* * *

It wasn't the pain. Pain didn't frighten Lamar; it was the helplessness and the pain. He lay flat on his back, under a big light. His chest had been shaved and scrubbed with astringent until it stung. Now what he saw was so weird: In the back room, he saw a one-eyed giant. That's what it looked like, at any rate. Really, it was only the old slope, bent over him with the needle, his eye swollen huge and bloodshot by the lens it wore. It was an operation, for now the surgeon's latex gloves were slippery with blood.

"You gotta lotta blood in you," the doctor laughed. It connected with something somewhere in Lamar's previous life, but he couldn't say what or when.

The only reality was the needle. It hummed and tapped as Jimmy Ky leaned over and worked it. Not a big pain, like the thrust of a blade or the channeling of a bullet, but a sharp, brief flash of explosion on his body, enough to make him jump or leap each time.

"No move, goddamn. Make you look like kitty cat, not lion."

Lamar tried to ride it. Eleven more hours of this shit?

And this wasn't even the bad stuff. This was the easy part: doing the base colors, the larger shapes. The hard work would come later, when the little man got down to details and moved in with the tiniest of needles for the little drips of color that gave the piece life. And he was a careful craftsman, unmoved by the pain he caused his subject. He never looked hard at Lamar, but only at the design.

Lamar was afraid to breathe. He took strength from one thing and one thing alone: his cousin Odell, Baby Odell, sitting with the implacable patience and loyalty of the retarded, watching and waiting and playing sentry at the door to the back room.

* * *

It was so goddamn dark! Ruta Beth couldn't see a thing. The truck was just a truck, the man just a man, standing there, as if deciding. When he finally moved, he walked toward the door and there was something familiar in the gait. Where did she recognize it from?

"H-he's going in," came Richard's sing-songy voice. "What should we do?"

"Shut up," she barked, but herself thinking, *What should I do?*

She watched as the man approached the door, paused again, adjusted his hat as if he were stepping into a fancy restaurant. He was a big guy, well packed with bulk and girth, but no damned youngster. Something familiar to him, goddammit.

She reached under the car seat and pulled out her ski mask. She pulled it over her face, feeling the scratch of wool, the stink of her own sweat, its warmth, its closeness. Her mouth tasted pennies.

"It's nothing," said Richard wanly. "He's just a cowboy. He wants to get tattooed. He's some oil-field hand. He wants 'I Love Susie-Q' on his biceps, that's all."

"Shut up, you pussy boy," she said. She slid Lamar's cutdown Browning 12-gauge semiauto from the back seat, pushing the safety off. Her hands flew to her waist, where she'd tucked Lamar's .45 SIG.

"It's all right," said Richard. "Please make it be all right."

The man stepped in, closed the door behind him. There was a glorious, blessed moment of silence.

"Whew," said Richard. "It's all—"

Then the sound of shots, lots of them, fast and wild, and from where they sat they could see the gun flashes illuminate the darkness of the tattoo house.

CHAPTER 23

Animals!

Zoo!

Odell's eyes roamed the extravagant figures on the wall, utterly transfixed.

Magic!

He saw lion. He saw birdie.

Big birdie and snake. Tiger.
Grrrrr! *Tiger bad! Bear.* Growlllll!

He began to make animal sounds and shake just a little. So many animals. It touched a far-off and not coherent shard of memory: He was very small and Mama took him over to Mrs. Bean's farm and let him pet the goats. Odell remembered the goats all round him, the funny funny sounds they made, the thickness of their animal odors, the soft wetness of their tongues as they licked his face, and his mama saying, "Oh, I ain't seen him smile like that ever."

But then they had to go back to Daddy; Daddy was mad. Daddy whipped and hit Odell.

"That goddamn stupid boy, ugly as shit, no brain in his

goddamn head nowheres,'' Daddy screamed, beating him with the belt while Mama cried. But Odell never cried.

The door opened.

Bud paused at the door, put his hand on the knob, and was surprised that it yielded to let him enter. He stepped into a small, darkened chamber awash with the smells of incense, disinfectant, and sweat.

He felt enveloped in quiet. It was as if he'd entered a religious shrine. He blinked in the low light, half in and half out of the door, and his eyes quickly sped to sinuous forms in sheer bursts of color on the walls. Was it a museum, like earlier today? Snakes, he saw snakes, and strange, stylized beasts, ornate and muscular, formal and alive at once. Eyes of beasts bore savagely down at him. He heard breathing, the low sounds of a tinny radio, and looked across the room to the primary source of radiance, a doorway behind a counter, which revealed portions of still another chamber, well-lit, like an operating theater. He could see a form splayed out in white seminudity and another form bent across him, with bloody-fingered latex gloves holding a strange implement that must have been a tattoo needle. And slouched in the doorway like a sleepy dog was another form.

Bud looked, said, ''Say, I'm—,'' and then focused on the slack but puzzled face of Odell Pye. Odell grinned absurdly, and his tongue flicked out. There was a black hole in the center of his face, just under his nose, and his eyes had the guileless stupidity of a young boy drunk for the first time.

Bud looked at Odell, all his instincts clotted up in his heart, but he knew he was in big trouble.

The moment seemed to last forever, like a breath taken and held. Then it exploded.

Odell stirred into action, yanking a shotgun from somewhere, but without willing it Bud had drawn his Colt Commander from the high hip holster and hit the thumb safety, and he and Odell fired almost simultaneously.

The flash from the gun muzzles filled the room with incandescence; the snakes seethed and pounced in its blinding whiteness. Bud was not hit and did not know if he had hit Odell—he doubted it, as he had pointed, not aimed, and had fired with one hand—and without a conscious thought anywhere in his head, he jacked the trigger seven more times, pumping .45s at Odell in a burst that sounded like a tommy gun. And like a tommy gun, it was evidently inaccurate, for Bud saw clouds of plaster flying, large chunks of masonry ripped up, the flashes blotting details from his vision. Then the gun came up dry, Bud cursing, for only an idiot shoots a gun empty without counting shots to reload with one in the spout and less vulnerability.

He dived into the room, ripping a fresh mag off the pouch on his belt, slamming it home, and thumbing off the slide release to prime the pistol once again. He came to rest behind a counter that now atomized into shreds before his very eyes. He saw the glass liquify as buckshot pulverized it, and the stuff blew into his face, knocking him back, blinking. But he felt no pain, and in response fired three fast times at the gun flash, receiving on the middle shot the impression of a yowl. Odell had disappeared. Smoke hung in the air. There was a moment of silence.

Then a small, blue Asian man came crashing from the open doorway. Bud tracked and nearly fired at him but didn't and instead redirected himself toward the opening itself, to see the low, hunched form of Lamar Pye bent in a combat crouch, good two-hand hold, but apparently unable to see Bud.

Bud couldn't see his sights, it was so dark, so he just put

the back of the pistol against what little he could see of Lamar and fired three more times, fast, reloading his last .45 mag with one shot left in the chamber, just as he knew he should.

He also understood that in firing he'd given away his position. If Lamar wasn't hit mortally, he'd return fire in just a second, so Bud slithered to his left, coming hard against a wall, then backed spastically until he found what appeared to be a door, and slipped back into it.

Flashes lit the darkness. Both Lamar and Odell fired, Odell obviously not dead at all, maybe not even hit; and the counter behind which Bud had cowered simply evaporated as Lamar's .45s and Odell's buckshot remodeled it. He heard Lamar's pistol lock back dry and another sound— hollow, like someone blowing in a wand—seemed to suggest that Odell was reloading as well. He could see no part of Lamar, but he put the pistol before him in that segment of darkness out of which had sprung Odell's bursts and, convinced he saw a shape, squeezed off what he meant to be but two or three shots. But in shooting he banished the sudden demons of fear that had come from nowhere to tell him what a fool he'd been, how he'd walked in here without backup, without even a radio, and so he could not stop shooting until the gun was empty. Again, he thought he heard a cry, as he dumped the Colt, and his hand sped to and ripped his big new Beretta from the shoulder hoslter.

"Waharrrrr, Waharrrrr" came a gurgling cry from the dark. It was Odell, his voice veined with hurt.

"Goddamn it, boy, you stay put," cried Lamar in return, equally anguished. "Who the fuck are you, mister? What the hell, you ain't no cop, we don't mean you no goddamned harm."

Bud was silent. All he had to do was open his mouth and

Lamar would have a source of noise for him to bring fire on.

"*Wahh-arrrrrrr.* Mama. *Wah-marrrrrrrrrr,* pweezze. Mama."

"Odell, you stay down, Daddy come git you in a bit. Where's that goddamn car?"

A car? More of them? The criminals had backup. The cop didn't.

Shit, Bud thought.

Who the fuck was he?
Where had he come from?
Why was it happening like this?

Lamar hurt every damn place, and he felt so goddamned naked, his shirt off, blood all over his chest. But what had him worried was Odell. Odell sounded hit bad. He'd never heard that tone in the boy's voice. It was so pitiful, so animal. Odell, hurting. It just filled Lamar with rage.

If only he could clear his mind and think, or if only that goddamned Ruta Beth would get here. Where the hell was she?

"Wharrr?" came Odell's quavery voice.

"You shut up, Odell, we be out of here in a jif," he called back.

He had one goddamn magazine left, he'd fired the other two. Seven .45s. Where was goddamn Ruta Beth?

His breath came in wracking sobs. The room was so dark. He could see nothing.

Lamar looked about. How stupid that *he* was in the light and his enemy in the dark. Kind of goddamned mistake that could get you killed.

He slipped back in the room, jumped up, and with a light tap of his gun muzzle shattered the huge light over the table. The space plunged into darkness.

How long had it been?

Maybe thirty seconds?

Where was goddamn Ruta Beth?

He slid back to the door, edging out. He could see nothing. The guy was somewhere in the back of the shop, amid the destroyed counters that had just exploded as Odell's buckshot had blasted them. But where? Had he found cover? Was he dead himself already? Lamar couldn't see a thing, and he could hear nothing over Odell's labored breathing.

Lamar tried to clear his head. The main thing was to get out. Fuck this boy, let him live or die, but get out, go back to the farm and regroup. He wondered if the sounds had carried. All that gunfire in the little room in so short a time, the stink of gunpowder in the air.

Oh, who are you, you motherfucker.

"Who are you, goddammit?" Lamar bellowed to silence.

Smart boy, wasn't making a move.

"Wharr?" came Odell's wet voice. Then: "MAMA!"

See mama? Yes, he'd promised he'd take Baby Odell to his mother's grave and he'd never made good on it. How could he, with all the goddamned cops in the world on his ass?

Then, as his eyes adjusted to the dark, Lamar noticed something. There, just ahead of his eyes, light switches.

Turn on the lights, Lamar. Put this motherfucker in the lights, and kill him.

"Marrrrr," whispered Baby Odell.

Bud was squashed so low to the floor he could hardly move. The darkness was absolute. He could hear Odell moaning and breathing harshly, but since Lamar had turned out the lights, nothing from him.

He tried to gauge where the door back to the tattooing

room had been. That's where Lamar would be right now, waiting for him to make a sound. Or would he? Maybe Lamar was creeping toward him even now, to get close and cut open his windpipe.

No! He'd make noise moving across all that glass on the floor. There's no noise, only the wheezing and moaning of Odell. Maybe they're just waiting for their pals.

Suddenly the lights came on.

Bud blinked as his eyes filled with dazzle. A shot cracked out from the now-visible Lamar, but it hit a shard of wood blown loose from the counter, and danced away.

All Bud could see was that big gun in Lamar's hands, not part of Lamar but only the gun, the long-slide .45 gripped tightly. Time seemed to slow down, as if it were an accordion slowly being stretched.

Bud thought, *Front sight,* and fired.

Lamar's hand exploded in a burst of pink mist and the .45 fell away. Lamar slipped and fell, unarmed, fear on his face.

Front sight, Bud thought.

He tried to take his time, that is, to shoot in two-tenths of a second rather than one-tenth, placing the front sight on Lamar's face, now distended and swollen with fear as Lamar lay helpless before Bud's gunsights.

Baby Dell hurt so.
*Red juicy wet mushy everywhere! HURTY! Clicky BOOM
   go arm, BOOM go chest, BOOM go tummy, BOOM
   BOOM BOOM.*
Marrrrr?
Mar cry?
No Mar!
Bad man hurt Mar.
No, bad man. No hurt Mar. Mar Baby's friend.

No, man!
Bad man, HURT bad man!

As Bud fired, the world around him suddenly lost its stability as a cloud of dust showered down upon him.

He ducked, feeling a terrible sting in his leg, and turned.

Odell stood behind the counter. Part of his jaw had been blown away; Bud could see tiny teeth, the tongue squirming like a mouse. His eyes were wild and insane. He held the shotgun that he'd just fired at Bud in one hand, as the other was useless, soaked in blood that ran in torrents from a high chest hit.

Odell pulled the trigger again but nothing happened.

He started to walk toward Bud, raising the shotgun like a club.

Bud fired six times, aiming at center mass. Each shot tore a hole in Odell, and more blood spurted wetly down his shirt, but still he came.

Bud fired seven more times, the 9-mm hollowpoints punching at Odell, who halted, went to his knees, and with a look of utter agony climbed back to his feet.

"ODEEEEEEL," he could hear Lamar shout.

Bud aimed at the forehead and blew a big chunk of it out. He aimed at the eye and blew a blue hole just beneath it. He aimed at the throat and tore it open.

The Beretta locked dry.

Odell was on him, that huge weight, the rancid breath, blood spraying from the ruined mouth, the sound of breathing labored and wet and desperate like an animal's. Odell's big hands were on Bud's neck, but the medium of their grappling was liquid. Blood was everywhere, slippery and almost comical, as Bud squirmed for purchase under the huge man. Then he remembered his belly gun.

Bud got the .380 out from his shirt, not even remembering pulling it, and stuck it under Odell's armpit and squeezed the trigger. He fired and fired, until at last Odell slumped against him, slack.

Bud pulled himself out and stood.

Lamar had climbed to his feet. He held his left hand in his right, another bouquet of roses that was blood.

"You," said Lamar. "You goddamned Bud Pewtie. You done killed a baby."

Bud aimed at Lamar's head—amazed and impressed that Lamar didn't flinch or cower, so intense was his hate—and pulled the trigger.

The gun didn't fire.

He looked at it. He'd shot it empty against Odell's bulk.

In the next instant, a huge billow of dust flew into the room, and the thunder of collision mixed with the roar of an automobile engine. A car literally stove through the front of the shop, blasting glass and wood everywhere.

In the driver's seat, a figure in a black hood leveled a shotgun at Bud, who dropped just a fraction of a second before the gun fired. He felt the sting of another pellet, this one lodging in his scalp. Bud thrust himself backward down the stairwell, felt himself float in darkness, and then hit the steps with the sensation of a beating delivered by six cons, which took the breath out of him and filled his eyes with stars.

He rolled over and slithered deep into the darkness, totally animal now, intent only on escape.

But no one followed him down the steps.

Instead he heard the roar of the car as it backed out, presumably with Lamar now aboard, and then howled away.

Bud listened to the sudden silence.

He felt chilled, and missed his sons. He wasn't sure if

he'd done right or wrong. He yearned to call Jen or Holly or have his old life back.

He began to shiver.

Richard had never heard anyone howl in such pure animal pain before.

"AAAAAAAH!" Lamar cried, bucking and sobbing in the back seat, holding his crippled and bloody hand. There was blood everywhere, all over the seats, on the sideboards, everywhere.

Meanwhile, curled in total concentration, her face grim and unyielding, Ruta Beth drove mindlessly onward.

"Slow down, goddammit," yelled Lamar once through his pain, when he thought she was going too fast.

But if they expected squad cars rushing their way, the howl of sirens, ambulances, helicopters, whatever, it didn't happen. They drove on through darkness.

"We've got to find him help," said Richard. "He'll bleed to death."

Again, through his pain, Lamar screamed out. "You shut up, Richard, goddammit. It ain't bleeding no more. It's only pain. I kin git through pain. Ruta Beth, you git us home, you hear?"

"He'll bleed to death," shrieked Richard. "It *is* bleeding."

"Shut up, Richard," said Ruta Beth, "let Daddy decide."

Lamar tried to lie still but the pain was intense.

"Should we dump the car, Lamar?" asked Richard. "Maybe they have a description."

"And what then, you moron. They'll find it and trace it and beat us to the farm. I don't think that sonofabitch got a good lookiesee, he was so goddamned busy jumping down those goddamned stairs. He didn't have no time to get no read on the license plate, tell you that. Oh—''

A sudden spurt of pain seemed to jack through him; he tensed and wailed. It seemed to come like that, in spurts; or when they took a corner and the centrifugal force spun blood toward his wound and the pain flamed again.

''Daddy, you sure you're all right?''

''Just drive, goddamn it, Ruta Beth. Where'n the hell was you? We's in there shooting it out with that johnny for a *hour* before you came in. Whyn't you jump him in the goddamn lot?''

''Lamar, baby, we didn't know he was a cop. He looked like a cowboy, in a pickup truck, that's all. Then all hell's breakin' loose and Richard and I are trying to figure out what the hell to do. So I just finally goose her, figuring any other way, either you or he shoots us as we come through the doorway. Couldn't a been more than a minute.''

''Felt like a goddamn *day*. Oh, that fucker was good, shoots me in the goddamned hand.''

There was a silence.

Then Ruta Beth said, ''What about the baby?''

''The baby is dead. That goddamned Smokey must have hit him fifty goddamned times. I never saw a boy soak up so much lead and keep a-going. Goddamn, Odell, he was a man, Odell was—AWWWWWWWW.''

A spark of pain erupted somewhere inside him. Then he was quiet.

Ruta Beth began to cry.

''Poor Odell,'' she said, ''he never meant no harm to nobody. If the world had left him alone, he'da left it alone. Oh, that's so sad. He never got to see his mama's grave neither. Oh, Lamar, oh Daddy, that's so *wrong* what they done to him.''

Richard just looked out at the dark Oklahoma countryside as it flowed by, more emptiness than he'd ever seen before in his life.

"How that fucker got there, that's what I want to know. *How* did he know we'd be there?"

"Maybe it was just bad luck," said Richard.

"No luck is that bad, Richard. It was that goddamned Bud Pewtie, that trooper sergeant. Fuck has more lives on him than a goddamn black cat. I blowed him away *twice* at that farm and *still* he mantracks me down, that fucker. How'd he do it? How'd he know? He some kind of Dick Tracy or somethin'? Is he goddamn Columbo? Is he the Pink Panther? What the fuck? How'd he know?"

The question hung in the silence.

Lamar lay back, rocking gently.

Then he sat back up.

"Only one goddamned way a cop know *anything* these days. Someone drops a fucking dime to buy some time off. You got that gun, Richard? That heavy one?"

"Yes I do, Lamar."

"Well, give her here."

Awkwardly, Richard handed it to Lamar, who sat up in the seat to take it. He cocked it and pointed it at Richard's head.

"God, Lamar, you—"

"You sure you ain't been talking to anybody, boy? You sure? I ought to blow your head off just to be sure."

"Please Lamar. Oh, please, please. I *swear* to you. When would I? How could I? I didn't even *know* we'd end up there. Who knew? You wait, the papers will say why he's there."

"Ahh, it ain't that. You don't have the *guts* to betray me," Lamar said. He uncocked the Smith and chucked it on the seat. Then he lay back again.

"Goddamn, it hurts," he said. "Oh, Christ, it hurts so bad. That goddamned Bud Pewtie!"

Bud had no sense of time. He hid in the basement for what felt like hours and hours. His scalp wound began to sting unbearably and would not go away, but at the same time his leg wound throbbed; the second was somehow a deeper and more troubling pain. At one point he touched his face and realized it had been ripped to shreds. The vision in one eye was blurred, as if he had a stone the size of a cinder block in it. His mind blacked out into shock, but he never really lost consciousness.

He remembered the last camping trip, in the Wichita Mountain Preserve. It would have been about 1991. It was the last time they were really a family. Russ was a freshman and little Jeff would have been in the seventh grade, already having troubles, grades that just weren't happening and serious self-doubts. Bud remembered wishing he could reach the boy, cut through whatever ailed him, could put his hands on him, and say, Hey, it'll be all right.

Bud lost himself in this world for quite a bit: he remembered how green the world had seemed up there, how pure. They camped in a Nimrod that he'd pulled behind his truck, high up on a ridge, with much of the state spread out before him, and the air so clean it almost ached to breathe it in. He'd been so happy. They'd loved each other so much, even if no one had said a thing about it. He remembered the shouts of the kids and Jen's pleasure in being out of the house, and the sense of the world being forgiving and wide with possibility.

Then he saw the light.

The beam caught him and he blinked. Behind it he made out crouched shapes, the Weaver position, shooting arm

straight, support arm locked underneath, the posture somewhat bending the body shape.

"Don't you twitch, mister, goddammit. Show me your
hands."

"I don't think I can move 'em."

"You *better* move 'em, goddammit."

Bud brought his hands into the light.

"Who are you?"

"Sergeant Bud Pewtie, Oklahoma Highway Patrol. I've
been hit."

"You got a shield?"

"Yes sir. Don't you do nothing tricky now with that gun.
I'm going to reach in my pocket and get my shield out. I'm
unarmed. I mean, my guns are all upstairs. You got medics
on the way?"

"The whole world is on the way. That's goddamned
Odell Pye lying up there with a mess of holes in him."

"He took some killing, I'll say," said Bud, getting the
badge out, opening the folio to show it. Another light came
on from the top of the steps.

"Bud? Jesus Christ, ain't you a sight. He's one of ours,
Sheriff. Medic. MEDIC! Get them medics down here, we
got an officer down. Goddammit, ASAP! Get 'em DOWN
HERE NOW!"

The trooper came to him first and asked him where he
was hit, but in seconds two medics had arrived. They gave
him the quick once-over and determined that he hadn't
taken any solid, life-threatening hits.

"But you sure are cut to hell and gone," one of them
said, and Bud thought he recognized the man from various
turnpike accidents. "Looks like you got a face full of glass
slivers. And goddamn, I can see something stuck under
your skin up top your head."

"That's the one that hurts."

"Boy, I'll bet she do, Trooper. Goddamn, I'll bet she do."

The medics got him on a stretcher and a team of sheriff's deputies and troopers labored to get him up the stairs, out of the cellar.

He was pulled into a jubilee of lights. More cars and trucks were arriving even as they wheeled his gantry toward the ambulance, and now a van of FBI agents pulled up. A TV truck had already shown.

"Hold on," somebody said. "You Pewtie?"

"Yes sir," said Bud.

"Lon Perry, sheriff, Jackson County. Trooper, I can't have you boys turning my county into a goddamned shooting gallery when some goddamned undercover op goes dead-dick on you, 'specially since you ain't even had the goddamned courtesy to tell me you's working my territory."

"You're out of line, Sheriff," a trooper sergeant barked. "He's hurt, he just got the second most wanted man in the state and probably put a goddamned hole in the first most wanted, and no citizen even got scratched. You back off."

There were heated words, but soon another man came over and separated the warring sides. It was Colonel Supenski, looking like he'd just been dragged out of bed.

"Goddamn, Bud, you get around, don't you?"

Bud didn't feel much like answering any questions. He just said, "What the hell took everybody so long to get here? We had us a goddamned World War. Nobody called it in?"

"Not a goddamned soul, Bud. Nobody *to* call it in. Jimmy Ky crawled out of the bushes after Lamar and pals departed, waited ten minutes, tried to call, found out the goddamned car had torn out the phone lines, and walked two miles into town to tell the sheriff's department. Lamar, goddamn his soul, got away.''

"Damn," said Bud. "I know I hit him, I seen blood. I seen him drop his piece. I hurt him bad."

"That you did, Bud. Wilie, bring 'em here. Bud, take a look at your trophies.''

A highway patrol technician came over with a plastic bag. It seemed to contain two grisly pickles, each somewhat tattered at one end.

"What the hell are those?" Bud wanted to know.

"Lamar's fingers. His last and second-to-last left hand digits. You shot his fingers off, Bud. You killed his cousin, you stopped his tattoo, and you shot off two fingers. Say you done a hell of a night's work, Bud."

CHAPTER 24

At Comanche Memorial Hospital, a young doctor and two nurses bent over Bud in the emergency room operating theater and picked pieces of glass out of his face for nearly two hours. During this time they also removed a ragged piece of bullet jacket from Bud's scalp, where it had lodged just under the skin, and a double-ought buckshot pellet that had drilled into the meat of his left calf. That was the nasty one. It hurt like a sonofabitch. The painkillers they gave him helped some, but nothing could blunt the force of the pain of a foreign missile blown deep into the muscle tissue.

By the time the first team was done, an ophthalmologic surgeon had arrived by helicopter from Tulsa to work on his blurry eye. This gentleman probed for several minutes and then removed a particularly gruesome glass sliver from inside his left orbit, where it had sunk into the subcutaneous tissue just under the orb itself.

He held it out for Bud to see: It looked like a blade of pure glass, a vivid little knife.

"You're lucky, Sergeant. A millimeter to the right and you might have lost your vision permanently. I'm going to prescribe antibiotics and give you an eyepatch, but in a few days your vision will return to normal.''

"Thank you, Doctor.''

"No, thank *you*. It's an honor to work on a man as brave as you,'' and he went on with some blah-blah about Bud being a hero.

But Bud didn't feel like a hero. It wasn't a thing of heroes; it had no heroics to it; that was for the movies, where things happened clearly, you could follow them, they made sense, the cleverness was apparent. This was just a mad scramble, like cats in a bag fighting, luck happening or not happening, no strength, no cunning, just the blind happenstance of where so many bullets happened to end up. And, knowing that, he had to think: You could have done better. It was true.

If he'd just taken a look through the window and made out who Jimmy Ky was decorating, he could have gotten to a phone and called for backup, and all of them would be locked up or in the morgue, not just poor, dumb Odell. No one had directly confronted him yet, except for the odd nods from the troopers on the scene. Had he done well? Someone once said, if you're still alive at the end of a gunfight, you've won. But Bud didn't quite buy it. He'd almost gotten Lamar. Almost!

Once the doctors were done and Bud was washed and dried, he was rolled to a private room. There, Jen and Jeff waited. She came over and just touched him, lightly, on the arm; she didn't look quite real, because with the patch he had no stereoscopic vision; she looked like a picture. And she was haggard, having been awakened from a sleep at nearly five in the morning with the sketchy news that once again her husband had been shot up. Fortunately, the news soon followed that he wasn't hurt bad.

"Oh, Bud,'' she said.

He smiled wanly, feeling his dry lips crack.

"Oh, Bud," she said again.

Jeff stood aloof in the corner of the room.

"Where's Russ?"

"He's not coming," she said, "He went up to the lake with his friends. I didn't call him. They said you'd be all right."

"That's good. Let him enjoy the Princeton thing. This ain't nothing."

"When is it going to end?"

"It has ended," he said. "I swear it."

Presently, a nurse came along and shooed them out. They had to wait in the hall. He needed his rest; he was still in danger of shock and he'd need to be sharp the next day, anyway.

But, alone in the dark at last, he couldn't rest. He lay there unsettled. He tried not to think about it. Images from the fight kept flashing back on him. He'd think he was done with it and then it would come back to him, blown up and in slow motion. The slack look on Odell's face in that first second. Goddamn, must have beat him to the draw by just a fraction of an instant, that's how goddamn close it was. It made him almost physically sick; he'd drawn the Colt and thumb-wiped the safety off and fired at a speed that had no place in time. But it was so easy to screw up a presentation like that; suppose he hadn't gotten his grip right and hadn't depressed the grip safety, or he'd missed the safety with the thumb, or he'd missed the shot. But goddamn, he'd put out the telling shot and it kept him fighting. Any single little muff in that complex of movements, and he was a goner.

He'd fired so much! Suppose he'd held back on the shooting? Maybe if he'd placed his shots better and aimed more. He remembered aiming once, at Lamar's big hands on the Colt. How the blood exploded from them on the hit, the gun flying. Funny, in a gunfight they say that you concentrate on your opponent's weapon and that hand and arm wounds are the rule, not the exception. That was it exactly, there.

It was such a close goddamn thing, is what it added up to. Physical violence with guns at close range always involved the fantastic, the unbelievable. Every shooting was a Kennedy assassination in replica, a twisted mess of events where everybody was operating in an ozone layer of stress and nothing made sense. Funny, Bud had done all that shooting and had all that shooting directed back at him, and he couldn't remember hearing a single shot! But his ears rang like somebody was beating on them with a bat. He had no sense of how long it took, either. An hour? More likely three minutes, or two. All that shooting, so much shooting, and how few bullets actually found targets. Even the great Lamar hadn't shot very well. So much for your gunfighter myth.

It was the flashes that haunted him. When the guns fired, they produced huge clouds of burning gas that in the dark blossomed like starbursts, blinding and disorienting everybody. Maybe that's why in all the shooting, so few rounds had gone home? Who could see in the middle of the Fourth of July? But those flashes, cruelly flaring out in the dark, each blindingly white and hot, each a potential death sentence. He'd see them for the rest of his life, he thought; he'd never be finished with them.

But mostly, Bud couldn't get Odell out of his mind. It was like something from some horror movie, the way Odell kept eating up the lead and coming for him. He'd seen the boy's heart explode, seen his throat blown out, seen part of his brain fly away. But still Odell came, like some robot or something, outside of pain, beyond death. What kept him going, what reserve of pure animal fury? Or maybe it wasn't fury. Maybe fury couldn't get you through something like that. Maybe it was love. Only person in the world poor Odell cared about was Lamar, and by all reports Lamar cared back just as hard. That kept him going beyond the collapse of his nervous system. Finally finished him with the .380. And suppose he hadn't had the belly gun? Conceivably, dying, Odell had enough strength left to crush the life out of him. Goddamn, that little gun sure was worth the money he'd laid out for it!

The next morning, a new doctor came in and gave him a onceover, and confirmed that he probably wasn't going to die, at least not in the next thirty years. And then, one by one, the boys in suits came in. Colonel Supenski was there, representing the state police, as well as two highway patrol investigators and an investigator from the Jackson County sheriff's department. But Lt. Henderson, of the OSBI, was missing.

The chief questioner was a tough, young state's attorney.

How did he feel?

He felt fine.

Was he up to it?

He was up to it.

Did he want his own attorney present?

"Now hold on," started the colonel—

"Strictly a routine question in a case involving death by force," said the state's attorney.

That settled, it began.

Slowly Bud told the story, trying to leave nothing out of the lead-up, except the detail of Jack Antelope Runs. Then the gunfight, in excruciating detail.

"Did you warn them before shooting?"

"Warn them? I was trying to *kill* them."

"Strike that from the record, goddammit," said Colonel Supenski. "He didn't mean that."

"Did you mean that, Sergeant Pewtie?"

"No sir. I was merely trying to survive. There wasn't no time for a warning. I saw a weapon in the perpetrator's hands and I established that he meant to harm me, and so I opened fire."

It went on for several hours: where he'd been, what he remembered, where Lamar and Odell had been, and so forth and so on.

Bud had a curious moment here, as a realization reached him.

"You know, for three weeks I been packing three guns and spare magazines for each. I had fifty-eight rounds of ammunition, which I been bitching about like a old lady. Goddamn, if I'd had fifty-nine, Lamar would be dead meat today."

The lawyers left about six. The boss, after conferring with the investigators, gave him the good news.

"I think you did a great job, Sergeant. Mr. Uckley agrees with me. No state indictments. You're in the clear."

"Thank you."

That left Bud alone with the colonel.

"Okay, Bud," said the boss, who'd been holding his piece for a long time. "I have to say this. You got guts to burn and what you brought off is a masterpiece of police work. We're so very proud of you. But Bud, I told you, and it's beginning to grate on me—this ain't a goddamned private war. You ain't a cowboy. You understand me? It's modern times, we work in teams now. Bud, I *cannot* have a lone wolf operator working on some personal revenge agenda. I catch you on Lamar's tail again, by God, I'll prosecute you. I could even git you on carrying a concealed weapon, since by all lawful interpretation, you were not duly authorized to carry under those circumstances as you were formally on medical leave."

"Yes sir. But I can only repeat: It ain't personal. I never want to see that sonofabitch again, except when I testify against him."

"You understand then that you're on official administrative leave? You ain't to be hanging around or going places where you might run into Lamar? You are formally relieved of police duties. It's routine, it don't mean a thing, but I do mean to see that you hew to that line."

"Yes sir, that's fine. I just want to go home, is all."

"All right. I'll believe you on that. Another thing, I got the prelim on Odell. Want to hear it?"

"Yes."

"You hit him thirty-three times, Bud. Four .45s, thirteen .380s and sixteen 9s. And most of 'em were good, solid torso hits. You even hit him three times in the head. The doc says the hollowtips opened up like they should. There wasn't much of him left."

"He took a basket of killing, that's for sure."

Bud shivered a bit.

"Now what you don't know isn't going to make you happy. I've had a report from our press officer who's been watching the TV and seen the evening paper from Oklahoma City. The press people are all excited about you shooting Lamar's fingers off. Like it's a joke or something. Like you're Annie Oakley."

"Anyboy tell 'em how common hand hits are in gunfights?"

"You can tell 'em anything you want, but they only listen to what they already know from movies. That's how it is. But this stuff could make Lamar mad. We want to move you and your family to a safehouse."

"Oh, Lord."

"It's best, Bud."

"I have a boy hitting four hundred and another about to

graduate with honors. I can't take them out of their high school. It's the time of their lives. They can't never get it back.''

The colonel looked at him.

''Well,'' he finally said, ''maybe I'll just assign a full-time shift on your home. That be all right?''

''Most 'preciated.''

''I guess a tough old coot like yourself can look after himself.''

''Colonel, can I ask you something?''

''Sure, Bud, what is it?''

''The old man. C. D. Henderson? Where's he?''

''Well, they done retired him. He spent a lot of the state's money and came up with nothing. You got more from a drawing of a lion than he did from half a million dollars worth of overtime. He had a bad drinking problem, you know? It was time. I hope I go out better, though, than he did. Bitter old coot. Sad, actually, how ugly it became.''

They kept Bud three more nights, and he got through them with his old pal the bottle of Percodan. At ten on the fourth morning, he was released to Jen's care. The two of them drove home in her station wagon. His leg still throbbed, and though he no longer wore the eyepatch, the vision in the one eye was blurry. Moreover, it felt like every square inch of his body had a bruise or a cut on it.

''Now, you're supposed to take it easy.''

''Ain't any other way for me to take it. Plenty of naps, going to Jeff's games, that sort of thing.''

''Bud, the season's almost over. He's only got tomorrow night.''

''Oh. Well, that's another thing I didn't do very well, is it? I didn't pay attention to Jeff. Is that why he's so grumpy lately?''

''Bud, what's going on?''

"What you mean?"

"Something's going on. You aren't hardly there anymore. There in the house. Even when you're there. You're off somewheres else. You never talk to any of us. Like you're saving your best stuff for somebody else."

A flower of rage blossomed in Bud. He was at his worst when Jen was picking at his secrets. But he just clamped up.

"It's just this Lamar thing. Hell, I've been in two gunfights, had a partner killed, been on the road, into and out of hospitals, and killed a man myself. That's were I been."

"No, Bud, it's something else. I've been watching you for twenty-five years. I know something's going on. You have to tell me."

Bud was acutely uncomfortable. Here was the perfect chance, he thought. Tell her. Work it out now, civilized, friendly-like. It didn't have to be a mess, with screams and accusations of betrayal and tears. Begin to discuss it with her. Tell her: You met somebody, you care about her, it's time to make the change. It'll be all right. It's a new chance for everybody.

But Bud couldn't even begin to form the words. It was inconceivable to him.

"No," he insisted, "things are fine. Just want to get rested up and read in the papers that they got Lamar. I swear to you."

Her silence expanded to fill the air in the car and drive any other possiblity out.

They got home and Bud saw a state car parked out front.

"Been there long?" he asked.

"Yes. Two men from the OSBI. There's another car out back. I asked them in, but they said they'd stay in the car and keep a watch out. Do you think he'd try anything against us?"

"Lamar? I don't know. I doubt it."

"If you say so."

"Well, you can't predict. But these boys out front'll prevent anything bad from happening."

Bud waved at the two—sullen youngsters, under huge cowboy hats, with hooded eyes—who nodded in return and went back to eyeballing the neighborhood.

Bud went in—he had a moment of bliss, walking in his own front door, even if each step felt as if it pulled him through a bucket of glass. Still, it felt good: to survive a goddamned gunfight and come back to this and see that everything was just as it had been, that Jen's sense of order had made certain that it was neat, that it was still a house rank with the odor of boys. He felt as if a weight had been lifted.

He went to the gun safe in the downstairs closet, spun the dial, and the thing opened up: his guns, gleaming in the low light, three short of course, lay in there. He decided to get a short-barreled shotgun out just in case, removed it, slid five 12-gauge double-oughts down its tube, but didn't crank the slide to jack a round into the chamber. He locked the door and laid the shotgun to rest against the wall.

"Honey, I got a shotgun out. You just have to throw the pump if it comes to it. In the closet. Next to the safe."

"Okay, Bud."

"Where're the papers?"

"In the living room."

"I'm going to take them upstairs."

She didn't answer.

Bud got them and took them upstairs. He slid out of his boots, took another Percodan, and lay back in his bedroom. He read all about it, saw himself referred to by name as a highway patrol undercover officer—now there was a joke! —and read quotes by the colonel and half-a-dozen other officials on what a good job he'd done. There was a murky official photo of him.

Generally, the press business was pretty favorable. It treated him as some kind of hero, and none of them mentioned that he was the patrolman jumped by Lamar and Odell three months back; that was good, it didn't make it look like this "revenge" thing, as everybody seemed to think it would. Maybe the stupid reporters were too dumb to put it together but more likely, someone had said to them, don't stroke this angle and, for once, they'd agreed.

But he didn't like the games they played with the story of the fingers. They almost seemed to think it was funny, that he'd done it on purpose. If he'd been an expert shot, one bullet would have killed Odell, not thirty-three, and the second one would have killed Lamar.

Around one, he fell asleep. At three he awakened, saw that a note from Jen was on the bureau. She'd gone out on errands; Russ and Jeff would be back late; they wanted to go to the Meers Store tonight, was it all right? Or should they stay in?

Bud rolled over and dialed Holly's number.

"Hi," he said, "how're you?"

"Oh, Bud, they say you're a big hero! Bud, you're famous!"

"Oh, it'll go away, believe me. These buzzards forget as soon as they write something."

"You're all right?"

"I'm fine, I swear to you. I'm done with the eyepatch but I have scabs on my face and a bandage on my leg, where there's still swelling and some pain, but I seem to be tougher than beef jerky. Lamar just can't git me dead. I can't git him dead either."

"Bud, when can I see you? I want to be with you so bad. I want to help you through this."

"No help needed. I'm fine. Honey, I told you—it just depends. A day or two, when the ruckus settles down. You can wait, can't you? We're so damned close."

"Bud? You're going to do this, aren't you? You keep putting me off, but you're going to be with me. I couldn't stand to lose you, Bud. I just couldn't. I'm so afraid you're going to change your mind and go running back to what's easiest."

Bud had never promised he'd leave. He knew that. He couldn't force himself to. He'd promised to consider it. The distinction may have been slight, but it was powerful in his mind; it was the difference between adultery and blasphemy.

At the same time there was such eagerness and, underneath, such despair in Holly's voice. How could she love him so? Was she crazy? What would happen when she saw him as Jen saw him—a largely immobile and inert chunk of solitude, who didn't give much and took a lot, and whose idea of a good time was to reload .270s for the fall? It scared him a little. He wasn't quite sure he trusted it. But he didn't have it in him to hurt her.

"Well, I'm working on it. When them boys was shooting at me, it was you I was thinking about seeing. Okay?"

"Good, Bud. I have to hear that."

"Holly, soon. I swear to you."

He hung up and got up. He walked around the empty house, feeling the ache in each step. He looked out the window at the black OSBI car with its two radio antennae and the slouchy young men. He was once again at complete loose ends, too agitated to sleep, yet not really able to go anywhere. He went downstairs and turned on the TV for the six o'clock news, to see if there was anything on Lamar.

There wasn't. The big news was the Lamar cult. It had struck again that night at the high school.

Someone had painted ODELL WAS MURDERED in huge letters on the blank brick wall of the gymnasium. And next to that, LAMAR WILL BE BACK.

CHAPTER
25

Lamar thought he could get through anything. The hand wound coagulated and scabbed over, and no infection set in; it only hurt, hurt like the devil, but pain was no problem. And the disappointment that Lamar felt when he looked at his unfinished chest, with the outlines of a lion just barely sketched in, rough and crude, incomplete, was palpable, but a man who's spent most of his life in prison has trained himself at least to patience, and so he knew that his disappointment, too, would vanish eventually, as all things did.

The grief was something else. Lamar had not known grief in his violent thirty-eight years; his father died on the highway before he himself had even been born, so he never knew to miss him. Then there was his mother, a wan and sickly woman, without much in the way of personality, who passed him around to aunts and cousins and whatnot; he was in reform school when she died a drunkard's death in a ditch, with a bad man. He felt nothing, not even a stab of loneliness. When Odell's mama, Camilla, died when he and Odell were on a straight eighteen month slide for aggravated assault—plea-bargained down from second degree murder—he felt a twinge. She'd been the best woman he'd ever known, kind and gentle, and she had so loved her Baby Odell, though not quite enough to stop her husband from chaining him up in the barn and beating him with a razor strop. Lamar had stopped that himself. But that was more a single moment's passing, like a cold breeze through his insides. Here it came, there it went, it was gone forever.

But now Odell. He didn't think it would ever stop hurting. He thought of it as weight. It took the form of a fat black cat that crawled upon his chest, suffocating him. He got the idea that if he ever lay down and went to sleep, that cat would kill him. He imagined it having mousy breath and a white blaze between yellow saucer eyes that never blinked but only looked on him with utter stillness and without interest. But it wanted him dead. It would creep up during the night, warm and cuddly, and just plant itself on his chest, acquiring weight as the night passed until he clawed for air, but by that goddamned time the cat weighed a ton and its purrs had the quality of a file's gritty grasp, squashing him down into the feathers until he was no more.

"Goddamn cat" was all Lamar would say as to why he no longer slept but instead roamed the farm at night, striding grimly about on the rolling, open prairie, amid the craggy mesquite trees that seemed to be trying to claw the moon from the sky in black rage. Sometimes he ventured as far afield as across the highway into some farmer's grazing lands, where he walked madly between the cattle, who soon grew accustomed to his prescence.

As he walked he tried to reconstruct Odell in his mind, as if in doing so, he could keep that boy out of the cold and lonely grave. There had been something solid about Odell: He expected so little, he was almost unstoppable in most kinds of battle, he knew no fear or remorse; he simply lived each moment, then forgot it forever. Lamar had taken care of him for years. He understood his cousin's strange language full of twisted words and broken sentences; he understood the subtleties of Odell's face, which most people regarded as utterly impassive and blank. Not Lamar; he could read Odell's mood from the set of his mouth, the raggedness of his breathing through that incomplete septum, and the essential sweetness of his character.

For at heart, in some way, though he had done terrible things at Lamar's dark bidding, Odell had retained his innocence. He simply had done what Lamar said and taken no pleasure from it. He had had no need to dominate or kill or steal; he had only needed to be paid a little attention and be fed, and that had lasted him to the end of his days. But Lamar had dragged him along, made him a pale instrument of his own criminal will, and had now gotten him killed.

No, no, he told himself. *You can't believe that. You'da gone on for years, you and Odell, you thinking, Odell happily following, if it weren't for that goddamned Bud Pewtie.*

The thought of Pewtie recalled the gun flashes in the dark, and that made him think of Odell hit on the floor, his baby voice keening in pain and hurt, his mouth shot away so that his tiny store of words had been reduced to an animal howl.

"WAHRRRR!"

And then when the lights came on, he saw the blood all over Odell and the way his jaw was smashed and hanging, sections of bone blown out, and a torrent of blood squirting out of it. That must have been the very first shot, the jaw shot, the lucky jaw shot that changed the whole nature of the fight.

That Bud Pewtie seemed to have the Pye number all right! Something about him made him special to the Pyes. Lamar remembered turning with the shotgun after the .45 had run dry at the Stepford place and pumping one last shell into Pewtie. It was like his back exploded! Blood from a butchered pig, a big, fly-catching puddle of it! And the bastard wasn't even badly hurt! Flesh wounds from birdshot! Pretty goddamned suspicious.

And the second time. A second time Bud Pewtie, big as life and dumb as an elephant, came walking onto Ruta Beth's farm and was just ten feet away and all Lamar had to do was jump across that space and bury the hatchet in the lawman's brain! It would have been so easy! They could have stashed him, taken his truck, and driven to new digs in New Mexico or Texas or California or somesuch. But no— played it safe, and got poor Odell blown away.

What haunted him most, as it haunted Bud, was Odell's insane lumber across the tattoo shop while Pewtie shot pieces off him. He must have hit him two dozen times as Lamar just stared, his own hand blown to shit so that he could think of nothing; you could just see the bullets tearing through Odell, blowing off pieces of bone and flesh like he was nothing. Still, something in Odell drove him onward while Pewtie put them into him. Odell, goddamn was he a lot of man! He may have been a baby to the world, but to Lamar he was a man, because he had truly given up his life for Lamar's, a sacrifice that was all but unimaginable to Lamar. He'd never seen anything like it in all his years of prison. It just wasn't done. When a man's time came, it came, that was all.

So Lamar roamed the fields at night, thinking these things over, working himself deeper and deeper into a titanic rage. One night it rained and the lightning flashed all around, but Lamar didn't care. He went up on a ridge and stood in the pouring rain, his shirt off, the lightning bolts detonating like artillery shells all around him. When they went off, their illumination brought the world into sharp, instantaneous relief; he could see the farmhouse and the highway far away, and the abutments against the horizon that were the Wichitas; but the flashes were like gun flashes and the thunderclaps like the sounds of guns.

"He should see a doctor," said Richard. "He'll get a fever and die. Or he'll go insane out there in all that rain and lightning, and do something crazy and take us with him."

"You shut up now, Richard," said Ruta Beth, blinking as a particularly vivid flash filled the dark kitchen with sudden shadows. "Daddy's in pain. He's in real pain. He needs time to get a grip."

"He needs a doctor. You don't get two fingers shot off and *not* see a doctor."

"What little you know, Richard. I heard that back in fifty-four, my daddy's brother Cy lost a whole hand to a threshing machine and there wasn't no doctor in these here parts. So they just wrapped him up tighter'n a drum, and few days go by and he's up and spry as a weed. It's only goddamned city folks need a doctor ever time their nose git a little runny."

"How long did Cy live?"

"Well, he died the next year of a fever, but that don't have nothing to do with it."

"Ruta Beth, I—"

The door blew open; rain whistled in and at that moment, as if in a cheap movie, a lightning flash illuminated the ravaged features of Lamar, his hair a mottled and wild mess, his eyes crazed, his muscles tensed and hard against the sting of the rain, with just the faintest outline of lion on his chest.

"Richard," he commanded. "I want you to git your art stuff. I want you to draw me a picture. Boy, draw me a picture as if your life depended on it. I got to see that picture or I'm going to die, Richard."

Richard leaped up.

"Yes, Lamar. Tell me what it is. I can draw it. I'll draw like I drew before. You just tell me and I'll do it."

"Richard, I want to see Baby Odell happy in heaven. He's sitting at the Lord's right hand. He's playing with a cat, a little kitty. He's got a halo. Then on the Lord's other hand, there's Jesus, and he's just as pleased as punch because his new buddy Odell done joined him up."

"Y-yes," said Richard, thinking it seemed a little ambitious for his modest talents.

"Yeah, but that's only in heaven. That's going on up top. Down here on earth, Richard, down here on earth, that goddamned Bud Pewtie, he's being burned. You know what I mean? He's on fire. His flesh is burning in the everlasting fires of hell. He's screaming for mercy, but they ain't none. No mercy for him. Do you get that?"

"Yes, I do, Lamar. And you? You're in the picture?"

"Hell yes, boy," said Lamar. "I'm the one with the match."

Richard drew as if he were the one on fire. He knew it was an absurdity, but in some way it satisfied him to reach out and at last help Lamar, if only in this crazy way.

He tried to remember the Sistine Chapel, for it had that crazed scope to it—heaven and earth, reward and punishment, the duality of existences, a classical Renaissance theme. He of course was no Michelangelo, but he doubted if Lamar knew who Michelangelo was, so he doubted his plagiarism would get him in much trouble. That's how he envisioned it—an insane white-trash Sistine Chapel, full of pure rage and the criminal's need to dominate and hurt, and at the same time full of a kind of innocence. It would be a lunatic masterpiece, a crackpot pièce de résistance, of the sort that is rare but does in fact exist—the works of Céline, for example; or Mahler, a horrible man; or Sam Peckinpah, that deranged maker of nihilistic cowboy movies whom some actually believed to be a very great artist.

It was as if he had been liberated. His fingers flew and discovered new and interesting ideas as they plunged ahead, each new line leading to yet another line in a mad scramble, a helter-skelter, a kind of artistic release. Whatever Lamar had done for him or to him, he had now at last released Richard's inhibitions; no thought of what was "proper" attended his brain, no reluctance, no phony patina of "sophistication"; he let the work flow from his id—or from Lamar's.

Heaven was a mountaintop, purple and swarming with clouds. Our Lord was a benevolent biker king, a Daddy Cool aslouch on the throne of his Harley, his powerful features radiating justice and serenity; at his left foot was his only son, Jesus as Road Captain, his leathers glistening, his narrow, ascetic face made more prominent by a ponytail that hung down from a bandanna. He had a tattoo that said JESUS LOVES and he, too, radiated benevolence and forgiveness. And Baby Odell. It was with special affection that Richard evoked the Baby; he cured his harelip and gave his eyes focus and wit; he gave him not the slobby body of an overgrown farmboy but the sleek muscles of a weightlifter. His mouth was no longer small and overshadowed by the dark fissure above it, but firm and eloquent, just as he now had cheekbones and spine and the one thing that poor Odell never in life acquired, for it requires some kind of primitive self-awareness: dignity. It was about halfway through that he realized he was reinventing Odell as Al Capp's Li'l Abner, but that was okay: there was something barefoot and down-home to both Abner and Odell that made it appropriate.

It was nearly midnight when he finished the rough

sketching for the first half of the drawing; but now, in a fever, he could not stop. He was consumed with fire, as high as he'd ever, ever been before in his life.

Oh, Mother, he thought, *if you could see me now.*

For Bud Pewtie, he tried to imagine a pain so everlasting and consuming it would be almost beyond comprehension. How does one get the total squalor of torture, of ultimate and total degradation, into a mere representation? He tried to think of atrocity—the blown-away old people in this very house; but more, scenes from Auschwitz, the endless litter of scrawny corpses; or the famous photograph of the searing flame of napalm in Vietnam, out of which with such utter delicacy the little girl had run, leaving her mother and baby brother cooking behind; the Zapruder film frame in which Kennedy's skull explodes, a fragment launching into midair and trailing a plasma gossamer; a picture of the rent, headless corpse of a third-trimester abortion that an antichoice zealot had once sent him.

Yet none of this stuff really worked; it didn't get him where he needed to be.

What is the worst, he thought, the worst thing you know or have ever heard of? The screwball in *Silence of the Lambs* with his "woman suit"? The German officer who forces Sophie to choose which child shall live and which shall die? The cries of the Scottsboro boys as they were dragged to their trees, knowing they were innocent?

No, he thought, the worst thing you ever heard of was the boy who blinded his mother. He didn't have the guts to kill her. He wasn't strong enough, though he hated her almost as much as he loved her. He tried to remember the mechanics of his strokes with his stiff arms, his sudden explosiveness, the sound of the blade cutting into the skin and into the sockets. He remembered her wailing. God, how she wailed for mercy. But she was so weak. She had dominated him for so long, but she was so weak! The power he'd felt, the obscene sense of gratification after all those years.

"There, Mother, there! Now you know how it feels!"

That's what he'd said to her.

Now, trapping that sickness and storing it like a fossil fuel, he began once again to draw.

Lamar sat like Rodin's *Thinker,* watching the sun come up. It crept over the rim of the plains out beyond the highway, foreshadowing another hot, clear Oklahoma day. This early, it was still farmer's sun, appreciated wordlessly only by men who rose before it to get a good part of their immense day's labor finished before it got truly hot. It was swollen and bloodshot, and almost orange, but still cool. Lamar regarded it dully. It was as if he'd spent his rage and collapsed, finally, after so many long, sleepless days and nights battling fever and pain and that goddamned big cat that was still stalking him. His face was slack, his eyes dull. He was shirtless, the half-lion looking almost abstract, like a scribble, on the planes of his chest. His hair fanned wetly over his broad back. He breathed through his mouth, drawing the air over a dry, dead tongue. Nothing moved on his body; he looked as passive as a piece of stone, though the veins on his muscular right arm were distended and now and then a rogue impulse caused one of his remaining fingers to twitch.

He'd been sitting there since three o'clock, when he'd returned from another of his long night walks.

Richard approached gingerly. He felt as if he were a small boy in the presence of greatness.

He stood, waiting to be recognized.

After a long time, Lamar finally looked over.

Richard saw two glistening tracks running down his cheeks, which connected with no knowledge of Lamar that he'd ever had, until at last he recognized that tears had left their mark. Lamar was weeping silently.

"Lamar, are you all right?"

"Oh, I'm hurting something mighty, Richard," Lamar said. "I'm hurting so fierce I doubt if I'm a-going to make it."

"Please, Lamar. What would we do without you? You can't talk like that. You've got to make it. It always seems darkest just before the dawn."

"Goddamn Richard, that poor boy, he never'd done a thing wrong if I hadn't a-steered him to it. It's me should be lying on that slab, not him. And I promised him I'd take him to his mama's grave and I never done that. And now he ain't even going to git no funeral. They going to dump him in some goddamned pauper's grave and that's the end of it. It's so sad. It kills me how sad it is."

"Lamar, I finished the drawing. I'll put the colors in tomorrow if you like it."

He held it out to Lamar, who took it and examined it closely in silence for some time. Then Richard heard a shuffle, a choke, a sob, as Lamar broke down completely.

Richard stood there feeling as if he'd violated some immense privacy of Lamar's. To see a man so bold and strong and fearless weeping hysterically—it befuddled Richard. It was like seeing his own father crying, when all the signals always said that fathers don't cry. His never did. Mothers cry. But his never did, either.

But then Lamar looked over and said, "Richard, goddamn, what you done here, that's *wonderful*. The Baby in heaven, Bud Pewtie in hell. Goddamn, Richard, you are a great artist. Just looking at that lets me imagine it in some way I couldn't before. I do know that he's up there, a-waitin' on me. Goddamn, Richard, boy, it's like you done lifted a huge weight off my shoulders."

"Why thank you, Lamar," said Richard, stunned at the response.

Then Lamar looked at the bottom part, the hell part.

"Now what's this?" he said, his features darkening. "I thought I told you he was supposed to burn, like in hell."

"Lamar, Lamar, I thought hard about it, and I came up with something different. Something so . . . strange it would make you famous. Famous forever. It's so horrible."

Lamar's features knitted as he tried to penetrate the image. Gradually, they lightened.

"His face," he said. "You got me doing something to his face."

"Yes," Richard admitted shyly.

"I don't get it, Richard."

"What is a man, Lamar? A man is many things, and you can take them from him, but the one thing, if you take it, you take *everything*."

"Everything?"

"Yes. Everything. Not his life, not his family, not his balls, but—his face."

"I'm cutting his face off?"

"Everything. Eyes, nose, tongue, lips, teeth. You've taken his face. You've left him without a face. Consider it! It's so . . . extreme."

Lamar looked at Richard and a strange light came into his eyes. And then Richard saw that it was respect.

Lamar suddenly embraced Richard, held him tightly.

"Richard, I think you done helped me find the power. You and the Lord, Richard, you both done helped me find the power."

"You can go on?"

"Go on? Hell, boy, we gonna git us a Bud Pewtie. And his goddamned family. And this time, we'll leave a ruckus in the chicken coop they talk about in Oklahoma for a hundred years! You mess with the Pyes, they'll say, and the Pyes will have their day! And we'll leave him for all to find —without a face!''

CHAPTER 26

They began to come in the night. He could not deny them. He wasn't sure if they were dreams or fantasies, but they always came between the hours of four and six while he was in a semiwakeful state, involving visions and positions as yet untried: smoky memories, these visions, all of Holly. He'd roll over and see Jen sleeping, and wonder, *Why, oh why aren't you enough for me?*

But the fact was: She wasn't enough, or at least now that he'd had the other, younger woman so often and knew how she tasted (salty) and how she smelled (musky) and the consistency of her hair (tight) and all the secret parts of her that he could touch to make her squeal and moan.

Maybe it was just the closeness of the brush with death; whatever, now he needed flesh to confirm that he was unmistakably alive. He wanted Holly's flesh. He did not, goddamn his soul to hell and goddamn his allegiances to hell, want his wife's flesh.

"I have to go," he said to Jen in the morning.

She just looked up at him. She was a handsome woman, near his own age, with a square, beautiful face, now completely unimpressed and beyond surprise. Her eyes just bore into him. He sensed her remoteness and her passage into a zone beyond disappointment, as if to suggest there were few words left.

"My guns," he said. "I called that OSBI lieutenant, Henderson. They're out of the state ballistics lab now, they all been tested. He says I can sign for 'em. Sure would feel better with my own guns, and not somebody else's." He'd been given a department Smith .357 for self-defense, just in case, but somehow it lacked the proprietary intimacy of the ones he'd put so many holes in targets and Odell with.

"So you're going to go fetch them?" Jen said suspiciously.

"Yes, thought I might. Then I thought I'd stop at the range and run a box through each and see how it felt. Then I'll be right back."

"You haven't been 'right back' in four months, but I suppose if you have to go, you have to go."

Bud tried a smile. It didn't work. He knew he shouldn't appear too anxious, but whenever he "acted," he knew his movements seemed awkward and forced.

However, today he knew he had to have Holly and damn the consequences, and so after dawdling over another cup of coffee and reading a sports section whose scores he already knew by heart, he at last got up, threw on his hat, slid the generic Smith into a belt holster and a jacket over that, though it was hot, and set out.

He blinked. The Percodan knocked out the sharp jabs but couldn't reach deep enough into his nervous system to shut down the more general throbbing in his limbs and joints that made him aware of every movement; once again, he felt ancient. He no longer wore the eyepatch, but some moisture came and he blinked it back as he slid behind the Ford's wheel. As he climbed in, he fired something off in his leg wound, where the pellet had sunk so deep, and a momentary flare of pain blossomed inside. He shook it off and pulled the door shut.

It was bright now, June, and flecks of pollen hung in the air. Spring was a memory; full Oklahoma summer bore down, its weight crushing all movement from the air. He took an unair-conditioned breath, and it felt like sucking down steam. Then he turned the engine, backed out, and with a nod, passed the day-shift bodyguards.

He drove to the City Hall Annex. C.D. was not there to be found, but instead there was a younger OSBI detective, and some boys holding court in the task-force big room.

The boys wanted to meet Bud: two Texas Rangers still hoping to get a try at Lamar, two undercover state policemen from the headquarters unit, and two or three OSBI investigators, the names and hands all thrown at Bud in a hurry.

"Hell of a job you did there, Pewtie. Goddamn, that's the kind of shooting this here country needs more of by a damn sight"—that was the gist of the comments, offered in several variants.

"Well," said Bud modestly, "I was damned lucky."

The social palaver done, Bud went into the office where once C.D. had drunkenly held court, and the new boss opened a drawer and pulled his guns out one after another.

"One Colt Commander, .45 ACP, serial number FC34509, one Beretta 92F 9-mm, serial number D12097Z, and one Beretta 84 .380, serial number E259751Y. There, Sergeant Pewtie, just sign and they're yours. Got your Beretta shoulder holster and the Colt Galco, but I don't know what happened to the .380 holster. How the hell you carry that?"

"In my belly. Behind my belt buckle. No holster at all. Hurt like hell, but I was damn glad it was there when I needed it."

He looked at them: his three guns, all functional black combat pistols, without a grace note or a gleam to them. Just tools. A wave of sweetness came over him, so powerful it almost made him want to faint. No man whose life hasn't been saved by a gun can begin to imagine what a man whose life has feels when he confronts the instruments of his survival.

Bud headed out, but then he stopped, feeling he had a thing or two still to do.

"Where would I find C.D.?"

"Well, Sarge, he's got a place way south of town, out Thirty-eighth Street, south of MacMahon Park." He gave an address.

"I ought to drop on by," Bud said, learning that he felt it exactly as it popped out.

"The old boy'd probably appreciate that, assuming you get him early enough, before he's given himself up to the bottle."

Bud looked at his watch. Did he have time for this? Why was he doing it? If he got in and got out quick, it shouldn't matter. But time, as always, was the problem. It might help him cover; he went to see the lieutenant, they got to talking, the hours passed, *that's* why he was late.

It was a dingy little suburban tract house in an unappealing development, smaller even than Holly's place, way south of the airport, and now and then a big jet would roar overhead, its landing gear threatening to knock down aerials and chimneys. There were no trees in the neighborhood.

He waited just a second to determine if he really wanted to do this or not. It had the sense of a fool's errand. But there was something in the way it was shaking out he didn't like—that he, Bud Pewtie, had "found" Lamar, where the old man had not. It wasn't really a fair interpretation. He finally went up and knocked on the door.

The woman who answered was another bitter prune, without a lick of softness anywhere to her drawn features or her immense fatigue.

"I'm Pewtie," Bud said. "Is C.D. available?"

She just fixed him with a wordless glare, and then finally said, "You the lawyer about the settlement?"

"No ma'am. I'm a highway patrol officer that worked his last case."

"That damn Johnny Lawyer said he'd be here *yesterday*. We need the money. Damn fool C.D. lost all his two years back on a goddamn re-sort investment down at Lake Texoma."

"Sorry to hear that," Bud said.

"Well, you go on back then. But he's in a black mood, as usual."

"Has he been—"

"Of course. You can't take that man's bottle from him, but he don't get bad until around four."

Bud walked back into a dark little room and found C.D. sitting under a pyramid of cigarette smoke, his bourbon bottle, and a paper cup before him. He was watching a soap opera through squinty eyes, his face all knit up, a cigarette dangling from his lips. On a shelf to the left stood a brass army of pistol marksmanship awards.

"Howdy, there," said Bud.

"Bud, goddamn," the old man leaped up, "nice of you to drop by."

"Well, damn, just wanted to know how you's doing?"

"Oh, it's okay. Gits a little draggy toward the end of day, that's all."

"You need anything?"

"No sir, not a thing. I ain't quite as drunk as I was last time I saw you. Need a drink yourself, son?"

"No, lieutenant. I just wanted to drop by to say so long."

"Well, you're the only one of 'em man enough to do that. Close to fifty years, and nobody even come by. How 'bout a sandwich? Bud, you want a sandwich? *Honey!* Can you git Bud a sandwich?"

"No, it's all right, Lieutenant, I already ate."

"Sure, Bud. Say, that was good work on Odell. Pity you couldn't have gotten Lamar, too."

"I was one bullet shy, goddamn his luck."

"Now, Bud," Henderson said, "I'll be the only one of 'em who tells you the flat-out truth. You shouldn't have fired so much without aiming. Been in seven gunfights, won 'em all, only twice was I even hit. You got to aim, Bud. You can't spray and pray. That's what old Jelly Bryce taught me and no man was better with a gun than he was."

"You're right, Lieutenant. I just couldn't think fast enough."

"Another thing Jelly Bryce taught me, a man comes at you again, soaking up lead like that, you got to stay cool and break his pelvis with a big bore bullet. Break his pelvis, down he goes. Hit him three inches inside the hip. Puts him down every damn time. Under them circumstances, even a head shot is iffy; hell, you can blow out the top half of a man's brain and his heart, and he can still go for fifteen seconds on instinct."

"I'll remember that."

He took a drink from his glass. The soap opera whined onward. Bud could smell the liquor and the smoke. All of a sudden, he just wanted to get the hell out.

"Listen, Lieutenant, I do have to poke along. I just wanted to say I's sorry how it ended for you and I didn't

want no hard feelings. Some are saying I found Lamar and
you didn't, but we both know that's not how it was.''

"No, Bud, that is how it was. You *did* find Lamar and I
did not. Bud, you going to bring those boys over? I'd surely
like to meet those boys of yours. They sound like a damned
fine set of boys.''

"Sure, Lieutenant.''

"Let's set a date, Bud. I'll get my calendar out. Maybe
we could take 'em fishing. Let's pick a weekend in July, we
could go on up to the Wichitas, or no, no, out to Lake
Texoma. Used to own a nice piece of land there. I know
where the damn fish are hiding, that I can tell you!''

"Lieutenant,'' Bud said, "I'll have to check with them.
Jeff's got Legion Ball and I don't know when exactly Russ
has to go East. I'll have to call you back on that.''

"Sure, Bud. Now, you *positive* you don't want no
drink?''

"Lieutenant, I have to go.''

"Okay, Bud.''

"Anyways, I'm sorry—''

"Well, I's sorry too, Bud. I wanted that Lamar and by
God if I'd gotten another break or so, you can bet I'd have
nailed him.''

"Yes sir.''

"Yes sir,'' said the old man, less to Bud than to himself,
"yes sir, I'd have nailed him. Just couldn't get that last
damned break.''

When Bud finally got back to his truck, the full force of
the day's heat lay upon him. He checked his watch: Dammit, he'd spent close to half an hour with the pitiful old
goat, when he'd only meant to spend ten minutes. He shook
his head at what had become of the mighty Lieutenant Henderson. He still felt a little woozy from the smoke and the

dark claustrophobia of the place, or maybe it was the force of his sexual anticipation. Anyway, he got in and drove to Holly's, feeling he'd earned it.

It took him twenty extra minutes to find the place, and he'd have to come up with an excuse to account for the time, he knew. But by the time he got there, he wasn't thinking about such things. He thought he'd burst.

He pulled up, nodded at a black kid on a yellow plastic trike on the sidewalk, and bounded to the porch.

"Well, damn my soul," she said. "The hero himself."

Bud looked around theatrically. "Oh yeah? There's a hero here? Always wanted to meet one of them boys, shake his hand."

"Git you in here, Bud Pewtie, this very instant. You can tell me how much you like my house and how sorry you are I had to move in by myself . . . *later*."

She pulled him in and began to grope with him, immediately coming upon his guns.

"Oh, my, well sir, maybe we ought not to do a thing, so as you don't have to readjust all your equipment."

"I'd gladly dump 'em in the trash, darlin', for a few minutes with you."

"Well I *hope* it's longer than a few minutes."

And it was. Bud was in fine form today, released of all his inhibitions, driven forward by the peculiar intensity of his wants. His pains vanished; his legs were young again, his lungs full of stamina. The games started in the living room on a sofa, moved up the stairs, though pausing there for several minutes owing to the possibilities of the steep upward rake of the steps, then continued in her upstairs bedroom, where things got immensely tangled and complicated until at last the moment itself arrived, exploded, and then departed.

"Whooee, wasn't that a time?" Bud said.

"You should do more of this man-killing, Bud. It does wonders for you."

"Wasn't I the boy, though?" he said.

"You certainly were."

He laid around in her bed for another half an hour and then the mood came across him again. Squealing delightedly, she accommodated him; she was smooth and slippery as an eel.

And when that one was done, he said, "Well, I think we broke in the new house right nice."

"Would say so. Want to see it?"

Bud knew he shouldn't. Too much time, he was late already; but she was so proud of the damn thing.

"Sure," he said.

They dressed, and she lugged him around, room to room. Bud tried hard to keep his enthusiasm up, but he knew he was doing a poor job. And, there really wasn't much to see: her trailer furniture, spread throughout a six-room house, looked sparse. And for some reason, the house looked grayer and dirtier than he had remembered it looking. Could he live here? It wasn't nearly as nice as his wonderful and comfortable old place.

"It's a great little place, honey," he said.

"You'll help me paint it?"

Bud *hated* painting.

"Of course."

"Oh, Bud, we'll be so *happy* here. I know we will."

"Yes ma'am, I know we will. Now, uh, I've—"

"I know, Bud. And you don't want to do any *talking* at all. Okay, Bud. Will I see you tomorrow?"

"Of course you will," he said. "By god, of course you will."

* * *

Bud drove home, thinking of lies, or rather expansions on the truth. *Old C.D., now I had to go see him. It ain't right what they done to him and what they're saying about him. And you know how that man can talk* (she didn't, of course). *He just jaws onward and onward and you can't slow him down any. And he's so bitter I didn't want to insult him any further. Plus, he had to hear the story of my famous shootout. And of course he had a lot of comments and constructive criticism. The time just flew away on me.*

He actually mouthed the words out loud, so they'd feel familiar in his mind. You didn't want to be making stuff up in an escapade like this, because you could just as easy as pie come up with something that invalidated something you'd said before; pick a nice, simple, believable story, near to the truth as you can make it (not very, in this case, but believable) and stick to it. He had a laugh here, remembering an old story about a football quarterback who was out helling around and his wife caught him sneaking in around seven in the morning, and he had a dandy all set up. He told her he'd come back at about ten the night before, but since she was already asleep he didn't want to wake her so, since it was such a nice night out, he'd decided to sleep in the hammock out there in the front yard, and that's where he'd been. She said, "That's very nice, but I took the hammock down two weeks ago." So the fellow said, "Well, that's my story and I'm sticking to it."

Bud pulled in the driveway, and immediately one of the OSBI youngsters got out and came up to him.

"Sergeant Pewtie?"

"Yes?" he said, suddenly alerted by the youngster's gravity. Oh Christ: What was wrong?

"Sergeant, your wife has been looking all over hell and gone for you."

"What's wrong?" he said.

"It's your son."

"My son?"

Bud watched him in horror, thinking his whole life might be about to change: Lamar, his son, vengeance, it all came together in a single, horrifying moment.

"Your youngest boy, Jeff."

Oh, God, thought Bud.

"He just been arrested by the city police. Assault. He attacked two boys in school. Hurt 'em bad, too."

CHAPTER 27

The papers, in all their accounts of the famous gunfight at Jimmy Ky's, gave no personal details about this Bud Pewtie. Oklahoma highway patrol sergeant, forty-eight, that was all. His name was in no phone book either, but that was common: Cops seldom had listed phone numbers.

"How are we going to find him, Daddy?" Ruta Beth asked.

"Oh," said Lamar, "there're ways. He's left a trail. A sly old dog like me, hell, I'll sniff him out."

Lamar stared at the photo in the paper, and Bud Pewtie stared back. It was a grave, authoritarian face, the face of a manhunter. Lamar had seen it on a few cops in his time, but fewer and fewer of late, as the cops had gotten younger and somehow sweeter. But Pewtie had the gray eyes and flat mouth of a hero type, an ass-kicker, a shooter. And goddamn, he'd done some shooting. Lamar looked at the bandage swaddling his left hand. Two fingers, just gone, as if by surgery. Luck or talent? Lamar knew it was probably luck, but it left him a little uneasy. No man should be that lucky.

"He's a scary man," said Richard.

"Richard, when you hold a gun to a man's kid, he ain't scary no more. And when you blow that child's brains all over the sidewalk, let me tell you, he's going to bawl like a baby. Oh, then he'll know the true cost of mixing up with Lamar Pye. By God, he'll know."

Lamar thought: *He's probably a family man. Looks like the father of a whole tribe, lots of those square tough-guy sonsofbitches was like that—they were trained that the world was theirs for the taking and their job was to fill it with kids.* He thought of Pewtie as the head of a tribe, and saw him living on an estate, though of course he knew how little cops made. But the image was good; it stoked the cold rage Lamar knew he had to taste and hold to do the deeds that he had in mind, that would teach the world how dangerous it is to take something from Lamar Pye.

"Now," he said, "says here he's forty-eight years old. Wouldn't a stud like this one have kids? Wouldn't those kids be roughly in high school, figuring he got married in his late twenties, when he got out of the goddamned Marine Corps and got his training done?"

He looked around at Ruta Beth and Richard. No doubt about it, though Ruta Beth was as decent a girl as ever lived, she was not bright. She had some of Odell's dullness in the face, as she grappled with the idea.

Richard, on the other hand, was too goddamned smart. That was his whole goddamned trouble. He could figure everything out and do nothing. Richard was about the most worthless man he'd ever seen; a bad thief, gutless, a goddamned Mary Jane. He should have let the niggers make him their bitch before they killed him. But no. Not Lamar. Takes a boy under his wing and all these months later is still stuck with him.

Richard got it first, of course, but when he said it, Ruta

Beth got it, and her little dark eyes lit up with something like a baby's glee.

"Sports! His kids would do sports! You know they would!"

"Yes indeed, Richard, I think you got it. We go to the library, look through old newspapers, your high school sports page. Goddamn, I'll guarantee you, this one'd have a fullback or a pitcher or some other goddamned thing. We'll find his name in the paper and we'll know what school he goes to. Yessir. That gives us the place old Bud Pewtie lives in. We can hunt for that truck, which we all got a good look at when it was parked here, even though you two geniuses didn't recognize it in the parking lot."

"It was dark, Lamar," said Richard.

" 'It was dark, Lamar,' " repeated Lamar. "Or maybe we send the boy something—say, a basket of fruit, because he done pitched a no-hitter. Then we ID him when he comes out and follow him. Anyway you cut it, goddamn we'll have us the whole goddamn Pewtie clan, you betcha."

"Suppose he's guarded?"

"Well, then we wait a bit, and we catch us a Pewtie when the guard is down. Say a kid. Or maybe the mama. Then we call old Bud, and we say, you either come on out to play with us, or we going to start sending you fingers and ears. Oh, he'll come. Goddamn I know, he'll come."

It fell to Richard and Ruta Beth to enter Lawton's small branch library at Thirty-eighth and Cherry and take up the bound copies of the months of April, May, and June (not yet finished) for the *Lawton Constitution*.

Richard paged through the grim newsprint, his fingers darkening with inkstains. Every now and then a headline would reach out and snag his eye. GRANGE SLATES BAKE SALE, for example, or SAFETY RECORD SET AT WHIZ PLASTICS or RECITAL SET FOR TUESDAY—not news stories per se, but little announcements about this or that thing occurring somewhere in or about the greater Lawton area. They were like bulletins from another life: Richard had been raised to hold lower middle class society in utter contempt, but right then, it seemed the nicest thing he could ever imagine was to work accident-free in the Whiz Plastics plant his whole life, and go to the Grange bake sale on Saturday and his daughter's recital on Tuesday.

Never. Was gone. Couldn't happen. That life was sealed off. He was "special," he had been trained from an early age, smarter and more talented, and see what it had got him?

Why am I so damned smart? he wondered, pityingly. *Why do I have to see through so much? Why couldn't I be banal, like everyone else?*

"What the hell are you crying about?" Ruta Beth said. "You want us arrested for being weird? They do that in small towns, you know."

"No, it's just that it's so commonplace, the contents of a newspaper. There's nothing *meaningful* in it. It's so *ordinary.*"

"Goddamn, Richard, you are the goddamnedest weirdest man I ever did see. Don't see what Lamar sees in you. Go on, look for the goddamned name."

Richard pushed his way onward, his eyes roaming through the sports section, pulsing through dreary tales of dreary games played all across the city and surrounding counties. Why did boys love games so? It was a complete mystery to him. Take baseball, for example. What was the point? After all, if you hit the ball or you didn't hit the ball, in the long run, what was achieved? It was one of those self-defining systems, full of—

TWO PEWTIE HITS TAKE LAWTON HIGH PAST EUREKA

He'd almost missed it. But there it was, the name Pewtie, big as life. There couldn't be two of them.

"Sophomore Jeff Pewtie continued his hitting rampage," the breathless copy read, "with a single in the first and a bases-loaded double in the fifth. Since being promoted to Lawton varsity in mid-May, the 15-year-old sophomore has hit an amazing .457."

Richard rushed through the pages in search of this young Hercules' labors and found them nearly every week. When Jeff didn't deliver mighty clouts, his superb outfielding astonished the fans. Finally, yes, a picture: the boy being clapped on the back after delivering a game-winning hit, this just from last week! He looked carefully. The face was young and square and handsome, on a compact, muscular body, brimming with health and confidence. He looked hard into the bone structure and tried to match it with the sergeant's photo from the papers earlier that week, after the shooting. After a bit, he came to see it: It was the shape of the nose and the distribution of flesh between the eyes, the subtle architecture of a face or, rather, of a genetic pattern reiterated, though in a slight variant mutation, father to son.

"That's him," he said.

" 'Bout time," said Ruta Beth.

"That's the kid."

Richard looked at the boy; a shiver came across him. What a perfect gladiator, how confident of his place in the world and expectant of the future. And what woe awaited him.

In the parking lot, they showed Lamar a page they'd ripped from the newspaper, with Jeff's picture.

"You were right, Lamar. You were dead right. Now all's we have to do is go to the school like you said, and do what you said, and in a day or so, we'll—"

"Richard, goddamn, sometimes I don't think you got a brain in that head of yours. Not a one. How careful you look at this?"

Richard hung his head in shame.

"Not very," he said.

"Didn't think so, Richard. Tell me, Richard, you ever looked at a *sports page* in your life? Or you only look at books with pictures of naked women in 'em?"

"I-I-I don't like games," Richard said sullenly, punching out his lower lip.

"Well, on most sports pages, they got what they call a *schedule.* Yes, indeedy, and all you need to do is lookiesee and there it is."

"There what is?"

"The schedule. Of the games. Don't you think this old hero cop Bud Pewtie going to want to see his kid play ball? I mean, really, don't you think?"

"He would, Daddy," said Ruta Beth.

"You damned betcha," said Lamar. "And according to this here schedule . . . there's a goddamn game *tonight.*"

He looked at the two of them.

"Better git your mitts, boys and girls. We's going to a ball game."

CHAPTER
28

Bud got to the downtown police station—a two-story brick box on Fourth Street that only had a gaudy flower bed out front to break up its blankness—fast, made his inquiries, and was directed to Juvenile. He raced up the steps and down a bright green hall to discover the department, opened an opaque glassed door to find the same vision of a thousand American police stations: the cluttered bullpen room, the green walls, the bulletin boards littered with circulars that nobody ever looked at. And, in one corner, there was Jen standing next to an old friend, a police lieutenant named Howard, who had done ten years on the highway patrol with Bud before he'd missed out on a promotion and left the state agency with bitterness.

He walked up to them.

"Jen, my God, what the hell is going on? Is he all right?"

Jen just looked at him, something long and hurting in her eyes. Then she looked away.

"Now Bud, you'd best take it easy for now," said Howard. "I wouldn't let them put him in the tank with the scum. He's in a solitary cell and nobody's going to hurt him, that I guarantee. We got two detectives working on statements and witnesses and I've talked to both the other boys' mothers and I know the Juvenile Justice, and I think we can get everybody to agree to accept misdemeanor charges. Them boys was a part of it, too. Everyone's trying to behave well under the circumstances.''

''Just tell me what happened, Howard. Jeff isn't the kind of boy to assault strangers anywhere, much less in school. We didn't raise him like that and he never been in fights or had any JD records or nothing.''

''Bud, he did attack those boys. In front of others. In class, actually. He's a strong kid, you know. He punched the Jennings boy in the ribs and broke two and he broke the Chastain boy's nose.''

Bud just looked at Howard in disbelief. He couldn't begin to understand it.

''I just don't—''

''They were the spray painters, Bud,'' said Howard. ''They were the ones painting 'Long Live Lamar' and 'Odell Was a Martyr' and 'Go Lamar' on the walls. Two real smart boys, one going to Norman, the other going East like your son Russell. You know, smart-asses, show-offs. Well, it seems they have that angry edge all the young people have these days. Wanted to 'Question Authority,' they called it. Mischief, I suppose. Most everybody knew it was them, maybe even Russell. But Jeff found out today in the locker room. He just walked from classroom to classroom till he found them, and started pounding on them. I'll say this: They ain't going to paint no more signs on no more school walls.''

''If you ask me, Jeff deserves a medal,'' said Jen bitterly.

''No,'' said Bud, ''you can't think like that. What he did was wrong, no matter the reason. He has to take his punishment like a man and not let it wreck his life. We need a lawyer, a good lawyer. My record sure as hell won't hurt. The main thing is to avoid the felony conviction. Hell, he's only fifteen. You don't want a felony conviction on your record; it'll dog you for your whole life."

Bud felt an immense melancholy settle over him. Poor Jeff: He saw in a flash how his mind had worked and how he'd set out to avenge the family honor. Frankly, what those two boys did made him sick. He gritted his teeth and swore to himself that he'd fight like hell to see that his boy got every damn break he could. But he hated it: the troubles of his life, that he himself had invented, dumped square in his poor youngest son's lap.

He put his hand on Jen's shoulder and she recoiled.

So he found a phone and called an assistant prosecutor he knew and got the name of the best defense lawyer in town, a name he recognized as a man who was known for a good deal of flamboyance and charisma—and publicity. Quickly he called, and when he was told that Mr. O'Neill was in conference, he said, "Now listen here, young lady. This is Sergeant Bud Pewtie of the Oklahoma Highway Patrol, the cop that shot it out with the Pyes. I think Mr. O'Neill would appreciate the fact that an officer as famous as I am chose him to call in an hour of need and he'd want me to be put through right away."

It worked; in a minute the lawyer was on the phone, and in five, he'd promised to be down there before four.

"Got him a lawyer," said Bud. "Believe me, getting a good lawyer is nine tenths the battle. All the scum has the best legal talent around—no reason we shouldn't."

But Jen didn't respond and just looked out the window.

Bud walked up to her.

"What the hell is wrong?" he said. "You are treating me like a piece of shit."

"Where were you?" she finally said. "Just what the hell is going on?"

"I was—" He came up dry. "I was seeing—"

And then he realized his mistake.

He couldn't say he'd driven out to see C. D. Henderson in his bitter retirement because he'd already lied and told her he was going to see C.D. to get the guns back.

He hit the wall. He came up blank. He was out of lies.

"I was just driving around, thinking."

"About what?"

"About how used up I feel."

"Oh, stop it, Bud. I'm not a fool. I can tell when something's going on."

She glared out the window.

Then she turned.

"You wait for the lawyer. You get Jeff out. I can't stand this anymore. I'm going home."

It took another hour for the lawyer to arrive, the paperwork to be signed, a quick hearing with the magistrate to be arranged, and then at last, Jeff was released. He looked so small, so pale and wan. They'd made him change clothes into those green prison beltless pants and shirt, and given him paper slippers. He looked like an intern. He wouldn't meet Bud's eyes, but the warder, a hearty black man who also knew of Bud, acted as host of the party, got Jeff's clothes and took him into the men's room where he could change.

Bud waited in the office and then Jeff was brought back, now looking somewhat better in his jeans and boots. But still he wouldn't look at his father.

They walked down to the truck together.

"You know, Jeff," Bud finally said, "I can certainly understand why you did what you did. A certain part of me even says those boys had it coming. But you can't assault them. That sets you on a path that can lead to self-destruction, a fine young man like you. It goes contrary to all your teaching.''

Jeff said, ''Dad, I know.''

''Then why did—''

''No, I mean, I *know*. What you're doing. It's inexcusable.''

Bud looked at his son's profile across the seat from him, saw the strong lean face, the delicate lashes, the intensity buried in the eyes.

''About her,'' Jeff said.

Little thud in Bud's heart. The world fell out of focus, and then came back.

''Jeff, I—'' But again he came up dry.

''It was the phone, Dad. About three months ago, I heard you talking on the phone late at night. Low voice, hushed. The noise came up through the floorboards. The next morning I looked at the phone for an hour. And then I punched redial. Don't you know about redial? How could you not know about redial? It dialed the number and the voice answered, a woman's, and she said hello and I said hello, and I remembered her voice from the time you and Mom had them over for dinner. And I said 'Mrs. Pepper?' and she said yes and I hung up. And I heard you—every night, I heard you, heard that voice coming up through the vent. You had to call her from the house? You couldn't call her from someplace else but you had to do it from the house?''

''Jeff, I—''

''You're screwing this woman and then you're coming home and acting like everything's okay, and then at night you call her and make plans for the next day? And you've got it all figured out, I bet! How you and her are going off, and you're just going to leave poor Mom and the rest of us.

And we have to pick up your pieces and go on, while you're out partying. God, Dad, how could you do that to her? How *could* you?''

Bud swallowed hard.

''Jeff, these things aren't so black and white as you make them out to be.''

''No, it is simple. You got tired of us. We bored you. So you went somewhere else. And every morning I had to wake up and wonder if this was the night you were leaving us.''

He had begun to cry. The tears ran down his cheeks. His nose began to issue terrible liquids. He hated to cry, Bud knew, hated losing control, but now he did and in seconds he was sobbing hysterically. Bud pulled over and put out a hand to touch him.

''No!'' Jeff said, recoiling savagely.

''I'm sorry, Jeff,'' Bud said. ''I never meant to hurt you. I don't think I ever would have left, not really. It wasn't something I planned or dreamed about. It just happened.''

''Dad. Dad, Dad, Dad.''

''Jeff, one thing a son always has to learn is that his father ain't a hero, he's just another man trying hard and making mistakes like everybody else. Now I suppose I cut myself too much slack. My old man was a drunk and he beat me up a lot, too, and he drove my mama out early. So I always thought if I was better than *him* then I'd really accomplished something. But now I see that being better than that don't mean shit.''

They sat there for a long while.

''Well,'' Bud finally said, ''at least I figured out what I'm going to do.''

He took a deep breath and faced the future.

''I'll make it work. I can make it work. You know I can make it work.''

"Are you just *lying* again?"

"Jeff, I never told you no lies. Yes, I lied to your mother. Someday when you're an aging man and a pretty young woman takes an interest in you and you can't find it in your heart to say no, then maybe you'll know what it is."

The boy looked at him through a ravaged, swollen face and said nothing.

"Don't you have a game tonight?" Bud asked.

He nodded.

"Will they let you play?"

"I don't know."

"Well, how's this? I'll take you to the game. When the game is over, I'll go over to Holly's and I'll tell her the news. I owe her that much. I have to tell her straight up, you understand. Then I'll go to home, and I'll tell your mother what a bad husband I've been. And I'll ask her to forgive me, and maybe she will and maybe she won't. But the lying will be over, that I swear to you. All right? The lying and the cheating, it's all over. Then pretty soon, when school is out, we'll all go on a nice trip. We have some money saved up, but I think the whole family going on a trip, maybe that's more important. I will set my house in order, Jeff, I swear to you."

The boy said nothing. Then maybe he gave a nod.

CHAPTER 29

Lamar stole a '91 Trans Am out of the very same library parking lot and followed Ruta Beth and Richard back to the farm.

When they arrived, he had it all mapped out.

"Okay," he said, "this is how we do it. We don't do *nothing* at the game. Too many people, too much traffic, too much you can't control. We hook onto goddamn Bud Pewtie though, and we follow his ass home. We wait till he's all snug inside with his goddamn family. Then we blow the doors down and start shooting. We leave hair on them walls. I want that kid and the mama dead and whoever's else in that house. I want Bud Pewtie to know what loss is. I want him to suffer as I suffered. Then I'll cut his face off, Richard, and then we're out of here, you got that?"

"All of them?" said Richard queasily.

"Son, you ain't up for this work? It don't mean nothing to you that I save you from being the niggers' fuckboy, that I save your goddamn life in Denny's and in the goddamn river, and that this sonofabitch done shot poor Baby Odell full of holes? Richard, this is a raid. It's man's work. You got to go in hard and shoot straight and put all of them down. Yes, *all of them.* The whole goddamn family. Now, either you going with us, or we'll leave you here and you won't be a happy boy scout.''

''I can do it,'' Richard said. In a funny way, he now believed it. It was, after all, only a mechanical thing: You point the gun, you pull the trigger. There was no higher meaning.

''You, Ruta Beth. Can't do a job like this 'less you believe in it the whole goddamned way. You with me?''

''Yes, Daddy,'' she said. ''The kids, the women, all of them. It's for the baby. We'll show them what it means to hurt a baby.''

''Good. Now I want us to change into some uppity clothes. We got to look like we got a boy playing ourselves. Any clothes from your daddy and mommy left, honey?''

''There's a trunk.''

''Can you and Richard git it? Then we'll change and go.''

''What are you going to do, Daddy?''

Lamar smiled.

''The guns,'' he said. ''I'm checking the guns.''

Lamar went upstairs and saw what there was to see. The SIG .45 that he'd taken off the Texas Ranger, the Smith .357 Magnum from Pewtie and two other .45s from the Stepfords, and two sawed-off shotguns, the Browning automatic and the Mossberg that had come from Bud Pewtie's cop car. Ruta Beth had bought ammo: 185-grain hollowtips for the .45s, 125-grain hollowtips for the .357, and six boxes of double-ought buck for the two shotguns.

He lovingly threaded shells into chambers and magazines, thrilled, as always, at the fitting together of parts, the slick camming of slides and pumps and bolts, the heavy feel of them all, until each gun seemed alive with its charges. The SIG, one of the other .45s, and the Browning semiauto would be his; he'd give Ruta Beth the pumpgun and a .45, and poor Richard could carry the .357.

Then, gathering them, he went downstairs. Richard had washed up and changed into a nice pair of slacks and a striped sports shirt. He looked like a lawyer at a party. Ruta Beth looked almost cheery in a white polyester pantsuit that had once been her mama's and a pair of loafers. Lamar quickly changed into a nice leisure suit in gray and a colorful shirt; he could keep his handguns out of sight that way.

He went to the mirror in the bathroom. He saw the same old Lamar, with that thick, friendly face, that mashed nose where the Cherokee deputies had pounded him all those years ago, the open, alert eyes. What is wrong with this picture? The hair, that's what. Too much hair. Looked like a biker or an Indian, or some other kind of trash.

"Ruta Beth," he called. "Come cut all my hair off."

The team was already on the field in sweats when Bud and Jeff pulled in. It was the last game of the season, and already parents had begun to gather in the parking lot. Bud could see the other team's bus—EISENHOWER H.S., it said—and knew their players would probably be in the locker room suiting up.

"Well, here we are," said Jeff.

"Let me go 'long with you to talk to him. This goddamned hero business may do us some good."

The two walked under the bleachers, around a gap in the fence, and around the edge of the dugout. Ahead of them, on the diamond, a lean black assistant coach was fungoing grounders to the infielders. Bud watched the ball snap and hop across the green and watched as the boys bent gracefully to scoop it up, always magically snaring it on the right bounce then pirouetting as they fired across the diamond to the first baseman, who then fired the ball to the catcher who served it up to the coach. In the outfield, boys were drawing beads on descending balls, gathering them in and then launching long throws.

Bud and his son ducked into the dugout, where an elderly man sat crosslegged, fussing with a lineup card.

"Coach?"

The old man looked up.

"Well, hello there, Jeff. Sergeant Pewtie."

"I'm out, sir," Jeff said. "I was wondering if it was possible if I could play?"

"Technically, both boys' parents have dropped charges against Jeff," said Bud. "The magistrate released him in my care on my word we'd find some counseling for him. It turned out Jeff didn't do no serious damage, and their parents acknowledge that what they done was stupid and what Jeff done, while also stupid, was understandable."

"So you ain't going off to prison?"

"Doesn't look like it, sir," said Jeff.

"It'd mean a lot to Jeff if he got to play," said Bud.

"Well, I think it'd mean a lot to the team if Jeff got to play. Let me make a call."

The coach stood and went to a pay phone a few feet down under the bleachers and dropped his own quarter and did some asking and some listening and some more asking, and then came back.

"Well, Jeff," he said, "You're to be suspended. For three days. I can't legally allow a suspended boy to participate in athletics. That's the rule."

"I see," said Jeff, but the disappointment broke on his face like a wave. He swallowed and seemed to tear up just a bit, too.

"Well, sir," said Bud, "thanks for giving us a hearing. The rules are to be obeyed."

"That they are, Sergeant Pewtie," the coach said, "and

to a 'T.' And the 'T' says that the suspension doesn't begin formally until tomorrow. Far as I'm concerned this boy's still in school and he better get his ass out on that field before I start to chew on it.''

Jeff lit up like a candle.

"I'll go get my uniform.''

He raced off.

"You're not going to get in any trouble for this?'' Bud said.

"Hell,'' said the old man, "I been here for thirty-four years and won 'em seven state championships. What can they do? Yell at me?''

Bud shook his hand.

"I appreciate what you're doing for the boy. He's a good kid. He deserves a break.''

"Yes sir, Sergeant Pewtie, I agree—he is a good kid and he does deserve a break. I hope this helps him.''

Bud slipped out of the dugout.

The stands were beginning to fill. He checked his watch. It was five P.M. and the game began at six, would probably be over by eight-thirty.

An overwhelming melancholy came over him.

Well, it was time.

He went to a refreshment stand that had just opened and bought a Coke to fight the dust and the phlegm in his throat. Its cold sweetness plunged down his gullet, momentarily energizing him. But then it was gone, the cup tossed into a steel garbage barrel, and there it still was, what he had to do.

He walked over to the same phone the old coach had used to call the school, dropped in his quarter, and dialed the number.

She answered on the third ring.

"Hi,'' he said wanly.

"Well, Bud Pewtie, bless my heart, my parts are still abuzzing for all the attention you paid them today. Fact is, don't think they'll settle down until sun goes down. Ain't felt this good in years."

"Well, I'm glad" was all he could think to say.

"Now, what do I owe this honor to? Usually, I don't hear from such as yourself until late at night."

Her voice was so happy! He could see her face, all lit up, the way the joy came into her eyes. He had never been able to please a woman so. It had been that way with them from the start.

"Ah," he said, "I'm at Jeff's game. Probably be here, oh, till eight-thirty, nine o'clock. It's his last game of the season. I'm hoping he'll have a good one."

"I know he will, Bud."

"Anyway, Jeff'll probably go with some of the boys to a pizza place or something and I thought maybe I'd drop by after the game."

"Bud!" she said, squealing with delight. But then her delight stopped. "What is it? Is something wrong?"

He lied. What was the point of hurting her now, of making her suffer for three hours until he could get over there? He didn't have it in him.

"No, no, nothing like that. It's just, I have some time, no one's going to notice where I am or why, and I thought maybe we could have a beer or something."

"Oh, Bud, it's a *date*. You haven't taken me on a date in months! I don't believe you've *ever* taken me on a date. I'll see you then."

"Yes you will," he said, hanging up.

Lamar sat by himself, up top of the Lawton Senior High bleachers. He was aware of the cop nearly thirty rows away, on the other side of the horseshoe of scaffolds and seats that embraced the base-paths of the diamond. But he never looked directly at the man, for he had a feel for the magic power of eyes—whatever it is that makes some men *feel* the pressure of eyes on them, and turn at the last goddamn second to avoid the shank sweeping toward them to end their lives. He'd seen it on the yard enough times: men who tuned their nerves and were always right on the goddamned edge, prickly and fast and fucking dangerous. Others just didn't pay attention, and when the reaper came for them, they weren't ready and it just split them open, there where they stood. But Lamar knew from more than seeing it happen: Once a nigger trying to make a name for himself had jumped him blindside in the yard at Crabtree State, meaning to rip his guts out right there. Lamar often wondered if it was the hand of God or the breath of the Devil blowing in his ear or some kind of animal thing that felt a push in the air; he spun a cunt hair before the knife reached his spine, caught it with his left wrist (he would always wear the jagged scar), and headbutted the man to death in approximately thirty seconds, pile-driving the top of his skull into the bridge of the man's nose with all the power in his body until it was done.

It was judged self-defense, the only time Lamar had ever won anything at a hearing; he later heard the boy had come for him in order to impress the Tulsa Afriques, the baddest nigger gang in that pen. He was hoping to get in; Lamar sent him to his weeping mama in a bag, and oddly enough Toussaint Du Noir, as the leading black punk of the Afriques had renamed himself, sent Lamar a carton of cigarettes for getting rid of a wannabe. But they were only Kools, and Lamar traded them for a couple of blow jobs from a bitch named Roy.

But Lamar was sure that Bud would have such an intuition, too, and therefore wanted to steer clear. So he had told his crew to wait in the Trans Am, which was parked a couple of rows behind Bud's easy-to-identify Ford.

Lamar enjoyed sitting there. He was with the fans from the visiting team, Lawton Senior's crosstown rivals, all of them good hard-working people of the sort Lamar had no problem with.

That goddamn Pewtie kid was good. Lamar knew him almost right away, from the squareness of his head and the same alert way his father stood. He guessed Bud had been a good athlete, too, for such things tended to run in families, just as his daddy had been a hell of a prison ballplayer and he, Lamar, had once been a good prison leagues center-fielder when he still had his speed.

But this young Pewtie could run anything down in left field, and had a good arm. Christ, though, he could hit a ton; it was the fifth inning and he'd already drilled a double and a single. But it was the way he attacked the plate when he hit, unafraid, legs apart, head straight, just waiting for the ball to come toward him so he could demolish it. It was his hunger that Lamar felt up there in the bleachers.

And that somehow made him hate the lawman even more; it wasn't enough that he took from Lamar the one person that he'd cared about, but that he had so much: wife, great kid, a place in a world that would forever shun such as Lamar Pye. It was a world that would only know him through fear.

Lamar sipped a Coke, adjusted his baseball cap, looking for all the world like just another working-class dad watching the high school kids play ball, all the while nursing his rage into something so hot it was cold.

It felt delicious. It was coming.

As a present, he looked across the way to the big state policeman sitting in the stands, yelling after his boy, and he thought: *Goddamn, mister, what you got coming. What you got coming.*

A last pop-up seemed to rise until it would bring rain but then fell, accelerating lazily in the bright night lamps' light, and an infielder nabbed it. That was it. Game over.

Not a bad one, either. Jeff had gone two for four, stolen a base, and made two nice running catches in the deep outfield. He'd made a good throw, too, a special victory, because his arm was the problematical part of his game. Lawton won easily, eight to two, and the game had essentially been over since the fourth inning, when Lawton put six runs on the board. No drama.

That's how Bud wanted it.

He looked at his watch. It was eight thirty-five. Plenty of time.

He milled through the departing crowd, slipped through the fence, and ducked into the dugout, where boys and parents had gathered. The coach gave a nice little speech about what a great team this had been, even if they didn't make it to the state tournament, and he may have had more talented teams but he'd never had one that had worked so hard, and that next year looked really good, and he hoped all the sophomores and juniors would play Legion ball this summer. There was a polite smattering of applause.

Then the team broke into its cliques and the players began to filter out in twos and threes, some with parents, others without.

Jeff slipped up to him.

"We were going to meet at Nick's," he said. "You know, like we always do."

"You have a ride?"

"I'm going with Tom and Jack and Jack's girl."

"Don't stay out too late. Don't worry your mother any."

"I won't, Dad."

The moment hung between them.

"Okay," Bud said, "now I'm going to take care of that business I told you about. And everything's going to be all right."

"I know, Dad."

"You just go and have a good time. Don't stay too late. No beer."

"Yessir."

Jeff slipped away, engulfed in a tide of boys, and Bud knew it was time to go.

Lamar was just a little bit nervous. He left the parking lot and parked a hundred yards or so down the road, so that he wouldn't have to start out of the nearly empty lot exactly as Bud did, because such a thing might give him away to a sharp-eyed man. He swallowed.

He was driving himself because he didn't trust Ruta Beth or Richard. But still, it was a touchy thing: to follow Bud's truck through traffic, ever so gentle, never losing touch, never being too tight, just close enough to track his rabbit to its hole. It was plain, old-fashioned hunting.

But he'd helped things along; after leaving the game in the seventh inning, he'd placed a piece of reflecting tape flat under each of Bud's taillights, low on the bumper; that way, he could drop back a hundred or so yards and still keep sight of the truck by the unusual pattern. He didn't have to see the truck proper, only the lights.

He watched Bud now leave the rinky-dink stadium, among the last. The lawman was by himself, moving with something akin to melancholy that Lamar couldn't quite figure, though he read hesitancy and regret in the body language. Before the trooper had seemed to swagger. He was under a goddamn black cloud. Even Ruta Beth noticed it.

"What the hell he so down for?" she wondered.

"Yeah, Lamar," said Richard, "you said the boy got lots of hits."

"Who knows?" asked Lamar. He thought he was sad now, imagine what he was *going* to feel.

Bud got in, turned on the lights, pulled out. Lamar turned on his lights and sped down the road so that he actually beat Bud's entrance into traffic, making his man wait while he lazed on by. Bud pulled into traffic behind Lamar, but Lamar wouldn't let himself look; some little thing like that, a look at the wrong time, and the whole goddamned shaky thing could fall apart.

"There he—"

"Shut up, Richard. Goddamn it, boy, keep your mouth shut and look right straight ahead."

Lamar slowed just a little; with a hasty spurt, Bud dipped into the oncoming lane and shot by, lost in his own thoughts. Good—that meant Bud couldn't have picked up someone coming into the traffic behind him, then hooking up; he'd have to be a genius to pick up the cue.

Lamar dropped a few car lengths behind.

"Can we turn on the radio?" asked Richard.

"Shut up, Richard," said Ruta Beth.

The cars ambled through the early evening traffic in the fading light. Up and down the streets, the streetlamps and shop signs were coming on, blurring in the windshield, making it hard to track the set of lights that was Bud's truck. But his concentration was so intense it was as if he were some other man: he just saw the two red lights and the bright strips that were Bud's and nothing else in the universe.

Then Lamar saw a problem up ahead. It just came, all of

a sudden, from nowhere. Bud signaled a left just as his truck was moving into yellow. Lamar would never make the intersection before red, and he knew if he blew through the light, he might be spotted by a cop or even Bud. You can't be too careful.

Lamar calculated quickly, figuring the least risky of two very risky courses in a split second. He took his left now, down a side street that he didn't even know went through. Out of Bud's sight, he hit the pedal, raced wildly, swerved by a slowpoke who honked, frightened two women back on the curb, wheeled right up another street, and came to the street Bud had turned left down. There was a steady stream of traffic.

Shit!

Where was he?

He scanned the lights disappearing down the road, goddamn it, and saw nothing, and felt a raging emptiness.

"Lamar, I don't—"

"Shut *up,* Richard, Daddy's working."

Then he saw it, the small jot of red reflected light under a taillight that signaled Bud. Lamar gunned his Trans Am, slid through the traffic, darted through two left-hand passes, and soon enough fell in a hundred yards back in the right lane.

"He ain't seen shit," he said. "Hot damn."

Bud pulled up outside the little house, now glowing in the dark. It looked merry and friendly. The black kid with the trike was nowhere to be seen. He climbed out, waited by his car for a second.

That goddamn house. *She moved here to be with you and now you got to do this goddamn thing. You're going to hurt her so. You will hurt her and hurt her and then walk out.*

He tried to put a nice spin on things. It was better for her.

Really, she deserved a fresh start, not some half-life with a retread full of lead and freighted with kids and guilt and his own memories of a betrayed wife and a dead partner, who was her husband. She deserved so much. A little frog worked into Bud's throat as he looked at the house.

Then it was time and he went in.

He walked up the walk. It was only eight hours since his last trek up the walk. What it had led to that time was sex with her. Smoke rose in his mind as images came to him. There was the business in the living room, on the sofa; and then the business on the steps; and the final business in the bedroom. They had stretched it out, moving from room to room, as if to celebrate the freedom they now enjoyed after so many motel rooms. Interesting things happened in each room, but the stuff on the steps—he didn't think they'd done anything like that before.

Gone, all gone.

An enormous sense of loss suffused Bud.

Had to do it, he thought. His sons. His wife. His family. This was hard, the hardest thing yet, but he could do it and save his family and win it all back.

He climbed the steps and before he could reach the door, it popped open.

"Well, howdy there, Mr. Bud Pewtie himself," she said.

"Hi, Holly."

"Well, get you in."

Bud walked in. Same house, same Holly smell in it.

"Do you want a beer?"

"No, I don't think so."

"Bud, you have that do-I-have-to-go-to-church? look on your face. Why don't you spit it out so's we can get to the nut-cutting part."

"Oh, Holly."

She sensed the remorse in his voice. A grave look came

across her, as if she'd been slapped. She knew, instantly. He could tell.

"Bud, no. We're so close."

"We're not close."

"Bud—don't do this to me. Please, sweetie."

"Holly, I—"

He stopped, stuck for words again.

"You what?"

"I never meant to hurt you. That was the last thing I ever meant. I wanted everybody to be happy."

"But everybody can't be happy."

"No, they can't. Holly—Jeff's found out. My son is in so much pain. I'm going to try to put his life together again."

"Bud."

"Holly, you are a young and beautiful woman. You can have your whole life. You can have anything you want."

"Bud, I want you. I want us. I want what we said we'd have together."

"I can't give you that. I'm sorry."

"Bud—"

"Holly, I have to be a better father to my son than mine was to me. Without that, I ain't shit, and I know it. I took something from him. I want to give it back."

"Bud, it's not an either-or thing. You can have both. I'm not saying it'll be easy, but you can have both."

"Holly, I'm setting you free. Goddamn, you can have anything. *Anything.* You just wait. Your life is going to turn out swell, you'll see. You get through just this little bit, and then the good times start."

She stared at him furiously, and after a bit began to cry. He wanted to go to her and comfort her. She had given him such comfort over the months.

She sat down.

"I don't see how you can live a lie. You go back, and it's

some kind of fake thing where you're pretending to be noble, and then I'm gone, and you're stuck with a wife you don't love. So then what have you got? You'll end up with nothing.''

Bud himself sat down. Now she put her head in her hands and began to sob.

Help her, he thought. *Stop her hurting.*

Her face smeared and swelled and turned red and patchy. Her nose ran. Quiet, racking shudders raced through her shoulders. He'd seen women cry that way on the turnpike when they looked at the carnage that had been their husbands or their children. There was nothing you could do for them except hope that they healed and went on.

''Bud, I love you.''

''Holly, it ain't about love. My son can't get another father and I can't get another family.''

''Bud—''

''Holly, I can't be the kind of man who runs away. That's where all this crime comes from—everybody cutting and running. I can't be that kind of a man.''

''You lied to me. So many times.''

''Maybe I did. But I lied to myself, too. I thought we had a chance. I ain't the man to give you that chance. You deserve the man who'll give it to you.''

''It's so easy for you.''

''No ma'am, it's not. It's not anything like easy. Holly—I *love* you. Don't you see that?''

''Oh, Bud,'' she said. ''Why are you doing this to me?''

Lamar thought it would be a bigger house. He was disappointed. He knew cops weren't rich unless they were crooked, and he didn't think Bud was crooked. But he thought they did all right. This little, run-down house?

''He can't be doing too well,'' he said.

"He ain't doing as good as us," said Ruta Beth. "This is a shitty neighborhood."

"Really," said Richard from the back, "it's just a crummy civil service job. He doesn't make twenty-five thousand a year, I bet."

They were parked on the street, half a block down from Bud's house. They could see his big truck parked out front.

"We going to hit them now, Daddy? In, out, bang, bang?"

"Let me think some," said Lamar.

It was a sweet thought: blow through the door just like at the Stepfords', catch him completely flat-footed, and pump out 12-gauge until nothing in the house lived. Then head out fast.

But . . . he hadn't realized it would be in such a dense little neighborhood. At the sound of shots there'd be witnesses everywhere; they'd get a fast ID, and before Lamar could get them back to the farm, the law would be on him. Second, Pewtie was fast himself, that was the trouble. He was wearing a coat, he was probably carrying, Richard might panic, who knew what might happen? If he got to that goddamned Colt, all kinds of hell might happen.

Plus, he didn't know who was there. Maybe the whole goddamn SWAT team. It was a SWAT team birthday party or something.

Lamar had to fight to control that part of him that screamed to go in and leave hair and blood on the walls. But he held steady, letting the smart part of his brain take over.

"Okay," he said. "We just going to stay calm. Now Richard, I want you to get out and mosey on down the street. Don't stop, don't slow down none, don't stare, goddammit, don't *stare,* and then you come on back. You let me know what you can see, but don't you push it, boy, or I'll have your balls for breakfast.''

''Yes, Lamar.''

Richard got out of the car, did not slam but rather eased shut the door. Maybe he was beginning to learn a little something: he began to mosey on down.

''Daddy, what you thinking?''

''I just want to play this sucker really right. That's all, hon. Then we done our duty to Odell and we be off.''

''I can't wait. I'll do anything you want, you know that, Daddy.''

''I know, sweetie. You are the best.''

He felt her hand touch his neck, gently.

''I could come up front now and put my mouth to you. You could have me in the mouth,'' she said. ''It would help you relax a bit. I don't mind.''

The idea didn't appeal to him.

''Not now,'' he said. ''We got work to do.''

He watched as Richard shuffled along the sidewalk slowly, seemed to pause just a second, and then moved on down the road. Then he repeated himself, coming back. It seemed to take forever. But finally Richard got in.

Lamar started the car, drove down the block, and turned before he asked what he'd seen.

''They're having some kind of fight or something. He's yelling at her, she's crying. She came over to him, he yelled something and she went away.''

''Sounds like my mother and daddy,'' said Ruta Beth.

''You see anybody else?'' said Lamar, turning another corner.

''No sir. No one.''

''You didn't see that boy of his?''

''No. He must still be out.''

''Okay, okay.''

Lamar rounded another corner.

"Where we going, Daddy?"

"I'm just going to come in from another angle, and park in a new place. I don't want no citizen seeing peoples sitting in a car and calling the cops. That's all we need. Goddamn, I wish his boy was there. That's what would make it really good."

He returned to the street and parked on the other side, this time well beyond Bud's.

"Okay," he said. "What the hell. We go. We get 'em both, we blow 'em away, man and wife, and then it's finished. Fair enough?"

"Yessir."

"You up for this kind of man's work, there, Richard?"

"I can do it, Lamar."

"I want you in the back. You go in the back. Anything comes your way without calling out your name, you put a bullet in it. But no one's coming your way. I'm blowing them to hell and gone, that's it."

Lamar got out, went back to the trunk, opened it. He slid out the Browning semiauto, just peeled the bolt back a bit to see the green double-ought shell in there, and let the piece rest in his hand alongside his leg.

Ruta Beth had the other shotgun.

Richard took out his revolver.

"Not yet, you coon-brain. Not till you get in the house. You ready?"

"Yes sir."

"You, Baby Girl?"

"Yes Daddy."

"Then it's butcher day."

* * *

"We can't keep going over the same thing again and again. We're like cats in a damn bag. It ain't going to change."

"So that's it? You're just going to leave?"

"Holly, I—"

"I can't believe you can just leave."

"I can't stay here forever. It ain't going to change."

"Oh, Bud."

He rose, picked up his hat, and walked to the door.

He opened the door.

Then he turned.

She was still on the sofa. She looked like he'd beaten her. Her face was swollen and wet.

"God, Holly," he said. "I am so sorry. You deserve so much. You deserve so much more than I could ever give you."

She just sat there.

He tried to think of something more to say, some magic sentence that would make it all better. Of course there wasn't one. So in the end, he merely turned and walked out.

If she'd have cried out, what would he have done? A part of him badly wanted to go back. A part of him didn't know what the hell he was doing. He only knew he had to get out of there, or he'd never leave. So he walked as if in a tunnel to the truck.

Lamar was seventy-five feet away when the door of the house suddenly opened. He saw Bud, big as life, looking like John Wayne in the doorway of a hundred westerns, face grim, broad Stetson low over his eyes.

But Bud didn't see him. Instead he walked in a straight line to the truck.

It was too far to shoot. He could run at Bud, but Bud would see or hear him. Again, he fought his thirst for action, and melted back, sinking into the ground behind a hedge, with his hand driving the girl and Richard back.

They watched as Bud climbed into the truck. He was too far away to attack, and they couldn't get back to the car in time to follow him.

Bud started the truck and drove off.

"Where's he going?" whispered Richard.

"Shut up," said Lamar.

"What do we do, Daddy? What do we do?"

Lamar thought for a second and thought the same thing: *What do we do?*

Then he grinned.

"I know," he said.

Holly sat there. The sense of loss was on her like a heavy wool blanket. The whole thing played out before her eyes and the words *so close, so close* kept echoing in her mind.

But she could never get him to see it: how perfect they were, how they'd be more together than they ever would be apart.

Then someone knocked on the door, filling her heart with hope.

She rose and ran, thinking, *Bud, Bud, Bud,* and opened the door.

But it wasn't Bud. It was Lamar.

CHAPTER 30

Bud drove aimlessly through downtown Lawton in the dark, not really seeing anything except the blurred lights. He followed no particular path and at various times found himself nearing the airport, the Great Plains Coliseum, and Gate Number Three. Even Fort Sill Boulevard seemed desolate. Downtown, those amber lights caught everything in a particularly harsh brown glow, so that no true color stood out.

Bud felt exactly the opposite of how he expected. He thought he'd feel liberated at last, shorn of his secret life, ready and willing to embrace with all seriousness of high purpose his old life, which had been miraculously restored to him. But no. He just felt draggy, slow, morose, grouchy. He wanted to get in a fight. Impulses toward extreme anger flicked through him. A part of him wanted to lash out, maybe at Jen, maybe at Jeff, maybe at Russ, really at himself. It wasn't depression so much as plain old regret; images from all the sweet times with Holly kept playing on a movie screen in his head.

So little to show. She'd given him so much and she got so little.

Well, Holly, let that be a lesson to you that will stand you in good stead sometime in the future: no married men. Not worth it. All's you get is promises and sex up front, and pain and abandonment at the back end.

At last he turned down his own street and pulled into his own driveway. Jen's station wagon was there in the carport.

He got out, walked in. The house seemed especially small and cheesy. Wasn't much of a house. No room in it big as a motel room. The furniture, except what Jen had been given by her mother, was cheap, bought on time, in ruins before being paid off. The linoleum in the kitchen was dingy; the walls needed repainting; his shop was a mess; the lawn needed cutting.

For some reason it seemed to stink of a thousand meals tonight, of backed-up toilets and spilled beer and TV dinners and pizza kept in the refrigerator too long. God. How had all this happened? How did he end up in a house he didn't love with—

"Well," she said. "About time."

"All right, Jen," he said.

"So where is he?"

"He's with his friends. I got him out in time to play and drove him over. That coach said officially his suspension didn't start till *tomorrow* so the old geezer let him play. Git himself in a lot of trouble, you ask me. Anyway, Jeff did fine, a double and a single, made a nice running catch late in the game."

"It went into extra innings?"

"No, no, it didn't."

"He's with his friends. Bud, where *were* you?"

"Oh, I had some business."

"*What* business? Bud, what's going on?" Her face was grave and her eyes locked onto him. He could not meet their power.

"Ah—"

It hung in the air.

Finally he said, "Look, I understand I haven't been the best of husbands lately, Jen. I just had my head somewhere else. Okay. I've told you some lies, I've done some things I shouldn't have done. But, Jen, I want to tell you now, flat out, straight to your face, that's all over now. Now I am going to be father to my boys and husband to my wife. I want us to have our old life back, the one we loved for all those years."

"Bud?"

"What?"

"Bud, I won't ask you for details."

"I'm glad."

"I've heard things and I don't want to know if they're true or not. I just want you to tell me whatever it was, it's all over now. You have a good life, Bud, fine, strong, brave sons. No man could have better sons."

"I know that."

"I know I'm not so young as I once was. I can't help that. Like you I got old, and like you I got fat. I just got fatter."

"It's not that."

"Oh, who knows what it is, Bud. I do know that I can forgive you maybe once. But, Bud, don't you ever do anything like this again. If you want to be with her, just go and be with her. But no more of this running around."

"I will make it up. I'll make it so you won't notice there was a bad time. It was all good times, you, me, the boys."

"Okay, Bud. Then I don't want to hear of it again. We close the book and we lock it and I don't want to hear about it again. Is that clear?"

"I understand."

"Good. Now I think we should go to bed. I think you

should show me that you love me still. In the physical way, I mean. It's been nearly a year, are you aware?''

''I didn't know.''

''It's been a long, long time, Bud, and I have needs, too, though you don't like to face it.''

''Well, then let's go.''

They headed upstairs.

The phone pulled Bud from a blank and dreamless sleep, and he awoke in the dark of his bedroom, his wife breathing heavily beside him. All through the house it was quiet.

Groggily, he picked it up.

''Pewtie.''

''Well, howdy there, Bud'' came a voice from far, far away. It swam at Bud from lost memories, out of a pool of still green water. He fought to recall it but its identity lingered beyond his consciousness.

''Who is this?''

''Oh, you know who it is, Bud. It's your old goddamned buddy Lamar Pye.''

Bud's head cleared, fast.

''Pye. What the hell are you—''

''Missing anything?''

''What?''

''Missing anything?''

Bud thought: *My boys.*

''Lamar, so help me Christ—''

''Sure must be lonely in that bed tonight.''

Bud looked: He could see Jen stirring under her blankets.

''I don't—''

''I hope you didn't call nobody yet, there, Bud.''

''I—''

''She's damned pretty, your old lady. A bit young for a old goat like you. Bet she gits you to working hard.''

"Lamar, what the—"

"Here, say something to your baby. Bring her over, sweetie."

A faraway voice said, "Git over here, you bitch," and in the next second, another voice came on the line.

"Oh, Bud, oh God, they came in and got me, oh, Bud, I am *so* scared, Bud they've all got guns and he hit me, he hit me—" and then Holly was taken away.

"Who is it, Bud?" said Jen groggily.

"You hear that, trooper? We got your wife. Yes sir, got your goddamned wife. You take my baby cousin, and shoot him full of holes, I'm going to take your lady, for my pleasures. Let me tell you how it's going to be, okay? You call anyone, you tell anyone, you mention this to anyone, by God, I will kill her and you know I will. First though I'll fuck her in every hole she got. Every one."

"I swear—"

"Now, Bud, if you want this pretty gal back, you'd best come and do what I tell you. I want you to go to a pay phone. You got about a hour. It's at 124 and Shoulder Junction, outside of Geronimo. Exxon station. I'm going to bounce you from pay phone to pay phone before I bring you in, just to make goddamned sure you don't have no SWAT boys with you. Got that?"

"Lamar—"

"You miss that goddamned call and I'll cut her throat and cut her nose off, Bud, and then come git you and the rest of your family at my leisure."

"Don't hurt her, goddamn it," Bud barked.

"Oh, and Bud?" Lamar asked in a voice rich in charm. "You want her back? Tell you what. Bring some guns."

He hung up.

Bud jumped out of bed, fought to clear his head. But, really, there was no decision to make, not one he could face anyway. If he called headquarters, he could play the game and sooner or later close with Lamar with a SWAT team, choppers, snipers, the works; the professionals would handle it as well as they could, but it wouldn't matter. One look at other boys at his private party with Bud and Lamar would cut her up without so much as a by-your-leave and take his goddamned chances with the lawmen. He didn't give a damn; he didn't fear his own death, he only wanted Bud's.

Bud pulled on jeans, boots, and a black shirt. He grabbed a sports coat, only to cover the guns he'd be wearing.

"Bud, what is going on?"

"I have to go."

"Bud, you—"

He faced his wife.

"I'm sorry. I have to go one last time. If you love me, you let me go. You trust me, you let me go."

Then he raced downstairs, opened the gun safe. There they were. He pulled on his shoulder rig and the high hip holster and then busily threaded rounds into the magazines, all of them, jamming them up with hollowtips. If his thumbs hurt, he didn't notice; it just seemed to take so goddamned long. He holstered the Beretta and the .45; the .380 went behind his belt on his belly. Then he looked for a rifle, knowing only a fool fights with a pistol if he has the choice, but came up short until he remembered that .30-30 lever gun outside, still under the seat in his truck. He closed the safe.

A shape loomed in the dark.

"Dad?"

It was Jeff.

"Jeff, I've got to go, fast."

"Dad, what's—"

"Never you mind."

"Dad—"

"Jeff, I love you. No matter what you hear or what they tell you or what happens, I love you. I love your mother and your brother more than anything. Now I have something to handle and I have to handle it. You stay here and take care of your mother. It'll be fine, I swear to you."

"Dad—"

"Jeff, I have to go!"

"Dad . . . I love you."

Bud grabbed his youngest son and gave him a bone-squeezing hug. He felt the boy's ribs and beating heart under that sheathing of muscle.

"Go on, now," he said, and dashed out.

Bud got to the truck, worried now, absurdly, that he was low on gas. But he had gas. He gunned it, whirled out of the quiet neighborhood for Geronimo forty-five miles away. He had about fifty minutes.

But suddenly a thought came to him. Goddamnedest thing. From where he didn't know, but an idea just flashed into his head. He saw a gas station phone booth and stopped and ran to dial 411.

"You have a number for a C. D. Henderson, out on Thirty-eighth?"

It took a few seconds.

"That number isn't listed, sir."

"Goddammit, this is a police emergency, I'm Oklahoma highway patrol sergeant Russell B. Pewtie, ID number R–twenty-four, and I want that number. Give it to me or give me your supervisor."

Soon enough Bud had the number and called.

The phone seemed to ring and ring.

Then a groggy woman's voice answered, the old woman, and Bud asked for the lieutenant.

"Carl," he heard her say, "it's some old boy for you."

Henderson's raspy voice came on.

" 'Lo?'' he said.

"Lieutenant, it's Bud Pewtie.''

"Bud, my God!''

"You still have your keys, don't you? You can still get into that goddamned office?''

"I could break in if I had to. Now what—''

"Listen to me, you drunken old goat. You get your ass over there. You say you're a detective? Well, this here's the night you're going to prove it.''

"What are you talking about? What's going on?''

"You never mind what's going on. I got something for you. The mystery person in Lamar's gang. Wore the mask all the time. Here's why. It's a goddamned girl. A *young* girl. Heard him call her 'sweetie.' Heard her say, 'Get over here, bitch.' That's all. But . . . a *young* girl. Young, in her twenties, maybe. Now that's another dot for you to connect. That's your goddamned third point. You find me a category that ain't a category that's got a Toyota that's also got a young girl. You got to find me that girl and that goddamed location. Now get cracking, you old buzzard, and don't you let me down.''

"Bud.'' Something like a sob ran through the old man's voice. "Bud . . . I'll try. I ain't the man I once was.''

"Well, goddamn, which of us is, except for goddamned Lamar?''

Bud hung up, checked his watch, saw that he was down to forty-five minutes. He jumped in his truck and gunned it.

"So,'' said Lamar. "Your old man. What's he like, you know, in the sack?''

"You pig,'' she said.

Tell him, she thought. *He's made a mistake. He came to the wrong house. He got the wrong woman.*

And then what?

Then he just kills me, that's all. And he still gets Bud.

"How big is he? Is he real big? Or is he just normal? I'll bet he's just normal."

She shook her head with disgust.

"Yeah. He's just normal. Here. You want to see something? You want to see something like you never seen before? Look at this. Hold her, Ruta Beth."

They had Holly's hands tied behind her tightly, and her feet tied. She felt so helpless and sick. He was the man who'd killed her husband. It was this grotesque white-trash tough boy with stumps for fingers, some malnourished little weasel of a farm girl, and the other one, a soft and delicate man-boy with tussled hair and the look of no guts at all on his prissy, plump-lipped little face.

Now Ruta Beth went behind her and held her head.

Lamar stood and undid his trousers.

"Oh, God," moaned Holly, and fought to look away, but Ruta Beth had surprising strength and governed her head until it was locked in the proper direction.

Lamar pulled his shorts down and unfolded what looked like an electric cable. It was a penis the size of a reptile, slack and coiled, its foreskin capping it.

"Hah? You see anything like that?"

"You look at Daddy," said the girl. "Go on, you look at the king. You ain't never seen nothing like that. That's the king."

She thought she'd gag.

"You just dream about it, honey. You just go on and dream until your husband shows up."

Bud reached the Exxon station with a minute to spare. But Lamar's call was late by five minutes.

When it came, he ripped the phone off the hook.

"Yeah?"

"Well, howdy, Bud. How you doing? You have a rough old time?"

"Cut the shit, Pye."

"Bud, biggest mistake I done made is not walking over to you when you was belly-down and capping you with that .45. Think of the trouble it'd saved us both."

"Where are you?"

"Oh, I ain't a-telling. You got a long night ahead of you. Maybe I'll bring you to me and maybe I won't. Maybe I'll run you into an ambush. Maybe I'm on a goddamned cellular phone right now, looking at your ass through the scope of a rifle. Just twitch my finger and it's all over."

He laughed. He was extracting immense pleasure from it.

"You haven't hurt her?"

"Honey, you tell your husband what you just saw."

There was the muffled struggle of someone being pushed to the phone.

"Bud!"

"Holly!"

"Oh, Bud, he made me look. They forced me to look."

"Holly, I—"

"At his dick. They made me look at it."

The fury rose in Bud like steam. He wanted to slam the phone against the booth until it broke.

Don't lose it, he warned himself. That's what he wants. He'll toy with her. He'll torture her in infantile ways to show his power—the size of his pecker, petty pains, maybe drawing on her skin. He'll do it so that she can tell you, so that you go crazier and crazier, and at the end you are hopelessly jangled and unable to operate.

It doesn't mean a thing. The only thing that counts is getting there and getting her out.

But he knew, too, that Lamar expected him crazy. He

lost something if he didn't let Pye know how nuts this was making him.

"Pye," he screamed. "Pye, you sonofabitch, I'll kill you. Don't you fucking *touch* her. Don't you touch her!"

Lamar laughed again.

"Bud, you still there? You got to git all the way to Snyder. To the 7-eleven on 183 north of Snyder. You best git you going, old bubba. Yes you best git a move on, or I'll do more than show her the lizard, I'll make her pet it. Maybe even give it a li'l kiss."

Lamar hung up.

Quickly Bud dialed C. D. Henderson's old office in the City Hall Annex. But there was no answer.

The old detective heard the phone ring. He'd been there five minutes. What was the point of answering it?

He opened his coat and removed the bottle of I. W. Harper. Only about a third left. He opened it, took a taste. Liquid flame, bright and deep. Immediately a tremor passed through him, knocked him into a blurred state, and then pulled him out again. He reached under his coat and his fingers touched something hard and cold: It was the curvature of the grip of a revolver. He pulled it out, feeling its oily heft: a Colt Frontier model, with an ivory grip, in .44 special, as manufactured in New Haven, Connecticut, in the year 1903. The rainbow of the case-hardened colors had long since worn off, turning the piece almost brown. His grandaddy had carried that gun before Oklahoma was a state; and his daddy had carried it, too, both as lawmen.

C.D. opened the loading gate, pulled the hammer to half cock and rotated the cylinder to see the primers of five tarnished .44 rounds, sited in the cylinder so that the firing pin rested on an empty chamber, the way any sensible man carried a Colt. Only fools carried a six-shooter with six shots; sooner or later, they'd thump the hammer accidently and blow a foot off.

C.D. was no fool.

But he didn't think for a moment he could help Bud, and he had some idea that a terrible, terrible weight rode on all this. He'd fail, a drunken, wasted old man. People would die. Bud, whoever else was involved. And Lamar would go on.

And when that happened C.D. thought he might thumb back the hammer of the old Colt, put the muzzle in his mouth, and pull the trigger. He felt so used up, he was hardly there. His life was a waste, things were changing so fast that he couldn't keep up. He was sixty-eight years old and should have retired five years back and enjoyed his time. But no. Vanity, anger, whatever, had driven him.

Okay, you old goat, he told himself.

Do some detecting.

Think. *Think.*

You got a new dot to connect. A third point, a third piece of evidence. A girl. A *young* girl. How does that help?

A category that is not a category. A young girl.

How do they connect?

How could they connect?

Original theory: Lamar would go for help or find help in the criminal community in one of its forms. They would always go to their own kind. So: He would go to the cycle gangs or the Indian boys running scams against their own tribes on the reservations or the organized crime interests in Tulsa or OK City or the drug networks supplied by South American gangs but run by niggers in the inner city, Hispanics or Italian groups otherwise; or that small shifting, mobile culture of armed robbers, professional contract killers, enforcers, and tough guys who serviced the bigger gangs on a strictly freelance basis.

But he'd gone to none of those, or at least none of those that could be demonstrated to have corresponded with the one known empirical clue, the tire tread that could only be worn by a small Japanese car, a Hyundai or a Nissan or a Toyota, in three model years.

Nothing. Nada.

Maybe it was just wrong, the assumption. Maybe he'd found somebody not in the life at all.

But no: Lamar, however extravagant, was a type, and types run to pattern. And Lamar's pattern was simple: He was a professional criminal, a long-term convict, he would only feel comfortable with his peers. Whoever he was bunking with would in some way be in the culture, would have stepped beyond the parameters of the law. And would be on the computer network.

But there was nothing.

The old man snapped on his computer terminal. It had access to Oklahoma Department of Motor Vehicles and criminal records at the state felony level. He could define a field and see what he got.

So he tried the most basic thing: He requested that the computer churn out a listing of all females between the ages of sixteen and thirty who registered or had registered a car in the known range.

SEARCHING SEARCHING SEARCHING the computer blinked at him for a few minutes, and then a list of names rose against its blue background.

He was not adroit at the mechanics of the computer; he could not physically manipulate the cursor without thinking, so he simply ordered the goddamned thing to print out. It clicked and chattered across the room, and he went to the printer, ripped the page out, and then examined what he had.

It was a list of eighty-three names, all of them meaningless, all of them unknown. Maybe one of them? Maybe not.

He went next to the known felons listing—that is, the felons who also had registered the right cars—and hoped there might be some correspondence, a coregistration that possibly suggested a daughter-father thing.

There was none.

No young woman with a car in the range could be linked to a known felon with the same car, at least according to the records.

Then, very slowly, he typed each of the eighty-three names into the computer and commanded FELONY RECORD CHECK.

It took the better part of an hour.

Results—zero.

"Richard," said Lamar, "come over here."

Shyly almost, Richard advanced.

"Richard, how long since you had a woman?"

"Ah? Lamar, that's *private.*"

"Oh, God," moaned Holly.

"Now, lady, lookie here at Richard. Now what's he got this Bud Pewtie you married ain't got? He's a fine, upstanding man. He's got a true talent, a God-given thang. He's loyal and hardworking. He's educated. Richard, you went to a college, didn't you?"

Richard said yes.

"See. He's a smart man. He could do you proud. You know, if you play your cards right, when this is all over . . . I might be able to git you a . . . *date* with Richard."

Lamar exploded once again into laughter.

Then he said, "You know, Richard, you could touch her a little. Really. She wouldn't mind, would you, hon?"

"Please," said Holly. "Oh, God, don't hurt me or touch me."

"Oh, it wouldn't hurt a bit. Richard, would you like to touch this young woman some place. Or maybe just look at her. You could look at her all you wanted, at least for a little while. Have you ever seen a girl this pretty without no clothes on, Richard? I mean, a *real* one, not in no book?"

The terrible thing was, Richard *did* want to touch her and look at her. She was a really beautiful young thing. He'd never had any woman, of course. It just hadn't worked out. Not that he was a homosexual. He was sort of a zerosexual. But now he looked at her and the deep stirrings of lust tingled in him. It was her helplessness that excited him. The way the rope cut into her white, freckly skin, the way her flesh blossomed around the raw pressure of the rope, the way her neck was faintly reddish as she squirmed, the look of complete horror on her face, and her goddamned prettiness. She wore Bermuda shorts, Nikes without socks, and a polo shirt; she looked like some kind of coed or something.

But then he thought: *Why is she so young?*

"Lamar, why is she so young?"

"What you mean?"

"Look at her. She isn't thirty. She isn't twenty-five. How could she have that son who plays baseball. Did she marry him when she was ten?"

"She was in his house. She got a wedding ring. They was fighting. Who else could she be?"

But then Lamar squinted and looked closely at Holly.

"How old are you?"

"I'm twenty-six," she said. "I *am* his wife."

"But that ain't your kid?"

"No, Jeff is not my son. Bud and I haven't had our children yet. He had his two boys with his first wife. But she died and he married me two years ago. It's the happiest two years of my life. He's a wonderful, kind, decent man. He's brave, he's strong. You ought to be ashamed of what you're doing.''

''Well, ain't you a goddamned Miss Mouthful. That son-ofabitch shot my cousin over twenty-five times. Just blew the life out of that boy.''

''You are such scum,'' she said. ''You may get me and you may get Bud, but they will get you in the end.''

Lamar leaned close.

''Don't you get it?'' he said. ''I don't give a shit. I ain't got much of a string to play out anyways. I just want to settle up. You think I'm afraid to die? Boy, then you ain't never been in no hard places, I tell you, and you don't know what hard places do to a man. In this room we're all going to be dead tonight or by noon at least. But by God, I will settle my dues and leave this world without no uncashed IOUs in my jeans.''

Bud blew through speed limits like a man in flames, and toward the end gave up on red lights. It was near two forty-five, the streets deserted. He charged up and down hills, cut across dirt roads, traversing Tillman and Comanche Counties on sheer instinct, then hit 62 just beyond Cache for a straight-line run to Snyder. He hit the 7-Eleven just beyond the town and found it still open, and someone on the phone.

He pulled his badge.

''Police business. We need this phone free.''

An Indian boy looked at his badge and spat on the ground and went back to his call.

Bud pulled the .45 and rammed it into the boy's throat.

''You sonofabitch, you git or you and I will have serious business and you won't like that a goddamned bit!''

In the face of the weapon and Bud's fury, the boy melted, hung up the phone, and ran off into the dark. Now

Bud felt a moment of shame, having given in to the cop's worst temptation, the display of brute power to require obedience. You can't just pull guns on civilians. On another night, it was grounds for suspension. Not tonight. Fuck it, tonight.

He looked at his watch. It was five after three. Shit. Maybe Lamar had called while the Indian was on the phone. He sat, breathing hard, his mind empty. The seconds clicked by. Suddenly it was ten after.

Christ, he thought, *I blew it.*

But the phone rang.

"Pye?"

"Oh, Bud, sorry I's late. Just gittin' to know your lady here."

"Don't you hurt her."

"Damn, she's a pretty one."

"Let her go. You'll have me. Let her go."

"We'll see. If you're a good boy, who knows, maybe I'll cut you some slack. If you got attitude, Bud, I may have to let her have a taste of some discipline, you know? Shit, maybe she'll even like it."

"Goddamn you, Pye."

"Best hurry on, Bud. You got to get all the way to Toleens, by four. Oh, you going to be a busy boy."

Lamar hung up.

Bud stared at the phone in sick fury. Toleens? Toleens? Where the hell was that? He hoped he had a map in the truck.

But instead he dropped a quarter and dialed the police annex, Henderson's number.

"Hello?"

"Lt. Henderson?"

"Bud."

Bud could tell from the tragic tone in the old man's voice. Nothing.

"I'm trying," the old man said. "I just ain't had no luck."

"Christ," said Bud. "They have a hostage. They'll kill her. You've got to figure this thing out!"

"Bud, you give me the okay, I'll put the call in. You go 'bout your business. We can track by air. A chopper. I'll have two busloads of the best SWAT operators in the business ten minutes behind you. We'll take that place down and the hostage can walk free."

"He'd *hear* the goddamn chopper, you know he would, Lieutenant. You can't play straight and outsmart Lamar. He's too goddamned good. He may even be watching me now and knows I'm pulling something. You *have* to come through. You *have* to."

Only the sound of the lieutenant's raspy breathing came.

"You haven't been drinking?"

"Son, I drink every damn day of my life. I won four of my seven gunfights drunk."

"All right, all right. Oh—Toleens. You ever heard of it? A town?"

"It's on 54, between Gotebo and Cooperton. Had a murder there in fifty-nine."

"Yeah, got it. There's a pay phone in the town?"

"Hell, boy, the pay phone *is* the town. Git on your way."

The lieutenant stared at the phone, listening to the dial tone in the seconds after Bud hung up. Then he placed it down on the cradle and put his fingers on the bridge of his nose between his eyes and squeezed.

The flare of light as his optic nerves fired somehow pleased him; then the room returned, deserted, green, junky, a police station room like all the ones he'd spent a long life in.

He felt used up, lacking will. A woman at least would die tonight, maybe Bud, too. A woman, a policeman, dying too young. Why should tonight be any different than any other night? It happened the world over. Why was it his responsibility to intercede?

He tried to tell himself it didn't matter, not cosmically. But it did. It mattered so goddamn much he wanted to cry.

He looked at the list. Eight-three names of young women who owned a car possibly linked to the robbery. A category that wasn't a categoy. Was it all an illusion? Was he a vain fool trying to tease meaning out of random events? Was there no pattern at all?

Break it down. Two elements. Young and woman.

What did *woman* tell him? A daughter of a criminal *possibly*. A criminal herself? Not in the records. No correspondence to the records.

He had a laugh. How much of it depended on the records. So much of police work was simply accountancy, human accountancy, the recording of accessible fact that may on faith in some distant time tell us something when we most need it.

Woman. Nothing.

What about young? What could there be about *young,* about youth, about immaturity, that fit into this or that touched on any issue of the central conceit, "a category that isn't a category."

How would a young girl get to know Lamar, who had been in jail for years and years? How could she meet him? Only way: She could write him.

Hmmmm.

Why would she write him? How would she hear about him?

Maybe she was one of those strange, desperate creatures who wrote to convicts, sent them money, proposed to them. It was a sickness, but it was there; and if that was it, there'd be no category for her. Or: wouldn't prison officials have noted it? That was where they started their investigations when a prisoner escaped.

Once again: nothing.

He returned again to the component: Young? What could that have to do with it? A young woman would probably not be attracted to convicts, it was more of a twisted spinster thing. Why a young woman? She *had* to be a daughter.

But presume, he told himself, since the daughter route appeared to lead nowhere, presume she is not a daughter or a sister or a relationship. She is a young woman. She is involved with convicts. What would involve her with convicts, other than her relations?

What?

He paused.

Something floated in the dark, just beyond him, translucent, ghostly in the still air.

There seemed to be a sudden stillness, as if the night itself had ceased to function, time had stopped.

What would involve her, draw her to them?

What?

She was a victim?

That would drive her *away.*

What?

She committed a crime herself.

It was so simple, and in the next second, wholly, it detonated in all its beauty into his mind; he saw into it now, clearly and absolutely.

A category that isn't a category.

A minor who commits a capital crime . . . but the court records are sealed, because she's a minor. There's no category for that. One cannot access it through normal channels.

C.D. blinked, opened the bottle, and swallowed a well-earned blast of Harper's.

If the court records are sealed, I can't get into them. Maybe tomorrow, but not now.

It angered him. So close and yet so far. Who else would have records?

And then the next step, easy as pie.

The newspaper.

C.D. opened a little black book he carried with him always, and located the number of the managing editor of the *Lawton Constitution*. He didn't give a damn what time it was as he called.

"Hello," came the groggy voice.

"Parker? Parker, it's goddamned C. D. Henderson."

"C.D.? What in *hell*—"

"Never you mind. You got anybody down at the paper tonight?"

"Ah—sure, skeleton crew, night telegraph editor, night photo editor, late makeup, sports desk. Probably a few odd bodies lying around."

"Ain't you all on some sort of computer system?"

"Nexus, it's called."

"I thought. Listen here, I'll give you a scoop and a half, you do me a favor. You call whoever's in charge down here, you tell him I want the name of all convicted female teen-aged murderers in the last ten years. Out of your records. Not the court records, your records. I want it fast. Okay, Parker?"

"I—What is—"

"Never you mind, Parker. You just git me that information and I'll take care of you. Have them call me here—555-3321—soonest. I mean *soonest*. Lives at stake. We're going to try and save an innocent woman and put a guilty man into the ground, where he deserves to go.''

The joy of it was that he could watch Bud without risking himself, or even leaving.

Lamar lay in the gully with a pair of binoculars, just down the road from the red dirt turnoff that led to Ruta Beth's house. He looked at his watch. If Bud had left the Exxon station twenty, twenty-five minutes ago on the way to Toleens, the only road he could take was this one and he'd be heaving into sight in a few minutes. And then what? A chopper overhead, a SWAT bus and convoy ten minutes behind? Would his truck have an aerial, suggesting he was in radio contact?

It was all very interesting to Lamar.

But of course the hard part was not shooting.

Bud would roll by; it would be so easy to nail him with four or five 12-gauge blasts, take him down and do him here, on the spot. Lamar saw it: the crashed truck, the holes in the door, the smell of gasoline, broken glass everywhere. The lawman in pain, begging for mercy. Lamar putting the shotgun muzzle up close to him, feeling him squirm a bit, and then the blast, the blood spatters, pieces everywhere. Oh so nice it seemed. *I-mag-i-nation.* Big word: Pictures in your head.

But Lamar knew they could have done him at the ball game or at any of the pay phones. Lamar forced himself into the hunter's patience. *Check it out,* he told himself. *Use the edge you got yourself. Don't rush things. Do it right. Make him pay. Make him pay real bad. I-mag-i-nation.*

Far off, he saw headlights. Their swift approach indicated reckless speed. Lamar was able to tell quickly enough it was a Ford F250, blue and white, and as it approached, he dialed Bud's tense face into focus.

Square-headed man, eyes hooded under the Stetson, dark clothes, driving fast but well, steady as a rock. There was a set to his face that Lamar remembered from the Stepford farm, as poor Bud walked up toward the house and he and Odell prepared to take them down. He looked so body-proud, so full of his own self, and he still had that bull-necked swagger to him, though now cut through with so much tension that he hardly seemed human. He flashed by Lamar toward his destination still a good twenty miles down the road, not knowing how close he was to being reeled in.

Next Lamar looked at how the truck rode, which appeared to be normal; it didn't ride low on its tires, which meant he wasn't carrying a big load, which meant a Trooper SWAT team or gaggle of Texas Ranger snipers wasn't hunkered down in the truckbed. It had no extra aerial.

Lamar watched the taillights grow tiny, then fade, and listened till the whine of tires on asphalt died away. He put the glasses down and listened hard. No sound. He waited and watched. Only the low night wind pushing across the wide plains, now and then the squawk of some night creature. No choppers followed Bud a thousand feet up, and the road itself remained empty for the longest time, a flat blank ribbon glowing ever so slightly in starlight. No convoy appeared, nothing.

Satisfied, Lamar rose and headed back toward the farmhouse, enjoying the power he felt under the wide night sky. It was like being invisible, like being a god. He felt a stirring in his crotch at the promise of action.

He hardly ever thought about such things, for they were so much a part of the way he was. But now he felt it, pure and blood deep: He was the Lion, he was the king. And he was about to feed.

Bud hit Toleens, which was exactly one decrepit old general store, windblown and nearly barren of paint, with two gas pumps out front and a pay phone next to the front door. He pulled over and waited, checking his watch. Nearly four. He'd just made it.

He waited until ten after. Now what was wrong? Goddammit! He began to grow nervous. This was the perfect setup. At any moment gunshots might explode out of the dark, taking him down. Lamar might be just across the road, watching him twit nervously on the porch before blowing him away at leisure.

But the phone rang finally.

"Yes."

"Well, old Bud, how are you?"

"Cut the shit, Lamar. You haven't hurt her?"

"Not yet, anyway."

"Prove it."

"Now don't you go using that attitude on me, Lawman. I don't have to prove nothing. You want your woman, you better do what I say or the hell with her. And then I *will* hurt her."

"Where are you?"

"Oh, not yet, Pewtie. We ain't done playing tag. You got a bit more running around to do. I want to be real sure."

"Tell me."

"No sir. I want you headed east now, toward Chickasha. Town called Anadarko. That's your next stop. Another gas station. On 62, a Phillips. You got a hour."

"I'll never make it in an hour."

"Sure you will. Then we'll talk some more and maybe you can come git me and maybe you can't."

He hung up.

Quickly Bud dialed the annex.

He got a busy signal.

Goddamn!

He felt like throwing the phone. That old goat, what the hell was he up to?

Now what? Leave and drive like hell to Anadarko, which was just barely makable in an hour? Or give goddamned C. D. Henderson another few minutes, stretching it out even further?

He raced to the truck, started the engine.

But then he turned it off.

He ran back to the phone, dialed again.

The phone rang once, and C.D. picked it up.

"Bud?"

Who *else* would it be?

"Yes."

"Just got a call from a newspaper reporter. In 1983 a fifteen-year-old gal shot and killed her mama and her papa and served seven years before being released from the Kingsville Hospital for the Criminally Insane. I called there and talked to a night nurse who knew her well. She continually wrote to people who had killed or assaulted their parents."

"Richard!"

"Richard. She wrote to Richard, and no one never bothered to check on what letters came his way in prison, as he was the passive partner and only there a few months. But there's your connection. Bud, I checked her out against the list of car owners: She's registered in a ninety-one Toyota Tercel."

"Holy Christ."

"She lives on a place right off 54, in Kiowa County, way

out where it's empty and barren, just the far side of the Wichitas. Her name is Ruta Beth Tull.''

"I just drove by it. He ran me by it to check me out! Now he's going to bounce me around for a bit, just to get me completely tired. It's half an hour away.''

"You better get there, Bud. You got work to do.''

"Thank you, old man. You are one hell of a detective.''

"I believe I am, son. I believe I am. Now I'm going to give you ten minutes, that's all. That's what I owe you. Then the cavalry is coming.''

"Fair enough.''

"And Bud, remember: front sight. Center mass. Put 'em in the ground, Bud. All of 'em.''

CHAPTER
31

Holly tried to clear her head, but it buzzed with fright. She couldn't stop staring at them. Lamar was big and oily and somehow engorged with testosterone. He couldn't stop grinning. He was like a movie star.

On the other hand, that poor pitiful Sally who was his girl—Ruta something, some old-fashioned farm name—was nervous as a cat. She was really the scary one; a tight, grim, scrawny little mouse, with the small-featured face she associated with the inbred.

But the prize was the one they called Richard. God, she'd laugh if she wasn't so scared. Richard had dreamy, puffy, tussled hair, and though he was big, he was soft. He had creamy hands, like a piano player's, and a little dance in his walk; when he moved, all these rhythms were unleashed. He was of no known sex, with his prissy, parched little lips, and his strangely disaffected way of moving, as if he heard everything a second later.

What a trio! These insane fools had killed her own husband as he lay on the ground and then terrorized Oklahoma for two months? They seemed like some hill clan, white trash who hadn't ever seen a toilet that flushed. She almost laughed. They were so unbearably squalid.

And she knew they'd kill Bud. That was the terrible part. They'd take his life without hesitation and they'd take her life.

"What you looking at, baby girl?" Lamar suddenly demanded, bringing his face close to hers.

"What scum you are," she said. "You are the worst scum."

"Lady," he said, "you know, I could rape you. Did it for years and years to any woman I could find. Oh, the things I done. The law only knows but a third. They could punish me for a thousand years and be nowheres near even out on the deal."

"But you won't."

"Why's that?"

" 'Cause a tiny part of you is scared of Bud Pewtie. You only got the best of him once—then he got the best of you. It's third time coming up and maybe you ain't quite the stud you think you are."

Lamar laughed.

"Damn," he said. "You got a mouth on you! Half a mind to keep you around for comedy. You could help Ruta Beth with the cooking. Ruta Beth, you need a helper?"

"No, Daddy," said Ruta Beth, furiously.

"Sorry," said Lamar. "We ain't hiring today." Then he laughed again, eyes glinting in the low light.

Bud put his lights out and flew by the dirt road entrance. He saw nothing on 54 except the light of a beat-up old house a mile away against the darkness of the prairie, here and there the blotch of a grove of mesquites or scrub oaks, undulating prairies and crests and the far-off mountains.

He drove a half mile and slowed to a halt, careful not to

let his brakes squeak. He tried to think. Did he want to park by the road and come in over the fields? Did he want to try to go down the entrance road, slow, lights out? He could probably get pretty close. But surely Lamar would have someone looking out. As for the walk in, it seemed so long. He glanced at his watch. Ten to four. He wanted to make his move before they called and got no answer; going off the schedule just a little would set Lamar's hair to bristling; he'd begin to sniff things out.

You have to move now and fast, he thought. *You cannot fuck around. You have to go in and shoot Lamar in the first second.* Without Lamar, they would fall apart, though he thought he'd have to shoot the girl, too; he had no illusions. If she'd sold her soul to Lamar, she was a target and had to be hit. And maybe Richard, too, though he had fewer worries about Richard: Richard had no guts and would quit in an instant if Lamar was gone.

Bud eased ahead another quarter mile and came to another long, straight dirt road that seemed to lead nowhere. It simply vanished in the darkness. He thought: *It's only a half a mile down and roughly parallel. I can drive down it, turn right, go into four-wheel, buck my way through the grass and scrub and any barbed wire I find.* Then he'd close from the rear, shoot Lamar with the rifle from outside, kick in the door and take his chances with the girl and Richard. Maybe Holly would make it, maybe she wouldn't. It was the best chance she had, as long as he, committed to it, went in hard and shot to kill.

Okay, he thought, *time to go.*

His vest.

He hadn't taken time to put on his vest!

I hope my luck holds, he thought, but he doubted it would.

* * *

Lamar watched the slow tick of the minute hand as it swept its way around the face of the big clock on Ruta Beth's mantel. Round and round it went, sucking seconds off the face of the earth, drawing Bud Pewtie nearer to his fate. He'd done his homework. At four, Bud would be in Anadarko; Lamar would bring him back toward Odette, looking for a signal; Bud would never know where it would be so he'd be looking hard, spooked and tired. They'd bring him on in to the farm. He'd sit in the truck cab, with his wife trussed up in plain view. Then, slowly, he'd have to get out and go toward her. That's when they'd take him down, hard, with buckshot in the legs, under the vest he was sure to be wearing; then Lamar would crown him once, twice, maybe three times with the shotgun butt and drag him into the barn. The hard work would be done in the barn. It would take most of the morning. No one would hear the screams.

Then when he was gone, Lamar decided he'd have the woman. Have her all the ways there were to have her; it excited him that she'd know it would be her last thing. Maybe he'd give a taste to Richard. Didn't know yet. Then he'd kill her. Out of kindness, he'd decided to shoot her in the head.

"Daddy?"

"Yes?"

"It's about time."

He looked back toward the clock. Five till.

"Oh, give him a few more minutes, baby," he said. "Let him enjoy. He's got some things a-coming, like a freight train."

Richard was very nervous. He kept licking his lips and trying not to look at the woman, whose helplessness and fear excited him. He'd never had such a response to a

woman before; but he was also very frightened. This Pewtie
was a tough customer; he'd stood up to and killed Odell,
and not even the violent and fearless black inmates would
stand against Odell.

As usual, it was his imagination that betrayed him. He
could not quiet it. He saw that Lamar's great gift was his
ability to concentrate and act, whereas he, Richard, was
always bedeviled by rogue thoughts, erratic impulses. Suppose the buckshot didn't knock Pewtie down; suppose he
got a gun into action? Suppose Lamar tripped as he rushed
toward him. It could go wrong a hundred different ways,
although when Lamar planned something, it usually didn't
go wrong. Lamar just got things done, that was all.

But this was the last hard thing for a while. Lamar had
said they would leave, find new territory. Lamar wanted
also to find a skin artist to get the tattoo finished, and he
wanted Richard to work really hard at that. Richard didn't
want to disappoint Lamar. Lamar was a god to him; Lamar
stood above him and dominated the skyscape like a tyrant
king. Richard had yielded in all totality, replacing a mother
he feared and loved with a man he feared and loved.

I am a slave, he thought.

I love being a slave.

He looked at the girl again and felt a twitch in his dick.
Then he touched the heavy revolver in his belt and looked
at King Lamar on his throne and swore eternal fealty.

Bud drove without his lights on, in low gear, guided by
starlight, wishing there was a moon; but there was no
moon. He watched the tick of the odometer and when at last
the nine-tenths mark turned over into a new mile, he halted.
He got out and locked the Warn hubs on the front axle. It
was as dark as a convict's dream. The wind, always the
wind, snapped across the dry prairie. He looked, saw that

the gulch between the road and the field didn't look bad, climbed back in. He eased into four-wheel drive, pushed slowly ahead, and felt just the faintest sense of resistance. A fence, wire; it went down with the sound of metal pranging against metal. He lurched ahead and the truck sank abruptly at a wretched angle, shimmied down a bank, and seemed to come to a rest.

Shit, Bud thought, dropping into low range and giving the gas a feather touch. The engine's muttering deepened and the truck bucked a bit, then began to pull itself out of the gully. It shuddered free with a last grind of tire against earth, and he was on clear ground; he zoomed up into the field and began to pick his way across it.

No resistance; the truck rumbled almost silently along and he steered by a compass on the dashboard, avoiding the stunted mesquite trees, bypassing the low hollows clotted with scrub oak. The prairie was boundless, but like the surface of the sea, its flatness was illusion. Bud rose and fell through crests and dips in the earth itself, before him only the most basic of pictures: darkness that was air, and slightly less darkness that was land, and the line of demarcation between them too vague to make out.

But at last he seemed to come to a crest and he halted.

He could see Ruta Beth Tull's place. A flicker of heat lightning lit the sky, briefly illuminating the farm. It had a strange familiarity about it, as if from a dream. Why did he know it?

Then he realized he'd been here before, when they were searching for the tires. Lamar must have fooled him that day. He tried to remember the girl and got no image. Why couldn't he remember?

He saw the barn, he saw the house, freshly painted, white in the starlight. A single light was on. It was about three hundred yards away.

It occurred to him to try and drive closer. No, too risky; they wouldn't see a man approaching, particularly if he kept the barn between himself and them, but the truck might make a noise or create too much motion. It was too risky.

Bud returned to the cab. He slipped out of his coat and laid his hat on the seat. This wasn't hat work, no sir. Then he reached behind the seat and slid out the Winchester carbine, Model of 1894, though this one was manufactured in 1967. Gently he eased the lever forward, camming a .30-30 softpoint into the chamber. Closing the lever, he groped again behind the seat, found the box of ammunition, and extracted one more round, which he inserted in the loading gate. There, that brought it up to eight rounds. A .30-30 carbine wasn't the best for this kind of work, but it wasn't so bad either: He could fire fast, it was accurate, and that softpoint bullet would splatter like a pancake as it moved through whatever it hit, hopefully Lamar's brain. Hell, Texas Rangers had carried them for years and they always got their man.

He touched his other guns, counting them off: Beretta 9-mm, Colt .45, Beretta .380, all loaded, all with spare mags jammed with hollowpoints.

Bud returned to the ridge, studied the farm, glad that he recognized it and that he'd be making his fight on ground he'd at least seen before.

There was nothing else to think of or do.

Oh yeah: a prayer.

Hey, he said, looking upward. *Old man. Please help me tonight. You know I need it bad.*

Then he swallowed and went off to meet Lamar.

He scurried down the slope, jogging, trying not to breathe hard, watching as with surly inevitability the house and barn grew larger. As he moved down the slope, his angle on the house changed and it seemed to disappear behind the barn.

New fears assaulted him. What if Lamar had recruited a gang, what if not three awaited him but ten, twenty?

Well, then you die, he thought, *and so does Holly, but so be it.* In half an hour the SWAT people would arrive; the gunfight would leave no survivors at all, like that crazy thing in Waco—people eaten up in the insanity of the moment.

He got to the barn, again encountering familiarity. He saw the oven that was a kiln, the wood tables, the racks of drying vessels, the cans of paint, glaze, whatnot, the brushes stored carefully in jars, glinting softly in the starlight, all strange, all familiar. Yes, now he remembered: She was a potter. He bought a pot from her! He remembered the pot, with its jagged flashes of color. It was the only colorful thing about her. He now saw her: a drab, scrawny young woman. He saw exactly how she could fall for the power and the glory of a Lamar, especially as she herself had already known the sick thrill of standing over something that had been alive until just a very few seconds ago.

But still . . . she was a girl.

Bud hoped he could kill the girl.

Just kill her. Shoot her dead in the head or upper torso and think nothing of it.

But that little bit of doubt upset him; not that she was poignant and needy but only that she was such a drab little creature, unstirred by life's possibilities. He shook his head as he slid through the barn.

Crouching in its doorway he studied what was before him. The house was twenty-five yards off and he could see the back door and dim light from the first-floor windows. Two cars had been parked in the yard around toward the front of the house, and he could also make out what appeared to be a rickety porch out front.

He first thought of the cars: escape.

Backing out of the barn, he circled around again in a wide low arc, and slithered up to the cars. Neither was locked; one was the Toyota that had so bedeviled everybody, and the other a black Trans Am.

Gingerly Bud opened each, leaned in, and reached up under the dash to a nest of wires. He didn't have time to find the ignition wire, but simply, with a hard yank, pulled them all. Nobody was driving anywhere tonight.

He next crawled to the side of the house. The window was tall and he couldn't quite see in, but from the low secondary light, he gauged the room to be empty and dark, probably the kitchen, its only illumination a doorway into the larger room or hallway. He snaked around back to find a door. He tried it; it was locked. He looked around quickly for something to secure the door from this side, figuring after he shot Lamar, Richard would head for the nearest exit and could be counted on to come to rest against a locked door, ready to give up.

Clothesline!

He ran to it and cut it free with his pocketknife, then came back and swiftly wrapped loops about the doorknob, drew the rope tightly to the clothesline post and tied it securely, a good working cowman's knot. Richard wouldn't be able to get shit open.

Maybe he'd go out a window and into the fields. They'd find him thirty yards out, nursing a broken ankle.

Bud glimpsed at his watch. Four A.M., no two ways about it. Time to go.

He slid around the base of the house to the edge of the porch and peered in. The front door was open, though a screen door blocked entry. The screen would be easy to shoot through, though. He drew closer to the doorway and peered into the blaze of light and sensed bodies but couldn't get a clear look. He stepped out a bit further, until at last he saw Lamar Pye.

Big as life its own self, standing by the couch, Lamar gripped the phone tightly. Behind him was Ruta Beth, a dark blur; Bud couldn't see Richard but figured he was there somewheres. And he made out a head crumpled in one corner of the couch. Holly.

The rifle came up to Bud's shoulder. He kneeled, looking for support. The light wasn't great, but it was enough. He could see the bead of the front sight. It wobbled, described a filigree in the air, and Bud sought to capture it too hard, driving it wild. He exiled a chunk of air from his lungs and willed steadiness into his limbs.

Kill Lamar, throw lever, kill Ruta Beth. Two easy shots, a second apart. Lamar dies with his brains blown out, Ruta Beth won't react in time to move and she's the next easy target, into the chest. Then dump the rifle, draw the Beretta, and blow into the house. If you see Richard, pop him; otherwise grab Holly and flee.

Yet even now he paused just a second, dwarfed by the coldness of it all.

No, goddammit, he told himself. *Do his ass. Send him to hell for breakfast.*

Bud concentrated on the front sight as he pressed the trigger and the bead was right there on Lamar's broad, almost handsome face.

He felt it break, and there was perhaps a tenth of a second as the hammer fell when Bud sensed the world suspended, like a note held too long, beyond human endurance. Time had stopped. There was no sound, no movement, no sense of life anywhere.

The rifle fired, its flash draining details from the dark

night, and the door to the house shattered into a billion pieces, a sleet of bitter chaos—goddamn, not a screen but a goddamn glass storm door in the middle of hot summer, who'd ever have imagined *that?*—and Lamar sank instantly from view but with such goddamned energy and purpose that Bud knew the bullet had been deflected and that he had not been hit.

Lamar had tried again. The phone rang and rang. Now what the hell was wrong with that boy?

"Where'n fuck is he?" he demanded.

"Maybe he had a flat or an accident," said Richard.

"Not this old boy. He ain't that goddamn type. He *is* a accident."

Darkening with fury and frustration, he stood in the room.

What the fuck?

The ringing grated through the earpiece of the phone, but no one picked up.

He tried to run through ways it could have gone wrong. Had he been too fancy? Should he have done the fuck as he drove along the road? Is there any way, any way *at all* they could be on to him?

No. He'd been too careful. They weren't that clever.

He stood, watching the girl curled beneath him, bound and gagged helplessly. He could sense Ruta Beth behind him. Richard was off some goddamned place fretting over some goddamned thing.

The door exploded.

Next thing, Lamar was on the floor. How he got there he didn't know: just his fast reflexes taking over, getting him down there, flat and safe.

"Lamar!"

It was Ruta Beth, standing dumbly.

"GEDDOWN!" he screamed. "THEY HERE!"

Ruta Beth hit the floor.

"I'm hurt, Daddy."

"Goddamn," said Lamar.

"Oh, shit," said Richard from the kitchen.

"You hit bad, Baby Girl?"

"Neck. Oh, Daddy, it hurts."

"You gotta shoot back, goddammit, or we are cat piss."

He himself pulled Holly off the couch and to him, as a human shield. He felt her heart beating against her ribs like a trapped little bird. A temptation came to put a bullet in her head, but he knew that was stupid. He slithered to the window, dragging her with him, and snuck a peek out to see nothing, smelled just the faintest whisper of smoke hanging in the air. He calculated swiftly. A SWAT sniper wouldn't have missed, not hardly, and by now there'd have been dozens of gumballs flashing, big boys on loudspeakers, choppers, the goddamned whole world getting ready to kill him. But he didn't see a goddamned thing.

He knew who it was.

How the hell did he find him?

Goddamn!

"Richard, boy, the lights, get 'em out."

"Lamar, I—"

"GODDAMN BOY, GET THEM OUT!"

Only a scream would get Richard moving. Somehow the worthless piece of shit began to flutter around, and in a second the lights had vanished. Another second passed, and suddenly Lamar heard a high keening sound. Sounded like an animal being burned in a fireplace or something, but under the whine of fear and slobbery, pee-pants panic he recognized Richard's tones.

"Locked! Locked! Locked!" Richard was sobbing.

He meant the back door, Lamar thought. Fucking Pewtie

had locked off the back door. Smart motherfucker. No other way out, except the side window.

"Ruta Beth, you okay?"

"Oh, Daddy, it hurts so bad. I got blood every damned place."

"Can you shoot, Baby Girl?"

"What?"

"Can you *shoot,* goddammit, Ruta Beth. Got to answer him. It's that fucker Pewtie. You're all I got."

Not really; he had the girl, too. He felt her squirm under him.

"I don't think so, Lamar. I got blood on my hands. So slippery."

She was losing it fast.

"That's okay, Baby Girl. It don't matter. You're still the goddamn champ. Listen here, I want you to slide out the door. He ain't going to shoot, he sees you're wounded. You yell for help. He's going to say, Put your hands up, and when I hear his voice, I can nail him."

Ruta Beth crawled by him, leaving a black slime of blood. She got to the doorway and somehow pulled her way up. Then she stepped out on the porch, stood under the bright porch light. Lamar kneeled on Bud's wife's neck, calmed himself, and studied the darkness out the window, waiting for a scream. He had five double-oughts in the Browning cutdown. When it came, he'd flash to the area and pump the gun empty. If it was only one man as he now suspected, he'd at least hurt him.

Bud had fallen back behind the Trans Am almost directly to the left of the house.

Goddamn! Goddamn!

It had all fallen apart. Now what? Lamar knew he was

there and would just as sure as winter be calculating coun-
termoves, if he hadn't already cut Holly's throat.

But what Bud saw astonished him.

It was the girl, Ruta Beth Tull. She stood groggily, her
hands up. She was drenched with blood. He hadn't even
fired a second shot! Then he realized the Comedy King was
having a good time tonight with the play of whimsy: He
had decreed that the screen door turned out to be a storm
door and it would deflect Bud's bullet from Lamar, but the
same Laugher saw that it hit Ruta Beth.

"Don't shoot," she said. "I's bad hurt."

She took a step forward.

Bud put the front sight right on her head. The range was
thirty feet; he could hit her in the face easy.

"Don't shoot," she said, taking a wobbly step forward.

He felt the trigger strain against his finger.

Do it, he told himself. Do it and move on to the other.

"Keep your hands high and come out and lie face down
in the—"

The window lit bright with harsh flame as someone fired
five fast shotgun blasts at him. Bud had no consciousness of
drawing back, only a sense of an explosion all around him
as the buckshot tore into the hood of the car and spalled
spastically against the windshield, blowing shreds of glass
outward as it turned the sheet into webbed quicksilver.
Abruptly the left side of his face went to sleep for what
must have been a whole second, then began to sting.

He touched his face: blood. But had anything penetrated?
He felt a core of ache spread through his brain, and the
suffocating odor of gunpowder swirled around him. But he
seemed not to be mortally hit.

Next he heard the crash of a window from the other side
of the house. Lamar had jumped free.

* * *

Lamar knew the lawman would do the right thing, which was the wrong thing; he couldn't just shoot poor Ruta Beth.

And indeed, Lamar saw a shape hunkered by the left front fender of the Trans Am bending over a rifle and in a second he'd brought the sawed-off Browning up and unleashed its whole tube of shells. The bright fireworks of the gun flashes ate up the world and Lamar now wished for half a second he hadn't cut it down, for with a full-stocked and barreled weapon, the highway patrolman would have been easy meat. But the gun bucked in his hands and he struggled to bring it back on line and each fresh blast lit the night for what seemed miles, though curiously so intent was he on the mechanics of it, he didn't hear a thing.

Then the gun came up dry, the smoke seethed in the air, and he thought he'd hit but he wasn't sure. Only one thing remained now: to get clear, to get out. Nothing else mattered. If he got out of the house and across the fields, he could flag down a truck and commandeer it or steal a car from some square john or some such. But his ticket out was the goddamned girl, though she'd slow him somewhat; but Pewtie wouldn't spray in his direction with the little wife along.

"Come on, sweetheart," he said, rising and pulling her up. The now useless shotgun fell away. He had a SIG, with seven cartridges, but no reloads. Too bad. Didn't have time to look for other magazines now.

In one powerful motion he pulled her along to the side window and threw her out. She smashed through the glass, caught her foot, and fell with a horrible thud to the earth. He leaped out and pulled her up.

"Come on, goddammit, or I will put a bullet in your head and think no more of it."

He yanked her off into the darkness.

* * *

Bud stepped out from behind the car but then remembered Ruta Beth, still in the doorway. He drew back and put the rifle on her once again.

"GET OUT, GODDAMMIT AND GO FACE DOWN!"

But the woman just stared at him. Then slowly, she seemed to be raising her hands but she stopped midway, and pointed something at him. Was there a gun in it or what?

Bud didn't have time to think; the carbine fired, he threw the lever and fired again. He didn't see the bullets strike, but with the second one, Ruta Beth seemed to deflate; all the air went out of her as she tumbled sideways and she seemed to hit the floor with sickening force, her arms and legs flung loosely akimbo.

He wanted to race out after Lamar.

But where was Richard?

Where was Richard?

Was it a trap? Maybe it was Richard who had gone out the window, and Lamar, reloading, just waited for him to show himself.

No, it was Lamar. Only Lamar would be smart enough to get out the window that fast. Richard would be inside, in pieces. Richard wasn't a factor, that was clear.

Richard lay on the kitchen floor, sobbing.

It was so unfair. Why did things always have to happen to him? Now the police were here and they would kill him. He hadn't done anything. Didn't they understand that? He was innocent. No blame should be attached to him. It wasn't like he *wanted* any of this to happen. He actually tried to *prevent* it. In the restaurant, he had heroically screamed, trying to save the woman's life. Ruta Beth had killed her, not him.

Richard tugged on the door again. It wouldn't budge.

He turned and crawled to the door and peeked into the living room. The shooting had stopped. The windows were all blasted out and there was no sign of Lamar.

"Lamar?" he called.

No answer.

He looked toward the door and saw Ruta Beth's boots laying splayed on the floor of the porch. He suspected, after all the shooting, that Ruta Beth was still in them.

He crawled over and peeked around. Ruta Beth lay on her stomach, in a huge and spreading black, satiny puddle of blood. She was utterly inert, utterly without signs of life. He'd never seen anything so still in his life.

He faced the darkness.

He raised his hands.

"I surrender," he said.

There was no answer.

It was the worst possible thing. Now he had to pursue an armed and very violent man across unknown terrain in the dark. He couldn't shoot because he'd hit Holly. At any time, Lamar could double back to ambush him.

You fool, he told himself.

You stupid fool. You don't have the sense of a buckworm.

More out of anger than anything, he plunged ahead, trying to control his breathing, trying to regain his night vision after it was blown to hell by the gun flashes.

But then he thought: *Lamar is blind, too. Lamar won't be able to see shit for a good five minutes.*

Bud raced ahead, low. He tossed the carbine; it was useless in the close-quarter stuff that was coming up. This was straight cop work: an in-close gunfight with an innocent body in the way. He knew the statistics from *Police Marksman* magazine: The average gunfight now took place between twenty and twenty-three feet, with an exchange of between 2.3 and 5.5 shots. So he took out his .45 Commander, the bullet being a harder hitter and the gun being easier to shoot straight and well. It would be a close thing, if it happened at all: one, two shots, not like in the tattoo shop, with them all blazing away as if in a war movie.

The gun's familiar grip somewhat comforted him; its known contours, its safety exactly where the safety should be, its short trigger taut and sharp against his finger, the way it settled into his palm and the way his fingers clenched about it—all these things had their pleasures in the tension of the moment. He hunched, looking for signs in the field, thinking of course that Lamar would head for the nearest clump of trees so as not to be caught in the open. The prairie was empty and barren; but ahead, on the right, he saw a clump of trees in a fold, the only feature in the emptiness. There was no other place to go, no other route of escape, and he knew Lamar would move fast because he'd have figured there'd be fleets of cops there in no time.

Or maybe he said fuck it, strangled the girl, and now had just flattened himself into the earth and waited for his blood enemy to approach.

No. Lamar's not like that. He's a professional, whatever else he is, and would put first priority on escaping to steal and kill another day, on another chance to get Bud and get away. He wasn't one for sacrificing himself.

Bud crouched lower and hurried onward.

The girl was slowing him down. He wanted to smash her to the earth. But the girl was the only card he had, so he had to hold her.

He assumed Pewtie was following him. What choice did the lawman have? But when he looked back across the fields, he could see nothing, or nothing real; spangles of light, blue and orange like pinwheels from a Fourth of July when he was a boy, still danced before his eyes from the nearness of the shotgun's fireworks. *That's the trouble with a goddamned sawed-off.*

Once, the girl went to her knees, but he pulled her savagely up.

"You stay with me, girly, or I will finish you here, quietlike and then do your husband and go on my happy way."

He saw terror, and felt her squirm. She made a sound, low and raw, behind the gag. But she could not meet his power, and looked away, her eyes bugging, the veins in her throat standing out like ropes. She was bleeding, too, from the fall out the window; she'd hit her head hard. Tough shit. It was going to be a hard night on everybody.

He pulled her along. He could see the dark line of the trees ahead only a hundred or so yards, and happily accepted the fact that cop cars and choppers and whatever hadn't yet arrived. Maybe Pewtie hadn't called them, had tried to do the whole thing on his own, some John Wayne kind of deal. But no: Pewtie would call for backup and then come in alone. Lamar knew the plan: Kill him and walk out with the girl, knowing the others would fade.

Now Lamar was but fifty yards from the tree line. A sudden spurt of energy came to him, and he roared ahead, pulling the girl. She seemed wasted, without much fight, but in some mix-up of limbs, she went down and he got tangled in her and he went down, too, with a thud, tasting dirt as he fell. There was a slight moment of concussion, and suddenly she squirmed savagely and ripped away from him. With more power than he ever thought she had, she raced away.

"*Goddamn you!*" he hissed and brought the gun up and began to press the trigger, but stomped on the impulse, knowing the flash would give him away. Instead he rose and leaped after her, slipping once in the mud, but in three short bounds had her. He tackled her, feeling his weight and strength bring her down, but she kicked and bucked under him, and he tried to push her face in the mud, but somehow his hand slid off her face, just enough to dislodge the gag.

''BUD! BUD, OVER HERE!'' she screamed as he finally pushed her face into the mud, but before he could do anything more, he saw Pewtie on the crestline. He drew up the pistol and fired. He couldn't stop shooting, the mesmerizing pleasure of it drawing him onward as the gun leaped in his hand and the gun flashes blossomed like a tulip of light. Pewtie disappeared.

He didn't think he'd hit him.

''Come ON,'' he yelled, pulling her up, but again she pulled away and this time instead of running after, he simply watched her run and then himself turned and headed to the trees.

Bud saw movement and brought the gun up to fire.

He took the slack out of the trigger as the phantasm wobbled desperately to him but saw in the next second it was Holly.

''Holly. Here.''

She slipped as she turned, and he ran to her.

''I got away. He didn't shoot me. Oh, Bud, I knew you'd come.''

He got out his knife. He cut her arms free. She threw them about him.

''Oh, Jesus. Bud, you have saved my life sure.''

He said nothing.

''You do love me. You came for me. God bless you, mister, you are a man.''

''Yes, well,'' he said.

''Bud, you must love me, what you risked for me.''

''Holly—''

"Take me out of here."

"You have to do that yourself. I want you to go into the field and just lie down flat no matter what happens. We got everybody coming in on this thing in a minute or two. You're safe. You made it. I got you out."

"You're done, Bud. Oh please don't do what I think you're going to."

"I have to finish it up now. I've got to go get Lamar."

"Bud! He'll kill you!"

"I have to—"

"Bud!"

"I have to go."

But she pulled him toward her, as if to draw him in forever, to make him hers now that it was so close, so easy and—

He hit her with his open hand, hard, left side of the head, driving her down.

No one had ever hit her before.

His nostrils flared, his eyes were wide and strange and fierce. She saw nothing in them at all that she could recognize.

"Don't you get it yet?" he almost screamed. "It's over! Goddamn it, I am quit of you and you are quit of me! Now get out of here. I got man's work to do." And without looking back he set off down the crest for the trees, knowing that he had another few minutes until Lamar's eyes regained their night vision. He saw the dark band of vegetation up ahead, dense and beckoning and otherwise silent.

Wait for backup, the rules all said.

Not this time, he thought. *This time we get it done.*

Lamar crouched in the trees. No moon, no stars, it was so damned dark. His eyes still weren't working right. Shooting at the cop had been stupid. Like an amateur, like something little-bitty-dick Richard would do. The gun flashes again so close to his face had blasted his vision to hell and gone: everywhere he looked he saw stars and pinwheels, dragons breathing fire, lions' manes flashing in the sun.

Time. He had no time.

He also had almost no ammunition now. The gun hadn't locked back, but he slipped the magazine out and felt its lips and realized they were empty. That meant he had but one cartridge, the one in the chamber.

Damn!

He thought he saw the man coming down the slope through the strobe effect, but there was no way it was a clear-enough image to shoot at. And he couldn't even see his gun.

The only way was to get in close, real close, put the gun up to him so the muzzle touched flesh, and then blow him away with the last bullet.

But Lamar didn't like that either. It depended on Pewtie getting close and once he got in the goddamn trees there was no way of telling which way he would go. And Pewtie saw better than he did, because the rifle hadn't flashed nearly so much as the shotgun and he hadn't fired in quite a while. And Lamar couldn't just *wait*. The longer he was here, the surer it was he'd get caught.

No sir. Got to bring him to me and kill him fast and get on out of here before the posse shows.

An idea flashed before him.

The gun, the gun, the gun.

Yes. Secure the gun in the crotch of a tree. With a branch or something wedged into the trigger guard. Let Pewtie come. When he approaches, fire the last shot.

Pewtie will then fire back on the gun flash with every damn thing, blowing his own eyesight to hell and gone. Then *he's* blind and you ain't.

In the second after he's done, you hit him hard and low and take him down. It becomes a thing of man on man, strength against strength, and Lamar knew that there was no man who could stand against him one on one. If Pewtie had any doubts, he could ask Junior Jefferson.

Lamar slipped back and in not much time found what he needed: a young sapling with a stout crotch maybe five feet up. Lamar wedged the SIG into it, slipped off his belt, and secured the gun tightly. He looked around and then up and with a snap broke off a four-foot length of branch.

Ever so delicately he wedged the tip into the trigger guard so that it just about filled the gap between trigger and guard. Force it another half an inch and it would trip the trigger and the gun would fire.

Lamar slipped down, waiting for the sounds of his quarry.

I'll still get him, he thought.

Bud had reached the trees.

No sir, don't like this a bit.

He reasoned now that if he had to shoot, it would be in response to fire, and he wanted a lot of chances, not a few. So he restored the .45 Commander to his high hip holster and reached up and unslung his Beretta. With a thumb he snicked the hammer back. Then, finger on the trigger, he began to snake ahead.

He's in here, goddammit, just waiting till his vision clears enough. Got to move fast or I'm a dead man.

He slid into the brush. His night vision was clear as it could be. Before him he saw only a thin maze of trees, ground cover, the furrow that was a stream, beyond, a fence, and beyond, way beyond that, the humps of the Wichitas. But no Lamar.

He was so slow, he was sure Lamar couldn't see him.

He eased ahead, almost soundlessly, scanning as he went, seeing nothing.

"Lamar!" he called. "Lamar, give it up. They're on their way. You don't have to die tonight like your poor girlfriend."

Silence.

"Lamar, they'll just send you back to the House. You'll be a big man. You'll have it all. You'll be the king."

Lamar didn't respond.

Was he yelling to a ghost? Had Lamar sped through the trees and was he closing in on some fine family to murder and steal a Lincoln Continental and get clean away?

No. He couldn't have moved that fast.

"Lamar!"

A gun flash blossomed before him, spangling his vision, but Lamar's best shot missed, and Bud drew the Beretta onto the fire and returned. The gun bucked and rose in his hand, but Bud was in love with shooting it. The gun flashes illuminated the cathedral under the trees, etching each detail in the bright light if only for a millisecond.

Bud fired eight or nine times.

Now he was pretty much goddamn blind, but he heard the scrape of something moving before him and before he could stop himself, he fired again, the flashes even larger this time, like flares or star shells, that seemed to turn the night to day, catching in their shards of blaze the seething smoke.

Damn, he thought, and then Lamar hit him full in the chest.

Lamar watched him come. He had a moment of doubt in his course, for so slow and clumsy was the man, he seemed an easy target. But not at night, when you couldn't see your own gun to aim and you only had one shot. You'd have to wait until he was at contact distance and maybe he wouldn't ever come into contact distance.

You figured fine, he thought.

He watched as Pewtie hesitated, caught in doubt.

Can't make up your goddamn mind, boy.

Then Pewtie put one gun away and got another out. Now what was *that* all about? Some secret meaning in the guns? Didn't matter. What mattered was that Lamar now knew Bud was carrying two, one in hand, and one high on his right hip.

Bud gently entered the trees.

Then he halted, and yelled something at Lamar. Lamar couldn't quite make it out, because he was so low into the forest floor, about six feet to the right of where his pistol was wedged into the crotch of the tree. He controlled the sapling that reached its trigger with his left hand, but he was concentrating real hard on not making a sound, not hardly breathing, on not hardly being alive. At the same time he tried to focus his mind on Bud, to somehow reach out through the trees and take over the lawman's brain, to bring him on. So far it was working.

Bud moved in closer and yelled something else. He seemed to pause, unsure which way to head. Then he seemed to make up his mind, and pivoted as if to head off to the right. If he got too far, Lamar could never reach him.

Okay, Lamar, he told himself. *Do it now. Do it and be done with it.*

But something in Lamar now held back.

What? Fear, regret?

Whatever, Lamar just watched as the man, twenty-five feet away, seemed to turn in slow motion, just a dark shape in the woods, almost not there unless you'd seen him come in.

Do it, Lamar, he told himself.

With his hand, he nudged the stick forward, and it didn't take long. The report was crisp and not loud, the flash momentarily lighting the lawman's taut face and then disappearing.

Pewtie fired back almost instantaneously. Lamar looked into the earth to preserve his gradually returning night vision, and heard the cracks and the echoes lashing out, almost like a whip snapping over his head, so many, so fast.

Oh you scared. You so scared. Not two shots, not three, but six, seven. Pray and spray, motherfucker.

A moment of silence. Then absurdly, Pewtie fired again, like a crazy man, rushing forward on the surge of adrenaline and under the roar of the shots. Lamar rose like a lion and bounded the few feet to him on an oblique angle; and if Pewtie ever saw him coming, it was too late, for he thundered fully against the man and felt the surprise and the shock disorganizing Pewtie's body, turning it to water, and Lamar was on him, crushing his thrashing body under his own.

First thing was the gun hand, which he controlled with his own left, then, slithering up to gain control, he hit the cop a hammer blow in the face because with two fingers gone, no way could he make a fist; he hit him right over the eye, and thought he felt a bone in the face break as the man screamed and with his other hand rose to ward the blows off.

It was like terrible fag sex, the two strong men pumping against each other in a rising fog of body stink and fear. Lamar saw how it would go in a second and knew he'd win easy. He'd pound the head of the man he controlled for another ten seconds, smashing him into submission, then twist across the body to get both hands on the gun wrist and corkscrew the automatic out of his grip and pull it back and shoot the lawman with his own gun.

But Bud's hand shot up to his throat and began squeezing, the thumb driving desperately for the Adam's apple. Lamar gagged, then threaded his hand under Bud's and gave him a knuckle thrust to the fleshy side of the neck, feeling the body beneath him go rigid in the awful pain. He hit again and thought he felt the tremor of surrender quivering through his opponent. Quick as a big cat, he pivoted and now had both hands on Bud's gun wrist, cranking it counterclockwise to rip the pistol from the grip, seeing the hands turn white as they lost their purchase. Something hit him lightly in the leg and then the gun fired, its flash blinding him again, but it didn't matter, for the slide didn't lock back and the recoil further weakened the man's grip and now he had it. It was in his hand.

He leaned back, fiddling to get it in his hand right, and then thrust the muzzle against the man's body and pulled the trigger.

Richard heard shots. They seemed to come from out beyond, out on the prairie.

He looked around again, seeing nothingness, and then headed toward the sound. He walked in the darkness and paused for just a second, to see the farm spread behind him and before him only the darker band of the trees.

A shape suddenly appeared before him.

"Lamar?" he said, but it was only the girl, who looked at him in horror and then slipped off. He watched her disappear and wondered why she had such revulsion on her face.

He stood there for a few seconds, wondering what to do. The world had never seemed so empty to him as it did at that moment.

Then he saw a single shot coming from ahead in the trees; by a trick of fate he had been looking exactly where the flash so briefly blossomed.

It occurred to him: *Lamar may need help.*

He walked toward the shot.

I have to help Lamar.

He took out his gun.

Bud felt his strength vaporizing, and with it all his will. He had nothing left to fight with, and Lamar had hit him so hard in the face and throat he was seeing nothing but flares of light as his throbbing optic nerves shot off. But still he clung to the Beretta, knowing it held his purchase on survival.

Lamar was above him, over him, hitting him gigantic hammer blows against which he had no defense. His face swelled like a rotten grapefruit. He saw his sons before him in the strobe effect of the optic nerve and for just a second forgot where he was. Lamar's face was a savage mask, so rigid with hatred and power it seemed like something from ancient times. Lamar's dark eyes glowed and his nostrils flared and Bud could smell sweat and dirt and blood and then Lamar hit him a giant clout on the nose, breaking it, filling Bud's mind with red mist.

Lamar pivoted, and Bud felt Lamar's other hand coming onto his wrist, Lamar's weight still pinning him, and the gun was being corkscrewed from his grasp until it was only a second before he lost it.

Magazine button, he thought.

He pushed it with his thumb and felt the magazine slide out, and then he pulled the trigger, the gun firing pointlessly off toward nowhere, as Lamar then seized it and with a blast of triumph broke contact with Bud and pivoted to jam the pistol against his ribs and squeeze the trigger.

Lamar must have pulled the trigger ten times before he realized the gun wasn't going to fire. Couldn't. No magazine.

In the interim, Bud balled his fist. He hit Lamar in the throat and felt his antagonist sag back.

He rolled just a bit and grabbed his Commander from the high hip holster and tried to bring it up against Lamar, but Lamar was too fast on the recovery and with his own left hand grabbed at the pistol.

The two men began to slide through the mud down toward the stream, hopelessly locked, each desperately seeking leverage, strength, hope as they tried to control Bud's Commander. Bud's thumb was over the safety, trying to get it down, Lamar's below it, trying to keep it up. Their faces were inches apart.

Suddenly, fast as a snake, Lamar seemed to leap out. He sunk his teeth into Bud's nose. The pain scaled the heights of his spine and he screamed, but in the same terrible second he remembered: *I shot his fingers off.*

With a jab his thumb lanced out against Lamar's fist, hit bandage, dug through it, and felt scab yielding to blood and heard a new scream, not his own.

Bud tore the automatic free and rammed it into Lamar, but when he pulled the trigger it would not go. Lamar had got a finger between hammer and receiver.

"You fucker, you fucker, you fucker," Lamar was saying.

Bud got the gun free and with his thumb cranked back the hammer, but again Lamar snared his wrist.

The gun in Bud's hand was like a bayonet as each tried to gain control and drive it into the other's heart. It rose and rose, wavering this way and that, now Bud ahead, now Lamar, the two of them locked in each other's arms, squeezing and biting and batting at each other with their skulls.

Up and up the gun came until it seemed to touch Bud's chin; he felt it hard and cold and saw Lamar's merciless eyes but from somewhere some last ounce of rage unleashed a last ounce of strength.

The gun fired.

The flash erupted in Bud's face; the light was incandescent and unyielding and seemed to fill all the corners of the earth, and as the tide of brightness roared through his brain, it destroyed his vision. A thousand bits of powder and lead drove into his skin.

He fell backward, isolated in his blindness, seeing nothing, feeling nothing.

Bud was helpless.

He'd lost the gun, he was blind, his ears rang.

He's going to kill me, he thought, and waited for the next shot, almost welcoming it, for it would stop the pain that now began to throb in his head, and it would let him rest at last.

But no shot came. He blinked and groped and still saw nothing but only heard some unidentifiable sound, a rasping, a moaning, whatever.

He drove his fists into his eyes and pressed them hard, backing sightly up the bank.

He opened his eyes, waiting to die.

But ever so slowly he identified the sound. It came from a hulk just before him, sunk to the knees in the stream, hands clasped over face.

Lamar's hands came away and another flash of heat lightning crackled in the distance and Bud saw that the bullet, a hollowtip, had blown through Lamar's chin upward and like a plow had gouged a furrow up what had been a face. The teeth and most of the tongue were gone, the nose had been eviscerated, and as the bullet had opened and surged upward it had destroyed both of Lamar's eyes and opened his forehead so that pulsing dark matter showed amid the bone. It had erased his face.

"Iiilmu, iiilmu, iiilmu," Lamar moaned and Bud knew it was "Kill me, kill me, kill me."

Bud finally found the Beretta .380, though it had slipped down almost into his underpants in the struggle. He raised it and aimed. He was three feet away. He fired twice into Lamar's head, and he fell sideways into the creek and did not move.

Bud stared at him for just a second, then sat down as an exhaustion so total it seemed to penetrate to his heart overcame him. He felt numbness everywhere, except where he hurt. The little gun slipped out of his hand and he did not even look for it.

Holly, crying bitterly, had made it nearly all the way back to the farmhouse when she heard the roar. She turned to the west and saw them, or rather their lights; three helicopters roaring in over the tree line, lights flashing dramatically.

Then, from the other direction, she saw the vehicles—state police cruisers, vans, ambulances, a whole convoy—racing down the road to the farm. The vehicles and the helicopters reached the house almost simultaneously, and from each there poured a crowd of black-garbed men in hoods with fancy guns. It was all theater, like a movie; it had nothing to do with anything.

She walked toward them as the men completed their dramatic performance, kicking in doors, presumably racing through the house ready to hose anything that moved down with their machine guns. But there was nothing to hose down.

She reached the perimeter.

"Help," she said.

In seconds policemen surrounded her.

"They're out there," she said, pointing. "Bud Pewtie

and Lamar. Over there, in the trees. I heard some shots. You'd better hurry.''

"Let's go," said an old man, who seemed to be in charge.

"Please hurry," she said, but they were already gone.

We were so close, she thought.

Bud climbed up the bank through a fog of exhaustion; he could make no sense of the rising dust, the roar of the helicopters, the flashing of their navigation lights.

His mind worked imperfectly. It closed on one thought: It was over.

A light came onto him.

He blinked.

"There he is," shouted the pilot over the intercom.

C.D. looked, and yes, the light came onto Bud, who groped blindly, then sank to his knees. C.D. saw the blood all over him, focused a pair of binoculars on the face and saw how battered it was.

"Put it down, GODDAMMIT," he screamed.

The bird hit with a thud.

"Listen, you get back to the house and see if there's a goddamned doctor in the cars, or at least a goddamn paramedic. Get him here fast. That boy's hurt bad. Then you call Comanche Shocktrauma and tell them to expect incoming.''

"Mark the place with a flare, Lieutenant, so we can find it on the way back."

"Goddamn right I will," said C.D. "And bring some more men to secure the area."

He rolled from the deck of the Huey, and someone handed him a flare, which he ignited with a yank. The flare's red fire blossomed. Carrying it, he raced down to Bud as the helicopter roared away into the night.

He ran down the slope and came to Bud, dropping the flare.

"Bud, Bud—"

"Got him, Lieutenant. He's down there. Blew his face off. Oh, Christ I hurt."

"Take it easy, Bud."

He tried to comfort Bud, holding him close, putting his hand to the highway patrolman's chest to check the heartbeat. Bud fell forward, then caught himself. In the flickering magenta of the flare, the blood all over his face looked almost black, and the swelling had all but buried one of his eyes. The man was shivering, and saliva and phlegm ran out of his bloody mouth.

"I killed him. Oh, fuck, is he dead," Bud was saying.

"Good work, Bud. You got him. Great goddamn job. Now settle down. Help is—"

But suddenly someone else was before them.

He thought it was another cop, but as the figure drew nearer and acquired clarity out of the darkness he recognized its size.

"Where's Lamar?" asked Richard.

C.D. was close enough now to see how swollen the man's face was. Had he been hit? Did Lamar beat him? But Richard sniffled and C.D. knew he'd been crying.

"It's all over," he said. "It's finished."

"Where's Lamar?"

"Dead," said C.D.

Richard held something up. C.D. saw that it was a Smith & Wesson .357.

Bud almost laughed. Richard! With a big gun like that! His own gun!

"Richard, boy, it's all over. Put the gun down. You don't want to hurt nobody. Not now," C.D. was saying.

Richard looked at the gun, almost amazed to find it there.

Bud heard vehicles revving, roaring toward them. A chopper suddenly hovered overhead, throwing out a searchlight beam that lit the three of them and beating up a storm of dust.

Richard blinked.

"I—I—" began Richard.

"There now, Richard, it's all over. You just put that old gun down so nobody gets hurt," C.D. crooned.

Richard looked up at C.D. and then at Bud. In the light Bud saw huge eyes webbed with red and full of fear, trembling lips, drops of dew on the nose.

"Richard, put the gun down, those boys mean business. It's all over. Nobody has to get hurt now, not you, not nobody. You were a victim, too. He made you do them things."

Richard nodded numbly.

"Drop the gun, Richard," said Bud, suddenly anguished, afraid the troopers would shoot this poor, pitiful child. Richard took a step toward them, seemed to turn and watch the men from the helicopter racing at them, and turned back to Bud and C.D. He faltered, as though he were losing his grip. C.D. reached out to help him.

Richard started to bend to set the gun down as the troopers surrounded him, and it was fine, it was great, it was the happy ending everybody dreamed about.

But something suddenly came into Richard's eyes, from nowhere.

"Daddy!" he cried, and raised the pistol and fired.

CHAPTER 32

Long after the funeral, which was one of the biggest in the history of the state, long after the newspapers and the television had lost interest, long after people had stopped asking about it, the Ford F250 pulled into the parking lot of a small cemetery in Kiowa county. It was November, the day before Thanksgiving, when Oklahoma turns chilly and ocher and seems somehow drained of its brightness.

The wind snapped through the air and Russ Pewtie, stepping out of the passenger side, pulled his jacket tight around him; when he breathed, ragged plumes of breath leaked from his nostrils and his eyes began to issue tears from the cold. He'd just flown in that morning from a surprisingly more temperate New Jersey.

Beside him, his brother Jeff, who had driven up to Oklahoma City to pick him up, also shivered.

"Damned cold," said Russ.

"Damned cold," said Jeff.

Russ was back from his first two months in the East; he hadn't had an easy time of it and had already dropped a course; but he felt better and knew that somehow, he'd make it through. Jeff was looking good. He'd gotten his grades up and now, a junior with a driver's license, his own inherited truck, he even had a girlfriend, a pretty young woman who was the daughter of a colonel at the fort. He was working out every day after school to get ready for ball in the spring.

The two young men left the truck, which smelled so of their father. They looked around, shifting a little on their feet to stay warm, but without much luck.

Russ looked at his watch.

"We may as well go on out there," he said.

"Yeah," said Jeff. "Get it over with."

They stepped between gnarled scrub oaks and through a frail metal gate, and walked among the gravestones on the prairie. There were so many of them. The wind rose and whipped and snapped, and the high grass bent in its force. Out here: always the wind.

There was no wind like this back in New Jersey, thought Russ. There's no wind like it anywhere.

After some minutes of hunting, they came at last to the stone, which was one of but many in a neighborhood of stones. Like its companions, it was nondescript polished granite, about as austere a symbol of a life as could be imagined, completely without frill or sentimentality.

Russ tried to feel something but he really couldn't. He felt phony, ridiculous, absurd.

He looked down at the marker, which summed up a man's life in a set of years.

1926–1994.

And beneath that, the inscription: A LAW ENFORCEMENT OFFICER.

And beneath that another inscription: HE DID HIS DUTY.

"Poor old bastard," said Jeff.

"I wonder why he did it," said Russ.

And below that the name: CARL D. HENDERSON.

"He did it because he thought it went with the job," said their father, rising from the other side of C.D.'s gravestone, where he'd been alone for some time. And then he said, "Thank you boys for coming. I appreciate it much. Hi, Russ. You're looking great."

"Thanks Dad, I'm okay. I didn't see your car."

"I didn't feel like driving today, that little thing with its piddly automatic. Mommy dropped me off. She had to go to pick up the turkey."

Russ looked at his father and remembered the last time he'd seen him, near death in the hospital. The survivor was a graver man, thin and solemn, his skin still almost gray. Now and then a faraway look would come over him. The bullet that had gone through C.D. Henderson's aorta had then struck Bud, breaking his clavicle and destroying the nerves in his right arm, then coursing downward to destroy a lung before coming to rest behind his spleen.

Thank God there'd been a doctor on the chopper; he'd taken one look at C.D. and known it was all over, cut Bud's chest open there in the grass and massaged his heart back to life before they medevacked him to Comanche General Shocktrauma where he'd fought the reaper for three months until finally pulling out of it.

"You're looking great, Dad," lied Russ.

"This goddamn retirement's got me cranky as a mule," Bud said. "But I'll get used it. Well, you boys ready for the party?"

"Yes sir," said Jeff.

Bud pulled out a fresh bottle of I. W. Harper and cracked it open. Without much ceremony he took a long, smoky swallow. He passed it to Russ and then to Jeff, who each took a gulp.

"Wow," said Jeff, blinking at the power of the fluid.

"I ever catch you doing that on your own, I'll wale the hide off you!" Bud said, taking the bottle from Jeff.

Then he turned and poured the rest of the liquor into the ground next to C.D.'s stone.

"The old goat was always trying to git me to drink with him," Bud said. "Well, now I finally got around to it. And I brought my boys, too, just like he wanted. This one's on you, old man."

Then he turned, and looked at his two sons. Russ for once wasn't wearing the habitual scowl of the young intellectual; and Jeff looked a little wobbly for his first taste of hard liquor.

"All right," he said. "Let's go home."

Some time that same week, Richard blinked, and blinked again, as the doors opened and he stepped out of the ambulance onto the sidewalk of Prison Boulevard with his guards. He had a little impulse to shield his eyes, though it was impossible; handcuffs and anklecuffs bound to an iron belt held his limbs secure.

The wind was chilly, the sky bright. He shivered, and felt phantom aches. He, too, had recovered from his wounds, which were surprisingly minor given the fact that four state troopers had fired at him in almost the same second that he had fired into Henderson and Pewtie. What was it Lamar had said? "Ain't nobody knows how to shoot no more"? Well, another thing Lamar had been right about.

One bullet broke his rib; another passed cleanly through his chest, and two more through the fleshy part of his leg. He'd known he wasn't going to die. In fact what hurt the most was that one trooper had kicked him in the head as he lay on the ground. He thought they were going to let him bleed to death. But he disappointed them and would not die.

Most of the last months had been passed in the confines

of a friendly institution, the Kingsville Hospital for the Criminally Insane, where loving doctors had tended him and cared for him, but something had changed. He was remote and unresponsive and they'd tried so hard to reach him, but he just looked at them. They seemed from another planet somehow. And in the last months, when he was ambulatory, they'd urged him to draw again. But he just stared at the pencils and the paper and saw blankness.

The adjudication was simple. Sparing the state the expense of trying him, his lawyer pled him guilty to first degree murder on the proviso that he not be given the death penalty. His lawyer told him he couldn't be considered for parole for seventeen years. He wasn't charged in the escape, because his lawyer convinced the court that Lamar had forced him to go along, and he wasn't charged in the murder of the guard or the delivery man or any of the citizens or policemen in the robbery of the Wichita Falls Denny's. His greatest character witness was old John Stepford, who told prosecutors, "He didn't do a thing. He just sat there and cried while Lamar and Odell did the terrible things to my poor wife and I. Richard was a damned coward. Couldn't hurt a flea."

If Richard had an opinion, he kept it to himself. He had become a near mute, a sullen watcher, slow to move, his face sealed off from human expression. Who knew what danced behind his eyes, for they, too, had become dull and hooded.

"There it is, Richard," said the head of the guard detail, "just like you left it."

It hadn't changed a bit.

McAlester State Penitentiary loomed above him, its high, white walls blazing in the sun, giving it the aspect of a Camelot, a fabled Moorish city, a walled fortress in Tibet. The Mac. The Big Mac. It would have him back at last.

He blinked again: from here he could only see the walls, and just the briefest half a top story of the cellblock that had been his world for four months before Lamar had taken him on that mad, crazed dash. He looked around, but there was nothing to see except walls.

The Mac, he thought. *I am back.*

Now I have to pay.

He knew he would probably die.

The blacks would get him. Probably it would be the blacks. His whiteness would inflame them; they'd be on him in a second, fuck his ass and kill him and laugh about it. He could try and punk for a big con but . . . seventeen years of blow jobs?

Maybe the Mexicans, the *cholos.* They loved to cut up gringos in the showers. They would get him fast. Or the red guys, those impassive mongol savages with their elaborate tattooed biceps bracelet, N-D-N-Z.

But he knew: It would be the blacks.

The doors clanked open.

A lieutenant he recognized waited.

"Well, howdy there, Richard. Known you'd come back, sooner or later. They all do."

Richard said nothing.

"Hell, Lamar and Odell are back. They're over there, in the goddamned prison cemetery. Who else'd have 'em? Ain't going into a graveyard with quality folks, that's for sure."

Richard remembered the cemetery vaguely. A nondescript parcel of junk land off to the west, beyond the agriculture center, where members of the prison community, bull and con alike, were interred.

"I'd like to see them sometime," Richard said.

"Well, we'll have to see about that, Richard," said the

guard. "Some things are more possible than others. They ain't going anywheres, that's for sure."

Richard just nodded bitterly, wondering how it would happen.

Processing was indifferent and efficient; he had no belongings, really, to confiscate, and just gave himself over to the institution.

Now, with an armful of clothes and in new prison dungarees, he entered the cellblock and walked along the catwalk to where he would spend the rest of his life.

Again, the immensity of it. It towered over him; he thought of a cobra's flared hood, the sense of darkness enveloping. There was no daylight. Out on the yard, things were progressing as normal. He heard the shouts from the basketball and handball courts, the clunk of heavy iron being pumped by inmate bodybuilders. Other rogue sounds: Latino music, cheesy and loud; soul music; country; and the yammer, the gibber of many men talking, seething, bucking, clawing for space and individuality and . . . survival in the most primeval of places. Smells: farts, sweat, bile, vomit, shit. Iron and stone everywhere, the slight vibration of the grid of the catwalk beneath him, the cells slipping by on the right, each festooned with pictures of various saints and sluts.

Until at last . . . home.

"Here you go, Richard. D–fifty-eight. Sorry, there ain't no doubles. You in with a rapist, a road captain of a cycle gang and a guy who likes to cut people. Not your average Sunday school choir."

Richard knew where they'd put him, too. Back bunk, upper, where the farts coalesced in the air and in hot weather the atmosphere was most like the inside of a sub, while in the winter it was the coldest. Every square inch of wall would be taken up with pictures from the inner lives of other men, and he'd have no say in anything. His own cellmates might even kill him, just for the shit of it, when they got tired of jacking off or buttslamming each other.

Richard slipped in.

Hmmmmm.

It must be some mistake.

He didn't get it.

"Don't ask me, Richard. We let you boys work out who sleeps where."

There was an open bunk, but it wasn't the rear upper but the front lower.

Hmmmmmmm.

The best bunk in the cell.

And all the pictures had been scraped off the wall; he could hang anything he wanted.

He looked at it dully. Nothing showed on his face.

"Okay, Richard. You on your own. You be a good boy now, and if you git in trouble, you call us."

"Sure."

The detail left and Richard was alone.

He sat on the bunk.

Then he looked at the two desks and again was astounded. Normally the desks belonged to the two strongest men and fuck the two weakest. Sometimes a deal could be worked out where all four shared, if all four were of equal power. But . . . *both* desks stood vacant, the materials they had previously contained stacked neatly over to one side of the room, as if it was up to him to choose the best one.

Richard sat for a number of hours trying to work out the puzzle. He had one little task to perform. He carefully unfolded a print he'd ordered, and then hung it, Scotch-taping it precisely centered above the desk.

Then, in time, he had to go to the bathroom.

It used to terrify him. In the stall-less bathrooms, naked to the world, you were at maximum vulnerability. He'd trained himself only to go when Lamar or Odell went. But there was no Lamar and Odell. They were in the ground a mile away.

Yet once again, he was amazed at his own torpor. The trip to the bathrooms didn't particularly frighten him. He just got up and went. What would happen would happen, and maybe sooner was better than later.

He stood, left his cell, and walked along the catwalk until he reached the john. He ducked in. A scrawny black man looked at him, said nothing, and departed.

Richard sat and shat. Then he rose, buckled his pants, and took his time washing his hands.

He walked out and then he saw them.

There were four of them, big and black.

They came from nowhere—or actually, out of a cell. Suddenly they blocked off the catwalk ahead of him.

He looked about. Far above, a guard with a Mini-14 patrolled on the shooting walk, but he was looking in another direction.

And so, he thought: *Here it is. At last. My fate.*

One of them was immensely puffed up from working out; his ebony muscles, sculpted and glowing, stood out on his body like haunches of beef or inflated sausages. He wore a red bandanna. Another was lanky and sullen, with Michael Jackson's pretty hair, a gold necklace, and ropey, veiny arms. His eyes were deader than coal. The third was just a kid, eager to impress, his face drawn in tight and impassive to broadcast the word *tough* to the world. He looked at Richard with haughty eyes. And the fourth was the famous head-boss nigger, Rodney Smalls. Rodney looked at him through narrow eyes.

Rodney was an immense man, sagacious and violent, a magnificent despot, who ruled with an iron hand. Rodney rarely ventured out of his cell, preferring to run things among the blacks from there.

But now Richard got it: He had to pay for Junior Jefferson. He had inherited Lamar's burden of guilt.

He tried to keep his own face dull. He just stared at them as they approached.

Okay, he thought. *Is this it?* He wasn't particularly frightened for some odd reason.

They were on him.

"Hey, Richard."

"Yeah?" *Give them nothing. Don't let them see your fear.*

"What you say, man?"

"I'm okay," he said.

"How you doin'? You need anything, man? You need smokes? I can get you smokes."

"Cool," Richard said.

"Shit, man, we ain't got no beef with you. Just want you to know that up front, Richard. You okay."

"That Richard," said Rodney to his young charge, "he smoked two goddamned troopers. A lieutenant and a sergeant. Blew their E.T.-looking white motherfucking asses away cold. Stood up there like the motherfucking man and put them Smokey-Bear cocksuckers down. You git 'em both, Richard?"

"I capped the lieutenant," said Richard. "Goddamned sergeant had more lives than a cat. But I'll tell you this: He hasn't had a good night's sleep since he ran into me!"

The four black men laughed.

"Richard, you okay. Man, you got the stones. You cold, motherfucker. You ice, man."

Someone clapped him on the back. He felt their warmth, their love, their respect.

"You go cool, Richard. For a dirty white boy, you ain't half bad."

He watched them walk away. The young one made a gun from a finger and aped blowing a state trooper away and they all burst out laughing.

"Richard?"

He turned. A pale white man stood before him, maybe five years younger.

"Richard, my name is Aaron Miles. I'm one of your cellmates. I was wondering—"

"Did I talk to you, motherfucker?" said Richard.

"Ah—no. It's just that—"

"It's just that nothing, motherfucker. *If* we talk, and note I don't say *when* we talk but only *if* we talk, we talk when *I* say so. Do you understand, fuckboy?"

"Yes sir."

"Now I want half your cigarettes," instructed Richard. "Every week, I get half. Get it? Or I become interested in you. And you don't want that."

"Yes sir."

"Now get the fuck out of my sight."

The boy scurried away. Richard watched him go. He had a nice ass.

Now, for the first time in months, he felt something: an actual sensation slid through his bones, a small, tight smile played across his face.

He stepped back into his cell and saw his print.

Captured in a few deft pen strokes, the creature crouched on some featureless plain, swaddled in muscle, its head twisted almost as if in a feeding frenzy, its tiny eyes black and cunning, a spasm of blood lust throbbing through it. *Lion tourné vers la gauche, la tête levée,* by Delacroix, who, Richard realized, had gotten the neck right.

Ah: lions.

ACKNOWLEDGMENTS

The author would like to thank the following friends and colleagues for their assistance, while at the same time absolving them of all blame for its excesses and inaccuracies. Besides dedicatees Mike Hill, Bob Lopez, Steve Wigler, Lenne Miller and, especially, Weyman Swagger, all of whom gave good counsel when desperately needed, the others are: Steve Woods, Pat McGuire, Floyd Jones, Jean Marbella, John Feamster, Mike Mayo, Jim Horan, and the countless Oklahomans who were indefatigably polite and hospitable as I poked around their state for several weeks.

My agent, Esther Newberg of ICM, is the true heroine of the book, as abetted by my editor, David Rosenthal: special thanks to both of them for ''getting it.'' My wife Lucy, as usual, did the dishes and the bills so that I could slip off and pretend to be an Oklahoma state trooper and a badass escaped convict, which was much more fun than dishes and bills; my children—teenagers, by now, actually, Jake and Amy—were reasonably behaved throughout it all.

Finally, I should say that though I represent certain Oklahoma State Agencies—notably the Oklahoma Highway Patrol, the Oklahoma State Bureau of Investigation, and the Oklahoma Bureau of Prisons—the preceding work is entirely fictional and not in any way intended to reflect upon their performance of their duties.

Look for

BLACK
LIGHT

the new novel from

STEPHEN
HUNTER

Coming in June 1996 from Doubleday